The K...

Louise Brindley

CORGI BOOKS

THE KERRY DANCE
A CORGI BOOK : 0 552 14309 X

First publication in Great Britain

PRINTING HISTORY
Corgi edition published 1996

Set in 10/11pt Adobe Times by Kestrel Data, Exeter.

Corgi Books are published by Transworld Publishers Ltd,
61–63 Uxbridge Road, London W5 5SA,
in Australia by Transworld Publishers (Australia) Pty Ltd,
15–25 Helles Avenue, Moorebank, NSW 2170
and in New Zealand by Transworld Publishers (NZ) Ltd,
3 William Pickering Drive, Albany, Auckland.

Reproduced, printed and bound in Great Britain by
Cox & Wyman Ltd, Reading, Berks.

Louise Brindley was born in Darlington, County Durham, and at the age of four moved with her family to Scarborough in North Yorkshire. All Louise Brindley's writings reflect her knowledge of, and deep affection for, North Yorkshire, where she still lives. This is her seventh novel to be published by Corgi.

Also by Louise Brindley

MOVING AWAY
OUR SUMMER FACES
TANQUILLAN
THE INCONSTANT MOON
THE SMOKE SCREEN
STARLIGHT

For M.E. and Alice

Prologue

It would seem, in years to come, that time had gift-wrapped that era in golden days tied with silver ribbons of moonlight.

Looking back, Grace would think that they had all stepped into the spotlight for a brief moment to dance on the stage of life, not knowing how soon the curtain would fall. The Kerry Dance? Bob had laughed and called her fanciful when she told him she wanted to call their fourth child Kerry.

They had chosen quite ordinary names for the older children. Their elder son was Daniel – his mother's maiden name. The second boy, conceived during a brief spell of leave from the trenches, had been christened Robert James, after his father. The third child, a girl, had been given her grandmother Kingsley's Christian name, Dulcie – to even things up with Grace's side of the family.

Kerry was called after a haunting song which conjured up, for Grace, vague memories of a childhood holiday in Ireland, lush grass and softly contoured hills, a dusk-deepened glen on a summer night, handsome lads and pretty colleens joining hands in the Kerry Dance: the ring of the piper's tune.

Growing old, memories remained an integral part of life. Memories and dreams. Had Grace really seen the Kerry Dance, imagined or dreamt that she had?

Her mother told her she must have dreamt it. There was no way a child of her age could have been out alone after dark. The house would have been in an uproar. A search party would have gone out to look for her.

'But Mamma, I *did* see it.'

A warning look. An upheld finger. If only she could remember more clearly.

'Don't talk nonsense, child.'

7

But it had seemed so real, the music and laughter, the lantern light shining on the faces of the dancers.

Memories . . .

Life hadn't been easy for herself and Bob, Grace remembered, struggling to bring up their two little boys – Dulcie and Kerry hadn't been born then – in the aftermath of the 1914–18 war. Unable to afford a home of their own, they had rented furnished rooms in a Victorian villa in Roscoe Street. How she had managed to cook nourishing meals on a couple of gas-burners, she would never know. A matter of common sense, she supposed. A kind of balancing act, of setting a scrag-end of mutton stew to simmer very gently on one of the rings, stew containing lots of cheap vegetables – onions, carrots and parsnips. A steamed pudding cooked on the other, while a panful of potatoes sat on the banked-down sitting-room fire. Just as long as Bob had something satisfying to sit down to when he came home from work, and their two little boys did not go to bed hungry.

They had been desperately poor, but every Monday morning, as regular as clockwork, no matter how thin her purse might feel, she had paid half-a-crown to the Co-op club man to make certain they had decent shoes to wear. Bob's small Army gratuity had long been spent in the lean months when he had searched in vain for employment after the war. Then at last he had been given a menial job as a sweeper-up at the local market, a job which had no bearing whatsoever on his real trade as a barber.

Making do had become a way of life for both of them, a kind of challenge at the time. Grace had not minded one iota. Bob had come back to her safely after the war, thank God, and that was all she really cared about. In any event, nothing could ever be worse for Grace than telling her parents, before Bob went off to war, that she wanted their consent to marry as quickly as possible.

'At sixteen? You must be out of your mind!' Her mother's face, Grace remembered, had been a study in pained disbelief. 'No, it's out of the question! Who is this man anyway? Where did you meet him? How long has this affair been going on behind our backs?'

When the moment of truth had finally arrived, Grace said quietly, 'Does it really matter? The fact is, I am . . . I am going to have a baby.'

The wedding ceremony had taken place at the Jubilee Chapel in Aberdeen Walk. Grace knew she had forfeited her right to a white wedding. She had not realized that her day of days would be ruined by her parents uncompromisingly harsh attitude towards the bridegroom. It had made no difference that Bob was decent, clean and God-fearing, she might just as well have taken up with the devil in disguise. Her mother had decreed that the wedding should take place at nine o'clock in the morning, to save the embarrassment of onlookers outside the chapel.

Bob had suggested the Register Office as an alternative, at which Mrs Daniel had thrown up her hands in horror. And so Grace had appeared, in a place of God, wearing her Sunday-best, navy-blue costume, a white starched blouse, and a straw hat trimmed with an artificial rose. But, holding Bob's hand, smiling into his eyes, she felt no sense of shame or disgrace at being pregnant, rather an overwhelming feeling of relief that they were now as one in the eyes of the Lord.

They had been meeting secretly for some time past, and he had given her a ring which she had kept hidden, knowing that her parents would put a stop to those meetings if they found out about them, saying she was far too young to start courting. This Bob had accepted and understood. They planned to marry when she was older, by which time Grace would have introduced Bob to her parents and gained their consent to the courtship, or so she imagined. But things had not worked out that way. When war came, Bob had joined up. Faced with the sorrow of parting, they had made love. It had seemed the right and natural thing to do, and never till her dying day would she forget the joy and simplicity of that act of love at a time of heightened emotion when, for all they knew, they might never meet again in this world.

But never for one moment had Mrs Daniel let her daughter forget what she regarded as the disgrace of having to get married, and when Bob came home for good after the war, she had lost no opportunity of reminding Grace that, had she married a man with some kind of social standing and a nice bit of money in the bank, she might not have ended up in four poorly furnished rooms in Roscoe Street. Nor had she shown much affection for her grandchildren, whom she regarded as ill-fated, particularly the elder, little Danny, who had been conceived out of wedlock.

A long-cherished dream of Bob's had been to set up in business for himself as a barber. He had served his apprenticeship before the war and knew the trade like the back of his hand. All he needed was fifty pounds or so to purchase a second-hair chair, a shampoo basin and so on. He would soon build up a clientele. But what was the use of talking? He hadn't five pounds, let alone fifty.

'Don't worry, love. Something will turn up, you'll see.' Grace had no idea, when she uttered those words, how soon her prediction would come true. The death of Bob's father from a sudden heart attack had come as a shock to both of them. The funeral was a sorrowful affair. Afterwards, Bob's mother had given her son an envelope containing a paid-up insurance policy.

'Your dad asked me to give you this if anything should happen to him,' she said tearfully. 'I think he must have had a premonition.'

The policy was worth seventy-five pounds.

With the money his father had left him, Bob rented a shop in North Marine Road – on the other side of town – purchased a second-hand barber's chair, a wash-basin, several brand-new cut-throat razors, a small keg of green soft soap, and a dozen bottles of what he laughingly called 'brilliongtong'.

Moving closer to the shop to live had not occurred to Grace until the following winter, when Bob would come home half frozen from long bicycle rides to work and back, and she had begun to worry that his health might suffer as a result of his exposure to sleet, wind and rain. And so she had not demurred when he took her to look round an unfurnished house to let in Castle Road – not until she had seen the size of it, when she had stared in dismay at the big, empty rooms.

'Don't worry, love,' Bob said cheerfully when she voiced her opinion that it was far too big. 'The shop's doing nicely now. Far better than I expected. Anyway, it's high time we had a place of our own. Our own furniture and stuff.'

Stuff? Really, men had no idea how much 'stuff' would be needed to fill the kitchen cupboards alone: pots, pans, pudding basins . . .

'The thing is,' he said eagerly, 'we could get the essentials from the Co-op, and there's plenty of good second-hand furniture available at Ward Price's sale room. Of course we'd have to creep first, then walk. We'll manage somehow. The main thing is, do you like the house?'

'I haven't seen all of it yet,' Grace murmured, fearful that they might bite off more than they could chew.

He had then taken her upstairs to look at the views from the upper windows, and she had seen, with a feeling of wonderment, the whole of Scarborough's South Bay spread before her, the long line of cliffs to the far point of Flamborough Head, the parish church of St Mary across the way, the grave of Anne Brontë in the broad green meadow nestling in the lee of the Castle Hill, the rugged stones of that ruined fortress overlooking the harbour and the street called Paradise, the house known as Castle-by-the-Sea where the painter John Atkinson Grimshaw had once lived. The back rooms faced the North Bay, more austere than the South, with views of rolling cliffs stretching to Ravenscar and Robin Hood's Bay.

With a sudden uplifting of the heart, Grace knew that she belonged here in this house. Standing near one of the top floor windows, close to tears of happiness, Bob was right, she thought, they would manage somehow. No matter how hard she had to work, she would make this big empty house into a home for her husband and children.

She had been young, strong and resourceful in those days, when life had seemed gift-wrapped in sunshine and moonlight.

The days of the Kerry Dance.

PART ONE

Chapter One

Kerry gazed entranced at the screen. Carried away by the swirling dresses, the lilt of the music, she felt as if she had left her body to become part of the waltz. In the arms of her partner, one hand resting lightly on his shoulder, she imagined the dip and sway of the petticoats beneath a satin ballgown, the skimming of her elegantly shod feet across the ballroom floor, the rippling of his back muscles beneath his tightly fitting uniform.

The music of the 'Merry Widow Waltz' seemed to be deep inside her, welling up, filling her with an intense pleasure akin, somehow, to pain. It was the same feeling she experienced reading 'Ode to a Nightingale', or seeing a pathway of moonlight on the sea, as if so much beauty could not be contained in her slender young body without spilling over in tears.

Her sister Dulcie, who preferred gangster films, rattled her bag of sweets, selected a bon-bon, unwrapped it, popped it into her mouth and crunched through the shell to the soft lime filling. 'Want one?' she hissed.

'No thanks.' Trust Dulcie to spoil a magic moment, Kerry thought, resentful of the crackling and crunching going on in the next seat, coming down to earth with a bump, no longer a crinolined lady whirling in the arms of a handsome hussar, just a 14-year-old girl in a print cotton dress and hand-knitted cardigan, her feet encased in Clark's sandals.

Before the film ended, Dulcie lumbered from her seat, grabbed Kerry by the elbow and hustled her towards the exit, not wanting to stand still for the National Anthem. Emergence from the darkness of the cinema into the world outside came as a shock to Kerry. The transition from make-believe to reality was too sudden. Dulcie had no such inhibition. This was her kind of scene, the seafront with its amusement arcades, candy-floss stalls and ice-cream parlours; visitors strolling along beneath the triple rows of coloured lights strung between the lamp-posts, the tantalizing smell of fish and chips wafting on the air, the sound of dance music emanating from the Olympia Ballroom further along the Foreshore; groups of lads on the look-out for pretty girls.

Piqued because the lads looked at Kerry, not her, Dulcie wondered if she should go on a diet. But there were rich pickings of food available at the Pavilion Hotel, where she worked as a waitress, especially after some special 'do': salmon mousse for instance, cold roast sirloin, mushroom vol-au-vents, and meringues with lots of whipped cream. Dulcie loved food. When she got married, she thought greedily, it would be to a rich man with a big house and lots of servants. She couldn't care less if he was as ugly as sin, as long as he could afford to feed her properly. Not that any man, rich or poor, had given her a second look so far. But it wasn't every man that wanted a girl who looked like two boards nailed together. Plenty of fat girls found themselves a husband. Her time would come.

Catching the scent of fish and chips, her tongue fairly tingled for the tangy taste of salt and vinegar about a coating of crispy batter, the feel of flaccid, fat-soaked potatoes between her lips. As usual, she felt desperately hungry, but Mum would be clock-watching, and the steep incline of Paradise lay before her.

It was all very well for the slenderly fashioned Kerry to float uphill like a zephyr, her sandalled feet seeming scarcely to touch the pavement, Dulcie thought crossly, puffing and panting as they reached the stiff bend in the road, but *she'd* be starting work soon, now she'd left school. She'd know all about aching feet then, right enough.

Unaware of her sister's feeling of resentment, it seemed to Kerry that the scent of smoke still lingered in the air. How gloriously that beacon on the Castle Hill had flared up against the velvet darkness of a summer night. Visitors had

16

arrived in droves from the mill towns of the West Riding to watch the lighting of the beacon, she remembered, and to marvel at the fireworks display, the showers of golden rain and rockets exploding against the night sky, to await, excitedly, the lighting of the next beacon on the cliffs at Ravenscar.

The newspapers had been full of pictures of King George and Queen Mary on the occasion of their Silver Jubilee, the lighting of beacons in their honour on high promontories the length and breadth of the British Isles.

Cresting the hill, Kerry recalled the thrill of it all, the orange-red flames shooting up from the brazier, the dancing and singing, the soft darkness of a May night. There were the smells of toffee-apples and baked potatoes, the sound of the sea in the distance, the raucous cries of the gulls disturbed by the fireworks, the brooding stones of an ancient fortress standing sentinel beneath the stars.

Overwhelmed by the many and varied thoughts and impressions flitting with butterfly-quickness through her brain, above all by the pathway of silver on the sea, she cried breathlessly, 'Oh, isn't life wonderful?'

'Eh? What's so wonderful about it, I should like to know?' Dulcie, hot, tired and cross, had one thought in mind: to get home as quickly as possible for something to eat.

Grace Kingsley paced the small back sitting-room, pausing now and then to glance at the clock, the minute hand of which was drooping towards half-past ten. 'I hope those girls will be in bed before their father comes home,' she said anxiously. 'He worries when they're out late on their own.'

She realized, as soon as she had spoken, the folly of her remark. Her mother, who had come to live with them five years ago after the death of her husband, made a meal of chance remarks which showed up her son-in-law in a bad light.

'More fool he for allowing two young girls out alone on a Saturday night,' Mrs Daniel countered sharply. 'You know what that Foreshore's like when the season begins: all kind

17

of queer folk about. If he's so worried, he should have gone to meet them instead of supping beer at the Albion till closing time.'

'Look here, Mother,' Grace said defensively, 'Bob works hard all week. He has a perfect right to a couple of pints of beer and a game of dominoes on a Saturday night if he feels like it.'

Stuffing her knitting into the capacious bag hanging on the chair arm, Mrs Daniel got up stiffly, bristling with self-righteous indignation. 'Well, all I can say, things were different in my day. Your father would no more have thought of entering a public house than fly in the air. You're too soft, my girl, that's your trouble.'

'Rather too soft than too hard!'

Grace hated these spats with her mother. In any case, what was the use of talking? Nan, as the children called her, belonged to a different, more hide-bound generation whose lives had been shattered by war. She must never forget that Nan had lost two brothers during that war. But this was a new age they were living in: a far more emancipated age than she had known as a child, when talking pictures were unheard of and Saturday nights had meant dreary concerts in the front room, her father playing the piano, his brother, Uncle Ambrose, scratching away on his violin, and Mother's sisters, Fanny and Rosa, singing duets.

'Jerusalem, Je-hursalem,' they had quavered, nervous of hitting the high notes, whilst Uncle Ambrose, squinting through his pince-nez spectacles at the music-stand in front of him, settling his chin deeper into the velvet pad on the bridge of his instrument, finished the piece two bars ahead of them.

Feeling guilty, Grace asked, 'Are you going to bed now, Mother?', wishing she had not spoken so sharply. An unnecessary question since Nan had stuck her knitting needles through her ball of wool and was already heading for the stairs. She added contritely, 'Sleep well.'

Determined to get in a final dig, 'I doubt I'll be able to sleep a wink,' Mrs Daniel replied. Laying a gnarled hand on the banister, she mounted the stairs slowly, one step at a time, like a French aristocrat mounting the steps of a guillotine. Clutching her bag of knitting in her free hand, she felt misunderstood, extraneous, wishing her husband was still alive, that she had gone to live with Fanny and Rosa after his passing, had not done her duty, as she saw it, in coming to live with her daughter and that sex-mad husband of hers. The passage of time had not softened or altered Mrs Daniel's poor opinion of Bob Kingsley.

Oh God, Grace thought bleakly as her mother went upstairs to her room on the first landing. Then the front door opened and the girls came in.

'And where do you think you've been till this time of night?' she said heatedly, venting her feelings of guilt on her daughters. 'When I say you're to be home by ten o'clock, I mean ten o'clock, not half past! Now go and have your suppers before Dad comes home, or there'll be trouble.'

Immediately, Dulcie hurried through to the kitchen to make inroads on a plateful of salmon-paste sandwiches.

'I'm sorry we're late,' Kerry said, facing their mother. 'We came home as quickly as we could.'

Looking at her younger daughter's flushed young face, rose-petal skin, enormous blue-grey eyes fringed with dark lashes, her honey-blonde hair, Grace's anger evaporated. Never had Kerry irritated her in the way that Dulcie often did. The girl possessed a charm all her own, impossible to define. Kerry was not merely lovely to look at, she was kind. But there was more to it than that. It seemed to Grace Kingsley that Kerry danced through life to music that no-one else could hear. No-one except herself, perhaps?

Emerging from the Albion, Bob thought what a marvellous evening this had been. He had been sitting in his usual corner, playing dominoes, when the door opened and in walked Herbie Barrass; not that he'd recognized him at first, not after all these years. Frowning, he'd tried to put a name to the face. It wasn't until Herbie had slapped him on the shoulder and said warmly, 'Well, as I live and breathe, if it isn't my old mate Bob Kingsley. The Green Howards, remember?' that the penny had dropped.

Then, getting up so quickly he'd nearly upskittled the dominoes, he'd wrung Herbie's hand as fiercely as he had done the last time he'd seen him, seventeen years ago.

Memories flooded in thick and fast then. Memories of France, the trenches, the Armistice, their return to England, home and beauty, of celebrating their return in a pub near King's Cross Station prior to boarding a train for York, where they had gone their separate ways, Herbie to Leeds, he to Scarborough.

They had vowed to keep in touch. Of course they had not done so, apart from the odd Christmas card now and then, when memories remained at full spate, before memories faded away and died in the day-to-day business of living. In Bob's case, a married man with a growing family to feed and clothe, he had wanted to forget the war as quickly as possible. Even so, it was great to see Herbie again.

'Sit down, man. Let me get you a drink.' Both had uttered the same words at the same time, and laughed uproariously as they had done that lunch-time in the pub near King's Cross all those years ago, from which they had emerged, so euphoric, the wonder was they had boarded the right train at the right time.

'This is an old army pal of mine,' Bob had explained proudly to his friends gathered round the dominoes' board.

'Pleased to meet you, I'm sure.' Sitting down, in his element, Herbie had regaled them with risqué stories about his profession as a salesman in ladies' underwear, causing gales of laughter, until the dominoes' team was in such an uproar that the landlord's voice calling 'Time, gentlemen please', could scarcely be heard above the din.

Lord, yes, it had been a marvellous evening, Bob thought, standing on the pavement outside the Albion with his friend Herbie. So great that he couldn't bear the thought of saying good night to his good old pal.

Aware that he had drunk more than usual, he asked

carefully, 'Where are you staying?', anxious not to slur his consonants.

'Not to worry about that, old son.' Herbie laughed. 'I dare say I'll find somewhere to lay my weary head. I'll just pick up my bags and depart.'

He had deposited a couple of cases on the pavement, one of which contained his personal gear, the other his samples: corsets, brassières, petticoats and directoire knickers.

'Nothing of the kind,' Bob said expansively, with an uprush of affection for this man who had been his strength and stay during the war. 'You are coming home with me. My wife will make you welcome, I'm sure.' He added owlishly, 'A wunnerful woman, my wife.'

It was a glorious night, warm and fragrant, lit with stars and moonlight, with the sound of the sea in the background; the coloured lights of the Foreshore shimmering down into the creamy waves frilling in on the sand. The girl beside him looked lovely in the softly glowing darkness of the St Nicholas Gardens: ghostly, insubstantial, a little unreal. Her hand in his felt like a child's hand, making him feel protective towards her. Danny Kingsley, who preferred slim girls with delicate hands and feet, had spotted her standing on the edge of the dance floor earlier that evening, wearing a blue dress with an organdie collar and jabot, her pale blonde hair fluffed out about her youthfully pretty face.

Sizing her up, she looked a bit lonely and dejected, he thought. And so he had pushed his way towards her through the crowd of girls hovering near the cloakroom door, and asked her to dance with him. She had looked more animated then, smiled her acceptance, and they moved across the floor to the music of Leon Hampson's Crystal Band playing 'Lovely to Look At'.

Later, he had treated her to an ice-cream in the café overlooking the dance floor. Dipping her spoon delicately into the blob of vanilla ice contained in a thickly ridged melba glass, she told him her name was Wilma Burton, that she had come to the dance with friends from work who

21

had gone off with a couple of boyfriends, leaving her on her own.

'That wasn't very nice of them,' Danny remarked, liking the way she used her spoon, her ladylike way of speaking, the colour of her dress and the fragrance of eau-de-cologne emanating from the frothy organdie jabot.

'No. I suppose not, but they're not real friends, just girls I work with. We haven't much in common.'

She had china-blue eyes, he noticed, full pink lips, small even teeth and a retroussé nose. He particularly liked her air of fragility, of self-containment. She told him she worked at the Meadow Dairy and lived with her parents in Aberdeen Terrace. He told her his name was Daniel Kingsley and he worked at the Town Hall.

'Oh,' she said, deeply impressed, 'I've never met anyone who worked at the Town Hall before.'

They had danced together the rest of the evening. During the last waltz, he asked if he could see her home. Walking up through the gardens, he had taken her hand to guide her. He knew the gardens well, all the paths and flights of steps, and where the shelters were situated, having been this way many times before with other girls he had escorted home from the Olympia Ballroom, most of whom had expected a bit of a kiss and a cuddle along the way. But this girl was different. He wondered how she would react if he drew her into a shelter. There was only one way to find out. But dare he?

Wilma knew full well what was going on in his mind. A bit prim and old-fashioned she may be, she was certainly not daft. Besides, she liked him, and he was very good looking. Not tall, but she didn't care for tall men who made her feel even smaller than she was. One could tell a lot from dancing with a man. He hadn't tugged her round the floor, ogled other girls over her shoulder, bragged or told smutty jokes. And he hadn't been drinking, she could tell by his breath. She wouldn't have let him see her home if he had.

He had a clear but somewhat sallow complexion, a straight nose, white teeth, an abundance of brown curly hair which he had attempted to straighten with Brylcreem, and he must be responsible and clever because they didn't employ duds at the Town Hall.

Did he intend kissing her or not? He wanted to, she knew that, and she wished he would before the shelters ran out. Perhaps he needed a little encouragement? With this in mind, she managed to stumble near the entrance of a particularly inviting refuge. Suddenly his arm was about her waist, and he was saying she'd best sit down for a while in case she'd sprained her ankle.

'Oh, it's nothing much, really,' she murmured, extending her foot. 'It's my own fault for wearing such high-heeled shoes. But I'm only four-foot eleven in my stockinged feet.' She sighed deeply. 'I wish I was taller.'

'I don't,' Danny said fervently, 'I think you're just right as you are. I don't like tall girls.'

His kiss sent something akin to an electric shock coursing through Wilma's immature body, fulfilling her dreams of what a kiss should be, tender but firm, dry not wet. Closing her eyes, she succumbed to his embrace, the witchery of the night, aware of the soft breeze rustling the branches of the trees beyond the shelter.

Sitting close to him, so close she felt that she might easily become a part of him, aware of his increasingly rapid breathing, she drew back suddenly in alarm, afraid of what might happen if she let him go on kissing her. 'It's getting late,' she quavered, standing up. 'My father will be waiting up for me. I really must go now.'

'Yes, of course.' Danny experienced the painful dwindling of his manhood as, taking Wilma's hand, he guided her towards the safety of the town centre, her home in a side road leading off from Aberdeen Walk.

'I'm sorry, Danny,' she said huskily at the garden gate. 'I really do like you, you know.'

'And I like you.'

'Perhaps we'll meet again some time?' Her voice held a wistful, appealing note.

'Sure. Why not?' Taking the bull by the horns, 'How

about Wednesday night?' He spoke carelessly, as if it didn't matter one way or the other if they met again or not. 'I was thinking of going to the Capitol to see *The Lives of a Bengal Lancer*. You can come with me, if you like.'

'Oh yes,' she said eagerly, 'I'd love to. I *adore* Gary Cooper.'

'What time shall I call for you?'

'Oh, well, don't bother to call. I'll meet you outside. Say seven o'clock?'

'Fine by me,' Danny said huskily, badly wanting to kiss her again, deciding not to. Walking away, he called over his shoulder, 'See you on Wednesday night then?'

Mrs Daniel undressed slowly for bed. The furniture contained in her room on the first landing had come from her old home in Alma Square. Not that one room proved adequate to harbour the contents of an entire house, and so she had been obliged to pick and choose the items she could not have borne to part with under any circumstances whatsoever.

The double bed she had shared with her husband for many a long year had taken priority, along with her dressing table and wardrobe, a favourite rocking chair, and a carved oak chest which she now used as a bedside table, upon which stood an electric lamp with a parchment shade, a bottle of dyspepsia tablets, a carafe of water, and a shallow dish of saline solution into which she popped her dentures for a good overnight soak.

Propped up with pillows and wearing a high-necked flannelette nightgown, her skimpy grey hair braided into something resembling a Chinaman's cue, she mulled over her present situation. She had always believed, and would continue to do so, that Grace had married beneath her. Never would she forget that Bob Kingsley had taken advantage of an innocent young girl. But Grace thought far more of her husband than she had ever done about herself or her father, which did not seem fair. John Daniel had been a good man through and through, a pillar of the Methodist Church which he had served faithfully all the days of his life, a shining example, clean living, a good provider. All in all, he was a fastidious man who, having passed on his seed, had made no further demands on the mother of his child apart from a wholesome desire to brush, at bedtime, her long brown hair, had thereafter sought to comfort and fulfil her by reading from the works of William Wordsworth.

Mrs Daniel could truthfully say that their marriage had been satisfactory on the whole, based on mutual understanding of each other's sexual inhibitions, Mr Daniel's considerate nature, sensitivity, and his enlarged prostate gland.

Fanny and Rosa's invitation to live with them was still open, and she might be happier there than here, she mulled, where she was so little thought of.

In his attic room, James Kingsley – he had refused, lately, to answer to Jimmy – put the finishing touches to the article he'd written on the role of the poet in modern society, making sure he'd put all the full-stops and commas in the right places. Taller than his brother, lanky, bespectacled, clad in a disreputable pair of trousers, open-neck shirt and Fair Isle pullover that his grandmother had knitted him, he regarded himself as slightly bohemian, his attic as a studio.

There was much of his mother in this, her second born: the same hair colouring and fresh complexion, combined with something less tangible, a certain depth of vision lacking in Danny and Dulcie. Their father also, come to think of it. Bob had never understood why a lad of Jimmy's age should choose to shut himself away for hours on end when he could be outdoors playing cricket or football. Grace understood, and it was she who had bought him a work-table and chair from a second-hand furniture shop in town, and encouraged him to line the walls with bookshelves. No problem there. He'd been apprenticed to a firm of joiners and cabinet makers since leaving school at 14. It was a job he hated and was not cut out for, but his father had insisted upon his having a good trade at his fingertips.

What James longed to have at his fingertips was a typewriter. His course tutor at the Acme Agency of Journalism and Creative Writing had advised him to purchase a typewriter as soon as possible. Editors preferred typewritten to hand-written work, and the machine would pay for itself once he had mastered the keyboard and the art of writing saleable material.

Discussing the matter with his mother, Grace had told him not to worry, there were plenty of second-hand typewriters for sale at the junk shop. But James did not want a second-hand machine. He wanted a new one: a matter of pride, of professionalism. There was not much left over from his weekly wage-packet, however, when he'd forked out a couple of quid for his keep, had paid his fees to the Acme Agency, and bought all the notebooks and scribbling pads he required to further his ambition of becoming a world-famous writer.

Ah well, he thought, stretching himself full length on his narrow bed beneath the slates, men of letters must suffer a little for their art. One day, when he was rich and famous, he would look back on all this as part and parcel of the rich tapestry of life. Gosh, that wasn't bad. Jumping up, crossing to his desk, he scribbled down the phrase, 'rich tapestry of life', lest it escaped him. Not that he was likely to forget it. A thought like that was worth remembering.

Returning to his bed, he lay flat out and gazed up at the pale wash of moonlight on his attic ceiling. He considered the tapestry of his own life, by no means rich in his opinion, not in the full meaning of the word. To him, rich meant abounding in natural resources: fertile, abundant, ample – wealthy. And he couldn't even afford to buy a typewriter.

Lying in the narrow single bed in the room she shared with her sister, Kerry relived the magic of *The Merry Widow*. Silently, so as not to disturb Dulcie, she slipped out of bed to gaze out of the window at the silent, moonlit world beyond, a slender figure in a white cotton nightdress, fair shoulder-length hair framing her tender young face, lips slightly parted. Eyes aglow with happiness, she imagined, once more, the soft feel of the multi-layered petticoats beneath a swirling ball gown.

Imagination faded as Dulcie flopped over in bed, opened her eyes and said crossly, 'What the heck are you doing staring out of the window at this time of night?'

'I – I couldn't sleep, that's all.' Guiltily, Kerry hopped back into bed.

Suddenly came a soft creaking of the stairs, the murmur of voices, footsteps on the landing outside their room. Sitting bolt upright, 'Who's that?' Dulcie quavered, her eyebrows touching her fringe of mouse-brown hair.

'Perhaps it's burglars,' Kerry whispered, her imagination running riot. 'I'm going to look!' Hopping out of bed as quickly as she had hopped into it, she crept towards the door, opened it a crack, and peeped out.

'Well?' Dulcie demanded.

'Oh, it's nothing,' Kerry said, with a trace of disappointment, 'just Dad taking someone along to the spare room. I wonder who he is?'

'I dare say we'll find out in the morning,' Dulcie muttered ungraciously. Then, thumping her pillows, humping herself back into a sleeping position and feeling hungry again, she wished she had treated herself to cod and a pennorth after all.

Seriously annoyed, Grace conveyed her displeasure by the simple expedient of saying nothing at all when Bob came into the bedroom. Words were unnecessary in any case. He knew all the signs, betrayed by the ramrod straightness of her back, pursed lips and tensed shoulder muscles.

'Oh, come on love,' he wheedled, 'Herbie's not such a bad fellow. A bit too talkative perhaps, but it isn't every day an old pal turns up out of the blue.'

No reply. Grace was undressing beneath her nightgown, another bad sign.

Continuing his plea of self-justification, uncertain why she was so angry with him, Bob said mildly, 'Maybe I shouldn't have brought him home with me, but what else could I have done?'

No reply. Getting into bed, Grace turned her back on him.

Undressing quickly, Bob slipped in beside her, wishing he knew what he had done to upset her. Deeply aware of the soft womanly shape of her untrammeled figure beneath a covering of flower-sprigged cotton, he felt the sudden upsurge of his manhood, a strong desire to make love to her.

'Don't!'

He was shocked beyond belief as she pulled away from him. 'But *why*? What have I done?'

'You dare to ask me that?' Words came tumbling from Grace in a flood. 'That man you brought here tonight. He was using you, but you hadn't the sense to see it. You say he turned up out of the blue. I don't believe it. He'd been looking for you, I dare say. Looking for a soft touch. Why else would he have had his luggage with him?'

'Grace, love, this isn't like you.' Bob couldn't believe this was happening to him. He still had no idea why she was so upset. He said, 'The spare room bed was already made up, and all he wanted was a sandwich and a cup of tea.'

'I should think so too after all the beer he'd drunk!' Grace said hotly. 'You too, Bob Kingsley. Have you any idea the way you looked when you came home? Why, you couldn't even speak properly. I've never felt so ashamed in all my life!' She added bitterly, 'Mother told me I was too soft, and perhaps she was right after all!'

'Oh, so that's it. Your mother. I might have known she'd be at the bottom of it.'

'This has nothing to do with Mother, and you know it. It's all that man's fault. That old army pal of yours. Well, the sooner he's out of this house the better!' Grace turned over and closed her eyes, signalling the end of the conversation.

Bob sighed deeply. He knew his mother-in-law hated the sight of him, and why. But, damn it all, he'd done his best for the old girl, had taken her under his roof to live, and still she treated him as a pariah. It just wasn't fair. She was always harping on about how dreadful the war had been for people of her generation. Well, the war had been dreadful for him too, and Grace. Nan seemed to forget that. True, Mrs Daniel had lost two brothers during the war, much older men than himself. But what had age to do with it? Now he and Grace were at loggerheads, and all because he'd had a few drinks too many with his old pal Herbie Barrass.

Herbie knew he had made a bad impression on Grace. She was in the kitchen cooking breakfast when he came downstairs early next morning, carrying his cases, wearing grey flannel trousers and a tweed jacket that had seen better days.

She was a good-looking woman and no mistake, he thought, watching her as she forked rashers of bacon round the frying pan. Tall, but not too tall, well made but not fat, bright-eyed, with soft brown hair done up in a bun, and splendid ankles.

He coughed slightly to gain her attention. She turned away from the cooker and looked at him, surprised to see him standing there, his cases at his feet, dangling his trilby hat by its brim.

'Mr Barrass,' she said uncertainly. 'You're up early.'

'Yeah, well, I thought I'd best be on my way.'

'But you haven't had your breakfast.'

'That's all right, Grace – Mrs Kingsley – I'll have a bite to eat at the Commercial Hotel.'

'You're leaving without saying goodbye to Bob?'

'Might be better that way, don't you think?' Herbie grinned awkwardly, 'I reckon I've got him into enough trouble already.'

'Trouble? What do you mean – trouble?' Grace asked sharply.

'Let's just say I knew you weren't best pleased when I brought him home a little the worse for wear. But that was my fault entirely. We hadn't seen each other for such a long time, and . . .' His voice faded.

'What puzzles me,' Grace turned back to the cooker to lift the bacon onto a plate which she put in the oven to keep hot, 'is how you managed to find Bob in a place the size of Scarborough. That must have taken some doing.'

'It did,' Herbie confessed. 'The truth is, I went to the shop in North Marine Road first of all. I knew Bob had set up in business for himself from an old Christmas card he sent me years ago. I thought you might be living over the shop.'

'And when you discovered your mistake?' Grace insisted, cracking eggs into a bowl.

'Well, when the woman next door told me you lived in Castle Road, I dropped into the Albion on the off-chance of finding Bob there.'

'I see. So you had walked all the way from the station to North Marine Road carrying your luggage? Why didn't you leave it at the Commercial Hotel across the road from the station if that's where you intended staying the night?'

'The fact is,' Herbie admitted, 'I didn't come to Scarborough by train. I hitched a lift from Leeds with a lorry-driver pal of mine. Truth to tell, things haven't been too good in the ladies' underwear line just lately.' Another awkward smile. 'Must be losing my touch with the ladies. But that's my problem, not yours.' He picked up his cases. 'Well, now you know. Say goodbye to Bob for me, and thanks for everything.'

Touched by the man's vulnerability, understanding why all the risqué stories and his cocksureness of the night before, seeing them for what they really were – a defence against an innate sense of failure, a cry in the wilderness of forlorn hope, linked to the possibility of losing his job if his sales figures slumped below average – no longer angry, Grace said quietly, 'You're not leaving here without a good breakfast inside you, so you'd best leave those cases in the hall and go through to the dining-room over yonder.' She added with a smile, 'I've already set a place for you.'

Herbie swallowed hard, surprised by the sudden bobbing up of a lump in his throat. Putting down his luggage, he sat down at the dining-room table, unfolded a crisply starched serviette which he tucked into the waistband of his trousers, and pondered what the hell he had said or done to deserve such treatment from a woman whom he could have sworn had hated his guts the night before.

She came through in a few minutes with a pot of tea and his breakfast on a tray. He saw that she had given him several rashers, scrambled egg, and triangles of fried bread.

'Are you married, Herbie?' she asked, pouring the tea.

'Naw, who'd have a dozy bug . . . bloke like me? No oil-painting, am I?'

Sitting down at the table, she asked, 'Who looks after you?'

'I see to meself mainly.' Digging into his food, he added, 'I rent a furnished room over a pub in Chapeltown. I have the use of a kitchen and bathroom, but I don't bother with the kitchen. It's easier to nip out for a pie and a pint.'

'Who does your washing?'

'Oh, that? I wash my own shirts, take my collars to the Chinese laundry. Why?' He was eating like a starving man, speaking between mouthfuls of food.

'I just wondered.' She paused. 'How long have you been a salesman?'

'In this job, you mean? Not long. It isn't the doddle I thought it would be. Funny really, I've always had a nice line of patter with the ladies. Now they don't want to know.' He chased the dip on his plate with a slice of plain bread.

'Have you been to Scarborough before?'

'Naw, this is new territory for me. That's why I came early, to take a look-see at the shops I'm supposed to visit. Let's think. There's a shop called Boyes, another called Rowntrees. They're the important ones. I have a list somewhere. Don't suppose they'll cotton on to me though.' He grinned lopsidedly.

'Perhaps you're not taking the job seriously enough. What I mean is, you may be approaching it from the wrong angle.'

'How do you mean?' He looked puzzled, slightly hurt.

'Well, perhaps you're treating your samples as a kind of joke – the way you do when you're talking to men.'

'You could be right,' he admitted. 'Truth to tell, I'm a bit bloody embarrassed when I start trotting out the stays an' so on, so I make a joke of it.'

'I guessed as much.' Grace poured him another cup of tea. 'Appearance is important too.' She glanced at his shabby jacket without meaning to do so, but Herbie read her thoughts.

'I have a decent suit in my case,' he assured her. 'You didn't think I'd go touting for trade in this clobber?'

She stood up. 'You'd best give it to me, then. I'll have it sponged and pressed in no time. Then you'd best hang it upstairs in your room so it won't get all creased again by morning.'

'Why are you doing this for me?' Herbie's brown eyes held the look of an old spaniel dog uncertain of kindness.

Grace smiled. 'Let's just say that I'd like Bob to feel proud of his old army pal. I know you went through a lot together during the war. Besides, I wasn't very pleasant to you last night, and I'm sorry.'

'Like I said before, it was all my fault.'

And that, Grace thought, was the reason why she had changed her mind about Herbie Barrass, because he'd had the decency to admit he'd been in the wrong, had come down early with his suitcase packed, prepared to leave without saying goodbye to Bob rather than cause more trouble. More importantly, because she had seen, when she had stopped being angry, the frightened, insecure human being behind the façade of the cocky salesman in – ladies' underwear. For no apparent reason, she threw back her head and laughed.

God, what a woman, Herbie thought mistily, what a bloody marvellous woman.

Chapter Two

The family came down to breakfast in dribs and drabs: first Kerry, as bright as a sunbeam in a fresh cotton dress, ankle socks and sandals, her hair tied back with a black velvet ribbon, then her father, who, despite the miserable night he had spent in the dog-house, chucked her fondly under the chin and said, 'How's my little girl this morning?'

'I'm fine, Dad. But you don't look too hot.'

'Where on earth did you pick up that expression?'

Kerry giggled. 'They say it all the time in gangster films. That, and "You don't say?" "So what?" and "Look here, Buster!" Ask Dulcie if you don't believe me.'

'I believe you.' Bob Kingsley loved Kerry more than anyone else on earth apart from his wife, who was now in the kitchen cooking more bacon and scrambled eggs; who, to Bob's amazement, smiled at him and said, 'Herbie's in the dining-room. He came down early. Just take this fresh pot of tea through to him, will you?'

Fairly dancing with excitement, Kerry asked, 'Is Herbie the man who slept in the guest room last night? We thought he was a burglar.'

'Grace?' Bob said, a questioning look in his eyes.

'It's all right now,' she replied quietly, and his heart lifted with relief. He did not know how or why the miracle of forgiveness had happened, or when it had happened, and he didn't much care how, why or when, just as long as he had been forgiven.

'Hand me the tea-pot, love,' he said huskily.

Jimmy came downstairs like a runaway train, as hungry as a hunter. Danny came down more slowly, a faraway look on his face as he thought about Wilma Burton and wondered if he was in love with her. Dulcie came down looking like

33

an un-made feather bed, drawn from slumber by the tantalizing smell of bacon and eggs, followed by Nan, whose gleaming white dentures longed to bite into a couple of slices of toast smothered in marmalade.

Standing to attention, as though he was still on parade with the Green Howards, his serviette tucked into the waistband of his trousers, Herbie watched the disparate members of the Kingsley family as they entered the dining-room one by one, until, at last, Grace, the linchpin on which the wheel of the family revolved, came in with a tray of plates piled high with freshly cooked food. There was another breakfast for himself, which he tackled with gusto, pausing now and then to smile across the table at his old friend Bob, who had scarcely changed in appearance since they had first palled up together in France, during the war.

What a lucky sod Bob Kingsley was to be sure, Herbie thought, married to a fine woman like Grace, with four kids to his credit. Seemingly nice kids at that. The boy called Jimmy, and the younger girl, Kerry, were listening to their father intently as he recounted a few memories of the war – the lighter side of things, mainly connected with the odd characters they'd met during their training. The older boy, Danny, and his sister Dulcie, appeared to have other thoughts in mind, and the old girl sitting next to Grace obviously considered war talk in bad taste as a Sunday morning topic of conversation.

Knowing the danger signals by the look on her mother's face, Grace skilfully changed the conversation to what they'd all be doing after breakfast. Mrs Daniel's face darkened even more when Kerry said she was going to church, meaning St Mary's, not just because it was handy but because she loved the cool, dim interior, stained-glass windows, the great lectern eagle, the procession of clergy and choirboys down the aisle, and the glowing splashes of colour dappling the embroidered altar cloth.

'I don't hold with popery,' Mrs Daniel said briefly, to Kerry's consternation.

'But Nan,' she said artlessly, 'the vicar isn't a pope, he's just an ordinary man in trousers and a – a surplice.'

Herbie burst out laughing while Grace got up to clear the dishes. 'I can't see it matters all that much,' she said cheerfully, 'as long as we all go to heaven in the long run.'

'And you a Methodist,' Nan said sternly. But Grace wasn't listening, or pretended not to hear. 'When you've finished eating, Dulcie,' she said, 'you can give me a hand with the washing up. You too, Kerry. Bob, Mr Barrass would like to look round the town centre. Mother, why don't you go into the front room?' Jimmy, she knew, would spend the morning in his 'study'. 'Danny,' she said, 'if you've nothing else to do, you might as well go with your dad and Mr Barrass. The exercise will do you good.'

Grace knew that her Sunday morning would be spent in the kitchen preparing and cooking the one o'clock dinner. Not that she minded peeling potatoes, beating the Yorkshire pudding batter, basting the beef, paring apples and making pastry, just as long as she hadn't anyone under her feet, spoiling her enjoyment of the Sunday morning service on the wireless. She regarded it as a mental run-up to the Sunday afternoon ritual of a visit to her aunts, Fanny and Rosa, the recurring weekly horror of damp egg-and-cress sandwiches and Rosa's *spécialité de la maison*, Swiss roll with a smattering of raspberry jam encased in sponge cake made with plain flour. No baking powder.

When her mother came into the kitchen, looking pained, to ask, 'Who is that dreadful man you've given house-room to, and when is he leaving?' Grace said brightly, switching off the wireless, 'Oh, that reminds me. I promised to sponge and press his suit.'

'You did *what*?'

'Well, you see, he's a salesman, so he has to look smart,' Grace hedged, refusing to succumb to her mother's badgering, wishing she would go back to her knitting and leave her in peace to get on with the baking.

'He's common, if you want my opinion,' Nan said stiffly.

Grace sighed. 'If that's your opinion, you're entitled to it. Now please, Mother, I have work to do.'

'Oh, I know what's in your mind,' Mrs Daniel exclaimed bitterly. 'You wish I had never come here to live. Well, you needn't worry, I shan't be with you for very much longer. I've decided to move in with Fanny and Rosa.'

Grace looked at her mother in dismay. 'But *why*? Bob and I have done our best to give you a good home, to make you feel welcome.' Dusting the flour from her hands, 'I know we've had our ups and downs occasionally, but I thought you were happy here.'

'In that case, you thought wrong!' Mrs Daniel said harshly. 'I'll be far happier, much better off with Fanny and Rosa, people of my own generation who understand what it feels like to be old and unwanted.'

The beef spurted suddenly in the oven. Lowering the temperature automatically, scarcely realizing that she had done so, 'Unwanted? Mother, that's a terrible thing to say to your own daughter,' Grace replied hoarsely. 'Besides which, it simply isn't true! How could you even think such a thing?'

Mrs Daniel said bitterly, 'When your father was alive, I had him to lean on. Now he's gone, I have no-one to turn to.'

'You have me.'

'If that's what you think, you're much mistaken. The only person you've ever cared about is that husband of yours. How do you imagine your father and I felt when you told us you had to get married? Why, you weren't even ashamed of yourself.'

'Oh, for God's sake, Mother! Need we go through all that again?'

'No need to blaspheme! Fanny and Rosa want me, that's why I'm going to live with them. I'll tell them this afternoon when we go there for tea.'

Sitting stock still, Kerry gazed at the coloured rays of light dappling the altar, touched to the heart by some mystery beyond her power to understand. How silly and ignorant she was. She didn't even know which page to turn to in order to follow the service. All she really cared about was the loveliness of the great plumes of double white lilac spilling their fragrance into the air about her, the colours of the stained-glass windows shifting and changing as rapidly as the coloured pieces trapped within the kaleidoscope her father had given her on her tenth birthday – just as moonlight on the sea altered and changed with every movement of the restless tides and currents washing in on the shore.

No longer a child, not yet a woman, Kerry felt herself caught in the undertow of the two states of being, with nothing to cling to in the painful process of growing up apart from her parents whom she loved intensely, and something even deeper which she could not explain to anyone, not even herself. Deep within was a hidden well-spring of delight: a passionate love of beauty, words and music which belonged to her and her alone, which no-one could ever touch or destroy as long as they remained her secret source of happiness.

Sitting in front of the dressing-table mirror, Dulcie looked avidly at the secret store of make-up hidden away in the handkerchief sachet her grandmother Kingsley had given her last Christmas: sixpenny tins of Snowfire face cream and powder, a wand of Maybelline mascara, a pot of Bourjois rouge and a Tangee lipstick. At sixteen she was old enough, she reckoned, to begin wearing make-up. All the other waitresses at the Pavilion used it, so why not her? She knew why not: because her parents would have a fit if she did. So what? They need never know if she went about it the right way. True, Dad always came to meet her when she was on late duty at the hotel, but she could wash it off in the cloakroom beforehand, so he needn't know she had appeared in the dining-room looking reasonably attractive, despite her overweight body and her black-and-white uniform.

It was also high time she had her hair permed, Dulcie thought. Yes. She'd have it done first and worry about her parents' reaction later. And she really would try to curb her appetite, try to lose weight. As the thought occurred, she sniffed the air with glee at the scent of the Sunday dinner rising up from the kitchen, imagined the bliss of sitting down to a heaped plateful of roast beef and Yorkshire pudding, roast potatoes, carrots and onion gravy, with apple pie and custard to follow. Hurrying down to the dining-room, she bumped into Herbie Barrass on the half landing.

'Hey, beautiful, why the rush?' he asked mildly, reverting, without thinking, to his normal line of patter with the female sex, young or old.

Deeply offended despite having been called beautiful, pushing past him without a word, the day had not yet come, Dulcie thought prudishly, when she wished to be admired by a bandy-legged little man in a shabby tweed jacket and a pair of shapeless flannel bags, old enough to be her father.

After the dinner pots had been washed and put away, the Kingsley family and Mrs Daniel went to their various rooms to get ready for their afternoon excursion to the South Cliff, to visit Fanny and Rosa.

Putting on her best coat and hat, Grace told Bob that her mother had decided to live with her sisters.

'God help her digestion then,' Bob said light-heartedly, not pausing to consider the effect of his foolish remark on his wife, who burst into tears. 'I'm sorry, love,' he said contritely, 'but if that's the way she wants it . . .'

'You've never really liked her, though, have you?' Grace asked, wiping her eyes.

Searching his conscience, wishing to be entirely truthful and honest, Bob said slowly, 'I don't exactly love her, if that's what you mean, but I respect her. The boot's on the other foot, isn't it? She hates the sight of me.'

'Oh, come on, let's get it over and done with as quickly as possible,' Grace said stoically, dabbing her nose with *papier-poudre* tissue, too tired with all the cooking, clearing and washing up to think logically for the time being. 'What about Herbie? Is he coming with us?'

'Yes, of course. We couldn't very well expect him to stay on his own, now could we?'

'I suppose not.' At that moment, Grace wished she could slip into bed, cover her head with the bed-clothes, and sleep until Doomsday. Instead, head held high, she sailed downstairs, smiling, to fulfil her role as the mother of the family, the one they all looked to for guidance, love and understanding, with the possible exception of Mrs Daniel and Dulcie, who had got it into their heads that nobody at all really loved and understood them as they wished to be loved and understood.

In the spring and summer, or as long as the weather was fine, the little procession would wend its way down Paradise to the Foreshore and walk along the sea-front to the penny tramway which would swoop them up the stiff incline to the South Cliff promenade. From there it was simply a matter of crossing the road to South Street, where Fanny and Rosa lived above their fancy-work shop.

No-one, apart from Mrs Daniel, looked forward to these weekly visits. Bob suffered them for his wife's sake. Danny and Jimmy loathed them. Dulcie wriggled out of them whenever possible. Grace endured them for her mother's sake; Kerry saw the two aunts as tragic figures, and wove stories about them in her head. But she adored the South Cliff and the tram-ride; loved the breathless moment when the two carriages would meet, mid-way, and cross – one going up, the other down. Standing at the far end of the carriage with its slatted seats and straps for people to hold on to if the lift was packed with holidaymakers, she would feel like a bird in flight, watching, entranced, as the whole of the South Bay, the sands, the rocks, the sea, the lighthouse, the castle, and the Spa Gardens, were revealed to her in all their glory, toy-like in dimension.

On this occasion, Herbie Barrass wondered what the hell he had let himself in for. As a mark of respect, he had put on his sponged and pressed navy-blue suit, a clean shirt and a stiffly starched collar. But to sit down in the suit might crease the trousers, and so he stood beside Kerry, looking down at the panoramic view of the South Bay, feasting his eyes on the scene below, comparing it mentally with Chapeltown.

Taking afternoon tea with a couple of old biddies who lived above a fancy-goods shop seemed to him a poor way of spending a glorious summer afternoon. But, his heart told him, he would have gone anywhere, done anything, to please Grace Kingsley. Glancing over his shoulder at her, he saw that she was seated beside the old girl, her mother, looking straight ahead, her neatly gloved hands clasping the handbag on her lap, wearing a perched-forward straw hat, secured by a pearl-knobbed hat-pin and an elastic band beneath her bun of light brown hair.

Swallowing hard as the man in charge of the lift opened the gates and they filed out onto the promenade, Herbie imagined Grace's hair spread about her shoulders, at bed-time.

Aunt Rosa, a slightly built, fussy woman with curler-tortured hair arranged in a careful fringe on her forehead, opened the door to them and led them upstairs, chirruping like a canary. The room they entered resembled a furniture repository, Herbie thought. Never in his life had he seen so many overstuffed armchairs, occasional tables, ornaments, screens, pictures and photographs in the same place at the same time.

Amid this ruination of a room sat a very large lady wearing a tent-like, ankle-length gown of black georgette. It was hung about with multi-coloured bead necklaces, a lorgnette and a variety of floating ninon scarves over which she wore a deeply fringed, exotic shawl of Spanish origin, embroidered with brilliantly coloured birds of paradise.

'Forgive me, my dears,' Aunt Fanny murmured as they entered and ranged up before her, 'I'm feeling a little tired today. We've had such a busy week, haven't we, Rosa?'

'Oh yes,' Rosa lied bravely, 'a very busy week indeed, with the visitors and all.'

'You shouldn't be working so hard, not at your age,

Fanny,' Nan admonished gently, kissing her sister's cheek. 'You're not as strong as you pretend to be at times.'

Fanny smiled wanly. In her youth, she had been considered the beauty of the Mallory family, and she was still beautiful, Kerry thought. A bit like a fully opened rose whose petals were about to fall. Her skin was creamy white. She had heavily lidded blue eyes and a mass of faded fair hair caught back in a romantically floppy bun from which little tendrils escaped, to brush her well-upholstered shoulders.

In the manner of a queen holding court, she enquired, 'Who is this young man?' holding up her lorgnette to inspect Herbie, who was standing stiffly to attention.

Kerry said brightly, 'He's a friend of Dad's. His name's Herbie Barrass, and he's staying at our house.'

'I see. Well, do sit down.' With a wave of a plump, be-ringed hand, Fanny indicated the wealth of chairs ranged about the room. Not that the Kingsley family needed telling where to sit. They had occupied the same chairs every Sunday afternoon as far back as they could remember.

When Aunt Rosa had scuttled through to the kitchen to put the kettle on, Fanny began her usual question-and-answer session aimed at her great nephews and nieces in particular, and laced with comments regarding their appearance which they found harder to swallow than Rosa's Swiss roll.

'Are you sure you're getting enough to eat, Jimmy? You're as thin as a rake.'

'I'm all right,' he muttered, deeply embarrassed.

'Just mind you don't outgrow your strength, that's all. How tall are you now?'

'Five foot ten. The same as I was last week.' He coloured to the roots of his hair.

'And you, Danny. Have you found yourself a lady friend yet? High time you were thinking of settling down.'

'I'm not thinking of settling down just yet,' Danny said mutinously, put out because Fanny had unwittingly touched a sore spot, as if she had read his mind regarding Wilma Burton.

'You are obviously getting enough to eat, Dulcie.' Fanny

sighed deeply. 'I, too, was well built at your age. But, as my dear father would say, "Build up your constitution while you're young, Fanny my dear, then you'll have something to fall back on the rest of your life."'

Dulcie could have killed her.

'So you've left school now, have you Kerry?'

'Yes, Great Aunt Fanny.'

'Have you a job in mind?' Kerry was Fanny's favourite.

'No, not yet, though I wouldn't mind going to work in a sweet shop. I've always wanted to crack toffee with a hammer.' She smiled like a sunburst, a happy girl unaware of her potential, so glad to be alive that she couldn't care less what she did for a living, just as long as she could feast her eyes on moonlight and stars, borrow books from the public library, go to the pictures on Saturday night, breathe in the scent of white lilac, and listen to the sound of rain at night when she was safely tucked up in bed.

'No! Cracking toffee in a sweet shop is out of the question,' Fanny said, shaking her head so quickly that her bun nearly came unstuck. 'You must do something artistic.' Turning her attention to Grace, she said, 'You cannot possibly let Kerry work in a sweet shop! It's out of the question.'

'She'd probably eat all the profit,' Dulcie commented snidely. Fanny treated her to a withering look. Dulcie writhed inwardly.

'What have you in mind, Aunt Fanny?' Grace asked patiently.

'Simply this, my dear. You've heard of Hodnot's Decorative Accessories shop in St Nicholas Street? Well, the owner happens to be a friend of mine. I could put in a good word for Kerry, if you like.'

'Really? That is most generous of you,' Grace acknowledged in surprise. 'What do you think, Bob?'

'Sounds fine to me,' Bob conceded, equally surprised that the dithery Fanny had actually come up with a concrete suggestion for once in her life. 'What do you think, Kerry?'

42

'Oh yes,' Kerry said ecstatically, 'it's a lovely shop! I'd enjoy working there.'

When Rosa rustled into the room bearing a tray containing the violet-patterned cups and saucers that were part and parcel of the afternoon tea ritual, the menfolk rose to their feet to clear a space on the table near the window; Herbie felt that he had entered the pages of a novel by Charles Dickens. Not that he had ever read a novel by that celebrated Victorian author, but he knew all about him, just as he knew all about Admiral Lord Nelson and the Battle of Trafalgar.

Sitting down, the thing that worried him most was, how the hell was he supposed to hold a tea-cup in one hand, a plate in the other, and eat an egg-and-cress sandwich at the same time? Glancing across the crowded room, he caught Grace's eye, saw her amusement at his dilemma. Was it possible, he wondered, that old Mrs Daniel had given birth to the most beautiful woman in the world? The more he looked at the pair of them, the more unlikely it seemed. Time played havoc with some human beings, he knew, but it was difficult to imagine Mrs Daniel ever being young or remotely pretty. What had happened to dry up the sap in her veins? And yet she seemed inordinately fond of her sister Fanny.

Now the old girl was sitting like a ramrod in the chair next to her sister's, glaring across at him as if his presence prevented her saying something of importance not meant for the ears of an interloper, as though willing him to get up and leave the family circle.

He rose awkwardly to his feet when he had swallowed, albeit painfully, his portion of Swiss roll washed down with tea. 'If you'll excuse me,' Herbie said haltingly, 'I think I'll take a stroll along the promenade.'

'Oh, may I come with you?' Kerry asked brightly. 'You might get lost otherwise. Besides, I'd like to show you the Spa.'

Grace breathed a sigh of relief. 'You might as well all go,' she said, meaning the children. 'I'm sure your great aunts will excuse you.'

'I'll see you out,' Rosa chirruped nervously, wondering why the sudden exodus as she pecked each cheek in turn, apart from Herbie's. He, to her utter amazement and pleasure, kissed hers.

'You really made Great Aunt Rosa's day,' Danny said as they walked along South Street to the promenade. 'Did you notice the way she blushed when you kissed her? What made you do it, Mr Barrass?'

'Because I reckoned she deserved a kiss,' Herbie said simply.

'Ugh, that awful Swiss roll and those rotten egg sandwiches,' Dulcie complained. 'I felt like puking at the sight of them.'

'I'm not surprised,' Kerry said stalwartly in defence of the great aunts' tea-party, 'after all the food you put away at dinner-time.'

'I pay for my keep, which is more than you do,' Dulcie replied sharply.

'That's because I haven't started work yet,' Kerry retorted. 'How am I supposed to pay for my keep when I've only just left school?'

'Shut up, Dulcie,' Jimmy said levelly. 'You've never even begun to pay Mum for the amount of food she shovels into you, so you've no room to talk.'

'Oh, trust you to side with Babykins,' Dulcie snapped back at him, in high dudgeon, and flounced ahead of the party, at war with herself and the world in general.

As they turned the corner on to the Esplanade, Kerry murmured ecstatically, 'Oh, isn't the sea lovely?' Smiling at Herbie, she asked, 'Do you like Scarborough, Mr Barrass?'

'Yeah. It's great.'

'Just wait till you see the Spa.' Kerry skipped excitedly at the thought of the crowning of the Rose Queen ceremony that would take place there on the 25th of June. She could see it quite clearly in her mind's eye, the Rose Queen of Scarborough and her retinue walking down the long flight of steps to the lower promenade: the throne and the crowd awaiting the queen, the scattering of rose petals at her feet . . . If only she could be that girl, that chosen queen of Scarborough, walking down the long flight of steps wearing a rose-pink crinoline, holding a bouquet of long-stemmed roses in her hands, smiling left and then right at the crowds of people gathered together to watch her enthronement. But she was far too young.

Struck by the beauty of the girl, listening to her description of the crowning of the Rose Queen ceremony, knowing what was going on in her mind, Herbie said quietly, 'All you have to do is wait a little while longer. In four years from now, you'll be the loveliest Rose Queen of them all.'

In the room above the fancy-goods shop, Nan Daniel told her sisters that she intended to move in with them as soon as possible.

Stacking the violet-patterned cups, saucers and plates on a stout oak tray, Rosa Mallory's heart lifted suddenly with joy and relief intermingled at the thought of an influx of income sufficient to enable the payment of several long-overdue bills, not to mention the enhancement of her own and Fanny's daily intake of food, which consisted mainly of bread and potatoes, rice pudding, savoury ducks and lightly boiled eggs.

The trouble with Fanny was that she never seemed to realize the seriousness of their financial situation. All she cared about was stitching brightly coloured beads onto muslin jug-covers, embroidering lace-edged tray- and table-cloths, and sticking sea-shells on boxes and photograph frames. Not that Rosa had always seen eye-to-eye with Nancy, who could be overbearingly bossy at times. Even so . . .

Grace was saying that this was none of their doing. 'We want Mother to stay with us, don't we?' She glanced at Bob appealingly.

'Of course. But if her mind's made up, have we the right to stand in her way?'

Too attached to the past to care much about the present,

45

Fanny said dreamily, 'Nan knows she's welcome to live here if she wants to. We're not short of space.'

'It won't take long to clear the room on the top landing,' Rosa chipped in.

Nan's eyebrows shot up. 'The *top* landing?'

'Well yes. What's wrong with that?' Rosa's hands trembled on the tray she was holding. 'It's a very nice room.'

'Then I suggest you sleep there and let me have your room on the first landing,' Nan said forcefully. 'After all, Rosa, you have no furniture to speak of, and your wardrobe is half the size of mine.'

Rosa bridled. 'Small it may be, but it's solid mahogany, and . . .'

Oh God, Grace thought wearily – families.

The argument was hotting up now. 'Of course, if it's too much trouble,' Nan said, ready to do battle with Rosa.

'If *what* is too much trouble?'

'Having me to live here.'

Rosa's lips quivered. 'I said no such thing, I'm sure. I appeal to you, Fanny, did I say a word about trouble? All I said was . . .'

Why, Grace wondered, no matter how hard one tried to steer a steady course through life, came these constant reminders of whirlpools ahead? No sooner was one problem solved than another cropped up to take its place.

Chapter Three

Grace gave Herbie's shoulders a last-minute brush, and perked up a clean hanky in his breast pocket. She had washed his best shirt the day before when she came back from South Street, and Bob had hammered a couple of segs into the heels of his shoes before giving them a good old polish.

'There, you'll do,' she said, standing back to assess her handiwork. 'Now, remember your opening gambit?'

'Sure thing.' Herbie grinned. 'Good morning, madam, allow me to present my card.'

'Good. And just remember to let the buyer do most of the talking.'

'Be humble, you mean?'

'Not at all. You should feel proud of your samples. After all, you're not selling rubbish. Ambrose Wilson is a reputable firm, and the buyer will know that.'

Kerry came into the hall from the kitchen at that moment, looking more subdued than usual.

'Well, what do you think?' Herbie asked her. 'Will I pass muster?'

'Yes, you look fine.' She smiled, but the sparkle was missing. He wondered what was troubling her.

'Well, off you go, and good luck,' Grace said briskly. 'There's a bus due in a few minutes.'

Clean and decent, with a good breakfast inside him, samples case in hand, Herbie walked down the steps and crossed the road to the bus-stop feeling that he could sell ice-cubes to an Eskimo, seeing this glorious June morning as a new beginning, a freshly turned page in his life. In the space of a few hours, his faith in human nature had been restored. His parents had died young, leaving him at the mercy of the State to provide a series of homes for unwanted children, in which he had been clothed, fed and given a rudimentary education. Little else besides. Certainly not love.

When war came, he had been among the first to join up. For the first time in his life he had been imbued with a sense of purpose and identity, the feeling of being as good as the next man. Inured to discipline from an early age, he had experienced none of the traumas of nostalgia and home-sickness prevalent amongst men who had been torn from their families. Men like Bob Kingsley, for instance.

Private Barrass had been a good soldier, he reckoned, fearless in the face of enemy fire. After all, what had he to lose apart from his life? And what difference would his dying make to any living creature? Even so, his gorge had risen at the evidence of man's inhumanity to man when he saw the dying and the dead, the maimed and the blinded brought in by the stretcher bearers.

Thereafter, he had viewed his existence with a fatalistic attitude which ruled out commitment to any one person, principle or set of ideals, and when the war was over he had returned to civvy street to earn a living as best he could. He'd known many women whose company he had enjoyed to the full, had never married because he had nothing to offer. Love 'em and leave 'em was his motto.

Now, through a quirk of fate, he had been accepted, warts and all, by the kind of family he had never known before, never even knew existed. Moreover, he had fallen in love for the first time in his life. It made no difference that the woman he loved was as unreachable as the moon and stars. He would love Grace Kingsley till the day he died, lay down his life for her, if necessary.

On early duty at the Pavilion after her weekend off, Dulcie stared anxiously at her reflection in the cloakroom mirror. Had she put on too much rouge, she wondered, too much lipstick and powder? Her heart had beat quickly against her ribs as she applied items from her five shillings' worth of Woolworth's make-up, knowing her parents would strongly disapprove if they knew she was going behind their backs to make herself more attractive to members of the opposite sex. But surely every girl had the right to make the best of herself, Dulcie thought mutinously, to find her own place in the sun? The right to be admired?

She had been on duty on Friday night when a wealthy couple had entered the dining-room. The husband – fortyish, handsome, wearing a faultlessly tailored evening dress suit, pearl cufflinks, a gold wrist-watch and several ornate rings – possessed that air of authority common to very rich men, a certain smoothness and polish, as though he had been buffed with a chamois leather. But it was the man's wife who had made a far deeper impression on Dulcie.

Why, she's fatter than I am, she thought as the woman sailed into the room wearing a scarlet chiffon gown upheld with rhinestone shoulder straps, a dress so beautifully cut that it swirled about her as she moved. Her hair was dyed blonde, her skin glowed beneath perfectly applied make-up. She appeared not to give a damn about her size, and why should she? Everything about her suggested the cosseting of extreme wealth, the confidence that only wealth could impart, the couture gown, perfume, jewels, the mink stole about her shoulders.

I could look like that if I had her money, Dulcie thought enviously, making up her mind that she would, one day, *have* money, no matter what she had to do to get it.

Walking into the dining-room to begin serving breakfast, deeply conscious of her Maybelline mascaraed eyelashes and Tangee-reddened lips, she felt that she had taken a step in the right direction. And when she came off duty, she would go to that hairdresser's shop round the corner from the Odeon cinema, and book an appointment to have her hair permed.

Grace knew what was troubling Kerry. She had taken the news that Nan would soon be going to live with Fanny and Rosa badly. It was inevitable in Kerry's case, Grace realized, which was why she had imparted the news as gently as possible. Tender, growing girls of Kerry's age believed the world as they knew it would go on for ever, and it was right that they should think so. A sense of security, of continuity, was the greatest gift parents had to give to their children. God help the world if that should ever change. But, sadly, life had a way of moving on. Nothing remained static, and this was the hardest lesson of all to learn.

At least the Monday washday ritual never changed, Grace thought wryly as she went through to the scullery to sort through the mound of shirts, socks and underwear awaiting her attention. Kerry was in the kitchen, washing up the breakfast dishes. Nan had gone up to her room to start emptying drawers. When the pots had been dried and put away, Kerry came through to the scullery, looking lost. To take her daughter's mind off her troubles, Grace said briskly, 'If you've finished the washing up, you might as well go down to the market for me.'

Kerry was a good little shopper, and she loved the market. The girl brightened visibly. 'Just see if they have any nice firm tomatoes,' Grace went on, 'and you'd better buy a couple of heads of lettuce, a cucumber, and half a pound of butter. My purse is in the top drawer of the dresser – and you needn't hurry back.'

Joyfully, Kerry raced upstairs to put on her cardigan, her life restored to normality for the time being. Her mother was in the scullery doing the washing, and they'd be having cold meat and salad for tea. All was well with her world.

'Good morning, madam, allow me to present my card.'

The buyer of Boyes' lingerie department treated the presenter of the card to a searching look of appraisal before inviting him through to her office to display the contents of his samples case. 'You're new to this area, aren't you?' she enquired, looking at him intently through her pince-nez spectacles.

'Yes, madam, I have that – er – privilege.' He'd been about to make some jocular remark about new brooms sweeping cleanest and remembered, just in time, Grace's advice to let the buyer do most of the talking. Best leave out all the funny remarks, he decided. After all, he was a salesman, not a stand-up comedian.

'Tell me, Mr Barrass, are you a married man?' the buyer asked unexpectedly.

Thinking quickly, 'Oh yes, ma'am,' he replied, *sotto-voce*, 'and if my missus, that is my wife, was here with me now, she'd tell you that the goods I'm selling can't be bettered for quality, fit, or – dependability. Why, she swears by them – in the nicest possible way, of course. Take these corsets for example . . .' He choked back the words, 'They're her mainstays in life', wondering if he would ever get the hang of curbing his wicked sense of humour. At least, for Grace Kingsley's sake, he was doing his best. And he really wanted to keep this job, to keep on returning to Scarborough for the foreseeable future, not to lose touch with the Kingsley family. Especially not Grace, the wise and loving mother of the family.

Kerry wandered happily round the market, loving the long iron trestles set out with fresh farm produce: blocks of yellow butter, brown speckled eggs, and the jars of home-made marmalade and lemon curd produced by the farmers' wives who had brought them to the market early that morning. Plump, comfortable-looking women with worn hands and seamed yet smiling faces.

She loved equally the stalls piled high with fruit and vegetables: mounds of golden oranges and bananas imported from faraway countries, the boxes of Jersey-grown tomatoes, the long green cucumbers and the paler green heads of lettuce alongside the more mundane offerings of King Edward potatoes, carrots and parsnips. Above all, she loved the tapering green tin vases of flowers, in particular the clustering bunches of violets, green-leafed, bound with pale yellow raffia, costing tuppence a bunch. Only tuppence, Kerry thought bemusedly, for so much beauty and fragrance encapsulated within those shy and lovely blossoms, and her mother loved violets . . .

Leaving the market, Kerry walked down Eastborough to the Foreshore. The tide was out, the sand firm and wet near the water's edge. The summer season had not quite begun yet, although the first of the visitors were seated in deck-chairs on the sands, their faces turned to the sun. The beach was already dotted with green canvas ice-cream stands, and the donkeys had come down from their fields near Oliver's Mount to stand patiently awaiting the hoisting aboard their saddles of small, eager children, shouting, 'Gee-up, Neddy!'

The summer season would not truly begin until the opening of the Summer Shows, Kerry knew. Not until the commencement of the Rolling Stones Concert Party at the Floral Hall; the Bouquets, and the Spa Orchestra under the direction of Alick MacClean, the Miniature Railway at Peasholm, and the re-opening of the South Bay Bathing Pool – which she could see quite clearly from where she was standing – just beyond the South Cliff tramway and the moss-covered rocks of the Children's Corner.

Looking out to sea, her hands gripping the railings, watching the seagulls flying, strung between two states of being, Kerry wondered if she would ever be able to bridge the gap between the child she now was, and the woman she glimpsed just ahead of her: a stranger with whom she scarcely knew how to cope, a shadowy figure beckoning her on – herself in the years to come.

She walked home by way of St Nicholas Street, wanting to take a look at Mr Hodnot's shop. Decorative Accessories was a posh name, and this was a posh street, one of the finest in Scarborough, with the Town Hall at one end, the Royal Hotel, Bright's the jewellers, and a Colonial gents' outfitters, whatever that meant – perhaps only Colonels could shop there?

Boots the Chemist's shop was at the other end of the street, facing a phalanx of tall, impressive buildings, mainly banks, with Marshall and Snelgrove's exclusive department store halfway along. On the same side was Mr Hodnot's, into whose window she looked with a funny, tickly feeling of excitement at the wonderful goods on display: hand-made lampshades lavishly trimmed with tassels and gold braid, vases and Chinese bowls in glowing colours, silver cigarette boxes and jade ornaments, satin, velvet and brocade cushions laid upon a swag of emerald silk material.

Nothing more remote from Fanny's fancy-goods shop could be imagined, thought Kerry, with its window display of hand-knitted tea-cosies and dolls' clothes, shell-boxes and beaded milk-jug covers. Walking on past Marshall and Snelgrove's, she couldn't help wondering how her great aunt Fanny came to know Mr Hodnot well enough to put in a good word for her. Perhaps they were secretly in love? With that thought in mind, she fairly wafted home on a cloud of romance to find her mother and Nan in the kitchen, eating poached eggs on toast.

'Where have you been all this time?' Nan asked tetchily. 'Loitering as usual, I suppose? Well, you'll have to pull your socks up when you begin work, that's all I can say.'

'I told Kerry she needn't hurry back,' Grace said, on the defensive once more, trying to control her temper. Her mother had given her a hard time all morning, appearing in the scullery at intervals to complain about this and that, when all she wanted to do was get on with the washing. 'She's been to the market for me to do the shopping.'

'Huh,' Nan said, with a toss of her head. 'Knowing Kerry, she'll have forgotten what she went for, I dare say.'

Grace's temper flared, 'I'll have you know,' she began, but Kerry forestalled her. Laying the brown paper bag containing two bunches of violets beside her grandmother's plate, she said brightly, 'These are for you, Nan. I thought they'd look nice in that little cut-glass vase on your dressing table.'

'Oh well, I never . . . What a kind thought. Thank you. Yes, they will look very nice on my dressing table.' The old woman actually smiled, holding the violets.

Trust Kerry, Grace thought, getting up to put the kettle on, knowing full well the flowers had been meant for her.

*   *   *

Up at the crack of dawn, Grace had packed sandwiches for Bob and the boys, as she did every working day of the week, to save them time and money. Bob preferred not to close his shop at midday, when many an off-chance customer popped in for a shave or a haircut, and her sons could not afford to eat out, even at one of the cheaper cafés in the town centre.

Mondays were always tough and demanding for her, faced with all the washing and ironing, the reason why the Monday evening meal consisted of cold meat left over from the Sunday dinner, jacket potatoes and salad. Today had been a marvellous drying day, thank God. Standing at the ironing-board in the kitchen, listening with half an ear to music on the wireless, her hands busily engaged, her mind, nevertheless, was more busily engaged in thoughts of her family, her niggling worries concerning their welfare.

Pressing the collar of Danny's best shirt, she wondered what he got up to in his spare time. Difficult to tell with boys of his age. Boys? But Danny and his brother Jimmy were fully grown men now, she told herself, and what Danny, in particular, got up to away from home was his own business, not hers. Even so, she could not help worrying when he came home late, especially from the Olympia Ballroom on a Saturday night, with lipstick on his collar.

Thankfully, Jimmy seemed content enough with his attic room and his writing. But was he getting enough fresh air and exercise? And was it natural that a good-looking boy of eighteen evinced not the slightest interest in girls?

As for Dulcie . . . How could a child conceived with so much love and passion have grown into a plain, dull 16-year-old girl whose only interest in life appeared to be food?

Other young mothers from the Roscoe Street days had told her how lucky she was to have such a placid baby, when they had met occasionally in the street for a bit of a gossip, long after she and Bob had moved away from the area.

They'd have thought her crazy had she told them she preferred lively babies who bashed the sides of the pram with a rattle, kicked and squalled at bathtime, and splattered the tray of the high-chair with unwanted food. There was something unnerving about a placid baby who slept between meals and awoke to eat everything put before her. Where had she gone wrong with Dulcie? Somehow she had never been able to get close to the girl, as she had to Kerry. She realized, of course, that Dulcie was jealous of her sister, and she could see why. But Dulcie had never been bright or communicative, even as a small child before Kerry was born. And yet . . . It seemed to Grace that there were banked-down embers in Dulcie that might one day burst into flame.

Bob stopped to pick up a paper on his way home from work. So Stanley Baldwin had taken over as Prime Minister from Ramsay MacDonald? Not surprising really. MacDonald had been ill for some time. Not that Bob was all that interested in politics. Sport was more in his line. Cricket, football, boxing, and there were two great heavyweight fights in the offing – Primo Carnero versus Joe Louis in New York, and Walter Neusel versus Jack Petersen in London, later this month.

He walked home briskly, looking forward to his supper and an evening of relaxation. Perhaps he and Grace would take a walk along the Foreshore later, for a breath of sea air. She'd seemed a bit tense lately. No wonder, with that mother of hers to contend with. He wasn't sorry the old girl was leaving. Mrs Daniel had a way of putting people's backs up. Pity poor Fanny and Rosa when she moved in with them. She hadn't been very pleasant to Herbie, come to think of it. Herbie. Bob wondered how he'd got on that day. Well, he'd soon find out.

Danny and Jimmy walked home together, as usual. Danny in his working suit, collar and tie, Jimmy wearing his overalls; Jimmy taller than his brother, less compact, more intellectual. And yet a great bond of affection existed between them, although Danny couldn't understand his brother's lack of interest in the female sex. In fact, he'd asked him point blank one day, 'You're not "queer" are you?'

'How do you mean – "queer"?'

'Well, you know – a nancy boy?'

'How would you like your teeth rammed down your throat?'

'All right. Keep your hair on, I only asked.'

'Yes, well, don't ask again. Just because I don't go sniffing round girls like a randy dog doesn't mean I'm short of male hormones!'

They had punched each other affectionately afterwards.

Now Danny said, 'I've met this girl . . .'

'Oh yeah? What about her?'

'I dunno. I like her a lot. She's different. I – I think I might ask her to start going steady.'

'Oh? Well, who is she? Where did you meet her?'

'Her name's Wilma Burton. I met her at the Saturday night dance.'

'Come off it, Danny,' Jimmy said scornfully, 'you know as well as I do you fall in love with a new girl every week. What's so special about this one?'

'I don't really know, except I can't get her out of my mind. She's kind of – elegant.'

'Have you told Mum?'

'No, of course not. Don't be daft. There's nothing to tell her – yet.'

'When are you seeing her again?'

'Wilma? On Wednesday night. We're going to the Capitol to see *The Lives of a Bengal Lancer*.'

'Then what?' Jimmy insisted.

'How the hell should I know?' Danny exploded. 'It all depends how we get on together, if I like her as much on Wednesday as I did on Saturday! Oh, shut up, will you? And don't you dare say a word to Mum! I'll have your guts for garters if you do!'

'As if I would!' Jimmy grinned as they walked up the steps together.

*　　　*　　　*

Dulcie had come home much earlier, after luncheon at the Pavilion had been served, the dining-room vacuumed, the table-cloths changed, and the cutlery laid for dinner. Feeling guilty about the secretly arranged hairdressing appointment, after a brief word with her mother in the kitchen, she had gone upstairs to lie down, exhausted by the long morning shift and all the running about she'd done.

'You know, love,' Grace had said lightly, feeling as if she was treading on eggshells, 'you could find another, easier job, if you want to.'

'I *don't* want to,' Dulcie said snappishly, 'I like it fine at the Pavilion.'

Upstairs in her room she kicked off her sandals; lying down on the bed and sinking her head in the pillows, she wondered where else would she find a job likely to bring her into contact with rich people? Where else would she have been given a lunch of roast pork, cauliflower cheese, steamed chocolate pudding and hot chocolate sauce? So thinking, she belched windily before falling fast asleep with her mouth wide open.

Meanwhile, Kerry had set the dining-room table, washed the lettuce, prodded the jacket potatoes, and filled various glass dishes with pickled onions, beetroot, chutney and cucumber, whilst her mother finished the ironing and hung the clothes on the ceiling-rack to air. Grace carved the remains of the Sunday joint in readiness for the jacket potatoes when they were done, pleased that all would be waiting when her family came home from work. And ah, here they came now, first Bob then the boys. But where was Herbie?

Weary but happy, he entered the dining-room when the family had almost finished eating.

'Well, old son, how did it go today?' Bob asked jovially.

'Great. Just – great.'

'Go on then, tell us about it,' Bob insisted.

'Not until the poor man has had something to eat first,' Grace said, realizing that Herbie was close to tears. 'Danny, pass Mr Barrass the bread and butter. You, Jimmy, hand him the salad cream.'

Reading the look of gratitude in Herbie's eyes, Grace thought what a very nice man he was. Not at all the kind of person she had at first imagined him to be, but a warm-hearted, sensitive human being, overwhelmed by his first taste of success.

Herbie went back to Leeds like a giant refreshed, anxious to present to his employers the well-filled order book in his samples case. Bob had slapped him on the back and told him to come back soon. Grace said, 'You must promise to take better care of yourself from now on. No more pie-and-pint lunches, remember?'

Chapter Four

Worried that Rosa might find the clearing of the room on the top landing too much for her, Bob went up to South Street one evening after work, to lend her a hand. Nan had already begun packing her belongings in the tea-chest he'd lugged upstairs from the shed, even though the removal date had not yet been decided. This was the way with old people, he thought wryly, wanting everything done at the double. It was the same with his own mother when she had decided to move away from Scarborough after the death of his father, to live with her sister in Bridlington.

To his dismay, Rosa burst into tears when she saw him standing on the doorstep. 'No need to cry,' he said awkwardly, patting her shoulder.

'But if you only knew . . .' Her lips quivered. She blew her nose on a lace-edged hanky. 'What I mean is, everything's getting on top of me just now. I scarcely know where to begin.'

He'd always had a soft spot for poor Aunt Rosa with her pinched, reddened nostrils, myopic blue eyes, and her gallantly curled fringe of wizened grey hair. 'That's why I'm here,' he said cheerfully, following slowly in her footsteps as she led him up the winding stairs to the top floor, understanding what she meant by her remark when he saw the amount of rubbish which had been allowed to accumulate in his mother-in-law's future accommodation: an old dressmaker's dummy, off-cuts of carpet, stacks of cardboard boxes, wire mattresses, piles of newspapers dating back to the war; odd items of broken furniture and china, bundles of old clothing and worn-out domestic appliances.

Ye gods, Bob thought, what a shambles. What was needed here was a lorry to take all this stuff to the Council tip. But things were never that simple where old folk were concerned. Even as he hefted the off-cuts of carpet onto his shoulders with a view to taking them down to the back-yard, Rosa was wringing her hands and saying they might come in useful some time in the future, until Fanny appeared on the landing, a bizarre figure in her black get-up, multi-coloured scarves and dangling bead necklaces, her feet encased in fur-trimmed bedroom slippers, to thwart her sister's twittering with a wave of the hand.

'Oh, do stop fussing, Rosa dear,' she said airily, 'and go and put the kettle on for a nice cup of tea, otherwise we shall end up nowhere.'

Bob could not have agreed more, at the same time thinking that Fanny, despite her air of other-worldliness, probably possessed more common sense than Nan and Rosa rolled into one.

Now the time had come to have her hair permed, Dulcie entered the salon, head held high despite the dryness of her mouth, the slight trembling of her legs, and the clamouring of her guilty conscience that she had not told her parents she was about to have her straight brown hair made curly. But what the heck? This was *her* hair, *her* life, her own money she was spending . . .

Never had she imagined such a faffing going on. First the cutting and shampooing process, followed by the drying of her hair with a scorching hot hand-drier, the hooking of her hair through rubber pads placed next to her scalp, the winding of her hair on aluminium rods bound with crêpe hair and string, until her head resembled a porcupine: the dipping of the permanent wave sachets in a smelly solution: sachets tightened with clamps to hold them in place during the baking process.

She viewed with alarm the long black cylinders and wires of the perming machine, the placement of the cylinders over the sachets, the plugging in of the machine to the electricity supply.

'Please, miss, try not to fidget,' the assistant advised her as the machine grew hotter and hotter, standing by with a roll of cotton wool to stuff under the rubber pads if the heat became unbearable. 'As the saying goes, pride must bear a pinch now and then.'

A pinch? Dulcie could not even begin to tell the girl which heater was too hot to bear. Her whole head seemed to be on fire. Then, suddenly, the ordeal was over, the machine was unplugged and she staggered back to the chair in front of the shampoo basin to have the paraphernalia of sachets, clips, aluminium rods, string, crêpe hair and rubber pads removed; to have her hair shampooed once more, then fingerwaved and pin-curled into the latest style, after which she was obliged to sit, for the next half hour, under a hood-drier, from which she eventually emerged to stare in horror at her new coiffure, which resembled a set of tramlines soldered to her scalp with setting lotion.

A fine drizzle of summer rain had begun to fall when she left the salon, and she had nothing to put over her head. By the time she had walked home, Dulcie's permanent wave had frizzed into a kind of bush about her face.

Unfortunately her mother was in the hall when she came in. 'My God,' Grace uttered despairingly, 'what on earth have you done to yourself?'

'I've had my hair permed, that's all,' Dulcie retorted quickly, defensively, heading for the stairs.

'I can see that. But *why*? Just you come back here, my girl! I want an explanation.'

'There's nothing to explain,' Dulcie said defiantly. 'I decided to have my hair permed. I paid for it myself, so why the fuss?'

'Paying for it yourself is beside the point,' Grace said heatedly. 'What worries me is that you went behind our backs to have it done in the first place! *Why*, Dulcie? Why did you do that?'

Dulcie's mouth quivered. 'Because I'm sixteen years old, a woman, not a child any longer. You have no right to dictate to me what I should or shouldn't do!' She fled upstairs to her room.

Grace's first instinct to follow the girl, to continue the argument, subsided as she realized the folly of driving an even deeper wedge of misunderstanding between herself and Dulcie. Perhaps *she* was at fault. After all, she had been married at sixteen, pregnant with Danny – a fully grown woman in her own eyes, if not in the eyes of her parents. In which case, how could she possibly condemn a 16-year-old girl's right to have her hair permed?

Even so, returning to the kitchen to put the finishing touches to the evening meal, Grace could not help wishing that Dulcie's perm had enhanced her appearance, that the money she spent had not been entirely wasted. What Bob and the boys would say when they saw the new-look Dulcie, she could not imagine.

In the event, Bob told her in no uncertain terms that she should have prepared them for the shock, whilst Danny and Jimmy teased her unmercifully, asking which tribe she intended joining up with in the Congo. Nan's comments were uttered on a note of sharp disapproval of silly young girls who saw too many gangster films and ended up looking as common as dirt.

Goaded past bearing, Dulcie rushed out of the dining-room, crying hysterically that she was sick and tired of the lot of them.

'Well, I hope you're pleased with yourselves.' Grace got up from the table. 'I'd best go up to her.'

'I'll go, if you like,' Kerry said. Putting herself in Dulcie's shoes, the least said soonest mended. Perhaps she could persuade her sister to go for a walk along the Foreshore, to soothe her injured feelings.

On the back row of the Capitol cinema, during the showing of *The Lives of a Bengal Lancer*, Danny groped for and held Wilma's hand in the torture scene, when slivers of bamboo were driven beneath Gary Cooper's fingernails. Truth to tell, he was far more interested in the girl beside him than what was happening on the screen: her face, seen in profile, the delicate perfume of 4711 eau-de-cologne emanating from the collar of the pink blouse she wore beneath her pink, hand-knitted cardigan.

After 'God Save the King', he led her masterfully towards the Londesborough Lodge Gardens, another old stamping-ground of his from previous encounters with many a former girlfriend. But this time was different. He really fancied Wilma, desperately wanted to make love to her, to break down her maddening air of prim self-containment, and remembering that he had almost done so the night of their first meeting. Almost, but not quite.

These gardens, once the private property of Lord Londes-borough, were far more secluded than the St Nicholas gardens, much prettier too, and more romantic, overlooked by the Lodge – now a medical baths – where King Edward VII had once stayed, as a guest of the Londesborough family. That was in the heyday of his affair with the actress Lillie Langtry, the 'Jersey Lily'.

A broad terrace with a stone balustrade led down to a lawn with a splashing fountain set amidst floating lily-pads, from which radiated a series of pathways overhung with summertime trees in new leaf, one of which passed beneath a low, ivy-clad bridge, where the shadows lay deepest – a warm, enfolding darkness made for lovers.

It was there that Danny, holding Wilma in the circle of his arms, kissed her until, his senses swimming away from him, he uttered the fatal words, 'I love you'. Bemused by her fragrance and fragility, the taste of her moist pink mouth on his, he really believed that what he said was true.

Further inflamed by her slight withdrawal, the turning aside of her head, her whispered words that he should not say such a thing unless he really meant it, Danny protested vehemently that he *did* mean it.

'But we scarcely know each other. How can you be sure?' Wilma wanted everything cut and dried. Her mother had warned her often enough not to let any man take advantage of her, always to keep control of her feelings whatever the circumstances, to find out what was on offer before committing herself to a certain course of action, no matter how tempting that course of action may be.

She asked winsomely, 'Are you asking me to go steady with you?'

And, 'Yes,' Danny blurted, overwhelmed by a feeling of relief that he knew exactly where he stood with her at last; knowing that he wanted to go steady with Wilma more than anything else in the world. In the fullness of time he would buy her an engagement ring. But not yet. All he wanted right now was to hold her, kiss her, show her a good time, to take her dancing at the Olympia Ballroom every Saturday night, to the summer shows, to Peasholm Park where he would hire a canoe to paddle her, at dusk, beneath the Japanese lanterns strung along the shores of the lake.

With all these delights in mind, sweeping her into his arms once more, he said buoyantly, 'The sooner you meet my family, the better.'

On safe ground now, Wilma allowed him to kiss her quite passionately. Even so, common sense warned her not to let his lovemaking get out of hand. Remembering her mother's good advice to 'save herself' for her wedding night, she had no intention of allowing Danny to take liberties of an intimate nature before she had his wedding ring on her finger. Meeting his family would be the first step in the right direction and she must, of course, take him home to meet hers. Not that they were likely to raise objections to her going steady with someone who worked at the Town Hall, but her father could be cross-awkward at times, and he would need to be worked on in advance to put on his best suit and a clean collar and shirt to meet his future son-in-law.

Wilma had everything worked out in her mind's eye, even to the wedding dress, and how many bridesmaids she would have, as she responded to Danny's kisses beneath the stone bridge in the Londesborough Lodge gardens, until . . .

'If you think I'm that kind of girl,' she cried out as he attempted to undo the top button of her cardigan, 'well, I'm not, that's all!'

Deeply ashamed, 'I'm sorry, Wilma,' Danny uttered

contritely. 'I really am sorry. It's just that I love you so much I . . .' Words failed him. Aflame with desire and carried away by Wilma's response to his ardour, he had simply done what any normal, full-blooded man of twenty would have done in attempting to come closer to the object of his desire. He should have known, should have realized that Wilma Burton was a cut above all the other girls he had kissed and cuddled beneath the bridge, especially Annie Cooper, a worldly-wise young woman who, one cold December night, just prior to his nineteenth birthday, beneath this very bridge, had laughingly, expertly, robbed him of his virginity: had taught him everything he needed to know about sexual intercourse between a man and a woman.

Now, all he could do was repeat over and over again, 'I'm sorry, Wilma. Please say you forgive me. I just got carried away that's all!' Swallowing hard, 'It won't happen again, I promise!' He smiled awkwardly, 'Well, at least not until we're married.'

Seizing the opportunity with both hands, 'You mean you – that we are engaged?' Wilma asked breathlessly, 'That you are asking me to *marry* you?'

Vaguely aware that he had said far more than he meant to say for the time being, that he had become enmeshed in a far deeper net than he had envisaged in asking Wilma to go steady with him, giving up the unequal struggle, 'Yeah, I guess so,' Danny replied uncertainly, re-fastening the top button of her cardigan.

'For what it's worth, I think your hair looks quite nice,' Kerry told her sister. 'At least it will when it's settled down a bit. I dare say it went frizzy 'cos you walked home in the rain with nothing on your head.'

Linking arms with her misunderstood sibling, she continued, 'The boys were only teasing you. As for Nan, well, she has a way of saying things she doesn't really mean.'

'Oh, it's all very well for you to talk, but what do *you* know about the way I feel? You're just a kid,' Dulcie said bitterly. 'Miss Prim and Proper who never puts a foot wrong in the eyes of the family!'

Feeling in her pocket for her weekend sixpence, not yet broken into, Kerry said, 'Come on, I'll treat you to an ice-cream cornet at Jaconelli's!' She could not bear to see her sister so unhappy. True enough, she was just a kid, but that did not necessarily mean being blind to what was going on around her. In any event, a letter had arrived that morning from Mr Hodnot, fixing an appointment for the following Wednesday afternoon, for an interview arranged by Great Aunt Fanny. If she was successful in becoming an assistant at Decorative Accessories, she, Kerry, would begin to grow up in a hurry: no longer a kid, but a responsible young adult earning her own living.

Dulcie brightened a little as the scent of fish and chips struck her nostrils. 'Oh, put your pocket-money away,' she said loftily, secretly pleased with her new hairstyle, delighted that one or two people had actually turned round to stare at her as they passed by. 'I'll treat you to a fish-and-chip supper at the Golden Grid if you like.'

Entering the restaurant with Kerry in tow, she wasn't such a bad kid after all, Dulcie thought, despite her prissiness and barmy ideas about moonlight and romance. She, at least, had been the only one to stick up for her in her hour of need, to say that she liked her new hairstyle. With these thoughts in mind, Dulcie ordered with gay abandon: two fish-and-chip suppers, mushy peas, a plate of bread and butter, a pot of tea, and two knickerbocker glories for dessert. Last week had been a good week for tips at the Pavilion Hotel. And in Dulcie's view this was what life was all about: money. The possession of money. The power of money . . . Money to squander on the good things of life: food, clothes, make-up, a new hairstyle, if she felt so inclined. *Money*. She hadn't had her fill of it yet, but she *would*. In time to come, she would have all the money she needed to cock a snook at her present lifestyle, to her family – particularly her mother, her two brothers, and Nan, who had never even begun to understand her desperate desire to break away from the close-knit, inhibiting family circle of which she had never been anything more than an outsider, an onlooker.

Little wonder, she thought. As far back as she could remember, she had felt herself overshadowed by her boisterous older male siblings, who would tweak her hair if they felt like it, pinch the food from her plate when their mother wasn't looking, and run away from her so fast that she couldn't catch up with them. Playing ball, they would never throw the ball to her, so that she always seemed to be reaching up to grasp the unattainable. Then, to add to her frustration, a new baby had arrived to claim her parents' attention. Not that Dulcie's memory extended back that far. She had simply become aware, in the fullness of time, that the newcomer had supplanted her as the baby of the family. Thereafter, jealousy had reared its ugly head, especially since her brothers appeared to adore their enchanting baby sister with her quiff of golden hair, beautifully modelled face, and enormous blue-grey eyes.

From then on, it seemed to Dulcie that a hard shell of resistance had grown up inside her as a repellent against the unfairness of life. Times without number, staring at herself in the full-length wardrobe mirror, she would wonder why it was that she had been blessed with a lumpy body and a fat face without one redeeming feature? Why was her hair mouse-brown and straight? Her nose a blob?

Had she taken the trouble to smile more often, she might have noticed that she possessed fine teeth set within generously proportioned lips, that her brown hair was thickly abundant, in keeping with the similarly-coloured, boldly-etched eyebrows above her pale blue eyes. But, having got it into her head that everything in the world was wrong with her, she hadn't the sense to see what was right with her. She had fallen into the trap of wishing to alter her appearance, her lifestyle, beyond recognition, hence her preoccupation with money. Money, which she saw as the only means of release from her present bondage. Money to spend, at will, in beauty parlours, on massage and mud-packs.

It never even occurred to her, as she wolfed down a

plateful of fish and chips, bread and butter, and a knicker-bocker glory, that she was adding to her troubles: her avoirdupois.

When they returned home, Dad was sitting in the back room, his ears glued to the wireless, listening to a boxing match. Nan was casting on a new jumper, her lips firmly clenched as she counted the stitches, Mum was in the kitchen making a pot of tea, Jimmy was upstairs in his room, writing, and there was no sign of Danny, who had gone to the Capitol to see *The Lives of a Bengal Lancer*.

'Did you enjoy your walk?' Mum asked, pretending not to notice Dulcie's hair as she scattered the contents of a packet of chocolate digestive biscuits onto a plate.

'Oh, yes,' Kerry replied brightly. 'Dulcie treated me to fish and chips at the Golden Grid, didn't you, Dulcie?' (Nudging her sister in the ribs with her elbow.)

And, 'Yes,' Dulcie said sullenly, awaiting the onset of another lecture about her hair, which, to her surprise, was not forthcoming.

'In that case, you won't be wanting any supper,' Grace ventured light-heartedly, 'so why don't you pop off to bed, the pair of you? Just say good night to your dad and Nan before you go.'

When they had done as they were bidden, standing at the foot of the stairs as they went up to their bedroom, Grace wished she had possessed the wit and wisdom to hold Dulcie close in her arms and tell her it didn't matter a damn about her hair. What she could not have borne was her elder daughter's rejection of her warm, conciliatory embrace, the coldness of her eyes as she shrugged aside that embrace.

Meanwhile, at the Wembley Stadium in London, the German boxer, Walter Neusel, was beating the hell out of the British-born boxer, Jack Petersen, and in New York the reigning champion, Primo Carnero, was about to face defeat at the hands of the coloured fighter, Joe Louis, soon to become the undisputed heavyweight boxing champion of the world.

* * *

'Now, darling, there's no need to feel nervous,' Grace told Kerry, *sotto-voce*, as they entered Mr Hodnot's shop the following Wednesday afternoon. 'Just answer his questions quite naturally. Above all, don't fidget. Keep your hands in your lap, and your feet close together.'

'Yes, Mother,' Kerry murmured obediently, stifling a giggle at the thought of herself running amok in Mr Hodnot's emporium of good taste; swinging from a crystal chandelier or ripping open his feather-filled cushions with a penknife. As if she *would*!

'Ah, you must be Mrs Kingsley, and this your daughter Kerry?' Mr Hodnot, a tall man in his sixties, extremely well dressed, hair carefully arranged to cover the bald spots, emerged from his office to shake hands with Grace. 'If you would care to come this way. Please sit down.' Ensconced behind his desk, he continued, 'Miss Mallory suggested that Kerry might like to work here. May I ask why?'

Remembering to keep her hands and feet together, 'Because I think your shop is the bee's knees,' Kerry replied brightly. 'It's so – interesting and colourful. All those gorgeous swags of material in the window, and those lovely Chinese bowls and vases. Oh, working here would be far better than clattering butter or cracking toffee with a hammer!'

Grace's heart sank. Mr Hodnot coughed drily. 'I'm glad you approve.'

'Oh, I *do*!' Kerry assured him. 'I'd give my eye-teeth to work here!' Losing control of her hands, she spread them in an all-embracing gesture of delight, almost knocking over a jade ornament on Mr Hodnot's desk. 'I mean, it's all so – lovely!'

Fearing that her daughter might suddenly spring to her feet and begin waltzing about the office, causing mayhem, Grace said despairingly, 'Please, Mr Hodnot, you must forgive her. She *is* very young, you know.' Then, between gritted teeth, '*Kerry!*'

Kerry's lips quivered, her eyes filled with tears. Returning her hands to her lap where they belonged, 'I'm sorry, I got

69

a bit carried away, that's all,' she quavered, miserable because she had disobeyed her mother. Moreover, her own stupidity had cost her a job she wanted so much. Mr Hodnot would never employ her now, she felt sure, despite Great Aunt Fanny's recommendation.

Mr Hodnot was dabbing his mouth with a pristine handkerchief from his top pocket. Perhaps the poor man had a cold? He certainly had a nasty cough, and his eyes were watering. She could scarcely believe her ears when, replacing the hanky in his breast pocket, he said calmly, his coughing fit over, 'Enthusiasm for work is rare in most cases, believe me, but no job is as glamorous as it may seem at first glance. We do have lovely objects for sale, but they all need dusting. That would be your main responsibility as a junior assistant, Miss Kingsley.'

Kerry's eyes opened wide in surprise. So all was not lost?

'I should also expect you to find out about the goods on offer, where they were manufactured, and so on. In the case of antique items, something of their history. Customers are often quite knowledgeable, and I insist that my employees learn as much about the stock as possible.'

'Kerry was good at history at school, weren't you?' Grace supplied eagerly, glancing at her daughter for confirmation.

'Oh yes. I got ten out of ten for the Battle of Trafalgar.'

'Quite so.' Mr Hodnot coughed drily to hide a smile at the girl's charming innocence, her obvious desire to please. 'Of course, you would also be expected to unpack the stock as it arrives at the warehouse. Not a pleasant job, I fear, for which you would be expected to wear an overall and something to cover your hair. Straw has a way of getting on to everything, in my experience. Furthermore, it would be your responsibility to sweep up the warehouse afterwards.' He paused. 'Still interested?'

'Oh yes,' Kerry said ecstatically.

'Very well, then. Your daughter's starting wage would be seven shillings and sixpence a week, her hours 8.30 to 5.30 from Monday to Saturday – apart from Wednesdays, when she would finish work at one o'clock, if that is acceptable?'

He was speaking to Grace now, saying that, in six months' time, if Kerry worked hard and did well, she would receive an extra half-crown a week.

Ten whole shillings a week! Come Christmas, she could be earning ten shillings a week! Kerry's face reflected a kind of inner radiance at the thought, not so much of the money but the glorious anticipation of becoming a real live wage-earner at last. No longer a schoolgirl but a working woman.

When Grace had accepted Mr Hodnot's offer on Kerry's behalf, and they had agreed she should start work the following Monday morning, he led the way from the office through a connecting door to the workroom where three young women machinists were busily engaged in making curtains, pelmets and cushions to his customers' requirements.

There were shelves stacked with bolts of furnishing fabric, some patterned, some plain, in a multiplicity of colours and textures. Pattern books hung from brass cup-hooks. Other shelves held stacks of lampshade frames in varying sizes, cards of tassels and braiding, and lightweight lampshade silks and satins from the palest shell pink to a glowing aubergine.

Mr Hodnot explained that he attended personally to the cutting out of material for curtains, cushions and loose covers on the long table which occupied the central floor space of the work-room.

'I had no idea all this went on behind the scenes,' Grace said brightly. Mr Hodnot smiled, well pleased that Fanny Mallory had written to him that letter of recommendation concerning her great niece. Kerry, with her pretty, intelligent face, would be an asset to his business. Obviously the mother's charm and good looks had been passed on to her daughter, he thought, leading the way to the warehouse where floor to ceiling shelves were chock-a-block with a dazzling array of *objets d'art*, which appeared, to the bemused eyes of a 14-year-old girl, to be an Aladdin's Cave of treasures.

Hands clasped, eyes shining, Kerry caught the scintillating

facets of cut-glass vases and wine-glasses, the lustre of Malin pottery bowls, deep blue with intense shades of green reminiscent of an evening sky in summer, all deep, dark and mysterious, yet luminous, lit with starshine.

And just to think that she was now a part of all this richness! Her cup of joy spilled over in tears of delight.

The heatwave came with such sudden intensity that the town and everyone in it seemed to have geared into slow motion.

Plump matrons on holiday cast aside hand-knitted cardigans to reveal sagging upper arms larded with fat. Their menfolk covered their heads with knotted handkerchiefs to prevent the blistering of their scalps from the fierce arrows of the sun.

The procession of decorated cars along the Spa peninsula seemed to be moving at a snail's pace. Flags hung limply in the breathless air. It was a perfect day for the crowning of the Rose Queen ceremony and the Battle of Flowers.

Pretty girls perching on lumbering flower-decked floats flung blossoms at the onlookers thronging the promenade. Rose petals rained down like confetti. It was a whirling spectacle of colour and movement against a background of sapphire blue sea, to the music of the Scots' Greys Band at the head of the procession.

Those poor bandsmen must be melting in their uniforms, Grace thought, keeping a watchful eye on Kerry in case she got lost in the crowd, smiling as the girl scooped up a handful of petals to throw at the retiring Rose Queen seated on one of the floats, wearing a rose pink gown, surrounded by her retinue of attendants dressed in the Victorian style and clasping posies of rosebuds in pink-mittened hands, their faces framed with silk-lined bonnets tied with satin bows.

The retiring Queen's crown of paste diamonds sparkled in the sunlight on this, her last public appearance as the Rose Queen of Scarborough. Soon it would be placed on the head of her successor. How sad she must feel, Kerry thought, knowing her year of glory was drawing to a close. Clasping her mother's hand, she tugged her along towards the forecourt where the crowning ceremony would take place. Two thrones were set side by side beneath the long flight of stone steps leading down to the terrace.

Crowds of laughing, excited people lined the staircase, awaiting eagerly the appearance of the new Queen, enjoying the thrill, the romance, the drama of it all; tense with expectation as the heralds at the head of the stairs blew a fanfare of trumpets to signal her arrival.

Kerry's heart skipped a beat as the silvery notes threaded the air and the slightly nervous figure of a tall young woman, dark-haired and smiling, wearing a stunning gown of gold lamé, with a train of gold lined with ruched oyster satin, and carrying a bouquet of yellow roses, began the long descent to her throne, her crown.

Grace knew exactly what Kerry was thinking at that moment. But one day, perhaps, in the fullness of time, she might also walk down that flight of steps wearing a beautiful dress, carrying a bouquet of roses.

Chapter Five

Danny was acting strangely, mooning about the house like a dying duck in a thunderstorm. Girl trouble, Grace thought, correctly assessing the situation. He was a handsome young devil, and he knew it. Moreover, he knew that half the female population of his own generation in Scarborough thought so too. Washing up one evening after tea, she recalled his High School days, when he would swagger down Westborough trailing a wake of giggling girls in gym-slips, jockeying for position. She had seen him more than once, unbeknown to him; had felt sorry for the plain, pig-tailed little lasses to the rear of the procession, who stood no chance at all of getting closer to their idol.

Empying the washing-up bowl, turning to put away the pots, she bumped into him. 'Good gracious, Danny,' she said crossly, 'you nearly gave me a heart-attack!'

'Sorry, Mum.' He grinned sheepishly. 'The fact is, there's something I've been meaning to ask you.'

'I gathered as much. Well, what is it?'

'I've met this girl, you see,' Danny said haltingly. 'Her name's Wilma Burton, and I just wondered . . . What I mean is, I'd like to invite her to supper next Sunday.' He added, defiantly, 'I've asked her to go steady with me!'

'You've done *what*?' Grace looked at him aghast. Asking a girl to go steady was tantamount, almost, to a proposal of marriage. Her motherly instincts were fully aroused. 'But who is this girl? Does she come from a decent home? Decent parents?'

'Of course she does!' Danny turned prickly in defence of his girlfriend. 'Wilma is a perfect little lady. Very genteel.' He couldn't very well tell his mother that Wilma had refused to bare her bosom to him that night in the Londesborough

Lodge Gardens and so he sought refuge in a nettled hauteur that he was deemed incapable of choosing a decent girl to go steady with.

Weighing up the pros and cons, accepting the inevitable, Grace conceded. 'Of course you can bring her to supper if you want to. We'll look forward to meeting her.'

'Thanks, Mum. I'm sure you'll like her,' Danny sighed blissfully.

Bob took the news philosophically. 'Knowing Danny, it won't last five minutes,' he said, getting into bed.

Grace wasn't so sure. Seated at the dressing table to brush her hair, she saw in the mirror the face of a woman trying hard to accept that her son was growing away from her, that she no longer occupied the first place in his heart. How did the saying go? 'A son's a son till he gets a wife.' Bob hadn't seen the look on Danny's face when he spoke the name, Wilma Burton.

'Come to bed, love, and stop worrying,' Bob said tenderly.

But how could she help worrying? She'd have felt marginally better had not Danny already asked this – Wilma – to go steady with him. To add to her troubles, Nan had fixed the date of her removal on the day following Wilma's visit. Of all the days in the week, why had Nan chosen a Monday, Grace thought irritably, smack bang in the middle of a wash-day?

Getting into bed beside her husband, glad of his warmth, his strength, his arms about her, she said, 'Oh, Bob, whatever should I do without you?'

'Worry yourself into an early grave, I expect.' He held her close. 'Look love, we're in this together, remember. That's what marriage is all about, isn't it?'

And, yes, she thought sleepily – a covenant between two people to love and to cherish one another all the days of their lives.

*   *   *

Bob had been up to the South Cliff every evening after work for the past week, to decorate the room on the top landing, pressing Jimmy into service as his assistant. Thankfully, all the rubbish had now been got rid of, despite Rosa's protestations. The old spring-busted mattresses, bits of broken furniture, and the rest of the junk were stacked in the yard. Fanny had caused its disappearance by the simple expedient of tipping the dustmen to take it away, saying in that throaty voice of hers that, for an extra sixpence, they would probably have taken away the contents of the entire house.

Then Rosa and Nan had almost come to blows over who should occupy the room on the top landing. The weaker willed of the two, Rosa had lost the argument, which entailed the humping of her furniture upstairs and re-decorating the room Nan would occupy. Reluctant to enter into a family argument, Bob said patiently, 'Just tell me what you want done, and I'll do it,' thinking what a relief it would be when the removal was over and done with, and Nan was settled in her new abode. Then, perhaps, he and Grace would have a bit of peace. More time for each other.

Grace had finally decided on tinned red salmon, salad, new potatoes and sherry trifle for the supper party. Nan said it was too bad of Danny to invite some silly girl to supper on the eve of her removal. Biting back the retort that it was too bad of Nan to fix her removal on wash-day, Grace said she couldn't see why having Danny's lady friend to supper on Sunday should make the slightest difference one way or the other.

'Oh, trust you to take his side. Next thing you know, he'll be wanting to get married in a hurry,' Nan said snidely, put out because Grace had cancelled the Sunday visit to South Street in order to make preparations for the supper party. 'Anyone would think the King and Queen were coming to visit.'

'Please, Mother, not now! Can't you see I'm busy?' Grace hurried upstairs to the bathroom carrying a pile of fluffy

76

white towels and a tablet of Lifebuoy soap, just in case Danny's genteel girlfriend wished to spend a penny and wash her hands afterwards. Then, not *Lifebuoy*, she thought distractedly, with its connotation of body odour. Far better a tablet of Knight's Castile – hustling her menfolk's shaving gear out of sight in the airing cupboard.

After the midday meal had been cleared away and the washing up done, Grace set the dining-room table with her best lace-edged cloth, starched damask serviettes, and the Chinese Rose dinner service which was only trotted out on special occasions such as birthdays and Christmas. Every fork and spoon had been silver polished and buffed to perfection. 'Do you think it looks all right?' Grace enquired anxiously of Kerry, suddenly fearful of meeting Danny's young lady. 'Have we forgotten anything?'

'No, I don't think so. And the table looks – elegant,' Kerry said blissfully.

They went through to the kitchen together, Grace to open the large, expensive tins of sockeye salmon she had bought to honour the occasion, to pick out of them all the bits of bone and skin, and to patiently scrape the new potatoes which she placed in a pan of cold, salted water, to which she added, with a flourish, a sprig of fresh garden mint.

Meanwhile, Kerry was seeing to the salad, washing the lettuce, slicing the tomatoes and beetroot, skinning the spring onions, and whipping the cream for the trifle, the makings of which – sponge fingers, apricot jam, sliced peaches, jelly, sherry and custard – had been placed in the larder to cool and set overnight. No use cutting the bread and butter just yet, she thought, dolloping the cream on top of the trifle, on which she created a dashing design of glacé cherries, blanched almonds and strips of angelica. She could cut the bread and butter later, and see to the potatoes whilst Mum was busy entertaining Wilma. Suddenly, she burst out laughing.

'What's the matter?' Grace wanted to know.

'I was just thinking,' Kerry giggled, 'what a funny name, Wilma.'

Grace could have kissed her. Kerry had a way of putting things into perspective.

'Mother, this is Wilma,' Danny said. They entered the hall together, his hand firmly clasping her elbow – a proprietorial gesture which said it all so far as Grace was concerned. She experienced a queer ache deep inside at his protective air towards his young lady. She could see why. Wilma looked as if a puff of wind might blow her away. Not that she could fault her appearance. The girl looked as if she had stepped out of a band-box.

'How do you do, Mrs Kingsley?' Wilma extended a daintily gloved hand. She was wearing her favourite blue dress with the organdie jabot, high-heeled sandals, and pearl earrings. Her newly washed hair, fluffed out about her pale, wedge-shaped face, reminded Grace of candy-floss. She spoke in a thin, high-pitched, girlish voice, which set Grace's teeth on edge.

'How do you do, Wilma?' Asked why she had taken an instant dislike to the girl, Grace could not have come up with a satisfactory explanation. She seemed too good to be true, far too composed and self-possessed. Or could it be that the girl was shy, trying too hard to make a good impression? Really, Grace berated herself severely, she must give the lass the benefit of the doubt. It couldn't be easy for her, faced with the prospect of meeting the Kingsley family at one go.

Bob came into the hall at that moment, smiling and relaxed despite having been inveigled into wearing his best suit and a starched collar to honour the occasion. Accustomed to putting folk at their ease by reason of his profession, adept at making small talk, he prised Wilma away from Danny, guiding her to the front room where the family were assembled. He put the girl at her ease – or so he imagined – by making a jocular remark about Daniel and the lion's den, not realizing that Wilma was totally in command of herself and the situation. In any case, his remark had fallen on stony ground, as she hadn't a clue what he meant.

'This is my mother-in-law, Mrs Daniel,' Bob said heartily.

'How do you do?' Wilma's face remained blank.

'Er, Mrs Daniel is leaving us tomorrow to live with her sisters.'

'That's right! Tell the world and his wife my business!' Nan snapped.

In the hall, 'Well, what do you think of her?' Danny asked his mother, face aglow.

'She seems very – genteel,' Grace said helplessly, at a loss for words.

'Oh, she is. A perfect little lady,' Danny enthused, following in the wake of his beloved, leaving his mother on her own.

A feeling of intense loneliness swept over Grace. The inevitable had happened. She no longer occupied the first place in her son's heart. If only he had held out his hand to her, said, 'Come on, Mum, let's go in together, shall we?' Close to tears, Oh God, she thought, she mustn't cry. This, after all, was supposed to be a joyous occasion. Was she being a dog in the manger, an overly possessive mother envious of her son's happiness?

Of course not; she wanted him to be happy. It was high time he thought of going steady with the girl of his choice. It was the girl herself who worried her. She was too self-assured, too neat, too self-contained.

If only Wilma Burton had tripped over the doorstep, removed her gloves before shaking hands, dropped one of them, laughed and apologized, or if her petticoat had hung down a little at one side, Grace might have felt differently towards her. She mistrusted seeming perfection in any human being, especially, God forbid, in a future daughter-in-law. Alone in the hall, blinking back tears, struggling for composure before entering the front room to face the assembled family, Grace thought of the kind of girl she had envisaged for her son. She would, for instance, have welcomed to the family circle Meg Jenkins, who helped her father with his Friday morning fish round, taking the orders whilst her dad did the weighing up. A nice lass, Meg, bright-eyed, with a ready smile and a buxom figure, who served in Mr Jenkins's wet fish shop when she had finished helping him push his handcart round town. No airy-fairy nonsense about Meg, Grace thought, not like this – kewpie-doll Danny had brought home with him, but a real flesh-and-blood girl with a heart of gold and a bubbling sense of humour.

She'd been surprised to learn from Mr Jenkins that Danny had taken Meg to the pictures two or three times last summer, before their friendship had fizzled out. 'A pity really,' Mr Jenkins said regretfully. 'Meg seemed quite keen on him, and he's a nice lad, your son. But you know what young folk are like nowadays! Don't know their own minds for two minutes put together.'

Kerry emerged from the sitting-room, looking anxious. 'Are you all right, Mum?' she asked.

'Of course I am. Why?'

Kerry thought differently. Her mother looked troubled. Unhappy. Lonely. She said, 'I thought I'd best get started on the bread and butter, and put the potatoes on to boil. Nan's getting shirty.'

Oh God, Grace thought. Trust Nan.

'And I think Dad could do with a bit of help,' Kerry went on. 'He's doing his best, but . . . What I mean is, Wilma's just sitting there like a statue, and Danny looks as if he's been mesmerized.'

Mesmerized? Kerry's command and usage of language startled Grace at times. It was a pity she hadn't won a scholarship to the Girls' High School, Grace thought, just because she had failed so miserably at maths. But above and beyond all that lay the rapport between herself and her younger daughter, Grace realized, as if they had been cut from the same bolt of cloth. Kerry had known at once that she was troubled. But what right had the older generation to burden the younger with their problems?

Squaring her shoulders, she smiled. 'You see to the potatoes, love,' Grace said. 'I'll go and give Dad a helping hand.'

'Well, what did you make of that?' Bob winced slightly, removing his collar. A couple of raw spots had appeared where the darned thing had chafed his flesh during the evening.

Grace knew what he meant right enough. Letting down her hair, unwilling to have first say, she countered, 'Make of what?', knowing she was about to be told anyway.

'What the hell does he see in the girl, that's what I'd like to know!' His anger was at full throttle. 'Of all the prissy, self-satisfied little ninnies, she takes the biscuit! It made my blood boil, the way she treated you, picking at her food as if it would poison her, after all the trouble you went to. Ha!' Buttoning his pyjamas, he got into bed, thumped his pillows and lay on his back, glowering at the ceiling. 'But just you wait till I get a moment alone with him, I'll tell him what I think of his fakey girlfriend, the silly young fool.'

Bob had had his say, now it was Grace's turn. Getting into bed, she said, 'The state he's in, he wouldn't even listen. He's in love with the girl.'

'In love?' Bob burst forth. 'In love with that stuck-up young madam? What *she* needs is a lesson in manners!'

Tossing and turning in bed, unable to sleep, Kerry felt that a barrier had sprung up between herself and Danny. They had always been so close, sharing a special, teasingly affectionate relationship. Last night he had seemed a different person entirely – a Samson shorn of his hair. As for Wilma, talking to her had been like trying to get blood out of a stone. Kerry had felt like sticking a pin in her to wake her up a bit. Even Dad had stopped trying to be jolly. If only she'd smiled once in a while, but her face had remained an unsmiling mask of indifference throughout the meal, except when she looked at Danny, seated next to her, when she'd looked plain soppy. *Ugh!*

She might at least have said the table looked nice, after all Mum's hard work, Kerry thought mutinously. But no, all the daft thing had done was pick and poke at the food set before her. Worst of all, Danny had appeared not to notice his girlfriend's bad manners as she inspected, minutely, each lettuce leaf on her plate to make certain it had been washed properly before conveying it to her prim little mouth. As for the salmon, trust Wilma to find the one and only leftover bone from two tins of sockeye salmon, which she had pushed to the side of her plate as a kind of reproach to her hostess. Kerry couldn't help wishing the silly fool had choked on it.

Halfway through the meal, in a valiant attempt at breaking the conversational deadlock, Jimmy had asked Wilma if she liked poetry.

'Oh yes,' she replied non-committally, regarding him as if he had just escaped from the nearest lunatic asylum.

Obviously thinking he was getting somewhere at last, 'Which do you prefer?' Jimmy continued. 'Keats? Shelley, Byron or Rupert Brooke?'

'Huh?' Wilma said blankly.

'I mean, which is your favourite?' Jimmy persisted.

'Patience Strong,' Wilma said coldly.

At least Wilma had been out-matched in non-communication by Dulcie, a mistress of the game, who had ploughed her way through the meal in complete silence, and by Nan, whose thoughts were centred on herself and tomorrow's removal to South Street. Kerry's tender heart quivered with disappointment that her beloved Danny had not once smiled at her across the table, had not treated her to his special wink of approval of her presence in his life.

Crying into her pillow, Kerry concluded that if love turned people, particularly Danny, into strangers, she didn't want ever to fall in love, and pulled the eiderdown over her head.

The minute the meal was over, Jimmy had ducked quickly out of sight and dashed upstairs to the haven of his room beneath the stars. Writers, he had long since decided, need not adhere to set patterns of social behaviour. In any case, no-one would miss him, especially not Danny. And yet he felt sick at heart that his much admired older brother had fallen under the spell of a bit of a lass totally lacking in either brains or personality. Why? he wondered bitterly. *Why?* What the hell did Danny see in her?

Lying flat on his back, pillows bunched beneath his head, and pondering the situation, he reached the conclusion that Wilma was playing hard to get.

Yes, of course, that must be it. Danny had always enjoyed a battle of the sexes, much as he enjoyed hitting a cricket ball for six in the last over, or sending a rugger ball soaring between the goal-posts to win a narrow victory over the opposing team in the final moments of the game. What Jimmy could not bear to contemplate was that, Danny, Danny of all people, had succumbed to the dictates of some silly little lass who, crudely speaking, wouldn't drop her knickers for him until they were married.

Walking Wilma home, aware of her tenseness, 'What's wrong?' Danny asked her. 'Didn't you like my family?'

'That's not quite the point, is it?' she flung back at him, walking two paces ahead.

Genuinely puzzled, 'I'm sorry, I don't understand.'

Shrugging away from his touch, 'Why hadn't you the guts to tell them we're engaged to be married?'

Shocked to the core, 'Because we're not,' he blurted out.

'You'll be saying next that you didn't ask me to marry you that night in the Londesborough Lodge Gardens, I suppose?' Wilma said icily.

Truth to tell, Danny could not remember exactly what he had said to her that night, in the heat of his desire to make love to her. Searching his memory, 'Well, yes, perhaps I did, in a roundabout way,' he admitted unhappily, 'but—'

'But *what*, Danny? Either you want to marry me, or you don't. It's as simple as that. If you don't, then we might just as well say goodbye right here and now!'

Unable to face the thought of losing her, he said wretchedly, 'Of course I want to marry you. But why the rush? Frankly, I couldn't afford to get married at the moment. All I have is my salary, and twenty pounds in the Yorkshire Penny Bank.'

'But if you spent that twenty pounds on an engagement ring,' Wilma said coolly, 'we could start saving in earnest for a home of our own.' She added, more warmly, guiding his hand into the crook of her elbow, 'Just think of it, Danny. A home of our own. Wouldn't that be marvellous?'

And yes, Danny thought, being married to Wilma would be marvellous. Moreover, knowing he had access to her slim, fragrant body whenever he wished, would be more than marvellous. Nothing short of a bloody miracle.

Chapter Six

Nan was in the hall, hovering, unnerving the removal men. 'Oh, be careful with that wardrobe,' she cried out as they manoeuvred it past the half landing. The piece was a towering mahogany edifice with a full-length mirror in the centre panel. 'Mind that glass!'

'Come into the kitchen, Mother.' Clasping Nan's arm, Grace propelled her away from the danger zone. 'The men know what they're doing.' She spoke calmly, despite her inner turmoil and the wash-house full of steam. 'I'll make some tea.'

Now the time had come, she couldn't believe that her mother was really leaving, and felt that she had failed her in some way, had not done enough to make her happy: the kind of guilt feeling experienced when someone dies and people wish they'd said and done more during that person's lifetime.

'You might have left the washing till tomorrow,' Nan said.

'I know, but I wanted to get it out of the way.' Grace had been up since the crack of dawn to make an early start.

'Now you can't wait to get *me* out of the way, I suppose?'

'That's not true!' Grace could have wept. 'I want you to be happy. I hope you will be, with Aunt Fanny and Rosa.' She put the kettle on to boil.

'I dare say we'll rub along well enough together.' Nan sighed deeply. 'Of course, they'll never understand, how could they, what it's like to be a widow?'

Trying hard to keep cheerful, 'But at least you had a husband, a happy married life,' Grace reminded her mother, getting out the cups and saucers, mugs for the removal men. 'Remember the time we went on holiday to Ireland?'

'Huh, shall I ever forget it?' Nan pursed her lips

85

disapprovingly. 'Why your father wanted to go there in the first place, I shall never know. All those dreadful rough roads and donkey carts.'

'I'm sorry. I never knew . . .' She gazed through the mists of time, 'I've always thought how happy we were there. I couldn't have been more than six or seven at the time, but I've never forgotten it – the little whitewashed cottages, the hills, the colour of the grass, the places we stayed.' Making the tea, with a quickening heartbeat, she said, 'There was one place in particular. In County Kerry. Do you remember? A small hotel set back from the road. I had a bedroom at the head of the stairs.'

'Hotel?' Nan said indignantly, 'It was nothing of the kind! Just a nasty public house. We would never have put up there in the first place had we realized that beer and strong spirits were sold on the premises! No wonder you had bad dreams with all that noise going on downstairs. All that raucous singing, and some wretched man tuning up his bagpipes.'

Mrs Daniel wrinkled her nose distastefully. 'Apparently there was some kind of celebration afoot. A human sacrifice, I shouldn't wonder! I was never so frightened in all my life.'

The Kerry Dance, Grace thought. Those warm-hearted Irish folk in the public bar had gathered together to join hands in the Kerry Dance – a celebration of life, not death. She had heard their laughter on the night air. Standing on tiptoe to look out of the window, she had seen a trail of winking lanterns between the trees leading down to the glen. And then what? She couldn't for the life of her remember what had happened next. Perhaps she had imagined or dreamt that she had witnessed the Kerry Dance? But if she *had* imagined or dreamt it, why had it stayed so vividly in her mind all these years?

Filling the mugs, she took them through to the hall to revive the removal men, and asked them how much longer they would be.

'Another half hour should do it,' the foreman said. He added heavily, 'I suppose the missis in yonder will be coming with us?'

'I'll keep her here for as long as possible,' Grace promised, thinking it wise not to mention he'd have Aunt Rosa to contend with at the other end.

Finishing her tea, 'I'd best go and see what those removal men are up to,' Nan said, getting up from the table.

'No need to hurry. Let them have their tea in peace. Sit down. Let me pour you another cup,' Grace suggested. Thankfully, her mother complied. But how to break down the barrier of resistance which had sprung up between them, all those years ago, when she had told her she was pregnant?

Their time together was fast running out. Grace said hesitantly, 'I wish you could find it in your heart to forgive me. You know what I mean? When I told you I had to get married.'

Nan's cheeks reddened. 'I don't want to talk about it,' she said flatly.

'But don't you see, Mother, I want you to talk about it? To understand why it happened. How *I* felt?'

'That is so like you,' Nan said, 'always seeking justification for something you knew to be wrong at the time.' Her voice rose. 'Never a thought to spare for the way your father and I felt when we knew what you'd been up to behind our backs. Behaving like a common servant girl. Ha! And your dear father a respected member of the Methodist Church.'

The foreman poked his head round the door at that moment. 'Thanks for the tea, missis,' he said, handing Grace the empty mugs. 'We'll be on our way quite soon now.'

'About time too.' Nan got up from the table. Grace went through to the wash-house. 'Where are you going?' her mother called after her.

'To hang out the washing.'

'But you can't. Not now. There isn't time!'

'Then I'll *make* time!' Grace picked up the clothes' basket. Deriving comfort from the soft warm summer day, she stepped out into the yard where the clothes' lines were strung between the posts, her eyes blurred with tears. Deeply distressed by her mother's lack of understanding, it was little wonder, she thought, that she had ceased to find solace in religion. Had she really behaved like a common servant girl all those years ago? On the other hand, why bracket all servant girls as 'common'?

Pegging out the washing, she remembered her father, and wished that she had known him better during his lifetime. Had she loved him or not? She couldn't honestly remember. He seemed a remote, shadowy figure to her now: a small, neat man, far less robust than her mother, forever writing sermons in his study, or dashing off to some prayer-meeting or other, whose eyes had never squarely met hers just prior to, and forever after, her wedding day. Yet surely, by reason of his calling, he was the one person she should have turned to for understanding?

Treading the paths of memory, she remembered him best on that Irish holiday long ago, seated in a donkey cart: he was laughing, his hair blowing in the wind, holding her hand, and she knew that she *had* loved him then, as a laughing child secure in the knowledge of his love for her. So what had happened to change all that? She knew the answer. A war had happened.

The bright summer day was drawing to a close. Now that Nan was safely ensconced with her sisters, Bob had planned an outing. He and Grace, Kerry and Jimmy were going to the seafront to watch the passing of the *Mauretania* on her way to the breakers' yard at Rosyth.

Dulcie was working late, Danny was taking Wilma to the pictures, and so, after tea, Grace and Bob walked arm-in-arm down Paradise, Jimmy and Kerry just ahead of them. It was a warm, pellucid evening. Grace felt like a schoolgirl neglectful of her homework. It had seemed so odd, locking the front door behind them, not having to leave Nan alone in the house. She certainly wouldn't have wanted to come with them, in which case, Bob knew, Grace would have made some excuse to stay with her mother – that she was too tired, or wanted to finish the ironing. There had been a kind of emotional blackmail on Nan's part, that reproachful look of hers, that air of, 'Oh, go out and enjoy yourselves, I dare say I'll still be here when you get back.' The inference being that she might have 'popped off' in the interim.

Even now, remnants of guilt clung to Grace like seaweed to a rock. Perhaps, she suggested, they should take the tramway to the South Cliff to make sure that Nan had settled in.

'We'll go tomorrow night,' Bob said firmly.

Fairly dancing with excitement, Kerry thought about the *Mauretania*. She had seen ocean liners on celluloid many a time, but never a real one, close to.

'She won the Blue Riband, you know,' Jimmy said loftily.

'She? Who?' Kerry wanted to know. 'What's the Blue Riband?'

'The *Mauretania*, of course. And you mean to say you've never heard of the Blue Riband?'

'I only asked,' Kerry responded mildly. 'How am I supposed to learn if I don't ask questions?'

Jimmy was fond of his sister, an intelligent kid on the whole, and she liked poetry. Real poetry, not that dreadful doggerel penned by Patience Strong. Striding along beside her, the thought occurred to him that Kerry's intellect was far greater than his had been at the same age, her imagination much keener than his: a bitter pill for a budding author to swallow. No wonder he chose to talk down to her occasionally. He plodded doggedly through life. Kerry appeared to dance through it. Therein lay the difference between them.

Walking along the Foreshore, Grace gasped in amazement at the number of people thronging the pavements, weaving and interweaving like the threads in a tapestry. Turning her head, she saw that the lighthouse pier was thronged with visitors awaiting their turn to board the *Coronia* and the *Royal Lady* for a closer look at the *Mauretania* when she sailed into view, and the bay was alive with smaller craft awaiting the coming of the leviathan.

Now the summer sky was fading quietly to the deepening dusk of an English twilight, the colour of a robin's egg-shell:

the palest turquoise, lit with a tremulous star or two, a hint of saffron on the far-flung horizon.

A feeling of peace washed over Grace, an inexplicable sensation that she had stepped back in time to recapture the magic of summer evenings long ago, when she and Bob had walked together in the Italian Gardens, wondering what life held in store for them, two young lovers on the threshold of life, lost in the mystery of love, two shadows beneath the trees, catching the heady scent of roses and lavender, watching the moon rise over the sea. Tomorrow night, she thought, hugging Bob's arm, after they had been to South Street to see Nan, they would walk home by way of the Italian Gardens, then down the winding paths to the shore where they would stand for a little while watching the waves crumpling in on the sand, and see the myriad twinkling lights of the Foreshore necklacing the bay.

They paused near the railings, gazing out to sea. Waiting. Waiting for what? They scarcely knew. A ship. An ocean liner which, for all they knew, might pass like a shadow to her graveyard at Rosyth, for all the world like a tired, defeated old lady shorn of her former glory, her days in the sun.

Suddenly, *'There!'* Kerry cried breathlessly. 'She's coming. Look. She's *coming*!'

They saw the ship, at first, as an optical illusion, a vision suspended in time and space, a trick of the imagination, as unreal, as ghostly and insubstantial as a mirage in some far-off desert, a shimmering phantom in the heat-haze rising from the sea. Was she coming closer or not? No-one could tell for certain if she was real, or just a dream. Kerry's heart throbbed painfully with excitement as the great liner sailed slowly into view, her four massive red and grey funnels towering above her mammoth superstructure, blazing light from stem to stern.

Tears rolled down her cheeks unchecked as the proud mistress of the sea fired three rockets into the still night air, and dipped her flag in salute to those gathered together to pay homage to her passing.

'I don't understand,' Kerry said, clinging tightly to Jimmy's hand, her voice harsh with tears, 'why anyone would want to destroy something so lovely; so – magnificent.'

Understanding her distress, 'Neither do I,' he admitted. 'It's just the way of the world, I guess. Something the powers-that-be call progress.' Placing his arm about her shoulders, 'Never mind, kiddo,' he added compassionately, 'at least they can't get rid of the stars!'

An overwhelming sense of loss assailed Kerry as the great ship passed the castle headland and was lost to sight. Then the four of them turned to walk back along the seafront, to form part of the pattern of humanity, Kerry in the polka-dot summer dress her mother had made for her, and the cardigan that Nan had given her on her fourteenth birthday.

Nan. Kerry had known, when she came home from work, that her grandmother's room would be empty, that she would not be there at the tea table. She had not fully realized, until it happened, how much she would miss Nan's daunting presence, her sharp tongue, the precise clicking of her knitting needles in the small back room; she felt as if part of the tapestry of life had been torn away, leaving a gaping hole in the familiar pattern of her days. The passing of the *Mauretania* had heightened her sense of loss.

Leaving the Odeon cinema, Danny and Wilma walked to the Londesborough Lodge Gardens, their favourite haunt. The film they'd seen hadn't been particularly inspiring, and although they had held hands, Danny felt depressed. Wilma, he knew, had her mind set on becoming engaged, and she would not give him a minute's peace until he had bought her a ring.

'Let's sit here,' she suggested, choosing a bench on the terrace overlooking the fish-pond, spreading out and smoothing her skirt as though her hands were flat-irons.

'What's wrong with the bridge?' he asked moodily, wanting to hold her, to kiss her in the shadowy darkness, not to sit beside her in full view of passers-by – summer visitors out for a final breath of fresh air before going back to their hotel rooms, other young couples strolling hand-in-hand towards more secluded benches.

'I need to talk to you very seriously, Danny,' Wilma said coolly, 'about the future.'

'Look, Wilma,' he said impatiently, 'I've already told you I can't afford to get married just yet. We've only just started going steady.'

'Oh well, if that's your attitude. If you don't love me—'

'Of course I love you!'

'No need to raise your voice.'

'I'm sorry.' He ran his fingers through his hair distractedly.

'You're afraid of your mother, that's it, isn't it?' Wilma persisted. 'Afraid of cutting the apron strings?' She gave a snorting little laugh of contempt. 'I knew, of course, she had you under her thumb the minute I walked in the house!'

'That simply isn't true!' He stared at Wilma in amazement, as if she had stuck a knife between his ribs, as if he tasted blood in his mouth. Rising quickly to his feet, 'I think we'd better be going now,' he said briefly.

Climbing down from her high horse, realizing she had gone too far, she dabbed her eyes with a cologne-scented handkerchief plucked from the sleeve of her cardigan and murmured brokenly, looking up at him, 'I do love you. Ever so much.' She really meant what she said. Danny was everything she had ever wanted or expected from life: handsome, charming, and with good prospects. She knew he wanted her physically, and she wanted him too, in the same way, but not until they were married.

A fervent disciple of women's magazines, which she read avidly from cover to cover, Wilma knew that virginity was the strongest weapon in every girl's armoury. She had not, therefore, really needed her mother's advice on the subject. Moreover, she knew from her workmates' intimate chatter about their boyfriends, that those who had 'given in' to them had been dropped like hot bricks afterwards.

Unable to resist the anguished expression in Wilma's tear-filled eyes, sliding down beside her to take her in his arms, he gave up the struggle. 'Very well,' he whispered, no longer tasting blood but the scent of Amami shampoo in his mouth, 'we'll get engaged, if that's what you want.'

'I could meet you on Wednesday afternoon, when you leave work,' she said matter-of-factly, her moment of panic over now she had got what she wanted. 'That will give you time to draw out the money for the ring.' Snuggling close to him, 'I've seen just the ring I'd like, in Lowson's window. Sapphire and diamonds.'

'How much?' Danny swallowed hard.

'Twenty-five pounds. But not to worry, I'll put the extra five pounds towards it myself.'

Today was Monday. On Wednesday he'd be an engaged man, bankrupt into the bargain. Tomorrow, he thought, he would have to face his parents. No question of gaining their consent to his engagement, thank God, but conscience forbade his taking such a step without telling them.

If only Wilma had been content to wait a little while longer, he thought, dragging his feet on the homeward path, to get them used to the idea of his going steady with the girl of his choice, wondering if what Wilma said about being attached to his mother's apron strings was true? But no, surely not? She'd just been a bit upset at the time. As for being under his mother's thumb, that was ridiculous. Even so, he couldn't help wishing that Wilma hadn't said it. But if she hadn't, he reasoned, crossing the road near St Mary's Church, she might never have cried and told him she loved him, and he might not have relented towards her, taken her in his arms, and agreed to their becoming engaged.

Oh dammit, he thought suddenly. Of course, Dulcie had been on late duty at the Pavilion. Crossing the road, he saw his father opening the front door with his latchkey. Dulcie and his dad must have been ahead of him all the way from town, and he hadn't even noticed.

Useless now to hang back. His father had already spotted him in the empty roadway. 'Hello, son,' Bob said cheerfully as Danny walked up the front steps behind them, 'did you enjoy the picture?'

'Oh yes, it was fine,' Danny lied bravely as the three of them entered the hall. Dulcie treated him to a baleful look over the banisters as she traipsed upstairs to bed with a muttered, 'Good night,' tired out with serving rich food to rich people, her face curiously blotched, as if it had just received a scrubbing with carbolic soap, and framed with an unbecoming nimbus of frizzy, mouse-brown hair.

When she had gone, 'Dad,' Danny said uncertainly.

'Yes, son. What is it?'

It was now or never. Squaring his shoulders, 'I think you should know that – that Wilma and I are getting engaged,' he blurted. 'The day after tomorrow, as a matter of fact.'

'Engaged? But you haven't known her five minutes!' Bob had to speak his mind. 'I'd have given you credit for more sense! Have you any idea what you're letting yourself in for?'

'We're in love,' Danny said stubbornly. 'We want to get married.'

'All well and good,' Bob acknowledged. 'But have you thought what you'll be giving up?'

'I don't know what you mean.'

'Then you're in for a shock, my lad! Marriage costs money.'

'I don't get it. Wilma's parents will pay for the wedding.'

'That goes without saying,' Bob said, 'but that isn't the end of the story, not by a long chalk! Their commitment will end there. It's you who will have to provide a home for Wilma, pay for the furniture; houses and furniture cost a hell of a lot of money, believe me. You'll need to save every penny you earn from now on to make that possible; give up all the things you enjoy, like dancing, having a good time, visits to the cinema, cricket and football—'

'I can't see why!' Danny was prickly now, on the defensive. 'Wilma wouldn't want me to give up sport.'

'Have you talked it over with her?'

'Well, no, but . . . What I mean is, Wilma would never try to stop me doing the things I enjoy.'

'You're quite sure about that?'

94

'Look here, Dad, if you're trying to put me off getting married, it won't work,' Danny said heatedly. 'What's wrong with wanting a home of my own?'

'Nothing at all, lad, as long as you realize what's entailed. All I'm saying is, why the rush?'

'In case you hadn't noticed, Wilma's a very attractive girl,' Danny said sharply. 'The last thing I want is to lose her.'

'Would that be possible, if she really loves you?' Bob asked gently, seeing his son, momentarily, as the child he used to be in the Roscoe Street days, a bright-eyed, curly-haired little lad toddling to meet him when he came home from work.

Grace, who had gone to bed when Bob went to meet Dulcie from the Pavilion, appeared suddenly on the landing, wearing a dressing-gown, her hair about her shoulders. 'I heard voices,' she said wearily. 'What is it? What's wrong?'

'Go back to bed, love,' Bob advised her, 'I'll tell you later.' The poor lass had had a hell of a day one way and another. The last thing she needed right now was a midnight confrontation with an angry young man unwilling to see sense.

'Tell me what?' Grace came slowly downstairs. 'Why were you quarrelling?'

'We weren't,' Bob said, 'I was just trying to make him realize that marriage isn't something to be rushed into—'

'*Marriage?*' Grace frowned. 'I don't understand.'

'Wilma and I are getting engaged,' Danny said flatly.

'So soon?' Grace's hand tightened on the banister. 'But *why*?' She shook her head confusedly. 'I thought you'd be going steady for a while, getting to know each other better before . . .' Her legs were shaking.

'Dad's already read me the Riot Act. I don't want to hear any more. I'm a man, for God's sake, not a child!' Danny spoke more sharply than he had intended, unwilling to admit, even to himself, that he'd been hustled into this engagement. He couldn't very well say that it was all Wilma's idea. What kind of a heel would that make him?

He had, at least, the grace to apologize for his outburst. 'I'm sorry,' he said gruffly. 'But getting engaged doesn't mean we'll be getting married right away. We couldn't anyway, not until we've saved up enough money for a place of our own. What's wrong with that?' He smiled awkwardly, 'After all, Great Aunt Fanny said it was high time I found myself a lady friend, remember?'

'Yes,' Bob said caustically, 'and you as good as told her to mind her own business!'

'Please, no more tonight! It's late, and I'm tired,' Grace said. 'I'm going back to bed.' Pausing at the turn of the stairs, 'Good night, son,' she murmured 'and God bless.'

Looking up at her, 'Good night, Mother,' Danny replied. 'Sleep well.'

Bob came up to bed. 'I may have been a bit hard with the lad,' he admitted. 'The truth is, it came as a bit of a shock – about the engagement, I mean. Not that anything I said made the slightest difference.' He laughed suddenly. 'I wonder what he'd think if he knew what circumstances were like for us when we got married?' Then, more seriously, 'All I can say is, I hope that Danny will be as happy with Wilma as I have been with you all these years.' Nestling beside his wife, feeling the soft curve of her body against his, he heard her sobbing intake of breath. 'Don't cry, darling,' he said tenderly.

'I can't help it! Oh, Bob, I'm so tired.'

'I know, love. I know.' Cradling her in his arms, he held her until he knew, by the soft expellation of breath against her pillow, that she was fast asleep.

Watching over her as she slept, he knew she would be up tomorrow, at the crack of dawn, to set the wheels of living in motion, to face whatever life threw up at her with her own special brand of courage.

Chapter Seven

Wilma's mother, a small-boned woman, sharp featured, with Marcel-waved hair, and a habit of sniffing, was fond of telling people, 'My husband's in transport, you know,' implying that he sat behind a desk all day, directing the running of the local bus company. True, Arthur Burton, twice the size of his wife, had, apart from a brief spell in the Army during the war, spent most of his adult life ferrying the general public from place to place. His first four-wheeled vehicle had been a horse-drawn landau plying for trade in the station forecourt. Then, when landaus became a novelty rather than a necessity, forsaking whip, bowler hat, leggings and frock-coat, plaid rugs, nose-bags, and muffler, he had become a tram driver, trading his bowler hat for a peaked cap bearing the Scarborough Tramways Company badge.

Not that he had relished the transition. Standing up in the driver's compartment, wind whipping past his ears in the bad weather, was far worse than sitting perched up on the driving seat of a landau, nor were tram drivers encouraged to wear mufflers or suck at a pipe of tobacco while manipulating the brakes and brass handles of the vehicle. But the tramway system had proved unpopular with the general public, not to mention the Town Council. In any case, motor transport was proving more convenient, far more flexible than the lumbering trams with their overhead wires and sparking antennas, so that when the system finally ground to a halt and the tramlines were dug up, Arthur Burton had become an employee of the United Automobile Company. In short, a bus-driver.

The Burtons were at home, Arthur enjoying a fish-and-chip supper, his wife Mabel reading an Ethel M. Dell novel, when Wilma breezed into the overfurnished back room of the house in Aberdeen Terrace like a zephyr.

'Guess what?' she burst forth. 'Danny and I are getting engaged!'

'Eh?' Arthur's mouth sagged open, emitting a few crumbs of batter. 'But we ain't even met the bloke yet! You can't get yourself engaged to someone we don't know! Who is this fellah? Why all the bloody rush?' His heavy eyebrows beetled alarmingly. Laying down his cutlery, he demanded, 'Has he taken advantage of you? Is that it? If so, I'll have his hide, the dirty young devil!'

'Oh, do be quiet, Arthur!' Flinging aside Ethel M. Dell, Mabel clasped her hands together delightedly. 'Wilma has told me all about her young man! Well, go on love, tell us more about it; what he said, and so on!' Real romance was better than fiction any day of the week. 'Did he get down on one knee?'

'Don't be so daft, Mum!' Wilma blushed becomingly. 'Of course he didn't! What's more,' she added for her father's benefit, 'he hasn't taken advantage of me! He does work at the Town Hall, remember?'

'Oh, I suppose he's one of them lad-di-dah chaps, then, who thinks himself a cut above the rest? But that don't alter the fact that you shouldn't have got yourself engaged to marry a bloke your ma an' me ain't even met yet!'

'Well, you'll soon have your chance,' Wilma said heatedly, 'because I've invited him to tea on Sunday!'

'Huh, a bit like locking the stable door after the horse has bolted, if you ask me,' Arthur said sourly, returning to his plate of fish and chips.

'Oh, take no notice of your father,' Mabel sniffed contemptuously. 'Let's go upstairs to your room. You can tell me all about it there!'

Now the boot was on the other foot. It was Danny's turn to be given the once-over by the Burton family. Entering the house in Aberdeen Terrace, it struck him how small and cramped it seemed compared with the Castle Road house. There was a funny smell about it, too, which he could not clearly define, as if the various food smells from the kitchen had permeated the wallpaper.

At least he'd managed to winkle out of the great aunts' Sunday afternoon tea-party, he consoled himself, following Wilma down the narrow passage to the back premises where her parents awaited his arrival. Nervously, he straightened his tie and smoothed back his hair in anticipation of this momentous meeting with his future in-laws.

Conscience had forbidden his acceptance of Wilma's proffered five pounds towards the purchase of her engagement ring; conscience linked to pride. The thought of accepting money from a woman had seemed utterly repugnant to him, and so he had borrowed the five quid from Jimmy, with a solemn promise to repay the loan from his next wage-packet. Now Danny was virtually skint, but it had been worth all the financial wheeling and dealing when he had opened his wallet and forked out the cash for the ring with a kind of millionaire flourish.

Of course he'd had to tell Jimmy why he wanted the money; had felt a bit put out by his brother's lack of enthusiasm. 'Are you sure you know what you're doing?' he'd asked.

'Oh, don't *you* start! I've already had a penny lecture from Mum and Dad,' Danny said sharply. 'Anyone would think I was committing a crime. What's wrong with getting engaged?'

'Nothing, I suppose. It's what it leads to that gets me,' Jimmy said gloomily. 'Next thing you know, you'll be up in front of a parson saying "I do", and "with all my worldly goods I thee endow". Not that that should take much doing. You haven't got any worldly goods to endow.'

'A fat lot of help you are,' Danny said irritably. 'I'm not planning to get married for ages yet.'

'I bet Wilma is,' Jimmy muttered. 'What I mean to say is, that's all girls think about, isn't it?'

'That's fine, coming from you,' Danny flared back at him,

'you've never had a girl, so how do you know what they think?'

Wilma had wanted to wear the ring right away, to walk out of Lowson's with the small diamond and sapphire cluster on the third finger of her left hand. They'd had a bit of an argument in the shop when Danny said he'd prefer to give it to her after he'd met her parents, which seemed the decent thing to do, less of a *fait accompli*. Wilma said they already knew she was getting engaged, so what did it matter? But he'd remained adamant. Also, he said, when he had been to her house for tea, they had better go up to Castle Road and show his parents the ring. Things had got out of hand somewhere along the line, and he wished to make amends, pushing to the back of his mind that had he been firmer earlier on, things might not have got out of hand in the first place.

So thinking, he entered the Burtons' back room, the ring, in its morocco box, making a slight bulge in his trouser-pocket. With half an eye, he saw the well-filled table in front of the green-and-brown tiled fireplace, the green plush armchair in which was seated a burly individual wearing a striped shirt, elastic armbands, carpet slippers, and smoking a pipe. A sideboard was crowded with photographs, vases and brass ornaments, the residue from which appeared to have flowed onto the mantelpiece and the what-not in the corner, next to the green plush sofa under the starched lace and chintz curtains of the window that overlooked the back yard.

Danny smiled awkwardly at the man in the chair. 'Good afternoon, sir,' he ventured.

'Humph,' the man said, knocking out his pipe on the fender.

'Daddy, this is my fiancé, Danny Kingsley,' Wilma said brightly. The man stood up. 'How do?' he said briefly.

Danny gazed in fascination at his future father-in-law's front collar-stud. 'I – er . . .' he murmured, bereft of speech, as if his tongue had stuck to the roof of his mouth.

Suddenly there appeared from the kitchen a female

whirlwind, oozing charm. Danny breathed a sigh of relief as his hostess, edging towards him through the barricade of furniture, glanced up at him approvingly, fairly beamed and murmured, 'So you are Danny? Wilma has told us so much about you, hasn't she Albert?' Almost in the same breath, 'You'll forgive my hubby's appearance, won't you? You see,' with a slight sniff, 'Daddy's in transport, and he does like to relax somewhat on a Sunday.'

'Yes, of course.'

'Now, do sit down, dear. I've just put the kettle on to boil. We can have a nice little talk over tea.' She added proudly, 'It's all home-made. I do pride myself on keeping a good table, and Wilma's a nice little cook, aren't you, darling?'

Inching his legs beneath the table-cloth, Danny surveyed the wealth of buns, cakes and pastries set before him, not to mention the sandwiches and jellies, wondering how on earth he'd be able to swallow a bite of it in his present state of nervous tension, with Wilma's father seated directly opposite, and the morocco box in his trouser-pocket digging into his right testicle.

Returning with the tea-pot, sitting down at the head of the table, 'Now then,' Mrs Burton said, pouring out, 'Wilma tells us you've bought her a lovely engagement ring.'

'Show it to them, Danny,' Wilma said, all smiles, thinking how handsome he looked in his navy-blue blazer, crisp white shirt, starched collar and striped blue-and-white tie. Hastily, he complied. The relief was tremendous.

Mrs Burton, in her green bouclé dress, reminded Danny of a grasshopper. Not that he had ever seen a grasshopper. All he knew about the species, from biology lessons at the Boys' High School, was that they were imbued with remarkable powers of propulsion, of producing a shrill chirping noise by rubbing their fore wings against their hind legs. Not that he disliked the woman, she simply exhausted him with her constant flow of chatter, her propensity for hopping from one subject to another, accompanied by a series of sniffs, until he had begun to feel like the male counterpart of *Alice in Wonderland*, to understand and appreciate more fully Albert's need of relaxation on a Sunday. No wonder the poor chap had opted out of wearing a collar and tie.

After tea, Mrs Burton brought out the family photograph albums – by which time Wilma's engagement ring had found its way to where it rightly belonged. The transition, from box to finger, had been toasted with glasses of sweet sherry and the cutting of a Dundee cake perched atop a glass stand draped with a limp, hand-crocheted doily.

Turning the pages of the albums with alacrity, chirping with enthusiasm, Mabel had revealed to her future son-in-law photographs of his bride-to-be in varying stages of her development from childhood, which he found acutely embarrassing. At last, glancing at the black marble clock on the crowded mantelpiece, he indicated that it was high time he and Wilma went up to Castle Road to show his parents the engagement ring, adding, as a sop to his conscience, that he hoped the two families would meet quite soon, now that he and Wilma were officially engaged to be married.

'Oh, don't worry about that, my dear,' Mabel advised him, on the doorstep, 'there'll be plenty of time for us to meet and discuss the wedding between now and Christmas.'

Head swimming, walking along Aberdeen Walk, Wilma clinging to his arm, 'Christmas?' Danny asked confusedly. 'What has Christmas to do with our getting married?'

'Well, we – that is Mummy and I – thought how wonderful it would be if we got married on your 21st birthday,' Wilma said calmly.

'But that's impossible! You know it is!' He could scarcely believe that anyone could be so daft as to think he'd have saved up enough money for a house within the space of five months.

'No, it isn't,' Wilma continued, 'not if we move in with my parents until we've saved up enough money for a home of our own. We'd be living rent-free, just giving Mummy enough to pay for our food, and so on. Well, what do you think?' She looked up at him appealingly. 'You do want to make love to me, don't you?'

Danny didn't know what he wanted at that moment. He felt bemused by the speed with which things were happening to him. One thing for sure, he wasn't about to be hustled into living with his in-laws.

'We're Baptists,' Wilma said, meaning that when the Burton family felt obliged to attend divine worship, they went to the Baptist Church in Albemarle Crescent. 'What are you?'

'Well, I'm not too sure. My grandmother's a stern Methodist,' – a Freudian slip of the tongue, he meant staunch – 'Grandfather was a lay preacher. I guess that makes me a Methodist. Why?'

'I just wondered.' Wilma spread her left hand upon his sleeve to show off her engagement ring. Danny swallowed hard, wondering how much wedding rings cost. Expense stared him in the face. He felt inclined not to look.

'I'm starting our tea-set tomorrow,' Wilma said. 'I've seen ever such a pretty pattern in Tonks. Bone china, with roses. I'll get the tea-pot first, then the milk-jug and sugar basin. Or should I get the milk-jug and sugar basin first, then the tea-pot?'

'I really don't know, love,' Danny replied, feeling stunned, and did it matter all that much? His father's words, 'Marriage costs money' came back to him, and something else besides . . . He said, 'By the way, I'm playing cricket next Sunday afternoon. You will come and watch, won't you?'

'*Cricket?*' Wilma stared up at him in amazement. '*Cricket?*' she repeated. 'You're not serious? Of all the stupid, boring games.'

'But I'm the team captain.'

'Oh well, never mind. You'll be able to get out of it, I dare say, when they know you have something better to do with your Sundays,' she said airily. 'I thought we might take a charabanc trip to Forge Valley next Sunday afternoon, have tea there, and walk along by the river.' She sighed blissfully. 'They serve lovely cream teas at that cottage near the bridge.'

*   *   *

Kerry adored her job. Never had Mr Hodnot's shelves and show-cases enjoyed such dustings as she gave them. Nor did she mind, her employer noted, buckling down to hard work in the warehouse when the new consignment of stock came in. What a bright, pretty little lass she was to be sure, Hodnot thought tenderly, seeing her as the daughter he might have had if he had married. He had toyed with the idea of asking Fanny Mallory to marry him when she'd returned to Scarborough after the war to live with her sister above the fancy-goods shop in South Street, but nothing had come of it.

The truth was, he had felt dwarfed by her stronger personality, incapable of satisfying her appetite for life. Fanny had been slim, then, astonishingly beautiful, and he'd had a good head of hair. He often looked back on that romantic interlude in his life, and wondered if he'd done the right thing in remaining a bachelor. Too late now. Fanny had put on weight, and he'd lost his hair. At least their friendship had endured the onslaught of time. In any case, he doubted if Fanny would have accepted his proposal. Theirs had never been a world-shaking love affair, more in the nature of an in-depth flirtation across various candlelit dinner tables, she wearing black lace and lots of sparkling jewellery, ordering outlandish foreign dishes, choosing the most expensive wines, having trouble with her hair which threatened to escape from its loosely pinned chignon by reason of the quick, birdlike movements of her head as she talked.

On the whole, he felt he had done the right thing in clinging to his bachelorhood, in turning his full attention to the creation of his business, his little empire of exquisite *objets d'art*, which drew to his shop the *crème-de-la-crème* of wealthy women with money to squander on jade, crystal, silks and satins.

Lady Hawthorn was such a woman. Tall and slender, wearing a beige dress and jacket, crocodile shoes, and carrying a matching handbag, she came into the shop one morning with a young man in tow, a good-looking, fair-haired man, whom Mr Hodnot recognized as her son Ashley. The latter was casually dressed in brown flannel trousers and a well-cut, Donegal-tweed jacket. Hodnot guessed that he was down from Oxford for the summer vacation, and thought he looked bored, as well he might. Doubtless his mother had inveigled him into drinking coffee with her in Marshall and Snelgrove before continuing her shopping spree. But that was none of his business.

Moving forward to greet them, 'Good morning, your ladyship; sir,' he said graciously. 'A lovely morning. May I help you?'

Kerry, dusting a cut-glass fruit bowl, turned her head to glance at the customers, her mind elsewhere. Gosh, he was handsome, she thought, and he had actually looked *at* her, not through her.

Lady Hawthorn wished to refurbish her husband's study. 'Of course,' she said, in a voice that reminded Kerry of plain chocolate, 'Sir Charles is conservative about colour, so we mustn't change things too drastically, although a touch of green or deep orange in the curtain material would be acceptable. What do you think, Ashley?'

Her son had been wool-gathering, thinking how pretty the girl doing the dusting was. 'Oh yes,' he said quickly, fairly certain that his father wouldn't even notice the colour of his new study curtains.

'I think I know the kind of thing you have in mind,' Mr Hodnot said smoothly. 'Miss Kingsley, fetch the new-range pattern books, if you please. These are predominantly heavy quality materials,' he explained when the books had been laid on the counter for her ladyship's inspection, 'in what might be described as – er – masculine colours. Nothing *outré*, you understand?'

Ashley smiled at Kerry, a conspiratorial smile which she could not help but return. His eyes were a greenish hazel, she noticed, and his hair fell forward a little onto his forehead. The smile froze on her lips when she caught Mr Hodnot's disapproving glance across the pattern books.

After Lady Hawthorn and her son had departed to lunch

at the Royal Hotel, Mr Hodnot took Kerry to task. 'What I am about to say may sound harsh, but you'll do well to remember that business is business. Lady Hawthorn is a valued customer of mine. Once you had brought the pattern books, you should have got on with your work. Do I make myself clear?'

Kerry's eyes filled with tears at this, her first reprimand.

Touched by her innocence, her woebegone expression, Hodnot said kindly, 'Business dealings impose certain limitations. How shall I put it to make you understand? Sir Charles and Lady Hawthorn are rich people, their son is at Oxford. They live in a different world from us.'

'I only smiled at him 'cos he smiled at me first,' Kerry explained. 'I thought it was the polite thing to do.'

'Well then, we'll say no more about it. Now, take the pattern books back to the sewing room.'

'Yes, Mr Hodnot.'

She wondered if she should have told him that she wasn't in the least bit interested in Ashley Hawthorn, only in the sixth form High School boy whose eye she had caught walking down Westborough on her half-day off. Gosh, but he was handsome.

Chapter Eight

Herbie set pen to paper: *'Dear Friends,'* he wrote in the copperplate script he'd learned painstakingly from drawing pot-hooks during his orphanage days. *'Since you were kind enough as to ask me to stay with you on my next visit to Scarborough, would you mind putting up with me for the weekend commencing the 13th September?'* He paused to wipe away the perspiration on his forehead, accumulated there from the sheer effort of doing his best handwriting, worrying, at the same time, about his spelling.

Knowing that Grace would read the letter, he wanted it to be quite perfect. Getting on with the task in hand, he continued, *'This time I'll be selling Christmas lines to the customers, seeing as how the shops have to stock up well in advance.'*

Another pause, then, *'I must say that I am doing quite well at the moment, and my firm are well pleased with my progress as a salesman, which is a great relieve. Yours truely, Herbie.'*

He signed his name with a flourish: added a *P.S.* *'Please write to me, at the above address, if inconvient.'*

A letter in Bob's handwriting arrived two days later. *'Dear Herbie,'* it read, *'It was great to hear from you again and to know you are doing so well. Your room will be ready for you when you arrive, and Grace is planning a celebration supper in your honour. Your old pal, Bob.'*

There was an end-of-summer feeling about September, Herbie thought, alighting from the train, an indefinable feeling of loss, of nostalgia for the long bright days of summer-time now shortening and fading to the mists of autumn, heralding the onset of the cold, sharp days of winter.

107

Even so, his heart lifted with joy at the thought of seeing Grace and Bob again – especially Grace, whose memory had filled his mind with happiness every moment of his life since their last meeting, to whom he owed his success as a salesman, and much more besides. She had imbued in him an inexplicable feeling of pride by simply being there when he had needed someone to guide him through the maze of life; someone to provide him with shelter, to feed him, to perk up a handkerchief in the breast-pocket of his best suit of clothes. She was someone capable of making him realize that values of decency and goodness still did exist in a world he had once seen as a desert, an arid waste of despair, especially after the war, when beer had seemed the only way to blot out memories of those men he had seen on stretchers carried into the dressing stations from the bloody battlefields of the Somme.

It had taken a woman of the calibre of Grace Kingsley to stitch up his own, less spectacular wounds of the mind, to give him a reason for living, a feeling of decency and self-respect he had never known before until he came up against her own particular brand of courage, her un-questioning belief in family values. No matter what trials beset that family, love came uppermost in her mind: the kind of love which made allowances for whatever faults they happened to possess.

It was like a homecoming when, at the bus-stop near St Mary's, he saw lighted windows shining through the dusk. He had two samples cases with him this time, as well as his suitcase. The front door opened, and Bob was there to give him a hand. A rich, warm food smell floated from the kitchen.

Grace appeared, smiling, her cheeks flushed from the heat of the oven. 'Your room's ready, and so is supper,' she said. 'Everyone's home now.' Herbie could have cried, knowing that 'everyone' included him.

Grace had made a beef stew with baked dumplings, brown and crispy on top. Tureens were filled with mashed potatoes, turnips and sprouts. Carrots and onions had simmered along with the stew to enrich the gravy. They usually had fish on Friday, but Grace reckoned that Herbie would need something more substantial inside him after a day's work and a train journey besides. She'd cook the fish tomorrow.

Digging into the food, Herbie frowned slightly. Someone was missing from the family circle: Mrs Daniel, Grace's mother. Perhaps she'd 'passed on'. He didn't like to ask.

As if reading his mind, Grace said, 'Mother is living in South Street now, with her sisters. You remember? Aunt Fanny and Aunt Rosa?' (Could he ever forget them?)

'Oh, fancy,' he said lamely, uncertain if congratulations or commiserations were in order, 'I expect you miss her.' Strange, he thought, how circumstances could change in so short a time. People, too. Not Bob and Grace, but the younger generation. What had Dulcie done to change her appearance so drastically, for instance? He could have sworn she had straight hair the last time he saw her. Why did Kerry seem so much more grown-up now than she had done before? Why did Danny give the impression of having hoisted the weight of the world onto his shoulders? Why Jimmy's downcast expression? He would find out the answers to these questions in the fullness of time. Meanwhile, he contented himself with sinking his teeth into a light-as-air dumpling.

'I'm a working woman now, you know,' Kerry told him, after supper, when the pair of them were standing at the kitchen sink, Kerry doing the washing, Herbie the drying, 'and,' her voice sank conspiratorially, 'I have a boyfriend. His name's Sid, and he's ever so handsome.' She added truthfully, 'Well, we're not exactly going steady . . . What I mean is, he's still at school, but he did treat me to an ice-cream cornet during the school holidays.'

Herbie's heart bled for her. He said, 'What about your job?'

'Oh, it's lovely,' Kerry said ecstatically, handing him a plate, 'and, come Christmas, I'll be earning ten shillings a week! Can you imagine? Ten whole shillings a week!' She added, *sotto-voce*, when the last of the cutlery had been washed, dried, and put away, 'Please don't mention Sid to

Mum and Dad, they've enough on their plates with Danny and Wilma for the time being.'

'Danny and Wilma?' Herbie hadn't a clue what she meant.

'Oh, I thought you knew. Danny's engaged to be married. It all happened very suddenly. One minute they were going steady, next minute he'd bought her a ring, now Wilma wants to get married on Danny's twenty-first birthday in December.' Kerry sighed deeply. 'Mum and Dad are ever so upset about it. You see, Danny can't afford to get married just yet, and they can't bear the thought of him living with Wilma's parents after the wedding.'

'I see,' Herbie said thoughtfully, folding the damp tea-towel he was holding.

Grace entered the kitchen at that moment. 'Oh, I'm sorry, I meant to lend you a hand,' she said brightly, unwilling to admit that she had spent the last half hour with Danny, attempting to dissuade him from hasty decisions which he might later live to regret. To no avail. She, above all people, knew why. Love was like that, the be-all and end-all of living. Danny loved Wilma. So be it. She had not attempted the futility of telling him what she knew in her heart of hearts to be true, that he would never find happiness with a scrap of a girl with whom he had nothing in common. She had, quite simply, begged him to reconsider moving to Aberdeen Terrace to live after the wedding. The most bitter pill of all to swallow was that Danny had scarcely listened to her suggestion that he and Wilma should find a place of their own to live, however cramped and inconvenient. Possibly furnished rooms in Roscoe Street, just as long as they made their own way in the world, as she and Bob had done in the early days of their marriage.

Dulcie came into the back room a bit later on. She had been on breakfast duty at the hotel, wearing her make-up, when a man on her station had ogled her admiringly and asked her name.

'Dulcie Kingsley,' she said, keeping her voice down,

knowing the head waiter would have her guts for garters if he caught her chatting to one of the guests.

'And are you a good girl, Dulcie?'

'I like to think so, sir.' She'd blushed to the roots of her hair, uncertain how to cope with the situation, at the same time unwilling to give him the brush-off. He was quite good-looking, she decided, in an elderly kind of way, and very well dressed in a nattily tailored blazer, a Paisley silk cravat beneath his dew-laps. 'Why do you want to know?'

'Reasons!' He tapped his nose with a tobacco-stained forefinger. 'A little secret of mine. I happen to like good little girls.'

Perhaps he was a film producer, she thought wildly, scurrying to the kitchen to place his order, a Hollywood talent scout. Her dreams crashed about her ears when one of the other waitresses said in a bored voice, 'Don't tell me you've got yourself lumbered with "Dirty Bertie"? Better watch yourself, kid, or he'll have your knickers round your ankles in two seconds flat, then you won't be a "good little girl" any more! Got the picture?'

Finding himself alone with Dulcie momentarily, Herbie asked her how she was getting on.

'Fine,' she said disagreeably, 'if it's any of your business.'

He gave the girl a long, hard look. 'What is it with you?' he asked. 'Don't you want people to like you?'

'They can please themselves for all I care!'

'You're a selfish little beast, aren't you?' Herbie said mildly. 'Mind you, I've met your type before, bits of lasses who think the world owes them a living: Leeds is full of them. Poor sixteen-year-old kids trying to bluster their way through life, as you are doing; reaching out for their share of pie-in-the-sky, a pot of gold at the end of the rainbow. But there ain't any rainbows in this world we live in, not the kind you're after, believe me.'

Dulcie stared at him, aghast. Then, turning on her heel, she ran upstairs to her room to fling herself on her bed, outraged at being called a 'selfish little beast' by an ugly little man who sold women's underwear for a living. She'd a good mind to tell her parents what he'd said to her. He was rude and common and she hated him. Coming here, eating them out of house and home, being made such a fuss of.

Getting up, she stared at herself in the mirror. Her perm had reached the stage of growing out. Washing it herself, she didn't bother to set it, with the result the permed ends were kinky, not curly. Tears welled up, she'd had a rotten day. What was it that common Herbie Barrass said to her? Something about there not being any rainbows. But there might have been if only that man at the hotel had been a film producer. In any case, she thought despairingly, what if he had . . . What? Well, wanted to pull her knickers down. She was sick and tired of being looked down on, being made to feel small. Sick of everything. She wanted to be rich, loved, admired.

Herbie was in the back room smoking a cigarette when Jimmy drifted down looking like a spare part. 'Want one?' he offered the lad a fag.

'Yeah, why not?' Jimmy accepted the cigarette and a light, coughed when the smoke hit his windpipe.

'Your first?' Herbie enquired.

'Yes, as a matter of fact.' Jimmy grinned awkwardly.

'A nasty habit, smoking,' Herbie said, 'expensive, too.' He paused. 'What's up, mate?'

Jimmy groaned. 'Don't ask.' He flopped down on a chair.

'I *am* asking.'

'You wouldn't understand.'

'Try me.'

'It's just that I seem to be getting nowhere fast.'

Herbie handed him an ash-tray. 'Put that thing out before you burn a hole in your trousers,' he advised. 'Well, go on.'

'I need a typewriter,' Jimmy said harshly, 'only I can't afford a new one.' He added with a sigh, 'Truth to tell, I couldn't afford even a second-hand one the way things are going right now. I lent Danny five quid and he hasn't paid me back yet. Then there's my Course fees, and my keep.

The devil of it is, my Course tutor told me I could probably place the last few articles I submitted if they were typed, not hand-written.' He went on in a rush, 'I'd set my heart on a new typewriter, now I'd settle for anything. What I mean is, I could soon earn enough money for a new typewriter if my articles were accepted, and I could buy a second-hand one if Danny paid me back what he borrowed. I know he meant to, but he's in a bit of a mess at the moment with that – that Wilma on about saving up all the time.'

'So you're a writer, are you?' Herbie looked at him in admiration.

'Not yet. That is, I am, or I hope to be when I get going. The trouble is, I can't get going.' Jimmy buried his head in his hands.

'How's your spelling?' Herbie asked.

'Not bad. Of course, I need a dictionary to look words up occasionally!'

'What beats me,' Herbie said, feeling for his wallet, 'is how do you know where to look words up if you don't know how to spell them in the first place?' Unearthing five one pound notes, 'Here, lad,' he said, 'take this, and say nowt. You can pay me back when you're rich and famous.'

Jimmy looked up, startled. 'But I couldn't! Thanks, Mr Barrass, but I couldn't possibly take your money.'

'Look, lad,' Herbie said firmly, 'I owe this family more than I could ever hope to repay. Take it and welcome. You'll be doing me a favour. I'd only have wasted it on beer – or cigarettes.'

The season was virtually over. The Rolling Stones had rolled away from that vast conservatory, the Floral Hall, with its hanging baskets of ferns and ivies.

The Bouquets' Concert Party had gone, too, leaving behind them lingering memories of laughter and applause, a feeling of emptiness, of September. A curious, end-of-summer feeling, Kerry thought wistfully, walking towards Gala-Land with her parents and Herbie, to catch the final performance of Evelyn Hardy's All British Ladies' Band.

Kerry adored Gala-Land, a huge underground cavern of Moorish design, a bewildering complex of cream and red brick arches reminiscent of a mosque in some far-off country: of James Elroy Flecker's *The Golden Journey to Samarkand*, a poem which had stretched her imagination to the possibility of one day setting off on that golden journey all by herself. Not that she had a clue where Samarkand was. Meanwhile, she'd have to make do with Gala-Land. But ah, the beauty of the words: 'We are the pilgrims, master; we shall go always a little further: it may be beyond that last blue mountain barred with snow'.

Herbie clapped the swinging music of the ladies' band until his hands stung. Amazed by the mastery of their instruments, he had to admit that his initial mistrust of women musicians no longer existed.

When the concert was over, he walked with the Kingsleys beneath the mock-Byzantine arches, in a state of enthralment, deeply aware of the woman he loved beside him as they paused now and then near the various side-shows; the skittles and shooting alleys, the coconut shies and strength-testing machines.

When they came to the curtained booth of Madame Jean, a clairvoyant, he said gruffly, 'I'd like to have my fortune told, if you don't mind.'

Bob laughed. 'Why not? We'll all have our fortunes told!' He added, tongue-in-cheek, 'I for one would like to know what the future has in store for us.'

Madame Jean, a small, fair-haired woman, bore no resemblance whatsoever to Romany women of her ilk. She sat behind a green-baize-topped card table devoid of playing cards or crystal ball. She did not immediately ask Herbie to show her his hands, nor did she ask him to cross her palm with silver. She said, 'I shall need some small personal object of yours, a ring perhaps, something you normally wear or carry about with you.'

'Will this do?' He handed her his pocket-watch. The woman nodded. Cupping the watch in the palms of her hands, 'Your path through life has not been easy. You have

114

known many setbacks and disappointments.' She spoke quietly, dispassionately. 'Nor have you been lucky in love.'

True enough, he thought, not that that would take much deducing. Most men, lucky in love, wore a wedding or signet ring, and his pocket-watch was no family heirloom, he'd bought it second-hand from a pawnbroker's shop in Leeds.

Madame Jean went on, 'That does not mean to say you have never been in love. There is someone very close to your heart. Someone who will come to bless the day you entered her life.' Stroking the watch, she continued, 'You have experienced a change of fortune recently, something to do with business dealings. Soon there will come a change of address, a change for the better.' She lay down the watch on the table. 'Now, show me your hands.' Herbie did as he was told. The woman looked at them intently. 'You will travel abroad,' she said, 'in a position of trust, even authority.' Her voice deepened suddenly. 'I see a time of danger ahead of you. The danger will pass, but it will leave its mark on you in some way, it may even alter the course of your future. There will be difficult decisions to make, concerning your future at that time. I see you torn between love and duty.' She closed her eyes momentarily, then, releasing his hands, 'I'm sorry, that's all I can tell you.'

Retrieving his watch, Herbie stood up. Curiously shaken by the encounter, he said, 'This business you're in, it's all just a bit of fun, isn't it? Not meant to be taken seriously?'

The clairvoyant smiled faintly. 'If that is what you wish to believe.' As he turned to leave the booth, she said, 'Please tell your friends I am sorry to disappoint them, especially the graceful lady with fair hair. Good night, Mr B., and good luck!' She had picked up a *Closed* sign to pin to the curtains of the booth following his departure, a booth Madame Jean had not left before or during his consultation, Herbie realized, so how the hell . . . ? And how come she had known his surname began with a B? It didn't make sense.

'Well, was it worth a tanner?' Bob asked cheerfully when Herbie emerged from the booth.

'No, not really.' Herbie grinned shamefacedly, unwilling

to admit how shaken he felt. 'In any case, I was her last client.'

Moving away from the booth, Kerry felt downcast. She would have really liked to know if she would one day marry a man whose name began with S. Not that Sid had quite reached manhood yet. Even so . . . Walking along the Foreshore on the way home, she perked up a bit when she remembered the ice-cream cornet he had bought her from one of those green canvas stalls on the sands a few weeks ago. Not just a penny cornet but a threepenny one, and the way they had strolled together as far as the harbour, she in a seventh heaven of delight at being the chosen companion of a High School boy sporting his school tie and blazer. Not that she had known what to say to him, but he had done all the talking, so it hadn't really mattered. In any case, she'd had all her mind on keeping up with the drips from her ice-cream cornet.

Walking round Peasholm Park with his fiancée in tow, Danny felt miffed, to put it mildly, that Wilma had vetoed a visit to the Odeon cinema as a money-saving exercise. After all, she'd reminded him, the price of two one-and-nine tickets would be far better off in his bank account than the coffers of the Rank Organization. He might have felt marginally better taking a walk round the lake, had not the colourful strings of lights bordering the paths been switched off for the winter, the flotilla of canoes and rowing boats stacked up and covered with tarpaulin on the landing-stage near the ticket office, had not Wilma kept harping on about the wedding . . .

'Of course,' she said, linking his arm, 'I shall ask my cousin Bella to be my chief bridesmaid.' She added, less enthusiastically, 'And I suppose I shall have to ask your sisters.'

'I wouldn't count on Dulcie, if I were you,' Danny replied moodily, 'she's an awkward lass at the best of times.'

'So I've noticed,' Wilma replied, with an almighty sniff.

116

'Oh? So I suppose she's not good enough for you?'

'For heaven's sake, Danny! What on earth's the matter with you tonight? After all, it's your wedding too, and time's growing short.'

How he choked back the retort, 'A damn sight too short', he would never know. All very well for Wilma to prattle on about it being his wedding too. He'd scarcely had a say in the matter. Normally a level-headed man in command of himself, he felt that this rushed wedding was tantamount to putting the cart before the horse. He'd been saving like crazy the past few weeks, but the amount he'd managed to bank would mizzle like mist on a summer morning when he had forked out for the honeymoon, and bought himself a new suit of clothes.

The honeymoon! Wilma wanted a week in the Lake District, at a nice hotel. The Lake District, of all places, in December! On the other hand . . . His spirits lifted at the thought of himself and his bride incarcerated in some 'nice' hotel bedroom, doing what came naturally. Naturally to him, at any rate. Fed up with walking, he drew his wife-to-be into a shelter overlooking the dark, quivering water of Peasholm Lake.

Wilma said, 'By the way, Mummy is throwing an engagement party for us next weekend. She and Daddy are anxious to meet your parents. Well, that's only natural, isn't it? I mean to say, it does seem a bit daft, doesn't it, that they have never met each other yet, with the wedding only a few weeks away?'

'I guess so.' At that moment, holding Wilma in his arms, covering her mouth with kisses, Danny couldn't have cared less about the wedding. All he cared about was the feel of her slender young body against his, the touch of his lips on hers, and suddenly nothing else mattered a damn to him apart from her beauty, her fragility, her fragrance. He wanted her more than he had ever wanted a girl before. The thought that she would soon be his, when the rigmarole of the wedding was over and done with, filled him with a sense of euphoria in complete contrast to his former moodiness, when

117

she had driven him almost mad with her harping on about the wedding.

He wished she wouldn't talk so much. Kissing her, the fact that Wilma's tongue would keep on wagging long after the wedding did not occur to him. Nor had he the faintest idea that it was Wilma's high-pitched voice which had grated on his mother's nerves at their first meeting.

Sitting in the back room with Grace and Bob, the conversation led to Danny's wedding – the thought uppermost in their minds, Herbie realized.

'If only he'd given himself a breathing space,' Bob said forcefully. 'That lass has him hypnotized if you ask me! You know how much he likes sport? Well, he's given it up now, at her say-so. First cricket, now rugger and football. And that's not the worst of it. He'd only just started going steady, next thing we knew, he was getting engaged. We'd just got used to that, then came the real bombshell. That daft girl got it into her head they should get married on his twenty-first birthday and live with her parents after the wedding.

'Grace and I have done our best to talk him out of it, but he won't listen to reason.' He ran his fingers through his hair distractedly. 'We don't know the first thing about her parents except that her father's in transport, whatever that means.'

'I take it you're not all that keen on what's-her-name – Wilma?' Herbie said sympathetically, beginning to understand why Danny looked as if he had hoisted the weight of the world on his shoulders.

'Danny is keen on her,' Grace interposed quietly, 'and that's what really matters. We have no right to interfere, it's just that . . .' her voice faded, tears filled her eyes, 'we had such high hopes for him.'

Herbie's heart went out to her. He longed to hold her, to comfort her. Instead, he said cheerfully, 'Shall I put the kettle on for a nice cup of tea?' A bit of a cheek, he knew, offering to make tea in someone else's kitchen, the only alternative, however, to making a fool of himself.

The front door closed, and Danny came in, bringing with him a breath of cool night air. 'Oh,' he said, poking his head round the kitchen door, 'I thought I'd find Mum in here.'

Grasping the nettle, 'I understand that congratulations are in order,' Herbie said, waiting for the kettle to boil. 'I hear you're getting married in December.'

'Yes. Thanks, Mr Barrass.' Danny edged further into the room, encouraged by the warmth of Herbie's voice, sensing an ally. 'At the Baptist Church in Albemarle Crescent, as a matter of fact, on my twenty-first birthday.' His eagerness faded suddenly. 'The trouble is, my parents don't approve.'

'Oh?' Pouring boiling water into the tea-pot, 'Why not?'

Danny shrugged his shoulders. 'They're against my living with Wilma's parents after the wedding. They think we should wait to get married until we can afford a place of our own. But that could take years. Frankly, Mr Barrass, I don't want to wait that long.'

Herbie said casually, 'What's wrong with renting a place of your own? That's what I'd do in your situation.'

'Mum said much the same thing,' Danny confessed, 'but it isn't that simple. I wouldn't want to upset Wilma or her parents.' He added awkwardly, 'You see, I've already agreed to move in with them after the wedding.'

Herbie's heart went out to the lad, a victim of his own conscience, so much in love that he couldn't see straight.

'Besides,' Danny added, colouring up. 'I don't want to wait too long to start a family. If that happens – you know what I mean? If we start a baby fairly soon, that would be a good excuse to find a place to rent. There wouldn't be room for a baby in my in-law's house. It isn't very big.'

Chapter Nine

After breakfast next morning, when everyone except Dulcie had gone to work, Herbie gave Grace a preview of his Christmas samples – celanese nightgowns trimmed with lace, cami-knickers, petticoats in pastel colours, pure silk stockings, spectacular garters; Ladye Jayne boudoir caps, lace-trimmed modesty vests, dressing-gowns and slippers.

They were in the hall at the time, Herbie kneeling beside his samples case, Grace looking on as he produced each item like rabbits from a conjurer's top hat. 'Well, what do you think?' he asked.

'You'll do well, I'm sure,' she said confidently. 'I've never seen such pretty lingerie before.'

Scrambling to his feet, 'Of course I've brought the usual bread-and-butter lines as well,' he told her. 'You know the kind of thing? Winceyette nightgowns, corsets and the like, for the older generation.' He added, re-packing the case, 'By the way, I forgot to tell you, my area is being extended to include York and Northallerton in the new year.'

'Oh, Herbie, I'm so pleased for you. Congratulations!'

'Yeah, well, I couldn't have done it without your help. Yours and Bob's,' he said. 'You've been golden friends to me . . . Well, I'd best be on my way now.' He wondered if she had guessed how much he loved her?

Standing on the top step to see him safely on his way, 'Good luck,' Grace called after him, touched by his words of appreciation. When he had gone, she went through to the kitchen. Come hell or high water, the housework must be done. Saturdays meant changing bed-linen in readiness for washday and cleaning the bathroom and kitchen. Each and every day brought its own particular chores: polishing, washing paintwork, window-cleaning, swilling and sand-stoning the front steps. Her routine never varied. She was proud of her home.

Stripping and re-making the beds, scouring the bath, she wondered where Dulcie had got to. She might at least have stripped her bed, as Kerry had done. What ailed the girl? Why had she taken to leaving the house without a word of explanation? Talk about the 'elusive Pimpernel'.

'Dulcie!' she called over the banister. Then, 'Oh, there you are,' when the girl appeared in the hall and stood looking up at her, 'would you mind nipping down to the shops for me? I'll need more bread for the weekend, a bag of self-raising flour, and a dozen eggs. My purse is in the kitchen.'

Dulcie made no reply. Stalking into the kitchen to find her mother's purse and a shopping basket, she thought resentfully that it was too bad to be asked to run messages on her morning off.

Washing the bathroom floor, Grace thought about the Burtons so-called engagement-party invitation. Danny had been full of it last night when he came into the back room with Herbie. Obviously he thought it a good idea, and perhaps he was right. It had struck her as faintly ludicrous that two families, about to become related through marriage, had never met. Even so, she jibbed at the thought of a party. Far better would have been an informal meeting with the Burtons, from her own point of view at any rate, and Bob's, who had declared strongly, in the privacy of their bedroom, that he'd rather face a firing squad than an engagement party.

It had taken all her power of persuasion to make him realize this was something they must face for Danny's sake. 'Whatever we say or do,' she reminded him, 'doesn't alter the fact that he and Wilma are getting married in December. The last thing I want is to put up a barrier between us. Blood is thicker than water. The least we can do is stand by him, give him our love and support. The day may come when he'll need someone to turn to.'

121

'When he realizes what a hash he's made of his life, you mean?' Bob said grimly.

'Let's not cross bridges before we come to them,' Grace said, thinking ahead to Sunday – mentally crossing bridges of her own before she came to them – cooking and baking, and the Sunday afternoon visit to South Street . . .

Mrs Daniel's new accommodation suited her well enough. Smaller than her old room, she had nevertheless managed to fit into it her prized possessions, nor did the lack of a view worry her unduly. Frankly, she had detested at times the view of the Castle Hill from the window of her old room, especially in winter; and the clamour of the gulls had driven her almost mad with their squawking and screaming in the early hours of the morning.

There were other advantages too. South Street was closer to the shops, and there was a fine Methodist Church in Filey Road, a mere ten minutes walk away, to which she repaired purposefully on Sunday mornings with Rosa in tow, having first prepared the one o'clock dinner and baked a Swiss roll in readiness for the afternoon tea-party.

Stunned by Nan's high-handedness, Rosa complained bitterly that the kitchen had always been her province and she saw no reason to change that state of affairs. Fanny had never complained about her cooking, she said tearfully, to which Nan replied that Fanny would stand for coals breaking on her head.

Appealed to as arbiter in the culinary dispute, Fanny said sweetly that they should draw up a rota. Taking sides in an argument was far too exhausting from Fanny's viewpoint. She much preferred embroidering lazy-daisies on scraps of linen, a gentle occupation which left her mind free to wander down the avenues of time. It was nice to remember the parties she'd attended as a girl, the many passionate love affairs of her youth . . . thoughts which would shock her strait-laced sisters if they could read her mind.

*   *   *

The South Cliff tramway had closed for the winter, and so the Kingsleys – apart from Dulcie, who was on tea duty – walked across the Spa Bridge to South Street, accompanied by Herbie, whose springiness of step had to do with success. He had made a killing the day before with his samples, and he looked forward to an equally successful day tomorrow before returning to Leeds on the four o'clock train.

The only fly in the ointment of his success story was that tomorrow would mean parting from the woman he loved, his return to a place he no longer thought of as home, fending for himself in a lonely bedsitter in Chapeltown.

Gazing out to sea, he suddenly remembered the words of Madame Jean, the clairvoyant, that soon would come a change of address – a change for the better. Why not? he thought. He was earning good money now. Why not find himself a nicer place to live?

Dulcie quite enjoyed afternoon tea duty at the Pavilion. Working at the town's most prestigious hotel, she felt that a little of the glamour had rubbed off on herself. The entrance lounge, where afternoon tea was served, fulfilled her dreams of grandeur. With a quirk of the imagination, she could see herself seated in a deep armchair near the roaring coal fire, eating a plateful of daintily cut smoked salmon sandwiches; choosing a chocolate éclair or a slice of cream-filled gâteau from the pâtisserie trolley, amid the décor of pink-shaded lamps and magnificent flower arrangements; listening to the resident pianist playing a selection of Jerome Kern melodies on a Blüthner grand piano.

The hotel was less crowded now than in summer-time. The out-of- season guests were mainly older people enjoying a degree of solitude, now that the hordes of day trippers had returned to the West Riding, leaving the streets of Scarborough uncluttered. These more mature guests were of the ilk who enjoyed shopping at leisure at Rowntrees or Marshall and Snelgrove, sedate drives to Forge Valley, Helmsley, or Whitby, or promenading along the wide, upper-crust Esplanade to admire the sea views.

Crossing the foyer to take the order of an elderly gentleman seated at a table near the piano, Dulcie thought thank God she had escaped the Sunday afternoon tea-party in South Street.

Looking up at her, the man said, with the merest trace of a foreign accent, 'Return a little later, if you please. I await the arrival of my family.'

The pianist was was playing 'Smoke Gets in Your Eyes', at the time . . .

Well, here we go again, Herbie thought philosophically, entering the cluttered sitting-room of the Mallory sisters. To his infinite surprise, Mrs Daniel seemed much more affable. She had obviously benefited from her change of address. Putting two and two together, he realized that bossy people are happier when they have someone to boss. A pity that poor old Rosa had become the whipping boy, he thought. The old lady had appeared vaguely worried and disorientated at their first meeting, but she had coped well enough with the tea-tray, had worn a little mantle of pride and self-confidence as she bustled from kitchen to sitting-room with the violet-patterned cups and saucers and plates of food. Now, shorn of her role as hostess, watching her sister Nan ferrying in the food, she seemed drained of what little energy she had possessed in the first place. Herbie's heart went out to the poor old girl. Sitting beside her, recognizing a fellow misfit when he saw one, he conversed with her gently, told her how well she looked, admired the amethyst and seed-pearl brooch she was wearing, until her sallow cheeks flushed pink with pleasure and she began to perk up a little, to smile.

None of this was lost on Grace. Herbie Barrass may not be the handsomest man in the world, she thought, with his plain, weatherbeaten, irregular features scored with the lines of living, but he was a prince among men, worthy of love, of happiness. She said an inward prayer that, someday, he would find the happiness, the love he so richly deserved.

* * *

At the Pavilion Hotel, two small girls chased each other merrily round the revolving doors until the man near the piano rose to his feet to put an end to their game. Then appeared a plainly dressed elderly woman in a state of near-exhaustion. The man's wife, Dulcie supposed, standing near the service door, her order pad at the ready. But surely not? A handsome man like that would be married to a much smarter woman, not an elderly frump wearing an ill-fitting tweed skirt, a camel-hair coat, and a brown felt hat stabbed with a wilting pheasant feather?

Of course, the woman must be the children's nanny, the tall man their grandfather, she deduced as the frump removed the little girls' coats and tam-o-shanters and went upstairs in the lift. Now the pair of them were scrambling onto chairs, squirming and wriggling, and their grandfather was raising a finger to his lips, bidding them to listen to the music. They'd be about five, Dulcie reckoned, and they were obviously twins. Not that she knew much about children, nor was she interested in them as a rule. In this case, her curiosity had been aroused by the man's slightly foreign accent, his bearing and his looks. Patting her hair, smoothing her apron, she went back to the table.

The man ordered tea for two, milk for the children, egg-and-cress sandwiches, scones and jam. 'And cream cakes, Papa. Please, may we have cream cakes?' the children chorused.

'We shall see,' the man told them gravely, 'what Fräulein Stockmar has to say; whether or not you deserve such a treat.'

Returning to the still room, amazed by the revelation that he was not the children's grandfather, 'Who is that man near the piano?' Dulcie asked an elderly still-room assistant who had been at the hotel since 'Dick's' days, and knew everything worth knowing.

'Oh, *him*! His name's Bergmann. He's a German or somesuch.' Water hissed into a silver-plated tea-pot. 'Huh, he married an English lass young enough to be his daughter,

the randy old goat! Well, I ask you. Don't believe in mixed
marriages meself. Never have and never will.' Swopping the
tea-pot for a hot-water jug, she went on, 'They stayed here
on their honeymoon. Mind you, she wasn't a bad sort of girl
– about your build. They say she died giving birth to those
twins.'

Dulcie's heartbeat quickened imperceptibly. So the man
was a widower? She could not have cared less if he was
German, Russian or double Dutch. He was handsome and
rich, and he had been married to a plump young English
girl. Picking up the tray, checking that nothing had been
overlooked, she crossed the room like a Spanish galleon
under full sail, all pennants flying, well pleased with the
darker shade of Icilma cream and the box of Ponds rachel
powder she had bought from Woolworths the day before,
which had added a subtle glow to her complexion, especially
by lamplight.

She took it as a good omen that the pianist was now
playing, 'Lovely to Look At'.

Bob mistrusted his mother-in-law's false air of amiability
which smacked of, 'See how much better off I am here than
I was with you?' At least it made a refreshing change to be
treated to glazed looks rather than beetle-browed stares of
displeasure in his direction. Not that he cared one way or
the other. Her underlying motive, he suspected, was to
convey to Grace, in particular, her capability as a house-
keeper. Clearly, the old girl was now in complete charge of
her new environment – as she would have been of the Castle
Road house, had she been allowed to rule that particular
roost.

It was poor Rosa that Bob felt sorry for. Poor, well-
meaning Rosa – too compliant and weak-willed to challenge
Mrs Daniel's whip-cracking domination, the usurpation of
her role as hostess, not to mention her room on the first
landing. One facet of the charade at least seemed authentic
from Bob's point of view. Obviously, his mother-in-law had
now directed whatever maternal feelings she possessed

towards the faded rose Fanny, the 'baby' of the Mallory family. Some baby! Yet Bob had to hand it to her. Despite her age and avoirdupois, Fanny was still beautiful, imbued with a curious glamour, an air of mystery. Looking at her across the crowded room, he failed, as usual, to pinpoint the true nature of Grace's Aunt Fanny, and wondered what thoughts and memories stirred behind those heavily-lidded eyes. She must have been stunningly lovely in her youth, and she still moved gracefully, when she could be bothered to move at all. Nor was she as dithery and ineffectual as she pretended to be. So why the act?

Now she was asking Danny why he hadn't brought his fiancée to meet her. 'We're not infectious, you know,' she said with a quizzical lift of the eyebrows, 'unless you regard old age as a contagious disease.'

Danny nearly choked on a sandwich. 'No, of course not, Great Aunt. We've been a bit busy, that's all.'

'I shall give you a hand-embroidered table-cloth and matching napkins,' Fanny said graciously. 'I expect your lady friend has started her bottom drawer. I dare say you'll both appreciate nice linen in your new home.'

Dispensing slices of the well-risen Swiss roll she had baked earlier, 'She'll have time enough for that,' Nan chipped in. 'Her bottom drawer will be full to overflowing by the time they find a place of their own to live.' She added acerbically, 'I did tell you, Fanny, that they're moving in with the girl's parents after the wedding.'

'Did you? I don't remember.' Fanny shook her head bemusedly. 'Oh, that seems rather a pity. I imagined that most young married women would prefer to be alone with their husband after the wedding.'

Trust his mother-in-law to stir up trouble, Bob thought bitterly in the awkward ensuing silence. Fanny was wrong in thinking and saying that old age was not a contagious disease. Old age spread itself like moss, lichen on ancient graveyard elms, brown spots on wrinkled hands. Old age spouted venom between pale, narrow lips. Nan's lips.

He said firmly, in Danny's defence, 'It is up to my son and his fiancée to decide their future, so let's drop the subject, shall we?'

Catching his wife's eye, he smiled awkwardly in her direction. Her shining presence lit up the room. Impossible to imagine her ever growing old. It was high time they put paid to these awful Sunday afternoon tea-parties, he reckoned, pushing aside his untasted portion of Swiss roll, and hating the whole damned set-up now that his mother-in-law had assumed control of the household. Poor old Rosa, he thought compassionately. In her case it was quite clear that the meek would not inherit the earth.

What on earth was going on in Kerry's mind, Herbie wondered, sipping tea from his violet-patterned cup. The poor kid looked as if she was trying to work out a complicated maths problem in her head, and getting nowhere fast. Catching his eye, she gave a guilty little start.

To tell or not to tell? That was the question bugging Kerry. Sid Hannay had dropped a hint that he was going to the pictures next Wednesday night, and said she could come with him if she liked. If she *liked*? There was nothing on earth she would like better. But what if her parents said No?

On the other hand, if she told a whopper, said she was going to the pictures with one of the girls from Mr Hodnot's sewing room, what would be the Lord's reaction in church next Sunday morning? Suppose He smote her a mighty smite in full view of the congregation?

'Conscience doth make cowards of us all'. Kerry gleaned snippets, quotations which appealed to her, as a squirrel gathers nuts, which she wrote painstakingly in the feint-ruled exercise book she kept hidden beneath her underwear in the chest-of-drawers she shared with Dulcie.

What to do? What to *do*? No use seeking Dulcie's advice. Her sister had been acting so odd lately that she hardly dared speak to her for fear of getting her head snapped off. Why, she had no idea. Perhaps poor Dulcie was anaemic, at a 'funny' age for a girl?

Oh lord, Kerry thought fearfully, perhaps she, too, would be at a funny age for a girl in eighteen months from now, if she wasn't already? Or perhaps one never grew out of that 'funny' age at all, if her great aunts and her grandmother were anything to go by. She loved them all dearly, but did it matter all that much who served the tea when there were far more important issues at stake? Danny getting hitched to that dreadful Wilma Burton, for instance, Dulcie behaving like a bear with a sore head, and herself about to fall from grace in the eyes of the Lord if she went out with Sid on the sly. At least she now had an inkling of how Danny felt about Wilma. Love struck one amidships when least expected.

The first time she'd seen Sid Hannay, he'd been charging down the main street, his hair blowing in the wind, a satchel of books slung carelessly over one shoulder – the image of her latest screen hero Errol Flynn, whom she had seen three times in *Captain Blood*.

For the first time ever she had transferred her feelings to a living hero rather than a shadowy icon as remote as the moon and stars. Afterwards, she had taken to haunting the main street to catch a glimpse of the handsome High School boy whose name she didn't even know at the time; had begun taking more interest in her appearance, brushing her hair one hundred strokes at bedtime to make it shine, wearing elastic garters to keep her socks up, pestering her mother to buy her a brassière, putting forward the argument that Dulcie wore one, so why shouldn't she?

'Yes,' Mum said, 'but Dulcie *needs* to wear a brassière.' Then, with a deep sigh, 'Oh, very well then, if we can find one small enough to fit you.'

Her every thought centred on her real-life hero. Kerry imagined him diving into a rough sea to save her from drowning, dancing with him to the 'Merry Widow Waltz'; herself as the Rose Queen of Scarborough, walking down that long flight of steps to her throne, pausing momentarily to throw him a rose from her bouquet. Reality had not quite lived up to romantic daydreams. Even so, now that Sid had

129

asked her to go to the pictures with him, she would risk anything to sit with him on the back row of the one-and-nines. Would they hold hands? she wondered. Would he treat her to a box of chocolates?

The fraught tea-party over, she was walking across the Spa Bridge with Herbie at her side, dreamily aware of the shorelights springing up one by one against the background of indigo blue sea, and thinking of Sid. She did not at first notice him coming towards her in the dusk, his arm firmly clamped about the waist of a flashily dressed, buxom girl with dyed blonde hair. Indeed, she might not have noticed him at all, so lost in thought was she, had not the girl he was with uttered a piercing shriek of laughter, crying out, 'Oh, Sid, you are *awful*, really you are!'

Herbie would never forget the stricken look on Kerry's face, her sharp intake of breath, the way she suddenly stopped walking, as if her legs had lost their power of movement. His heart went out to the poor little kid. It didn't take a mental giant to realize what was happening. So this was the Sid she'd told him about? No doubt about *that*! The lass he was with might just as well have used a loud-hailer. Not that she needed one – not with a voice like a fog-horn, a laugh like a hyena.

Drawing Kerry's trembling hand into the crook of his arm, urging her forward, 'Chin up, girl,' Herbie muttered compassionately, 'he isn't fit to tie your shoe laces, and don't you forget it! Just hold onto me, love. Pretend you're the Rose Queen of Scarborough walking down that long flight of stairs. You wouldn't want to disappoint your audience, would you? To turn tail and run? Of course not. There's a good girl. Come on now, you're doing fine. Now, just keep your eyes straight ahead. Think of home. Think of supper. What are we having for supper, by the way?'

Her head held high, walking past Sid and his girlfriend without so much as a sideways glance in their direction, clinging to Herbie's arm, with tears running down her cheeks, 'Sausages and jacket potatoes, I expect,' she said bleakly.

Guiding her homeward, Herbie knew exactly what she was going through. After all, God help him, he should know better than most how to endure the pangs of a hopeless love.

Chapter Ten

'Oh, do come in! I'm Wilma's mother. Pleased to meet you, I'm sure.' Mrs Burton stood with her back to the lincrusta dado as the Kingsleys, *en masse*, crowded into the hall. 'My word, what a big family!'

Dulcie coloured to the roots of her hair. Always ready to take umbrage, she imagined the unfortunate adverb referred to her size. It wasn't fair, she thought bitterly, when she was doing her best to lose weight. She hadn't wanted to come to this stupid party anyway. Now she wished she'd stuck to her guns and stayed at home.

Worse was to come. Meeting Kerry, 'Oh, what a pretty little girl,' Mrs Burton burbled effusively, inflaming Dulcie's sense of injustice, at the same time upsetting Kerry who regarded herself as a grown woman, not a child; the tragic victim of an unrequited love affair.

Then came Jimmy's turn to face the humiliation of Mrs Burton's blundering comments. 'Oh, what a tall boy,' she gushed, as if he were a ruddy piece of bedroom furniture, he thought disgustedly.

'Well, do come into the front lounge,' their hostess continued. 'My hubby is so anxious to meet all of you. He's in transport, you know.' Edging her shoulders along the varnished fleur-de-lys-patterned wallpaper above the dado, she preceded her guests through the first door on the right along the narrow passage, calling brightly, 'Well, here we are, Daddy!'

Entering the room, Grace realized why Mr Burton had stayed put. 'Daddy's' presence in the hall would have rendered movement well nigh impossible. The man bestriding the hearthrug resembled a heavyweight boxer, or one of those burly fairground attendants in charge of the dodgem cars on the seafront, she thought. Stifling an hysterical urge to laugh, she wondered if dodgem cars constituted a form of transport? Deep down, she felt more like crying at the thought of Danny moving into this dreadful house to live with the scatterbrained Mrs Burton and her monosyllabic husband.

What was she doing here? What were any of them doing here, sitting, in varying degrees of discomfort, on hard-seated dining chairs ranged round the room, sipping glasses of cheap, sweet sherry doled out to them by their reluctant host? All except Danny, who had remained standing, his eyes fixed hungrily on the door. Wilma floated into the room at that moment. Grace closed her eyes momentarily. Having made her entrance, the girl drifted towards Danny, lifted her face to be kissed, and laid claim to him by anchoring his arm with her left hand, upon which shone the engagement ring he had given her.

'Oh, don't they make a lovely couple?' Mabel Burton breathed ecstatically. 'It's so romantic, don't you think, Mrs Kingsley? I mean, two young people setting sail on the sea of life together!'

Grace swallowed hard. Easy to see, now, where Wilma's 'gentility' sprang from. In years to come, Wilma would become more and more like her mother, seeing no fault or imperfection in herself, living a romantic dream, enclosed in a narrow world of her own creation.

Narrow was the operative word. The sight of so much furniture, so many ornaments and pictures crammed into so small a space, depressed Grace. Caught up in a cobweb of rose-patterned china, silver-plated tea-strainers, Ethel M. Dell novels, green plush chairs and starched lace curtains, Danny would find it increasingly difficult to free himself from its suffocating threads.

Before supper was served in the back parlour, Mrs Burton took Grace upstairs to show her Wilma's room. 'Of course,' Mabel said archly, 'we'll be moving the single bed into the spare room after the wedding.'

Grace looked aghast at the 'bridal chamber'. It was already

crammed to overflowing with furniture. The kidney-shaped dressing table in front of the window, bedecked with rose-patterned chintz frills and furbelows, bore a bewildering array of skin-lotion bottles, pots of skin-food, lipsticks and tubes of Woolworths make-up. Opposite the bed – similarly dressed overall in rose-patterned flounces – stood a massive fumed oak wardrobe filled to overflowing with Wilma's coats, hats, shoes and dresses, a fact revealed when, opening the doors, Mrs Burton said proudly, 'I make all Wilma's clothes myself . . . her coats, undies and dresses, that is. Though I say so as shouldn't, I'm a very good hand with a sewing-machine, and she's so easy to fit, bless her.'

A moment of dewy-eyed silence, then Mabel continued, 'Of course I shall make her wedding dress myself, and the bridesmaids' dresses.'

Grace had to say it. 'Where will Danny hang his clothes?'

'Oh, there's a single wardrobe in the spare room. He can use that. There isn't room for it in here.'

This much was abundantly clear to Grace. The double bed would create serious problems. Once installed, movement would be well nigh impossible. Danny would hate undressing in the spare room at the far end of the narrow landing. In any case, her son was proud of his clothes, meticulous about his personal appearance. Glancing at the mammoth chest of drawers on the wall opposite the window, she asked Mrs Burton if there would be room in it for his shirts, socks, collars and so on.

Mabel looked pained. 'I dare say Wilma will let him have the top drawer if he asks her nicely,' she said off-handedly. 'That's up to them to decide, isn't it? Mind you, Wilma is very particular about her things.'

'So is Danny,' Grace said quietly, beginning to dislike Mrs Burton intensely. Clearly, the woman had masterminded this rushed wedding for the sole purpose of keeping her daughter at home with her. Danny was merely a pawn in the game.

Reading Mabel Burton like a book, Grace could almost hear her saying proudly to anyone who cared to listen to her pathetic jabber, 'My daughter's hubby works at the Town Hall, you know.' Anger flared up in her. How dare this silly woman dice so dangerously with Danny's happiness? The warning signs were all there. Once married to Wilma, his status would be that of an unwelcome lodger in the Burton household.

Danny valued his freedom. Giving up sport to please his fiancée had proved a bitter pill to swallow. The honeymoon over, how would he react to asking his bride 'nicely' to give him drawer space for his laundry? Knowing Danny, there'd probably be ructions. Giving up sport for a fiancée was one thing, begging drawer space from a wife, a different matter entirely.

Likely as not, coming home tired from work, in need of the space and the freedom denied him in this overcrowded environment, resentful of the watchful eyes of his mother-in-law upon him, feeling himself trapped, he would lay claim to that top drawer by the simple expedient of tipping his bride's lingerie onto the floor. Then all hell would break loose!

But she was letting her imagination run away with her, Grace realized. Now Mrs Burton was on about the number of guests at the wedding, saying she had already booked the Baptist Church Hall for the reception.

'That's partly why I invited you here tonight,' Mabel said conspiratorially, 'to discuss things – numbers and so on.' She added brightly, 'Don't be afraid to say how many people you want to invite! What I mean is, Daddy and I are footing the bill, and we do so want to give our little girl a wedding day to remember!'

'Yes, of course, I'm sure you do.' Grace felt suddenly drained, washed-out, physically and mentally exhausted, overwhelmed by her hostess's upsurge of vitality, the realization that the die was cast, that nothing she could say or do would prevent the marriage of her son Danny to Wilma Burton. All she could possibly do now was hope and pray that they would be happy together. What more could any mother wish for a beloved son?

135

Even so, walking downstairs to the back room where the supper table was laid with food enough to feed an army, Grace saw, in her mind's eye, a future facsimile of this house, filled to overflowing with fumed oak bedroom furniture, fussily patterned carpets, rose-patterned curtains and wall-paper, a china cabinet stuffed with all manner of junk ornaments. A house presided over by a self-centred, smug young woman who had never looked up at the stars, had never even begun to understand the real meaning of love – that vital, divine spark which gave all, expected nothing in return, except love.

Forgetful of her diet, Dulcie was eating as though a famine warning had been broadcast. Kerry, on the other hand, appeared as one in a trance, not at all her usual happy self. Come to think of it, the girl had seemed strangely off-colour for the past week, Grace realized, wondering what ailed her, feeling guilty that the wedding had come uppermost in her mind to the exclusion of all else.

In her element, Mrs Burton was now twinkling as brightly as a 100 watt light bulb, mingling with her guests, passing the plates of sausage rolls and sandwiches – actually ogling Bob, Grace thought indignantly. Of all the nerve!

Edging closer to Kerry, Grace enquired anxiously, 'Are you all right, love?' at the same time keeping a weather eye on Mabel.

'Yes, Mum. I'm fine. Just fine.'

'Then why aren't you eating?'

'I'm not very hungry, that's all.' Kerry smiled wanly. She could not, for the life of her, have told anyone, not even her mother, the way she had felt last Sunday evening, as if her heart had shattered like broken glass. Herbie had told her later that, growing up, she would forget about Sid, or at least remember him as part and parcel of the growing-up process. She hadn't believed him, how could she?

'I'll buy you a jar of Cod Liver Oil and Malt tomorrow,' Grace said decisively. 'That'll do you good.'

Bob felt as uncomfortable as he looked. Seething beneath his hair, he saw no point or purpose in this particular social event. Burton, a brutish man in his opinion, had not even bothered to dress properly, nor had he spoken more than a few sentences to either himself or Jimmy since their arrival. Now he was being treated to flirtatious glances from the man's wife, whose face was growing pinker by the minute as she babbled inconsequentially about the wedding, saying how delightful to think they would soon be related by marriage, that he must call her Mabel from now on. 'More friendly like, don't you think?' she enquired roguishly.

Then, turning her attention to the embarrassed Jimmy standing next to his father, 'And you, young man, must call me Auntie Mabel,' she chortled. She added, 'Of course, Danny may call me Mummy after the wedding. You see, I feel I'm gaining a son, not losing a daughter!'

Bob stared at her wordlessly in shocked disbelief at her stupidity. Did she really imagine that Danny would even contemplate the use of such a childish soubriquet? His heart sank to his shoes when, after the buffet, the silly woman suggested a return to the front lounge for a little light entertainment. Catching Grace's eye across the crowded back parlour, Bob signalled his distress with his eyebrows. Grace raised her shoulders helplessly in response. Impossible, for Danny's sake, to eat and run, no matter how strong the temptation to do just that – to quit this dreadful party as quickly as possible.

Glancing at their son, she saw that he and Wilma appeared to be encapsulated in a world of their own, as they had been all evening. This was as it should be, Grace realized, and possibly she had been wrong in thinking that Danny would resent the intrusion of his in-laws after the wedding. How little one knew, after all, about one's own children, what they were really thinking or feeling. How easy for a mother to make assumptions. There was no charter expressly forbidding the right of children to develop in their own way. The act of love, of birth, the care and fostering of the family in the early years, belonged solely to herself and Bob. The most they could hope for now was that their own values, sown along the way, would bear fruit in years to come.

She noticed, with a tiny tug of distress, that Bob's hair was turning slightly grey at the temples. But then, so was hers. Imperceptibly, they were growing older together. A tiny cloud of fear invaded her heart that he might die suddenly, as his father before him had done. Then, giving herself a mental shake, she knew that her depression had to do with this cramped, overcrowded house, the indefatigably charming Mrs Burton, her morose husband, and Wilma's high-pitched voice which grated on her ears like the monotonous buzzing of a chainsaw. How much longer would the ghastly party continue, she wondered. What was the point and purpose of it all apart from meeting Danny's future in-laws? She was soon to find out.

The buffet supper over, Mabel Burton led them back to the front lounge where, seating herself at the upright piano, she proceeded to entertain her guests with solo renditions of 'One Alone' from *The Desert Song*, 'Vilia' from *The Merry Widow*, and 'My Hero' from *The Chocolate Soldier*. Her shrill soprano voice cracking on the high notes, she was totally oblivious of the row she was making, unaware of Kerry's distress at the murder of 'Vilia', Dulcie's desperate attempts not to break wind in public, Jimmy's stuffed-owl expression as he struggled valiantly to stifle his laughter, the wry looks exchanged between Grace and Bob as the entertainment went on and on and on.

Meanwhile, Danny, a soppy look on his face, gazed continuously at Wilma who was standing near the piano turning over the music pages at her mother's behest; sharing the limelight as it were, a picture of complacency, the apple of her parents' eye; wallowing, it seemed to Grace, in her own perfection of form and face, her unassailable position as a bride-to-be, with a ring to prove her desirability.

Suddenly, Dulcie belched, albeit restrainedly, Jimmy burst out laughing. The audience began, desultorily, to clap as Mabel, pink-cheeked and triumphant, stood up to take her bow, thankfully unaware of Dulcie's *faux-pas*.

'And now,' she trilled, 'let us drink a toast to the future of the happy couple! Arthur, hand round the port. There now.

Are we all fully charged?' She treated 'Daddy' to a baleful look of displeasure at his slowness, gave an almighty sniff, and continued: 'We all know why we are here, the reason why I decided to throw this little party. Or should I call it a get-together? Well, now that we have all got together, I'd like to wish our little girl and her hubby-to-be good luck for the future.' Raising her glass, 'Like I said, here's to the happy couple!'

Bob groaned, deeply embarrassed. Grace gave him a dig in the ribs, a warning glance of disapproval. Dutifully they rose to their feet to honour the toast: 'To the happy couple!' Grace's hand shook slightly on the stem of her glass. It all seemed so ludicrous, so pretentious, she thought, resentful of the term 'hubby' in connection with her son, totally out of keeping with the seriousness of his future role as a provider for his wife and family. Never in her life had she referred to Bob as 'my hubby', always 'my husband'.

Sitting down abruptly, a drop of her untasted glass of wine dripped onto her skirt; tears filled her eyes. 'Are you all right, love?' Bob enquired anxiously.

'Of course I am. Stop fussing,' she muttered, as Mabel continued brightly.

'Now a word or two about the wedding. Wilma has decided on three bridesmaids – her cousin Bella from Birmingham, Dulcie and Kerry, haven't you, darling?'

'Yes,' Wilma said flatly, with a haughty glance in Dulcie's direction, a look which said more clearly than words that this compromise had been forced upon her as a matter of expedience rather than choice. After all, what bride in her right senses would want her retinue made ridiculous by the inclusion of a heavyweight with frizzy brown hair?

Picking up Wilma's thought-waves, colouring to the roots of her hair, Dulcie said stubbornly, 'You can count me out!' She added, close to tears, 'I hate weddings, and I wouldn't be a bridesmaid for all the tea in China.'

Wilma breathed a sigh of relief. Mrs Burton looked

stunned. Then, quickly gaining her equilibrium, 'Oh, well, if that's the way you feel. But what about you, Kerry? You'd like to be a bridesmaid, wouldn't you?'

'Yeah, I guess so,' Kerry responded dully, thinking of her lost love, Sid Hannay, feeling pale and wan, a bit like Greta Garbo in the fade-out of *Queen Christina*, facing a future devoid of John Gilbert.

'That's settled then. I'll need to take your measurements,' Mabel told Kerry, 'but I can do that nearer the time, after I've finished the bridal gown.' Her face grew even pinker. 'My word, I *am* going to be a little busy bee, aren't I? But I do *like* to be busy, don't I Daddy? Oh, isn't it exciting?' She emitted a tinkling laugh. 'Now, Grace. I may call you Grace, mayn't I? You won't forget to let me have your list of invites, will you? I must let the caretaker know how many to set up for. I shall do the catering, of course, and make the wedding cake. That goes without saying. I wouldn't trust anyone else to make the cake. Though I say so as shouldn't, I'm a very good cook.' Turning her attention to Jimmy, 'You will be Danny's best man, I expect? Don't lose the ring, will you?'

Jimmy couldn't help it. 'No, Auntie Mabel,' he simpered. Danny shot him a look that could kill. Jimmy smiled broadly.

'Now I must show you my photograph albums,' Mabel said breathlessly.

Rising purposefully to his feet, 'Another time, perhaps?' Bob interposed heartily. 'Thank you for a memorable evening, Mrs Burton, but we'd better be making a move now. After all, tomorrow's a working day, and we're early risers. Ready, love?'

Grace could have kissed him. Mabel's charm deserted her momentarily. She said, with one of her sniffs, 'Oh, well if you must go, you must, I suppose!'

'Yes, we really must,' Grace responded warmly, her usual smiling self now that the ordeal was over.

Walking home, her hand tucked securely into the crook of Bob's arm, she saw the riding lights of ships far out on the horizon, and lifted her face to the cool, cleansing wind blowing in from the sea.

No need of words. No need to tell Bob how much she had hated the past few hours. The inquest on the party would come later in the privacy of their bedroom, and they would laugh about it. 'Don't ever leave me, Bob,' she murmured. *'Promise!'*

Chapter Eleven

Danny would be 21 on 14 December. A Saturday, as luck would have it. Bob expressed his opinion that luck had nothing to do with it. The scheming Mabel Burton would have known well in advance that her future son-in-law's coming of age would fall on a Saturday – the day on which most couples got hitched.

As much as Grace dreaded the event, preparations had to be made. She would need a new coat and hat, shoes, gloves; Bob, Danny and Jimmy new suits from the Fifty Shilling Tailors. As for Dulcie. *Well!* The girl flatly refused to change her mind about being a bridesmaid. After a few failed attempts to talk her round, Grace gave up the struggle. She would not, however, countenance Dulcie's foolishness in saying she had no intention of going to the wedding at all. 'Go you most certainly shall, my girl,' Grace told her severely. 'What's more, you'll come with me to Hopper and Masons to buy a decent outfit!' She wasn't having Mabel Burton making snide remarks about her family. Nor was she prepared to put up with any more of Dulcie's nonsense.

Kerry, usually the more amenable of the two, demurred when it came to the bridesmaid's get-up that Wilma had chosen for her. 'It's *awful*,' she wailed, following a visit to the Burtons' house to have her measurements taken. 'Pink satin with puffed sleeves and a *sash*!'

'Well, what's wrong with that?' Grace asked, getting the supper ready, beginning to wish that Danny and Wilma would elope to Gretna Green and have done with it.

'What's *wrong* with it?' Kerry's face puckered. 'Pink satin in December? Bella-from-Birmingham and I will probably freeze to death! And that's not all. We're to wear poke bonnets and lace mittens. I ask you.' Sitting at the kitchen

142

table, chin in hands, sighing deeply, Kerry continued, 'You should have seen the look on Mrs Burton's face when I said I rather fancied red velvet and muffs. Either that or lace crinoline dresses, with fur tippets and long suede gloves.'

Grace smiled, 'The trouble with you, love, is that you let your imagination run away with you at times. Now, don't just sit there. Make yourself useful. Start by setting the dining-room table, there's a good girl.'

'Yes, Mum.'

Doing as she was told, Kerry recalled that starlit October night when she had gone with one of the girls from work to see *Roberta* at the Futurist cinema, a film about fashion, starring the lovely Irene Dunne. Tears had filled her eyes and rolled down her cheeks when the heroine sang 'Smoke Gets in Your Eyes'. It was so poignant a reminder of her own abortive love affair with Sid Hannay, the memory of which touched a raw spot in her heart even now. Especially now, in this cold, foggy month of November, with the shops getting ready for Christmas, and Danny's wedding looming up through the mist.

She had seen Sid once or twice since that dreadful evening on the Spa Bridge; had hastily averted her eyes. It was a matter of pride. The jar of Cod Liver Oil and Malt that Mum had bought her hadn't done her a ha'porth of good. How could it? Sweet sticky stuff in a bottle was not likely to mend a broken heart, although it had picked up her appetite to some extent.

Placing the knives and forks, the cruet and the tablemats just so, Kerry thought about the wedding. Thank goodness Herbie was coming. She thought the world of Herbie, her knight in shining armour whose down-to-earth wisdom had helped her through the worst moments of her life so far – on whom she relied to help her through yet another crisis. Weddings were supposed to be romantic, happy events. Sugar and spice and all things nice. Why, then, this feeling that all the joy and happiness of life had suddenly drained away from her, leaving her bereft, a shadow of her former self?

'So I'll smile and say, when a lovely flame dies, Smoke gets in your eyes.'

Kerry had no way of knowing – how could she? – that her present state of highly charged emotions, the ebb and flow of happiness and despair were all part and parcel of the growing-up process.

A hard cross to bear was that the old rapport between herself and Danny had almost ceased to exist because of Wilma Burton. At least she still had Jimmy to turn to, even when he was upstairs in his room pounding away at his new typewriter. But he never minded her presence in his study, and she loved the sound of rain beating down on his skylight window on gloomy November Sunday evenings, after their visits to South Street, when the supper dishes had been washed and put away.

She would sit cross-legged on his bed listening to the patter of the rain, the howl of the wind, the muted roar of the sea in the distance. She derived comfort from the unleashed elements of Nature beating, howling and prowling about the house on the hill, and Jimmy's energy and concentration on his work, knowing that, despite the world outside, she was safe from harm within these walls, with the people she loved about her.

And then, slowly but surely began to dawn the awareness of the true nature of love, to do with warmth, comfort and familiarity, nothing whatever to do with a febrile longing for a High School boy who, truth to tell, didn't look all that much like Errol Flynn anyway. In any case, she was now more than a little in love with Randolph Scott, Irene Dunne's co-star in *Roberta*, who closely resembled her brother Jimmy, except that Jimmy wore glasses, and he was not exactly the romantic hero type in his weird assortment of pullovers, with a scarf slung round his neck for extra warmth.

Even so, there came now and then mental images of summer-time; herself and Sid walking together along the sands towards the harbour, then she would regress, momentarily, into a state of longing for something that was over and done with for ever, that first blissful moment of sexual awareness, of sublime happiness when every detail of the sky, the sea and the sand, had shimmered blue and golden into the deep recesses of her heart and mind.

Summer-time was over and done with, and so was her first ever love affair. But Herbie Barrass had been wrong about one thing, Kerry reckoned. Come winter-time, hail, rain or snow, she would always remember the ice-cream cornet Sid Hannay had bought her from that stall on the sands.

Grace had agonized over the list of 'invites', as Mrs Burton had put it. Family came first, of course. Her own mother, and Bob's, his Aunt Caroline; Fanny and Rosa; Herbie Barrass – who counted as family. Then came the difficult part. Should they invite Mr Hodnot? He was, after all, a friend of Fanny's, and Kerry's employer. And what about Mr Jenkins and his daughter Meg? No. Perhaps not.

Naturally enough, Danny wished to invite his office friends and colleagues, their wives and respective girlfriends. And why not? But a line had to be drawn somewhere. A good cook Mrs Burton may be, but she could not be expected to feed the five thousand, and Danny's list included not only half the Town Hall staff but his Cricket Club pals as well. Talk about Ali-Baba and the Forty Thieves! It just wasn't on, and she told him so, whereupon he turned sulky and said that this was his wedding, too, and he had every right to a good send-off.

'I know, love,' Grace demurred, 'but we have to be realistic. This *is* a church hall do, remember.'

'Yeah, more's the pity,' he remarked. 'Frankly, I'd have preferred a sit-down lunch at the Pavilion Hotel, or Rowntree's Rendezvous Restaurant. I hate the thought of sausage rolls and sandwiches in some seedy church hall!' He added savagely, 'In case everyone's forgotten, December the fourteenth just happens to be my twenty-first birthday as well as my wedding day!'

'*I* hadn't forgotten,' Grace reminded him gently, 'neither has your father. How could we? But combining the two was

145

your wish, not ours.' She steeled herself not to say, 'If only you had waited a little while longer.' After all, what was the use? She had reached the conclusion, albeit painfully, that silence was golden in the case of a headstrong young man so determined to have his own way that he had brushed aside his parents' advice, their concern for his future, as meaningless nonsense. So be it. Her son was now a man, in charge of his own destiny. If only her foolish heart would stop remembering the child he used to be.

As the grandmother of the bridegroom, Nan decided that she must treat herself to a brand-new outfit: dress, coat, shoes, hat, gloves, handbag. The lot! No way was she prepared to be outshone by Danny's other grandmother, Mrs Kingsley. A poor, spineless creature to her way of thinking. No wonder the stupid woman had given birth to such a dissolute son, the seducer of an innocent young girl, she thought bitterly, popping her dentures into the dish of saline solution at her bedside.

She had seen the outfit she wanted in Rowntrees department store, a mulberry-coloured tweed coat and dress. She had no patience with Rosa, who seemed to live in a dream world these days, moping about the house with scarcely a word to say for herself, a tiny, shrivelled figure with permanently watering eyes, whose lack of spirit and dry nervous cough she had developed recently, irritated Nan past bearing. This was exacerbated by the fact that Rosa had shown not the slightest interest in the proposed new outfit, had declined even to consider buying anything new for herself to wear at the wedding.

There had been quite a scene about that, Nan recalled grimly, reaching for her bottle of dyspepsia tablets. All Rosa's fault, of course, the stupid thing, bursting into tears at the tea-table the way she had done, crying shrilly that she was sick and tired of being bullied and badgered, and what did it matter what she wore at the wedding, no-one would notice her anyway, then blundering upstairs to her room and locking the door behind her.

146

Worst of all, Fanny, of all people, had sided with Rosa – so far as Fanny ever sided with anyone in an argument. 'You really must try to be kinder to Rosa,' she said mildly. Then she, Nan, had left the table and gone up to *her* room, thinking that Fanny would come up to apologise. But Fanny hadn't come, and when she had gone down to the kitchen next morning, the eggshells were still in their cups, the tea-pot was half full of cold tea, the scones she had baked were rock hard, and there was a dead fly in the strawberry jam. And all because she had tried to persuade Rosa to buy a new coat and hat.

It just wasn't fair. But she had made her feelings clear to the pair of them that morning by the simple expedient of maintaining a dignified silence, at the same time clattering yesterday's tea things into the enamel washing-up bowl when they emerged from their rooms – a far from silent reproach for having wounded her so deeply. Not that either Fanny or Rosa had appeared to notice that they were being given the silent treatment, or that breakfast was not on the table as usual.

Fanny had merely smiled and said, 'Good morning', picked an apple from the dish of fruit on the sideboard, and drifted downstairs to the shop, while Rosa had said nothing at all except, 'I'm going out'. And out she went. Furthermore, the silly creature had stayed out all day, and when she returned, she had gone straight up to her room. Well, *really*! After all she had done for them: taking over the housekeeping, doing the shopping, making sure they had something decent to eat; slaving her fingers to the bone for them. And what thanks did she receive for her efforts on their behalf?

Switching off her bedside lamp, lying rigidly against her pillows, Nan Daniel faced the possibility that she had made a wrong decision in coming to live with her sisters. Not dear Fanny, of course. Oh, heaven, it was all so difficult. A case of two's company, three's a crowd. She remembered their girlhood days before the war, long before she had started courting the Reverend John Daniel. As long ago as that,

Rosa had been the odd one out, the misfit of the Mallory sisters, invited to the various Christmas and birthday parties they'd attended, the modest musical evenings, and their friends' weddings, because, Nan imagined, the hostess would realize the impossibility of inviting herself and Fanny without Rosa. Plain, dull Rosa, the parasite, the unwanted guest at all those pre-war weddings, parties and musical soirees.

In Nan's case, charity certainly did not begin at home. Never had it occurred to her to feel grateful to Rosa for staying at home to look after their ailing parents until their deaths. She had simply seen Rosa in the light of eternal spinsterhood; a born spinster put on this earth to cater to the needs of the old and dying, to trot patiently from room to room clearing up messes, providing food – badly cooked food at that. She had seen no earthly reason why she and dear Fanny should be called upon to suffer Rosa's appallingly bad cooking, the reason why she had felt it incumbent upon herself to take charge of the kitchen upon her removal to the South Cliff establishment. To what purpose?

She adored Fanny. Had always adored her. Had loved playing the elder sister, helping to choose her dresses, enjoying her artless prattle about the colour of a bead necklace or a bow of ribbon for her long blond hair. Naturally she had felt envious, at times, that this baby sister of hers was far prettier than herself – envy soon dissipated by the advent of John Daniel into her life, the fact that she, not the wickedly beautiful Fanny had been the first, indeed the only sister, to marry. This she had worn as a badge of pride until that dreadful day when their 16-year-old daughter had told her she was two months' pregnant by Bob Kingsley.

Her daughter's pregnancy had hardened, not softened, her attitudes to life. Her fondness for Fanny remained the weak link in her armour. This, and her growing tendency to relive the past, drawing Fanny into a world of long gone summertimes, saying, 'Oh, Fanny dear, do you remember those pretty pink dresses we wore to the Halls' garden party?' or whatever the occasion may have been, excluding Rosa from the conversation entirely, as if Rosa's mind had been wiped clean of memories as chalk is wiped from a slate. As if she did not exist, Rosa thought bitterly. But even a worm could turn . . .

Danny went up to Jimmy's room one wild November evening, after supper. Kerry was there, sitting cross-legged on the bed.

'Behold, the bridegroom cometh,' Jimmy said laconically, when Danny came in.

'Oh, don't start spouting poetry.' Danny felt slightly aggrieved that two articles of his brother's on that very subject had appeared in print recently, reaping the handsome reward of a cheque for ten guineas.

'It isn't poetry, it's biblical,' Kerry said loftily. Jimmy laughed. Danny scowled. He had come for a word in private about the wedding, not to be lectured by his kid sister.

'Hop it, Kerry,' he said. Kerry 'hopped it' with a scornful glance at Danny. 'All right, I know when I'm not wanted,' she told him, hanging onto her pride. Not wanting him to see how deeply he had hurt her by his curt dismissal, she walked out of the room, her head held high.

'Did you have to do that?' Jimmy asked. 'The kid thinks the sun rises and sets in you, and all you can do is slap her in the eye, the way you have done ever since you and Wilma started courting!'

'Huh?' Genuinely surprised, 'I don't know what you're on about,' Danny blurted indignantly.

'No, well you wouldn't,' Jimmy stretched his arms to relax his shoulder muscles. 'With you it's self first, second and last these days.'

'I didn't come here for a row,' Danny retorted, deeply shaken by his brother's uncalled-for remarks, up in arms at being called selfish when he was bending over backwards to please everyone except himself. He added huffily, 'I don't know why I bothered to come at all—'

'Oh, sit down and get on with it.' Jimmy grinned amiably.

Revolving slowly on the swivel chair he had bought with the money he'd received from his publishers, he asked, 'Not getting cold feet about the wedding, are you?'

'No, of course not.' Danny perched on the end of the bed. 'I just wanted to make sure . . .' He tried another tack, 'About the wedding, the ring, and so forth.'

'I shan't lose it, if that's what's worrying you,' Jimmy reassured him. 'I'm not as daft as all that!'

'I know.' Deeply embarrassed, Danny continued. 'But about the speech. You won't say anything, well . . . anything about may all our troubles be little ones.'

'As if I *would*!' Taking off his glasses, Jimmy rubbed them clean with the tail end of his scarf. Jamming them back on his nose, 'What do you take me for? A comedian?' His eyes glittered fiercely behind the lenses. 'I thought you knew me better than that.'

'I do, Jimmy, believe me.' Drawing in a deep breath of despair, he ran his fingers through his hair, his shoulders drooping forward. 'It's just that I—'

'Go on, you can tell me,' Jimmy said sympathetically. Getting up, he sat beside Danny; placed a comforting arm about his shoulders. 'I can tell there's something bugging you. What is it, Danny? What's wrong?'

'If you really want to know!' Danny blurted out, 'I dread living with Wilma's parents after the wedding.' Brushing a hand across his eyes, 'I want her all to myself. That's understandable, isn't it? I'm crazy about her! When we're married, I shall want . . . well, you know . . . How do you think I'll feel knowing her parents are in the next room listening to every creak of the bed-springs?'

'Bloody awful, I imagine,' Jimmy acknowledged. Getting up, he paced the room for a while. 'But if you feel this way,' he said, 'why not find a place of your own to live?'

Raising his head, Danny said simply, 'It isn't as easy as that. You see, Wilma wants to live with her parents, for the time being at least. Furthermore, I'm skint, Jimmy. Stoney broke! At any rate I shall be when I've forked out for the bridesmaids' presents and the honeymoon. So you see I have no other choice than to move in with the Burtons after the wedding.'

Jimmy said forthrightly, 'The pity is that you couldn't have waited a while longer to get married. You do realize how Mum and Dad feel about you living with the Burtons?'

'We've never discussed it,' Danny said carefully.

'You mean you didn't want to discuss it,' Jimmy was fast losing patience. 'You're too pig-headed, that's your trouble.'

'Oh? And what would you have done in my situation?' Danny said heatedly.

'Ah well, I wouldn't have landed myself in such a mess in the first place.' Jimmy went back to his chair. 'I thought marriage was supposed to be about give and take. And how come you're skint? You've stopped going to the pictures, you don't go to the Olympia any more. You should have a nice little nest-egg by now.' He grinned amiably to take the sting from his remarks.

'A fat lot you know!' Danny headed for the door. 'Seems to me this writing lark's gone to your head.' He felt suddenly jealous of his brother's success, the ten-guinea cheque, with the promise of more to come. Jimmy's publishers had written that they liked his work and were prepared to consider further articles of a similar style and quality, should he care to submit them.

Now it was Jimmy's turn to feel aggrieved. 'That's bunkum and you know it,' he said fiercely. 'I happen to like writing.'

'And I happen to be in love, so now you know!'

'All right. You win. I'm sorry.' Jimmy meant what he said. Like Kerry, he missed the old rapport between himself and their brother, the blame for which he laid squarely on the doorstep of the wretched Wilma and her dreadful parents. He added jokingly, 'In which case, having made your own bed you'll have to lie in it, I guess. Creaking springs and all!'

This was the last straw. Failing to see the joke, Danny clattered downstairs to his room to dwell on the injustice of life. Bunching up his pillows, staring at the ceiling above his bed, he longed for a cigarette – but Wilma had made him give up smoking. A waste of money from her viewpoint. Oh, damn and blast, he thought angrily, contemplating his smokeless, sportless, penurious future with the shocked realization that, in three weeks' time, he would be a married man. Time seemed to be rushing past him with the force of a river in spate.

He loved Wilma, of course he did. From the night of their first meeting she had teased and tantalized him with her air of self-containment, her coolness and fragrance, her doll-like daintiness and fragility. It had taken him some time to discover that a calculating brain ticked beneath that fluffy fair hair of hers, by which time it was too late to even attempt forcing certain issues on which they had not, and never would see eye-to-eye. His love of sport, for instance, which he had given up rather than risk losing her.

This fear had been at the back of his mind all the time, he thought, pummelling his pillows until little puffs of feathers flew out of them and drifted onto the carpet like snowflakes. At the least sign of resistance on his part, Wilma would say off-handedly, 'Oh well, if you don't want to marry me.' A kind of emotional blackmail on her part, sheer cowardice on his, because he wanted her more than he had ever wanted a girl before, and she knew it. Wanted her so much that he had gone along with this barmy notion of hers to get married on his twenty-first birthday, to share a roof with her parents after the wedding . . .

Oh, what the hell? Things would be different after the wedding, Danny thought grimly. He'd make damn sure they were. Once his ring was safely on his bride's finger, and she had promised to love, honour and obey him, he would get her in the family way as quickly as possible, find somewhere of their own to rent, a small furnished flat or a couple of unfurnished rooms would do. The papers were full of *Accommodation to Let* notices, furnished or otherwise.

Looking into the windows of a furnishing store recently, he had made a mental note of their terms of credit, the goods on offer: bedroom suites from £5.19*s*.6*d*. to 40 guineas;

lounge suites from 7 to 35 guineas. Terms, 40s monthly for a £100 worth of furniture, as little as eight shillings a month for £20 worth of what he thought of as the bare necessities. But he could afford at least 16s a month from his salary, Danny reckoned, which would buy them far more than the bare necessities.

His heart lifted suddenly at the realization that, once Wilma became his wife, and pregnant, he would assume his rightful role as the head of the house; the husband, the provider. Master of his fate, captain of his soul. Of course. It was all so simple, so easy if one really stopped long enough to think about it calmly and clearly, as he was now doing for the first time since he had placed that diamond and sapphire engagement ring on Wilma's finger.

Turning on his side, hazy with sleep, he half imagined, half dreamt that he saw Wilma walking down the aisle towards him, a vision of loveliness in her white wedding dress and veil . . . Fully asleep, he saw her coming towards him, ankle-deep in feathers.

Chapter Twelve

The fourteenth of December brought with it a series of snow flurries chivvied by a cold north wind. Danny woke to a thick head, the feeling of something hanging over him. He had been out with his pals last night, to Wilma's disgust, who regarded the stag night custom as barbaric. They'd had 'words' about it. Even so, Danny would not be talked out of spending his last night of freedom with his friends. And what a night it had been, he reflected, easing himself out of bed with great care, wondering if his legs would support him.

They had started the celebration at the Golden Ball pub on the Foreshore and worked their way to town via Bland's Cliff, popping into several of his old haunts *en route* before that final, terrific session at the Talbot in Queen Street, where they had sung bawdy rugger songs until closing time.

Thrusting his feet into his slippers, he went along the passage to the bathroom where he gargled fiercely with TCP to sweeten his breath, and swallowed a couple of aspirin from the cupboard over the wash-basin to relieve his throbbing headache. Desperately in need of a hot drink, preferably tea, he went downstairs to the kitchen to put the kettle on.

Grace was there in her dressing-gown, pouring boiling water into the tea-pot. Turning away from the stove, she smiled at him. 'Happy birthday, son,' she said. Moving swiftly towards him and kissing him, she held him, thinking briefly of herself 21 years ago, a frightened 17-year-old girl racked with pain, bathed in perspiration, bearing down to expel her first-born son from her womb; the peace and joy she had experienced afterwards when the child she had given birth to was placed in her arms, and she had seen, as a miracle, his tiny hands complete with fingernails.

'Well,' she said, returning to the tea-pot, speaking light-heartedly, 'aren't you going to open your presents?'

'Presents?'

'Over there, on the dresser.'

'But you've already given me a canteen of cutlery.'

'That was a wedding present.'

He looked so young and vulnerable, she thought, in his old plaid dressing-gown, unshaven, with tousled hair. She knew he had come in late, the worse for wear, and she was glad. Glad that he had had one final fling with his pals, a taste of the old freedom. She watched him open his cards and birthday presents, wishing with all her heart that he had not flung aside his freedom so lightly.

'A wrist-watch! Oh, Mum, it's great! Just what I wanted.'

Jimmy had given him a cigarette lighter, Kerry a wallet stamped with his initials. There was a smart white shirt from Herbie, who had arrived yesterday, a set of cuff-links from Grandma Daniel, Irish linen hankies from Great Aunt Rosa, a cheque for 20 guineas from Fanny, a silver cigarette box from Gran Kingsley, a gold-plated tie-pin from Dulcie.

Pouring the tea, Grace said, 'Your Dad and I wanted you to have your presents first thing. We thought there wouldn't be time later on.'

He knew what she meant. The wedding ceremony was due to take place at eleven o'clock – four hours from now. He should be feeling buoyant, thrilled, excited at the thought of it, but he didn't. Truth to tell, he felt sick with nervous apprehension and the amount of beer he'd consumed the night before. Sitting down at the table to drink the tea, he said, 'I'm sorry, Mother. You and Dad were right. I should have listened to you. I should have waited.'

Seated at her dressing table, manicuring her nails, her face smothered in a Boncilla Clasmic Pack, Wilma glanced with satisfaction at her white satin wedding dress hanging from the door of her wardrobe alongside her diaphanous veil and seed-pearl headdress. She had bathed earlier, and smelt of Mornay's rose-geranium bath-cubes.

She would give Danny his birthday present, the gold signet ring she had bought him, engraved with their intertwined initials, after the wedding, when they were entrained together on their way to the Lake District. She, of course, had chosen the hotel overlooking Lake Windermere. The choice left to Danny, they might well have ended up in a common-or-garden boarding house near the station.

She thought, quirking the little finger of her left hand to allow the nail-polish to dry, how jealous the girls at work would be when she described to them the Hotel Ranelagh in all its glory, which offered, apart from breathtaking views of the lake from the bedroom windows, superb cuisine in a lamplit dining-room and the music of a string quartet.

Just to think, in a little over three hours from now she would no longer be Miss Wilma Burton but Mrs Daniel Kingsley. Her cousin Bella from Birmingham and her parents – Daddy's brother and sister-in-law – were staying at a small hotel in Albemarle Crescent, opposite the church. There had not been enough room for them here in Aberdeen Terrace, especially since the front lounge was chock-a-block with wedding presents, the back parlour table stacked high with cakes, jellies and trifles, sausage rolls and egg-and-bacon pies, along with the three-tier wedding cake, awaiting their removal to the church hall, by the caretaker, who had access to a bakers' van.

Mummy had provided a marvellous spread, Wilma thought, hurrying along to the bathroom to coax off the face pack before it hardened to the consistency of concrete. Naturally she would have preferred a sit-down luncheon of smoked salmon, lobster thermidore, boeuf-en-daube or roast chicken at the Pavilion or the Crown Hotel, but beggars could not be choosers. Money did not grow on trees, alas. Prudence was the name of the game. Daddy had, at least, lashed out on several bottles of Madeira and Sandeman's Port Wine to honour the occasion. A pity about the weather.

But this, after all, was a December wedding. Dabbing her face with a fluffy white towel, Wilma dismissed as ludicrous the deep-seated fear that, had she not coerced Danny into this winter wedding, he might have escaped her. No, it simply was not true. Danny loved her, would do anything to please her. She knew why. Because he wanted her physically. She wanted him too, of course, but on *her* terms, not his.

The doorbell jangled suddenly, and up the stairs came her cousin Bella, her bridesmaid's gear packed into a suitcase, agog for a bit of a laugh and a giggle.

She glanced at the clock; only two-and-a-half hours to wait now, Wilma thought, before she became Mrs Daniel Kingsley . . .

Nan Daniel was standing ramrod straight in her mulberry-coloured wedding ensemble when Fanny drifted downstairs from her room in her usual clutter of bizarre black garments overlaid with, not a brightly coloured Spanish shawl but a smooth black sealskin cape with a stand-up collar. Covering her wayward hair was a floppy, black velvet Rubenesque beret stabbed with a black ostrich feather.

'Where did you get *that*?' Nan looked askance at the fur cape. 'I've never seen it before!'

'I can't remember exactly where.' Fanny wrinkled her forehead. 'It may have been Harrods, or Swear and Wells in Bond Street. My London days, you know.'

Nan did *not* know, and this bothered her. What exactly had Fanny got up to in London during the war? Rosa came down at that moment, a red-eyed, sniffing, coughing figure in her usual apparel, a hat as unappealing as a slice of uncooked black pudding planked firmly on her head.

'I defy you to attend my grandson's wedding looking like that,' Nan said icily. 'The wonder is you're not taking a shopping basket!'

Turning the tide of resentment between her sisters, Fanny said kindly, 'Rosa, dear, why not borrow my grey squirrel tippet and let me find that grey silk scarf of mine to trim your hat? And wouldn't it be nice if you wore your amethyst brooch on your lapel?'

'Well, *really*!' Nan turned away in disgust, jealous of the attention Rosa was receiving. Not a word about *her* brand-new outfit, or how smart she looked in it. Now Rosa was standing there, like a child, letting Fanny adorn her hat brim with the silk scarf, a softly floating thing shot through with threads of mauve and pale lilac which would pick up the colour of the amethyst brooch. Moreover, Fanny had found a pair of mauve kid gloves for their sister to wear, and Rosa's face looked quite different, pink-cheeked, almost piquant, above the soft grey necklet of fur which Fanny had clasped under her chin. 'There now, you look very nice,' Fanny said, admiring her handiwork. 'Doesn't she look nice, Nan?'

Mrs Daniel did not answer. She couldn't. Her upper dentures, none too secure at the best at times, might have shot out of her mouth had she given vent to her feelings at the sight of the rejuvenated Rosa gazing at herself in the mirror over the mantelpiece, and uttering shrill little cries of pleasure at her appearance. One thing for certain, her pleasurable anticipation of coming events had been ruined at the outset – and all because of Rosa.

Lifting the roof of the house on the hill, one would have seen members of the Kingsley family, and Herbie, in their various rooms, or occasionally dashing past each other on the stairs in varying stages of *déshabille*, counting the hours, minutes and seconds until the arrival of the wedding cars.

Grace had provided an eight o'clock breakfast of eggs and bacon, thinking the menfolk, in particular, would need something substantial inside them on a cold morning. Also, Bob's mother and his Aunt Caroline, who had arrived yesterday and were staying on until Monday morning, must be accorded full honours as guests beneath their roof. In any case, it was much simpler, in the long run, to seat everyone at the dining table rather than have them hanging about in the kitchen wanting toast and marmalade or bacon sandwiches at the drop of a hat.

There had been alarms and excursions enough already, with Dulcie in tears over her wedding outfit which, she claimed, made her look like a house-end. 'Nonsense,' Grace told her, 'you look very nice.'

'Nice? I look dreadful, and you know it!' More tears. 'I'm not going, and that's that!'

Goaded past bearing, 'Please yourself,' Grace said grimly. Then, catching the smell of burnt toast from the grill-pan, 'Now look what you've made me do!'

'Oh, that's right, blame me! Everything that goes wrong in this house is my fault. It always has been.'

'That's enough, my girl.' Bob had entered the kitchen unnoticed. Speaking firmly to his recalcitrant elder daughter, 'There's nothing wrong with the way you look. You're just over-excited, that's all. We all are.' He shot an apologetic look at Grace. 'Look, Dulcie, love,' he added kindly, placing a comforting arm about her shoulders, 'how do you think Danny would feel if you didn't turn up at his wedding?'

'He wouldn't even notice,' Dulcie sobbed, spinning out the drama.

'Not notice? Of course he would!' Bob tried another tack. 'If you decide not to go to his wedding, I shan't go either. How's that?' Smiling into her tear-stained face, 'We'll stay at home together and play "Beggar My Neighbour"; miss all the dreary speeches, forego our slices of wedding cake. Well, Dulcie, what do you say?'

Dulcie said nothing. She simply went upstairs to her room to take another long, hard look at herself in the wardrobe mirror, thinking that she didn't look too bad after all. Above all, remembering all the lovely food that would go to waste if she wasn't there to eat her fair share of it.

Kerry had entered the room at that moment, looking downcast, hating the very sight of the pink, puff-sleeved bridesmaid's dress hanging from the wardrobe door, thinking what a sight she would look in that get-up. As for the beastly poke-bonnet lying on the bed alongside the pink lace mittens, for two pins she would have opened the window and watched them sail away on the wind. Instead, she went down to the kitchen in her dressing gown, to tell her mother she wasn't feeling very well.

Meanwhile, the bridegroom had shot into the recently vacated bathroom to shave, before climbing into a hot bath to kill every vestige of body odour with liberal applications of Lifebuoy soap. He felt curiously detached in both mind and body, as if what was about to happen was going to happen to some other person, not himself, as though his submerged, soap-smothered genitals were specimens pickled in brine in some natural-science museum or wherever those scientific johnnies kept their grisly exhibits.

Climbing out of the bath, briskly towelling his handsome young torso, Christ almighty, he thought bleakly, what if he was impotent? What if he couldn't . . . ? Oh, God!

Then Jimmy hammered at the door, demanding to be let in. Meanwhile, Mrs Kingsley and her sister Caroline, along with Herbie Barrass, who had bathed and dressed much earlier, were in the dining-room tucking into their bacon and eggs, alongside Bob, Kerry, Dulcie, and Grace. Nervous as a kitten, Grace kept on jumping up from the table to stand at the foot of the stairs, calling up to the bridegroom and his best man to come down and eat their breakfast before it got cold. To no avail.

Joining his wife at the newel post, holding her in his arms, Bob said compassionately, 'It's time to let go, love.'

Looking up at him, her eyes brimming with tears, she said fiercely, 'You think I don't know that?'

The Albemarle Baptist Chapel, dating back to the Victorian era, fronted an enclosed area of garden surrounded with iron railings in which photographs of the bridal couple, family and friends were usually taken after the ceremony. It looked bleak, cold and uninviting to the occupants of the various wedding cars drawing up, at intervals, to their moans and groans as a freshening wind, laced with hailstones, played havoc with their wedding finery. They dismounted, one by one, to hurry up the path to the church doors, flung wide open in anticipation of their arrival.

All was nervous tension at the house on the hill. Herbie had offered to clear away the breakfast things and do the washing up, to Grace's relief. Trust Herbie to be in the right place at the right time, she thought gratefully. Even so, a niggling sense of worry persisted as she hurried upstairs to get ready for a wedding she had prayed might never happen.

Danny's words, 'I should have waited,' had added to her sense of foreboding. If only he had come sooner to that conclusion. Had he meant what he said? Had the full understanding of his future commitment to one woman suddenly struck him amidships? Had the solemn and binding nature of the church ceremony itself overwhelmed him to such an extent that he wished himself far enough away? Did he mean that he wanted to cancel the wedding, or simply postpone it?

Bob's mother had come into the kitchen at that moment, putting an end to the conversation, and so the vital question, 'Why?' had not been asked. Danny had thanked his grandmother Kingsley for the silver cigarette box, kissed her, and gone upstairs to his room, taking with him his mug of tea, leaving his mother to listen to the old lady's recollections of her own wedding day.

Then had come Dulcie's moment of high drama, plus Kerry's nervous stomach-ache. Grace found herself talking Jimmy out of wearing his favourite Fair Isle pullover instead of a waistcoat, helping Bob to search for the tie he had bought especially to honour the occasion, which he later discovered, still in its wrapping paper, in the top drawer of the dressing chest. Finally, panic seized her when the flowers – the carnations for the men's buttonholes, the carnation corsages for herself, Mrs Kingsley, Aunt Caroline, and Dulcie, not to mention Kerry's posy of pink rosebuds – failed to arrive on time, necessitating an urgent telephone call to the florist's whose delivery van, the shop assistant explained, had been delayed because of the bad weather.

'But don't worry, it's on its way,' she said cheerfully, hanging up the receiver.

The flowers and the wedding cars had arrived within minutes of each other. The florist's van first, thank God.

Kerry cast an anguished glance at her mother as she walked down the front steps with the bridegroom and his best man, clutching her posy, shivering with cold in her pink satin dress, the poke bonnet framing her pale, pinched little face. Then she, Bob, Mrs Kingsley, Aunt Caroline and Dulcie had crowded together into the back of the second London taxi, whilst Herbie had climbed into the front seat beside the driver. Herbie, whose calm, reassuring presence had somehow willed all of them into a more relaxed state of mind, particularly when he had helped the older ladies to pin on their corsages just so before entering the taxi, then standing back a little to admire the effect; bothering to tell them how nice they looked in their wedding finery. Dear Herbie . . .

Kerry and Bella-from-Birmingham stood shivering at the back of the church, awaiting the arrival of the bride. Danny and his best man sat stoically, side by side, in their Fifty Shilling tailored suits, Danny as white as a sheet, anticipating the opening strains of the 'Wedding March'.

Nan, Fanny and Rosa sat upright on the bridegroom's side of the aisle, turning over the pages of their hymn-books, not speaking to one another. Nan did not deign to look at Rosa, who had ruined her day, who loved the feel of soft grey fur beneath her chin. Fanny was remembering the man who had made her the gift of the sealskin cape she was wearing, who had died amidst the blood and welter of the First Battle of the Somme, what seemed a million light years ago to her now, a fat old lady of many long-gone summers. But ah, how beautiful she had been in that long-ago summer, when she and James Courtenay had said goodbye to each other for the last time, in a hotel bedroom overlooking the River Thames . . .

Holding Bob's hand, Grace felt suddenly in need of

warmth and comfort, as she had done 21 years ago, on the day Danny was born. Bob had been far away from her then. But he was here now, thank God, an integral part of herself, as close and as dear to her as life itself, as necessary to her as her own heartbeats.

Mabel Burton entered the church with Bella-from-Birmingham's parents, a striking figure in a violet-coloured dress and jacket, a hat of artificial violets perched gaily atop her recently tinted and Marcel-waved hair, her cheeks rosy with Bourjois rouge and a soupçon of Icilma powder: lips courtesy of Tangee; perfume courtesy of Coty.

There had been some unpleasantness with Arthur earlier that morning, when the new bed had been delivered ahead of time. And, 'You can take that thing back to the shop,' he'd told the shivering delivery men. 'Where do you think we're going to put it, eh, with the damned house in an uproar!'

'T'ain't our fault, mister,' the foreman said. 'We has ter foller instructions, an' it says on this 'ere docket—'

'I don't give a damn what it says on the docket—'

'Arthur!' Mabel had given him a sharp dig in the ribs. 'Not today of all days!' With a conciliatory glance at the men, 'Our daughter's getting married in an hour's time, and we have guests.'

'Aye well then, no use us standing 'ere arguing the toss.' The men had lumped the bed back to the van.

'Can you bring it back on Monday?' Mabel called after them. Receiving no clear-cut reply, she rounded on her husband. A fierce exchange of words had ensued, after which Arthur had barged upstairs to wrestle with his collar and tie, fretting and fuming at the daftness of women, his wife in particular, wanting a wedding in bloody December, in the middle of a blizzard. Then Wilma came onto the landing in her dressing-gown to find out what the row was about, and saying her peace of mind had been shattered just when she needed to feel calm and relaxed.

'I wish now I'd waited till the summer to get married,' she sniffed, looking and sounding like a younger edition of her mother, leaving Mabel wondering why weddings were never as satisfactory in real life as they were in romantic novels. Now Daddy would be grumpy for the rest of the day, Wilma would be snappy, and as for herself, her feet were killing her with all the running about she'd done, and nobody *cared*.

Well, she'd show them! True to Ethel M. Dell, whose heroines always made the best of a bad job, she went up to her room to cover the ravages of cooking with as much rouge as she could possibly apply without looking 'tarty', pinned on her violet hat at an impossible angle, and doused herself so liberally with l'Aimant that Arthur, who had managed at last to secure his collar to both its back and front studs, moved away from the dressing table with a muttered, deeply significant, '*Phew!*'

The bride arrived in a flurry of snowflakes. She swore under her breath as her veil, fairly lifted from her head by the wind, unsettled her headdress and her carefully arranged hair.

'Well, you *would* get married in December,' Arthur reminded her, seeing nothing in the least romantic in a biting cold wind fit to freeze a brass monkey, wishing he was at home in front of a warm fire, not about to give away his only daughter to a bit of a jumped-up clerk at the Town Hall, hating the thought of giving houseroom to his son-in-law-to-be after the wedding. What kind of a bloke was he anyway? No need to conjecture. The world was full of rotten little spongers like Danny Kingsley. Him and his lah-di-dah family, making fun of him behind his back, just because he hadn't worn a bloody collar and tie at that so-called engagement party Mabel had laid on for them. But of course, he thought darkly, hurrying Wilma up the path to the church doors, Mabel was as daft as a brush, and no wonder, reading all those damned books she borrowed weekly from the public library.

The strains of the 'Wedding March' began.

'Are you quite sure I look all right?' Wilma demanded of her bridesmaids in a fierce whisper.

And, 'Yes, you look lovely,' Bella-from-Birmingham reassured her. Kerry said nothing, she could not for the life of her have said anything remotely sensible or reassuring as, following in the wake of the bride, hearing the solemn strains of the 'Wedding March', she saw her brother Danny, his face aglow, awaiting Wilma's arrival at the steps leading up to the altar. And this, she thought, was goodbye to childhood, goodbye to Danny. The end of their old loving relationship for ever and ever. She thanked God, then, for the poke-bonnet which hid her face from full view of the congregation, the tears that filled her eyes when Danny slipped the wedding ring onto his bride's finger, and the minister pronounced them man and wife.

Danny thought, thank God I'm not impotent. The sight of Wilma walking towards him down the aisle, her fair hair fluffed out about her face, as pretty as a picture in her white satin dress, carrying a bouquet of pink roses, had convinced him of that.

'Whom God hath joined, let no man put asunder . . .'

'Behold, the bridegroom cometh . . .'

Was he really married? Danny could not quite believe it. It had all happened so quickly, the placing of the ring on his bride's finger, the signing of the register, the photographs in the Albemarle Crescent garden taken after the ceremony, with Wilma's veil flying in the wind. He felt the benison of food and wine afterwards in the church hall – a surprising haven of light and warmth, of relaxation after the tension of all the longing, seeking, striving, waiting, yearning, leading up to this supreme moment in time. With his wife beside him, her slender hands beneath his as they cut the wedding cake together, he caught the tantalizing, mysterious combination of Mornay rose-geranium bath-cubes and 4711 eau-de-cologne, which had made his senses reel at their first meeting that magical night in the Olympia Ballroom.

There were so many people, so many faces, so many well-wishers crowding about them, that when it came to making his speech on behalf of himself and his bride, all he could possibly say was, 'Thank you all for making this the happiest day of my life.'

What he wanted most, at that moment, was to be alone with his bride, to travel with her to their honeymoon destination: to make love to her, to absorb the simple fact that this was not a dream but reality, that Wilma was no longer Miss Burton but Mrs Daniel Kingsley. He wanted to kiss her hands, her face, her cheeks, her lips – those tantalizing lips of hers – to possess her entirely, as he had longed to do from the first time he'd walked her home from the Olympia Ballroom. The Olympia Ballroom . . . He remembered, when the wedding reception was over and done with, when he and Wilma boarded the train which would bear them far away from their curiously fraught, winter wedding, how the shining facets of light from a spinning witchball had illuminated her shining eyes and face, her spun-gold hair.

And now it was all really over and done with at last, the wedding, the speeches, the dash to the station to catch the two o'clock train to York; the flung handfuls of confetti as the train drew away from the platform, the feeling he had that he should have kissed his mother once more before leaving her; should have told Kerry how much he loved her, had always loved her. Too late now. Later, perhaps? After the honeymoon?

166

Chapter Thirteen

There was an air of finality as the train drew away from the platform, a strange feeling of emptiness as the trail of steam eddied in the wind, and all that remained was a dwindling view of the rear carriages.

Now what? Grace wondered, as the wedding guests walked towards the barrier, herself included, knowing that all she really wanted right now was the warmth of her own fireside, a strong cup of tea; to rid herself of her wedding finery, put on her old, comfortable clothes and make a start on the evening meal.

Besides which, Kerry, shivering in her pink satin bridesmaid's dress, looked as though she needed a good hot bath to warm her and an early night to make up the arrears of lost sleep. The poor kid didn't look at all well. Danny had always been her idol. It must have been especially hard for her, the baby of the family, to accept that changing circumstances had altered the pattern of all their lives so that, after today, nothing in earth or heaven would come as it came before.

It seemed to Herbie Barrass, an onlooker of the game of life, that the station barrier had effectively separated the sheep from the goats – more realistically, that the two families concerned in the joining in holy wedlock of Danny Kingsley and Wilma Burton had about as much in common as Keir Hardy and Winston Churchill.

Frankly, he had hated every minute of the ceremony itself, and the curiously fraught atmosphere in the church hall afterwards, during which his mind had registered, in detail, the personal dramas enacted against the wedding backdrop. He had noticed, in particular, Grace's stricken face as the bride and groom stood together exchanging their wedding vows, the tears trickling down Kerry's cheeks as the service proceeded. Afterwards, in the church hall, the scarcely veiled hostility between Nan Daniel and her sister Rosa, the latter who had downed three glasses of Sandeman's Port so quickly that her face had flushed to the colour of a jar of pickled beetroot, necessitating the loosening of the fur collar about her throat, whereupon Mrs Daniel had turned away from Rosa in disgust. Rosa sat down abruptly on a Sunday School bench, deeply ashamed that she was, through her own grievious fault, unable to stand up any longer.

Well, hitting the bottle, Herbie thought compassionately, was an age-old, perhaps the only, solution to deep-seated unhappiness of the kind he discerned in this elderly woman, whose mainspring of existence had been broken by the usurpation of her quiet corner of life by a much stronger, far more dominant personality. Placing a hand beneath Rosa's elbow, he guided her gently towards the barrier. The poor old girl seemed bemused, disorientated, as well she might. Drifting along behind them, light of foot despite her overweight body, Fanny asked anxiously, 'Are you all right, Rosa?' Nan simply stalked, ramrod straight, along the platform, bitterly jealous that it was Rosa, not herself, gaining all the attention.

The Burtons were going to walk from the station to Aberdeen Terrace with a few close friends and relations whom Mabel had invited back for tea. She was inclined to be tearful now that Wilma had gone. Grace understood how the woman must be feeling. She would miss Danny when it dawned on her that he would not be coming home from work with Jimmy any more. Then she would miss hearing his laughter in the hall, his two-at-a-time footsteps on the stairs, as she would miss not having to make his bed, or call up to him to hurry down for breakfast or he'd be late for work, as she would miss his clothes from the wardrobe, his shaving gear from the bathroom.

The time was now half past two. Hating the feeling of anti-climax after the trauma and excitement of the previous days, Grace invited Nan, Fanny and Rosa, on impulse, back to the house for a cup of tea and a bite of supper afterwards. They would hire taxis from the station forecourt, Bob would soon have flames roaring up the sitting-room chimney, and when dusk came they would draw the curtains and be all together like the folk of Shields.

Meanwhile, Danny and Wilma would be jogging along in a cold train towards their honeymoon destination. Why Wilma had chosen the Lake District, of all places, at this time of year, Grace could not fathom, unless her choice had to do with wanting to be different from most other honeymoon couples who, in the deep mid-winter, would have been content with a week in York, Whitby, or Bridlington. Possibly London, where there was plenty going on.

They had had a carriage to themselves as far as York. Fellow passengers embarking at Malton, nonplussed by the drifts of confetti in the corridor, had backed out of the carriage at the sight of a stylishly dressed young woman and a sheepish-looking young man sitting close together like a couple of doves on a red-plush perch.

When the train had left Malton, Wilma opened her tan leather handbag – chosen especially to complement her green-and-tan checked coat – told her husband to close his eyes and hold out his hand.

'Hey! What the . . .' Opening his eyes, he saw with delight the gold signet ring his bride had pushed onto the third finger of his left hand. 'Oh, darling, it's beautiful,' he murmured, taking her in his arms to kiss her, wanting her so much it hurt.

'Oh, *don't*!' she cried out in alarm. 'Not now! Not *here*!' Fussily, she rearranged her hat and patted her hair into place beneath the tan felt brim. 'Someone might see us!'

'I couldn't give a damn who sees us,' he said sulkily. 'After all, we *are* married!'

Later, glancing at his brand new wrist-watch, sick and tired of the long, slow journey, he saw that the hands pointed to nine minutes past nine. Cold, tired, hungry and frustrated,

'How much longer?' he enquired irritably of his wife. It seemed to him, at that moment, that he had been born in the train; lived a lifetime and died in the bloody thing. He wanted food, warmth, to lie down, to jump up and down. even, anything to break the monotony of the total blackness beyond the carriage windows, lit here and there with faint pinpricks of light from far-off, invisible dwellings in which, presumably, lived sensible human beings eating their supper before getting ready for bed.

Bed. He ached and longed for bed! Hopefully an enormous double bed with a well-sprung mattress, huge feather pillows, a puffy eiderdown, lavender-scented sheets, and thick, warm woollen blankets, in which he and Wilma would lie beside one another, naked and unashamed, to make passionate love to each other until the light of a new day filtered through the drawn curtains of the room.

First, of course, they must eat. As the train came to a juddering halt at Ambleside station, his tastebuds thrilled at the very thought of a sirloin steak served with a smothering of fried onions, a generous portion of chips and lashings of bread and butter, washed down with a pint of strong beer, with a satisfying portion of steamed pudding and custard to follow. Money no object! He had his Great Aunt Fanny to thank for that. Her birthday cheque for 20 guineas had come as manna from heaven, to ensure the holiday of a lifetime, the honeymoon of a lifetime.

It occurred to him as he and Wilma stepped into a taxi in the station yard, the driver hoisting their luggage aboard, that his thought processes had gone haywire somewhere along the line. The holiday of a lifetime, fair enough, but there could only be one honeymoon, not just for a lifetime but for ever, through all eternity . . .

Oh God, he thought, as the taxi drew up outside the Hotel Ranelagh, he must be going soft in the head – through hunger, most probably, and he had forgotten to thank his father for cashing his great aunt's cheque from his week's takings, or had he? He couldn't quite remember. Of course he must have done so, but had he made his thanks clear enough at the time? If not, he would do so later, after the honeymoon.

They could have sandwiches and a pot of tea, the proprietress of the Ranelagh told them coolly, if they so wished. Nothing more substantial was available at this time of night.

'But my wife and I have been travelling since two o'clock,' Danny said desperately. He added appealingly, 'We got married this morning. This is our honeymoon.'

'I'm sorry, sir, but the restaurant closes early at this time of year,' the woman said impatiently. 'The staff – the chef, that is – goes off duty at seven o'clock.' A pause, 'Well, do you want sandwiches or not?'

'Yes of course we do. We're starving.' Sandwiches, he thought savagely. He'd had nothing but sandwiches and a few sausage rolls since breakfast. He wondered what his mother had given the family for supper. Something substantial, he felt sure, a casserole or a hot-pot.

Awaiting the arrival of the sandwiches, he looked round the lounge, deserted apart from himself and Wilma. He was not impressed. Where were the potted palms depicted in the brochure she had shown him? Perhaps they were wintering in the south of France? The red curtains drawn across a wide bay window were faded in places, he noticed; the brass bell on the reception desk had not been polished, and the door leading to the dining-room was as tightly closed as an oyster shell. He thought briefly of the *Marie Celeste*, a story which had always intrigued him. Where were the members of staff the proprietress had mentioned, who may have remained on duty to clear up in the kitchen and dining-room even after the chef had departed?

The distant sound of clattering pots and pans, the whirr of a vacuum cleaner, the sight of a hall-porter or a smart waitress would have cheered him up enormously. The silence was more oppressive than golden. Depression settled on him like a shroud when the proprietress appeared with the tea and sandwiches – two rounds containing thinly sliced

Cheddar cheese. Lacking the nerve of Oliver Twist, he daren't ask for more. The handle of the metal tea-pot burnt his fingers on contact, necessitating the use of the handkerchief in his breast-pocket as he did the pouring out into the thick white cups on the cheap tin tray. At least the tea was hot and strong, too strong for Wilma's liking, and she ate only two of the sandwiches, leaving the rest for him to devour . . .

All together like the folk of Shields. When the roaring flames had stopped leaping up the chimney, and the sitting-room fire had sunk to a more acceptable level of intensity, kneeling on the hearthrug, Kerry made toast for the afternoon tea. She loved the feeling of warmth and security after all the false gaiety of the wedding reception, which she had hated more than she had hated anything in her life before, including her traumatic September meeting with Sid Hannay on the Spa Bridge. Gazing into the heart of the fire as the thick slices of bread impaled on the toasting-fork turned golden, then brown, she nurtured the deep inner certainty that she was no longer a child but a woman, which was to do with facing up to reality, she supposed, no matter how harsh that reality may be.

Perhaps life itself was a kind of balancing act strung on a tight-rope between dreams and reality? And possibly, she reasoned with herself, dreams were necessary to lessen the harshness of reality? Well, not dreams exactly, but a kind of inner glow, an awareness of the beauty and wonder of life set apart from the pain of loss, of changing circumstances?

She remembered suddenly a stanza from 'To The Moon', by Shelley, which she had copied painstakingly into her feint-ruled exercise book: 'Art thou pale for weariness of climbing heaven, and gazing on the earth, Wandering companionless Among the stars that have a different birth' . . . ?

The time had come to march to her own drum-beat. Come Christmas, she reminded herself, as Grace buttered and handed round the fragrant slices of toast, she would be earning an extra half-crown a week.

She felt glad that her mother had decided not to invite Mr Hodnot to the wedding. A snob at heart, he would have hated the church hall reception, the bare wooden floorboards and the trestle tables piled high with home-made food. Mr Hodnot much preferred dining at the Royal Hotel where he could rub shoulders with the like of Lady Hawthorn. As for Mr Jenkins and his daughter, Kerry knew that Meg would not have accepted the invitation had it been sent, and why. Meg was in love with Danny. In which case, how could she have borne to witness his marriage to another woman? Right now, poor Meg must be feeling the way she, Kerry, had felt that September evening on the Spa Bridge.

What a funny-peculiar day this was, she thought wistfully, spearing another slice of bread on the toasting-fork, with everyone behaving so strangely, particularly her grandmother and Great Aunt Rosa. Great Aunt Fanny always behaved strangely, so that was no great novelty, and so did Dulcie and Jimmy. Even so, despite the drawn curtains and the warm fireglow, the comforting presence of her parents, and Herbie Barrass, she sensed an undercurrent of discontent that worried her deeply, as if a storm was about to break, as though the atmosphere was charged with the muttering of thunder heard from afar – the way storms happened in summer-time, when the sky grew dark before the first flash of lightning.

The storm broke suddenly, unexpectedly.

Rising shakily to her feet, her face as red as a turkey's wattles, 'I'm sorry,' Rosa quavered, 'I feel faint!'

'Hardly surprising, in my opinion,' Nan said scathingly, with a curious hitching movement of her shoulders, 'considering the amount of wine you drank at the reception!'

'Please, Nan, not now,' Fanny adjured her volatile sister. 'There's a time and place for everything. That time is not here and now.'

'Oh, trust you to side with Rosa.'

Meanwhile, Herbie, in quick response to the crisis, guided

Rosa from the room, his arm about her waist, exhorting her not to worry, that she'd be as right as a trivet once she'd had a breath of fresh air.

Standing beside her on the doorstep, 'There now, that's better, isn't it?' he said cheerfully.

'Yes, but . . .' She dissolved into tears, 'You don't understand – how could you? – how wicked I am . . .'

Turning to Grace and Bob behind them in the passage, he suggested, 'Perhaps a little sleep might do her good.'

'Of course. Danny's bed is made up,' Grace said quickly, thinking how fortunate it was that she had changed the sheets and pillow-cases that morning. 'Bob, you and Herbie had better see her safely upstairs. I'll come up in a minute to help her take her things off. I'd better tell Mother and Aunt Fanny what's happening.'

Fanny was standing near the fireplace when Grace came in. Nan had remained seated. Kerry scrambled up from the hearthrug. Jimmy was beside her, looking worried. Dulcie had also remained seated, to Grace's disgust, to finish off the toast. Had the girl no finer feelings? 'When you've quite finished eating,' Grace said sharply, 'you had better take the tea things through to the kitchen and begin the washing up.'

'Why pick on me?' Dulcie replied insolently. 'Why not Jimmy or Kerry?'

Jimmy took the initiative. 'You heard what Mother said. Or are you deaf as well as bone-idle?'

'You have no right to . . .' Dulcie's face flushed a dull red as she stared angrily at her brother.

Cutting short her words, he warned her, 'I'll count to three, and if you are not out of that chair in two seconds flat, I'll drag you out of it! One, two . . .'

Dulcie knew when she was beaten. There was no love lost between herself and Jimmy, there never had been. Hauling herself from the chair, she walked through to the kitchen in high dudgeon, carrying a cup, saucer and plate, closely followed by Jimmy with the rest of the china on a tray, and Kerry, whose instincts told her that trouble was brewing between Mother and Nan. Why, she had no clear idea. Something to do with poor Great Aunt Rosa, she supposed. Thank goodness Grandmother Kingsley and Auntie Caroline had gone up to their room earlier on, to rest before supper-time.

'Is Rosa all right?' Fanny asked anxiously, clinging to the mantelpiece for support. 'I've never known her to feel faint before.'

'Yes, Aunt Fanny,' Grace reassured her, 'the fresh air revived her, but we're putting her to bed in Danny's room for the time being.'

'*Ha!*' Again came that curious hitching motion of Nan's shoulders, 'Trust Rosa to make a spectacle of herself!'

'Aren't you being a bit uncharitable, Mother?' Grace asked levelly. 'It's not Aunt Rosa's fault that she felt ill. Everyone does from time to time.'

Nan bridled. 'That's just where you're wrong, my girl! Oh, I know you think the sun shines out of Rosa. It's always "poor Rosa" this and "poor Rosa" that! If you had the sense you were born with you'd realize that "poor Rosa" is suffering from a hangover! Oh yes, I saw her with my own two eyes drinking glass after glass of port wine at the wedding reception. I never felt so ashamed in all my life, to think that a member of the Mallory family could behave in such a way.'

'If what you say is true, why didn't you stop her?' Grace demanded hotly.

'Stop her? Why should I? If Rosa wishes to go to the devil she may do so for all I care. The wretched, complaining ninny!'

'That's enough, Mother!' Grace was coldly angry now. Despite all the signs to the contrary, she had never wanted to believe that Nan was totally lacking in compassion. 'You are making things worse, not better.'

'All very well for you to preach.' Nan struggled out of her chair to confront her daughter. 'You don't know what Rosa's been like lately; moping about the house, shutting herself in her room for hours on end, stalking out of the house, not saying where she's going or when she'll be back. Leaving everything to me.'

Fanny said mildly, 'But you love being in charge, Nan. You know you do.'

'Just as well I *am* in charge!' Nan snapped back at her. 'Things were in a sorry state when I took over the house-keeping.'

'Were they? I hadn't noticed.'

'No, well, you wouldn't. But don't tell me you enjoyed Rosa's cooking. Why, Rosa can't even boil eggs properly. All that nasty white stuff running down the egg-cups!'

'Oh, *that*?' Fanny chuckled.

'I'm glad you find it funny. I don't.'

'No, well, a sense of humour was never your strong point, Nan dear,' Fanny reminded her sister. 'You take things too much to heart, that's your trouble. All this because Rosa had a glass of wine too many at the wedding reception. But surely we were meant to enjoy ourselves?'

'Getting drunk and making a fool of oneself may constitute some people's idea of enjoyment,' Nan spat forth, 'but it's certainly not mine!' She was in full spate now, so angry that she scarcely knew or cared what she was saying. 'I wish I were dead! I've worked my fingers to the bone for you and Rosa, just as I worked my fingers to the bone for my husband and family. And what thanks do I get? Grace and that precious husband of hers couldn't wait to turn me out of house and home – after all the jumpers, scarves and pullovers I knitted for them, all the money I spent on wool.

'I suppose that you and Rosa have always been jealous of me because I got married and you didn't. No-one has ever cared about the cross I've borne through life, the base ingratitude, the treachery I've endured at the hands of those nearest to me. Well, I'm sick and tired of being neglected and overlooked. And to think I went out of my way to buy this wedding outfit, and no-one has even mentioned it!'

Appalled by the outburst, Grace excused herself and hurried upstairs to help Rosa undress, leaving Fanny to pour oil on troubled water. Deeply distressed by her mother's outburst, she was hating this day as she had seldom hated anything before. Her son's wedding day . . .

But this curiously fraught day was not over yet.

When she had helped Rosa into bed, the old lady said piteously, 'Oh please, let me stay here with you. Don't make me go back to South Street. Nan hates me so!'

'I'm sure that's not true,' Grace said, plumping up the eiderdown. 'Aunt Fanny would be lost without you.'

'You don't understand. Fanny and I were happy together before Nan came. Now Nan wants Fanny all to herself and,' tears streamed down Rosa's withered cheeks, 'I can't bear it any longer. I really can't bear being shut out, being made to feel an interloper in my own home.'

She continued hoarsely, between sobs, 'First Nan took over my room, then she took over the kitchen, the cooking. Now she has taken over dear Fanny! We were so happy once, alone together in our own little world. Oh, I know I'm a poor cook. Fanny knew it too, but she never seemed to mind. We just muddled along together somehow, and we had so much fun playing cards together in the evenings, or listening to the wireless. Or sometimes we would just sit quietly together embroidering hankies or tray-cloths to sell in the shop.' Searching frantically for a means of drying her eyes, gratefully accepting Grace's offer of her own handkerchief, 'That's all over and done with now, which is why I am begging you to let me stay here with you and that dear, kind husband of yours.'

Aware of Bob's presence on the threshold, glancing up at him for guidance in this new dilemma, Grace heard him say gently, 'Of course, love, Aunt Rosa is welcome to stay with us for as long as she wants.'

Here we go again, he thought wryly. More painting and decorating, more humping of furniture; another old lady living beneath their roof. But rather Rosa than Nan Daniel any day of the week.

Grace wondered just how she would break the news to her mother that, from now on, Rosa would occupy her old

177

room on the first landing. However, 'Sufficient unto the day is the evil thereof'. She would worry about that later.

'If you'll follow me, I'll show you to your room,' the proprietress of the Ranelagh said off-handedly, when he and Wilma had finished eating.

More than a little put-out at having to lump the luggage upstairs without the aid of a porter, what kind of a bloody hotel was this anyway? Danny wondered, with no grub worth mentioning, no potted palms, and no staff?

At least there was a bed, he thought, dumping the suitcases on the floor of the 'bridal chamber'. Not that it looked all that inviting – a brass-railed edifice flanked with worn strips of carpet, an eiderdown as flat as a fluke, a stiff bolster, and two pillows in cotton cases so thin that the ticking showed through.

When the proprietress had departed, Wilma burst into tears of tiredness and frustration. 'It's *awful*! Just *dreadful*,' she sobbed.

Overwhelmed with tenderness for his weeping bride, attempting to put his arms about her, to console her with whispered words of love, he received the shock of his life when, shrugging aside his embrace, she said tartly, 'Oh, for heaven's sake, Danny! I'm not in the mood.'

'But Wilma, love, this *is* our honeymoon, remember?'

'Oh yes, I remember right enough! And I suppose you think that gives you the right to mess about with me? Well, you're wrong, that's all.'

'Mess about with you?' Danny couldn't believe what he was hearing from the lips of the girl he loved, his bride of a few short hours. He said hoarsely, 'I don't understand. You are my wife now, I am your husband. I thought you'd want me to – to—'

'Well I don't, so now you know! I'm tired and cold, and I have a headache.'

Dredging up memories of his stag-night, his married pals' jocular remarks that women were inclined to 'play up a bit' on the wedding night, Danny went along to the bathroom to undress, stumbling into a broom cupboard before finding the right door, an incident which did nothing to bolster his deflated male ego. Washing his face in lukewarm water, so much for his dream of revealing his well-muscled torso to his admiring bride, he thought bitterly as he shivered into his pyjamas, dressing-gown and slippers.

Returning to the bedroom, hoping against hope that Wilma would be in bed when he entered, and in a better frame of mind, the poor kid, he thought tenderly, she must be scared stiff of the inevitable – when it happened. He dare not think *if* it happened, because he *wanted* it to happen so much, the longed-for intimacy between husband and wife, the culmination of their courtship, the wedding ceremony, the reception, the cutting of the cake; that seemingly endless train journey to the back of beyond: their poor reception, the lack of a proper meal.

The latter wouldn't matter a damn if only Wilma would turn to him with open arms. And he would be very gentle with her. Loving her so much, how could he be otherwise?

Entering the room, he saw that Wilma was in bed – a humped shape beneath the blankets and the rose-sprigged eiderdown. Slipping in beside her, he realized, with a sinking heart, that she had her back to him.

Switching off his bedside lamp, 'Hey, come on, love,' he whispered, kissing the nape of her neck, sliding his arms about her waist, drawing her closer to him, sighing deeply when his searching hands discovered the tiny mounds of her breasts beneath her satin nightdress, 'I know you're tired. So am I, but this is our wedding night, the reason why we're here together like this . . .'

The effect of his words was electrifying in more ways than one. Switching on the lamp on her side of the bed, sitting bolt upright, 'Get away from me, you beast!' Wilma cried out in a harsh voice, shaking with sobs, 'All this is your fault! Bringing me to a wretched place like this. Well, I'm not staying. First thing in the morning I shall ring for a taxi to the station. Go back home. And the sooner the better as far as I'm concerned!'

'*My* fault?' His voice rose indignantly, 'What the hell are you on about? This was your idea from start to finish!'

'Oh, that's right, start swearing at me, blaming me for everything.' Her teeth were chattering.

'For heaven's sake, Wilma, lie down. You'll catch your death of cold!'

'Ha! You'd like that, wouldn't you, so you can start pawing me again. I know what you're after, right enough. Well, I'm telling you here and now, I don't want a baby. Not now, not ever!'

'Why, you selfish, cheating little bitch you!' The words sprang to his lips from the depths of his wounded male pride. To be told on his wedding night, that the girl he had married did not want a child by him was more than flesh and blood could stand, the deepest insult to his manhood. 'Why didn't you tell me this before?' he demanded hoarsely. 'More to the point, why did you marry me in the first place?'

Swinging his legs out of bed, he crossed over to the chair on the back of which he had hung his jacket containing his cigarette case and lighter. Hands shaking, he lit a Craven A.

'What are you doing?'

'What does it look like?'

'You promised you'd give up smoking.' Shrilly, 'You told me you *had* given it up! And you accuse me of cheating—'

Rounding on her, 'There's a bit of a difference, isn't there, between smoking a cigarette and being told that you don't want a baby? What *do* you want, that's what I'd like to know?' The cigarette tasted awful. He stubbed it out fiercely in the fan-embellished hearth. 'I'm a man, for God's sake, not a bloody Eu . . . you know what!' Returning to the bed, gripping the brass rail, his knuckles showing white. 'I thought you loved me. And you can't say I haven't played fair with you. All this time, holding back because I respected you. Never laying a finger on you; wanting you so much it hurt. I thought you wanted me too. Apparently I was wrong. Well, do as you like, Wilma. Go home if you want to. I shan't try to stop you.' Grimly, 'Now, with your highness's permission, I'm getting into that bloody bed whether you like it or not.' Kicking off his slippers, 'Oh, you needn't worry, I shan't "mess about with you" as you so charmingly put it. Frankly, the way I feel about you now, I wouldn't touch you with a barge-pole!'

Ignoring Wilma's sniffles, he got into bed, beat his half of the bolster into submission, turned his back on her and lay down to sleep. Exhausted in mind and body, with a hunger pain in the pit of his stomach, deeply shocked that the wedding night he had dreamed of had degenerated into a nightmare of harsh words, knowing it was useless to add more fuel to the blazing bonfire of misunderstanding between them, he fell into a restless, nightmare-ridden sleep in which he appeared at a cricket match clad only in pyjamas and dressing-gown.

Switching off her bedside lamp, lying wide awake in the darkness, her clinical little brain ticking away beneath her candy-floss hair, Wilma realized that she had said too much. What a fool she'd been to tell him she didn't want a baby. She had been so sure, all along, that she could twist him round her little finger. Now she was not so sure.

'What *do* you want?' he'd asked her. Pondering the question, Wilma knew exactly what she wanted – an adoring, undemanding husband, the security of a wedding ring on her finger, to be envied, admired by the girls at work because of her handsome husband who had such a good job at the Town Hall.

Tears trickled down her cheeks. If only the hotel had come up to expectations. If only Danny had been kinder to her instead of trying to take advantage of her the minute he got into bed beside her. Tired, hungry and homesick, bewildered by the strangeness of the room, the ugliness of the furniture, irritated rather than charmed by Danny's presence in the marriage bed, incensed by his assumption that he now owned her, she had reacted violently against the touch of his hands at her breasts, what she considered a violation of her self-containment, before she was ready for intimacy.

His scornfully uttered words, 'The way I feel about you

181

now, I wouldn't touch you with a barge-pole,' had rung an alarm bell in her mind. Suppose he really meant what he said? How the girls at work would laugh and point the finger if they could see her now, a bride on her wedding night, red-eyed with weeping, her hair in disarray, her husband asleep with his back to her; still a virgin, and likely to remain so, unless . . .

The girls at work? That silly Gladys Smith, a bride of last summer, who had regaled them, unashamedly, with explicit details of her wedding night, to Wilma's disgust, who had pretended not to listen. Even so, she could not help recalling Gladys' revolting chatter about birth control, gleaned from the pages of an *Enquire Within*.

'Well, I told Bert right off,' she'd confided merrily, biting into a corned beef sandwich during the lunch-break, 'that no way did I want to get pregnant till we'd saved up a bit more money, an' he agreed with me: promised not to go all the way for the time being.

'It's what's called "quoits" or summat. Apparently Catholics do it all the time. The trick is to stop him doing what he's doing before – well, you know what!' Gulping down the remains of her sandwich, ''Course, he was a bit put out at first, but he soon got the hang of it, an' it worked right enough.'

'Danny.'

'Huh?' Emerging from the depths of sleep, he could scarcely believe his luck. Wilma was close beside him, snuggling up to him, saying she was sorry they had quarrelled. Turning towards her, he gathered her close in his arms. Inhaling her fragrance, kissing her lips, her hair, bemused with sleep and desire, wanting her with every fibre of his being, he scarcely heard her whispered proviso that he must not go all the way with her, must stop when she told him to.

'Did you hear what I said? I want you to promise!'

'Hmmm?' He wished she'd stop talking, especially now, at this, the tenderest moment of his life so far, the culmination of all his hopes, dreams and desires, centred on his strongest desire of all, to prove to his wife how much he loved her.

Why her panic reaction to his quickly reached climax, he had no clear idea. Why her vitriolic anger towards him when the loving was over, he could not imagine. What had he done wrong?

'I might have known, might have guessed that you wouldn't stop when I told you to,' she said bitterly. 'Oh no, not you, the high and mighty Danny Kingsley! As to why I married you, well I wish I hadn't, that's all! After what you just did to me, I couldn't care less if I never set eyes on you again for as long as I live!'

PART TWO

Chapter Fourteen

From his desk near the window, he watched the first of the summer flies crawling up a pane. It had been buzzing about all afternoon. Why not swat the irritating thing and have done with it? Somehow, he couldn't do that. The poor little devil deserved a moment in the sun to try out its wings. Putting himself in the fly's place, he knew what it felt like to be swatted, put paid to, maimed beyond hope of recovery on the window-pane of life.

Anyway, it was nearly home time. Home? Depression settled on him like a cloud as he tidied his desk, said a brief good night to his colleagues, shrugged on his jacket, and walked down the Town Hall steps into St Nicholas Street.

Deep in thought, he did not notice a fair-haired, buxom girl coming towards him until, 'Hello, Danny,' she said brightly.

'Meg! Meg Jenkins!' He hadn't seen her for ages. Warming to her smile, 'What are you doing here?'

'I'm on my way home from the shop to see to Mum and get the tea ready. I thought I'd walk down the gardens for a change. It's such a lovely day.'

'Oh. Mind if I walk with you?'

''Course not. It's a free country.' As he fell into step beside her, 'Well, how's married life treating you?' She pushed to the back of her mind that she had once been in love with him. But that was two years ago, in the summer of 1934.

'Fine. Just fine!' But he didn't look fine. He looked dreadful: tired and pale, lacking his old ebullience and charm, the charm which had captured her heart during their short-lived romance – if it could be called a romance. No, just a bit of a fling, that's all it was, Meg thought. She had not been Danny's type at all. He much preferred the china-doll kind of girl, small-boned and delicate. This she knew because he had told her as much on their last date, and she had cried afterwards, knowing she would never fit his mental picture of the kind of girl he wished to marry.

'Where are you living now?' Meg asked as they entered the St Nicholas Gardens and walked down the sloping paths together.

'In the Old Town. Princess Street as a matter of fact. We moved there a couple of months ago.' He added by way of explanation, and to give the impression that all was well with his marriage, 'We lived with Wilma's parents for a few weeks until we found a place of our own.'

'Oh?' Nothing wrong with that, Meg thought, except that the forceful Danny of two summers ago had told her he wouldn't think of getting married until he could make the grand gesture of carrying his bride across the threshold of their own house. But this was no longer the forceful, confident Danny she had known, and she couldn't help wondering what had happened to change him.

She said cheerfully, 'We're practically neighbours, then?' Princess Street was a mere stone's throw away from Paradise, where Meg lived with her parents. Danny had walked her home along the Foreshore from the Olympia Ballroom many a time in the past, the way they were walking now, heading for the Old Town of Scarborough nestling in the lee of the castle headland. It was mainly the province of fishermen, their wives and families, whose pink-pantiled cottages had belonged to generations of fishermen, handed down from father to son. The houses in Princess Street, Georgian in design and far superior in size, had belonged to the élite of the seafaring community: the master-mariners, ship-builders and merchants, who had once lived there in considerable style.

It crossed Meg's mind that Danny must have paid the earth for a property in Princess Street. She would not have been human had she not experienced a twinge of jealousy towards the girl Danny had married in preference to herself.

She *had* loved him, very much. More than he would ever know. But why punish herself with thoughts of what might have been? Thank goodness she had possessed enough common sense not to go on seeing him. How could she possibly have done so after he had made it abundantly clear that the kind of girl he wished to marry bore not the slightest resemblance to herself? She had her pride, and she was not the kind to run after a man who didn't want her.

There were a few early summer visitors about, threading their way towards the Penny Tram into town, ready for their teas: haddock and chips or whatever, with lashings of bread and butter, cakes, jam and scones to follow, a similar pattern to the meal she had planned for her semi-invalid mother and her father when he came home from work.

Knowing that she had more than enough fish in the bass bag she was carrying, for her own and her parents' needs, the thought occurred that Danny might be glad of the surplus, a couple of cod fillets, a wing of skate, a whiting, landed fresh from the cobles in the early hours of the morning.

'Thanks, but I'd rather not, if you don't mind,' Danny said awkwardly when she offered him the fish. 'You see my wife doesn't care much for – seafood, and I wouldn't want to upset her.' He added desperately, 'She's not very well at the moment.' They were standing outside his home in Princess Street at the time, a house Meg knew well, from which the *Furnished House to Let* sign had been removed recently from the front room window.

'Just as you like,' Meg said, with a shrug of the shoulders, unwilling to let him see how deeply she still cared for him, her concern that, despite his brave words to the contrary, he was now living in rented, furnished accommodation.

A less sensitive young woman would have asked him, point blank, what was wrong with his wife, the nature of her illness? Meg Jenkins did nothing of the kind. She said simply, over her shoulder, 'Well, goodbye, Danny, and good luck,' as she walked on along Princess Street into Paradise.

'Who was that girl you were talking to just now?' Wilma demanded, when her husband entered the house. 'Don't

189

bother to deny it because I saw you with my own two eyes, the pair of you standing out there on the pavement, making sheep's eyes at one another!' Suddenly, noisily, she burst into tears.

'For God's sake, Wilma,' he said irritably, 'Meg Jenkins is our fishmonger's daughter, if you must know. I met her on my way from work. We walked home together. She lives in Paradise.'

'And you're living in a fool's paradise if you think I'm going to swallow that story.'

'Don't be ridiculous!' He turned away in disgust, unable to equate the wild-eyed, sloppily dressed woman he could scarcely bear to look at, with the band-box neat, self-contained girl he had married last December.

'Oh? Ridiculous now, am I?' Her voice rose to a piercing shriek. 'Well, I wouldn't trust you as far as I could throw you, Danny Kingsley, and you know why!' Here it came again, he thought wearily, knowing exactly what she would say next, and he was right. 'It's all your fault we're in this mess, living in someone else's house, making do with other people's furniture . . . '

He said bitterly, 'You seem to forget it was your choice to live in someone else's house after the wedding.' But what was the use of talking? He awaited the inevitable reply.

'That was different! We could have saved money, living with my parents. I could have gone on working. But, oh no. That wasn't good enough for you, you selfish beast!' Her voice sank to a lower pitch, diluted with tears, 'I just hope you're satisfied, that's all.'

Turning to face her, he said more kindly, 'Of course I'm not satisfied that I've made you so unhappy. I never meant to, believe me.'

'Believe you?' Wilma snorted contemptuously, 'I wouldn't believe anything you say from now on if you swore on a stack of bibles!'

'In that case, there's nothing more to be said, is there?' he replied bitterly. 'There's just one thing I'd really like to know. Why, if what happened on our wedding night was so repugnant to you, did you stay on with me at the Ranelagh? Why didn't you carry out your threat to catch the early morning train back to Scarborough?'

'What? And risk everyone laughing at me? My work-mates pointing the finger at me behind my back? No fear!'

He had to speak the truth as he saw it. 'I made love to you that night because you were my·wife, because I'd held back so long I couldn't hold back any longer. Was that really such a crime?'

'You used me for your own selfish pleasure,' she threw back at him.

'No!' He saw everything quite clearly now. 'The shoe was on the other foot. *You* used *me!*'

'How dare you say that? It isn't true!'

But the blinkers were off. 'Oh yes it is,' he said dully. 'You married me knowing you didn't want children. You married me because I have a good job at the Town Hall.' His voice deepened suddenly with anger. 'Not satisfied with me the way I was, you couldn't wait to change me into a lap-dog. And I put up with it – put up with giving up sport to please you, going along with the rushed wedding, your half-baked idea to live with your parents afterwards, not to mention that bloody ridiculous notion of yours to spend our honeymoon in the Lake District.

'Well, what's done is done, but from now on I intend living the way it suits me, and the sooner you come to terms with the man I am, not the man you hoped I'd be when you'd patted me neatly into shape like a pound of butter, the better for the pair of us!' He continued angrily, 'I'm attending a Cricket Club meeting at Gibson's Boarding House tonight, putting my name forward as a member of the Yorkshire team – and if you don't like it, you can bloody well lump it!'

Staring at him, ashen-faced, 'Cricket! You mean you're starting that again, knowing how I feel about it? What about me? What am I supposed to do? You don't care tuppence, do you, about me being in the family way?'

'Of course I care,' Danny admitted roughly, riddled with

guilt, 'but how am I supposed to feel, knowing you never wanted a baby – my baby – in the first place?'

'And how am I supposed to feel,' Wilma responded bitterly, 'that you made me have a baby whether I wanted to or not?'

'I'm sorry,' was all Danny could say as, pushing past her, he went upstairs to get ready for the Cricket Club meeting, an angry, bewildered young man incapable of making sense from the ruination of his life, through no fault of his own. Shrugging into a clean shirt, arranging his County Cricket Club tie in front of a swing-mirror, he recalled the speed with which he and Wilma had been evicted from the Burtons' house in Aberdeen Terrace when his wife had broken the news to her parents that she was pregnant.

Mabel, jellified by the news, had made no secret of the fact that she and Daddy could not possibly contemplate giving house room to a baby. And so, he, Danny, had been obliged to find rented, furnished accommodation for himself and his wife – hence this house in Princess Street. A rather nice house, in his opinion, not that Wilma had a good word to say about it. Life had treated her cruelly, unfairly, she considered, and she never let him forget it.

Brushing his hair, he thought about Meg Jenkins; hoped he hadn't offended her in turning down her offer of the fish. Truth to tell, he'd jibbed at the idea of inviting her indoors, finding a plate for the fish, introducing her to Wilma of whom, deep down, he felt ashamed these days, who, when she knew she was 'expecting', had stopped caring about the way she looked.

The minute her waist had started to thicken, her breasts became fuller, she had thrown a tantrum over the dresses, skirts and blouses she could no longer get into.

Deeply distressed, and fearing for her sanity, he stood in the bedroom, watching her scooping armfuls of garments from her wardrobe and throwing them haphazardly onto the bed. 'Stop it, Wilma!' he'd said hoarsely. 'Stop behaving like a spoilt child and start acting like a woman!' Gripping her arms, restraining her forcefully, 'This isn't the end of the world, you know.'

Struggling to free herself, her eyes filled with hatred. 'Not for you, perhaps, but it is for me. I wish to God I'd never married you!'

The feeling was mutual.

Now, Wilma had taken to wearing voluminous skirts overhung with ill-fitting blouses, had stopped bothering about her hair which she wore scraped back from her pale, tired little face. Danny knew why. Because she no longer wished to please him, to tantalize him with her personal freshness he had loved so much. He failed to understand why a fragrant, lovely young girl intent on attracting a male partner, a husband, had reacted so violently to a husband's natural desire to make love to his wife on their wedding night.

If he had done wrong in wanting to possess her slim, fragrant body in that wretched bed in the Hotel Ranelagh; if he had unwittingly betrayed the rules of gentlemanly conduct in proving to Wilma how much he loved her on that God-awful, never-to-be-forgotten night in a freezing cold bedroom at the back of beyond, he had paid the price of his folly ever since, not to mention the price of a week's indifferent accommodation, *sans* the string quartet mentioned in the brochure. In short, his honeymoon had proved a complete failure. More distressingly, his marriage offered little hope of success. As things stood, he saw no ray of hope for the future. Wilma didn't want his child, and he no longer wanted Wilma. It was as simple, as complicated as that.

Clattering down the twisting stairs to the kitchen, he demanded, 'What are we having for tea?' Wilma was standing near the sink, staring out at the back yard. This wasn't one of those superior houses further along Princess Street in which masters of the fishing industry had lived, but one of a row of narrow houses with the front door leading directly into the sitting-room, a second door opening into the kitchen.

193

'You can get your own tea ready,' Wilma said, keeping her back to him. 'I don't want any. I'm not hungry.'

'Well I *am*! I've had nothing to eat since dinner-time – those measly meat-paste sandwiches you put up for me. Are you really telling me you've got nothing ready for me?' But he knew that she hadn't. There was no smell of cooking, no pans of potatoes and vegetables bubbling gently on the gas-cooker. She hadn't even bothered to set the table. And to think he'd turned down Meg Jenkins' offer of good fresh fish.

At least his mother-in-law had given him plenty to eat, he thought, during the few short weeks he'd endured beneath the Burtons' roof. Not that he'd intended going there after the honeymoon fiasco. He had done so to please Wilma, whose pride would not permit telling even her mother that their trip to the Lake District had been a disaster from start to finish. She had even lied about the string quartet, saying how romantic it had been listening to music in a lamplit dining-room.

Hungry and angry, he said bitterly, heading for the front door, 'Never mind. I'll call in home on my way to the meeting. Mother will give me something decent to eat!'

Turning away from the window, Wilma called after him, 'Danny!' Too late. She heard the slam of the front door, his footsteps hurrying away from her. Burying her face in her hands, Wilma wept for the loss of her youth and beauty, the sudden ending of all her hopes and dreams for the future which she had mapped out so clearly in her mind's eye. Dreams in which she had seen herself as the wife of an up-and-coming Town Hall executive, a credit to her husband, attending social evenings dressed in the height of fashion, creating a stir, an impression, inviting her husband's Town Hall associates to their own home filled with their own furniture; hearing the wives say, *sotto voce*, 'Oh, Mrs Kingsley, what good taste you have! What pretty china,' and 'What a good cook you are!'

But Danny hadn't played the game according to her rules. Now, here she was, stuck away in a rented house in what she considered a poor area of Scarborough, growing fatter by the minute, unable to wear pretty clothes any more, with nothing to look forward to except the pain and misery of giving birth to a squalling infant she had never wanted in the first place.

'Hello, Mum,' Danny called cheerfully, letting himself into the Castle Road house with his latchkey.

'Danny!' Grace emerged, smiling, from the kitchen, surprised yet pleased to see him. 'What are you doing here?'

He admitted, shamefacedly, 'I'm hungry! Wilma didn't feel up to cooking today. I thought you might have something on the go.'

'Of course, son. Go through to the dining-room. Your dad will be delighted to see you, so will Aunt Rosa, Jimmy and Kerry. Dulcie's working late. Mind you, it's only cottage-pie for supper, and there may not be much of it left. But I could cook you bacon and eggs, if you prefer, and I was just about to dish up the steamed chocolate pudding and custard.'

She thought how thin he looked, and how miserable, despite his air of pretended gaiety, and wondered what she could possibly say or do to ease his pain at having married the wrong woman at the wrong time. She knew this was so, not that Danny had ever uttered a word against Wilma. But mothers had a way of knowing the truth without truth being spelt out to them in words of one syllable.

'Well, son. Nice to see you!' Bob grinned amiably. 'Where's Wilma?'

'At home,' Danny mumbled, 'she didn't feel up to coming out this evening.' He couldn't very well tell the truth, that he and Wilma had had a blazing row and he'd walked out on her.

'I see you're wearing your Cricket Club tie,' Bob said, fetching knife, fork, and clean plate from the sideboard, taking for granted that his thin, edgy son would clear up the remains of the food left on the table.

'Yeah, well, I'm off to a meeting at Gibson's. Thought I might as well find out what's on offer: put my name

195

forward, get back into the game. You know what I mean?'

Bob knew exactly what he meant; decided to say nothing for the time being.

'You're looking well, Great Aunt Rosa,' Danny said brightly as he helped himself to the leftovers. 'You too, Kerry. How are your dancing lessons going, by the way?' He treated her to that special smile she had loved and known so well in the old days, before he had started courting Wilma Burton.

'Great, just great,' she assured him enthusiastically, passing him a tureen of lukewarm mashed potatoes. 'In fact, I've been chosen to dance at the crowning of the Rose Queen on the Spa, next month. I'm to be the chief butterfly! What do you think of that?'

'Move over, Anna Pavlova,' Jimmy uttered, tongue-in-cheek. Everyone laughed, except Jimmy, who wondered what the hell was wrong with his brother these days – as thin as a barber's pole and as hungry as a hunter. The news that Wilma was 'expecting' had come as a shock to him. Somehow, he had never cast Danny in the role of a prospective father. By the same token, he could scarcely imagine Wilma as a doting mother, engaged in the messy business of nappy-changing and so on. Hard luck on the poor kid, he thought, if 'it' was destined to draw nourishment from breasts the size of a couple of currant tea-cakes.

He knew he was being horrible, but writers had a way of getting to the heart of the matter, delving into the truth behind any given situation. How, otherwise, could their writing reflect reality? Encouraged by the cheques recently received from various newspapers and magazines, spurred on by the giants of his world – Thomas Mann, Theodore Dreiser, Ernest Hemingway, John Steinbeck – he now wished to write a novel in size and scope comparable to those stars of American literature, a near-impossible feat, he considered, unless he scratched beneath the surface of life to discover the true motivation of human beings hidden behind the bland exteriors they presented to the world in general.

But what could he possibly write of his own mundane family that was likely to cause a stir in literary circles? He loved his mother and father dearly, but they were just an ordinary, loving couple who had married early in life and raised four children. Nothing in the least extraordinary about that. His brother had married a selfish bitch of a girl who, apparently, could not be bothered to cook for him properly. And what about Kerry who was practising hard to become a butterfly? His other sister, Dulcie, was, he considered, about as interesting as a dead fish. As for his plain, dull, Great Aunt Rosa, he could scarcely blame her for wanting rid of his officious grandmother or her lumpy, myopic, ga-ga sister Fanny.

No, he would need to look elsewhere for the theme of a world-shaking first novel, Jimmy decided, smiling up at his mother as she heaped his side-plate with a generous helping of chocolate pudding and custard.

Suddenly, he remembered Herbie Barrass, who was coming to visit the Kingsley family next weekend. Now *there* was a man worth writing about.

Danny felt much better now, with a good meal inside him. Thanking his mother, he kissed her goodbye and set off for the meeting.

Bob was in the hall. 'Just a word, son,' he said, 'in here.' He led the way into the front room and closed the door.

'What's up, Dad?'

'I'm hoping you'll tell me that.'

'I don't know what you mean.'

'You know perfectly well what I mean.' Bob paused to frame his words. 'It's obvious that something is badly wrong between you and Wilma. I'd like to know what.'

Danny said awkwardly, 'She's a bit off-colour at the moment. Upset about the baby, that's all.'

'How do you mean, upset?'

'Well, you know—'

'I don't know, son. That's why I'm asking.'

'Oh, come off it, Dad!' Danny was irritable now. 'She's

bound to be upset, isn't she?' Glancing at his wrist-watch, 'I'll be late for the meeting.'

'Ah, yes, the meeting.' Bob drew in a deep breath. 'I take it, then, that Wilma raised no objections to being left on her own, despite feeling "off-colour"?'

'Look, Dad,' Danny blurted out, 'Wilma objects to everything I say or do these days! I'm sick and tired of trying to please her, so I might just as well please myself.'

'All right, son. No need to get hot under the collar. But there's more at stake here than either one of you. There's a child on the way, and that should be your main concern right now.'

'You think I don't know that?' Danny's face crumpled. He stopped being angry. He thought the world of his father, always had done. He had kept his feelings bottled up far too long. He said in a voice harsh with emotion, 'The truth is, Wilma doesn't want the baby. It's all my fault. I made her pregnant against her will. She hates me now. Oh, God, Dad, what the hell shall I do?' The floodgates opened. 'Wilma had everything cut and dried from the beginning, I see that now. I didn't at the time I asked her to go steady with me!' His eyes were wet with tears. 'I loved her so much, I couldn't bear the thought of losing her! I gave up everything to please her, and where has it got me?'

He continued shakily, ashamed of his emotion, 'I don't know which way to turn to make things right between us. She wanted a home of her own, and what has she got. A rented house in Princess Street. Now every penny I earn must go towards things for the baby she never wanted in the first place!'

Racked with pity for his son's dilemma, Bob said calmly, 'Take my advice, son. Forget about the Cricket Club meeting. Go back to Wilma; tell her you love her. Tell her how much you are looking forward to the baby.'

Puckering his forehead, 'But you don't understand, Dad,' Danny said haltingly, 'I don't want a baby any more than she does. That's the reason why I intend going to that meeting!'

There was nothing more to be said or done for the time being, Bob realized. His son was in no frame of mind to accept his responsibilities as a husband and father. All he longed for now was his old way of life, a return to his bachelor days. It would take time, and a wealth of heartache, perhaps, to make him aware of the fact that his freedom days were over and done with for ever.

Chapter Fifteen

Disillusioned and sad at heart in the wake of Danny's disastrous wedding day, Kerry had gone, with a girl from work, to see *Top Hat* at the Capitol cinema. Returning home, starry-eyed, uplifted by the dancing partnership of Ginger Rogers and Fred Astaire, she begged Grace, 'Oh, Mum, may I have dancing lessons? I want to learn to dance more than anything else in the world!'

'We'll see what your father has to say about it,' Grace replied non-committally.

Later, they had both agreed that the girl needed a new interest in life. She had seemed so peaky and off-colour lately. Besides which, she was a born dancer, betrayed by her every movement, the way she used her hands and held her shoulders, her inborn sense of rhythm.

'You don't think she's a bit too old to begin ballet lessons, do you?' Grace had demurred, at first, discussing the subject with her husband.

Bob laughed. 'Look, love, that daughter of ours has been dancing since the day she was born! Remember the way she used to kick her feet in the cradle? The thing is to find her a really good teacher.'

Their choice had fallen upon a Miss Isabel Williams, a teacher of the highest repute who, since her early, enforced retirement as the ballet mistress of a famous public girls school, near York, had opened a small academy in Scarborough.

Discreet enquiries had further convinced them that Miss Williams, who had sacrificed her school career in order to take care of her ageing mother, was the person best qualified to teach their daughter – if Miss Williams considered her worth teaching. If not, if she considered Kerry too old to begin lessons, they must abide by her decision, Grace decreed. 'You do understand, don't you, my love?' she added compassionately.

'Yes, of course I do,' Kerry replied meekly. 'I'm just going to pray, as hard as I can, that she'll accept me as a pupil.'

'You'll have to audition for her, I expect.'

'Really?' Kerry's face brightened. 'Oh, I should like that very much! I'll dance till I drop to please her!'

Overjoyed by her success, attending her first class early in the new year, Kerry had formed an instant rapport with Miss Williams. She knew that Miss Williams returned home each night to stay with her mother, that she had engaged a reliable woman to take care of her during the daytime when she, Miss Williams, was busy earning a living. She knew because Miss Williams had revealed as much during the initial interview preceding her enrolment as a pupil.

All had gone well until, one bitterly cold night in February, for no apparent reason, Kerry had burst into tears in the middle of a lesson. Then, 'You'd better go upstairs to my flat,' Miss Williams said quietly. 'I'll talk to you later.'

Later, 'What is it, child? What's wrong?' Miss Williams asked with concern.

'That's just it, I don't know what's wrong,' Kerry responded, drying her eyes on a proffered handkerchief, 'I just feel so miserable, that's all.'

'You find the lessons too difficult, perhaps? Is that it?'

'Oh *no*! Please don't think that. I want to learn to dance more than anything else in the world.' She drew in a deep breath. 'It's just that – well, it all began with Sid, I suppose. I thought he loved me, but he didn't. Then my brother got married, and there was a dreadful bust-up between Nan and my Great Aunt Rosa when Mother told Nan that Great Aunt Rosa was coming to live with us. Now my brother's wife is expecting a baby, but they're not happy together, I know they're not. Worst of all, I'm *glad* they're not happy! I just wish that Danny would come back home, where he belongs. I wish, I wish that nothing had changed, that I could wake up one morning to find that everything was just the same as it used to be!'

Miss Williams said calmly, 'So do I, Kerry. The fact remains that nothing in earth or heaven comes as it came before. "The moving finger writes; and, having writ, Moves on . . ." Believe me, my dear, if you fail to move with the world, life will pass you by unnoticed and uncaring.' She smiled sadly. 'I'm sorry, I imagine you haven't a clue what I'm talking about.'

'Oh yes I have,' Kerry responded warmly:

"The moving finger writes; and, having writ,
Moves on: nor all thy piety nor wit
Shall lure it back to cancel half a line,
Nor all thy tears wash out a word of it."

It's from the *Rubaiyat of Omar Khayyam,* isn't it? I copied it down in my exercise book.'

Startled, Miss Williams said, 'On a happier note, I have been invited to provide entertainment for the crowning of the Rose Queen ceremony in June, and I want you as my chief butterfly.'

'You *do*?' Kerry's heart lifted like a – butterfly. All she could do for the moment was gaze at her teacher, open-mouthed with surprise and joy. 'Oh, Miss Williams, I . . .' Then, conscience-stricken, 'I didn't mean what I said about my brother and his wife. I'm sorry, not glad, they're unhappy. That was a dreadful thing to say.'

The doorbell rang. 'That will be my father,' Kerry said in a fluster, 'I expect he's been waiting for me. Please don't tell him I've been crying.'

'You're a late scholar,' Bob said on their way home. Smiling, 'Did Miss Williams keep you in after class? The others left ages ago.'

'No, not exactly. That is . . .' Her conscience gained the upper hand, 'Oh, Dad, I made a fool of myself.' The whole story emerged, not very clearly or lucidly as the pair of them faced an uphill struggle on ice-filmed pavements in the face of a bitter, sleet-laden wind.

Bob said, understandingly, tucking her hand into the crook

of his elbow, 'A nice lady, that dancing teacher of yours.'
He paused, then asked, 'But who is this Sid you mentioned?'

'Oh, no-one in particular.' His name had slipped out
unawares.

'*Kerry!*'

'He's a High School boy. At least he was. Now he's
working in a bank in St Nicholas Street,' Kerry admitted.

'And is he the reason why you've been so off-colour of
late?'

Crestfallen, 'I guess so. I'm sorry, Dad, truly I am.'

'Why didn't you tell us this before?' Bob asked patiently.
'Mum and I have been worried sick about you lately.'

'There was nothing much to tell,' Kerry said bleakly. 'All
he did was buy me an ice-cream cornet and ask me to go
to the pictures with him.'

'And did you – go to the pictures with him?'

'No. I found out just in time that he was going steady
with someone else – a girl from Boots the Chemist.'

'I see.' But Bob was far more worried about Kerry's
distress concerning the family problems which had erupted
recently. How blind he'd been not to see how deeply they
had affected her. 'Even so.' Pressing his daughter's hand,
Bob said firmly but kindly, 'Look, love, I want you to
promise that, from now on, you will come to us whenever
you're in trouble. Promise?' He added tenderly, 'That's what
parents are for.'

'I promise,' Kerry said meekly as they walked up the
front steps together and Bob opened the door with his
latchkey.

Dulcie was already in bed and fast asleep when Kerry
entered their room, walking on tiptoe so as not to disturb
her, knowing that her sister must be up at the crack of dawn
to serve breakfast at the Pavilion.

Dulcie's heart lifted with joy the moment she entered the
dining-room to find the handsome, elderly German gentleman she had noticed, last autumn, sitting alone at a table
near a window.

'May I take your order, sir?' she enquired respectfully, 'Or are you waiting for your children?'

The man replied, with a smile, 'I am alone for the time being, Fräulein.' He did not remember the girl, but she obviously remembered him, and the twins. He said, when Dulcie came back with his order, 'It is my intention to bring my children for a holiday the first week in July. The fresh sea air is good for them, and they so like the beach and the rock-pools at – how do you express it?'

'The Children's Corner?' Dulcie ventured.

'Ah yes, the so aptly named Children's Corner.'

July, Dulcie thought. If she went on a starvation diet between now and then, she might shed a stone in weight, treat herself to a pretty cotton dress or two, take the first week of her holidays. The head waiter wouldn't be best pleased, but to hell with that! This was *her* life, *her* future at stake.

Later, at staff breakfast, when the dining-room had closed and the lunchtime setting-up of tables had been accomplished, she cast anguished eyes at the hefty plates of bacon, eggs, sausages, tomatoes and fried bread being devoured by her colleagues. 'I'm not very hungry,' she declared, plumping for a portion of scrambled egg and unbuttered toast. Worst of all, a cup of black coffee – *sans* sugar.

But how virtuous she felt afterwards . . .

She had really put the cat among the pigeons, Rosa thought, getting out of bed to open the curtains.

Gazing at the view spread before her, hearing the raucous cries of the gulls wheeling about the castle, feeling happier, more contented than she had done for many a long day, she seemed far distanced now from the terrible row that had blown up when Nan discovered that she, Rosa, had begged Grace and Bob for sanctuary.

Dear Fanny had been upset, of course, but understanding. Nan, on the other hand, had denounced her as a 'wicked, deceitful fool intent on causing trouble'. And, 'I suppose you'll be moving into *my* room?' she'd shouted, beside herself with anger.

It was useless to protest that Nan had quit this room of her own accord. Nan, who possessed a far louder voice than hers, had shouted down her reasons for wanting to live with Grace and Bob as 'arrant nonsense', a trick to gain sympathy, a slap in the eye to herself and Fanny. Worse still, Nan had then vented her anger on Grace and Bob, and, oh dear, what ugly skeletons had emerged from the family closet.

Rosa had often wondered why the last-minute wedding invitation, the nine o'clock ceremony – before the streets were aired – why dear Grace had not appeared, as a bride should, in a white dress and veil, why the rushed reception at the house in Alma Square. Of course, one knew that the bridegroom was on embarkation leave. Even so . . . Then Nan was saying hateful, horrid things about her own daughter, telling the world and his wife the reason why a hitherto innocent young girl had found it necessary to get married in such a hurry; turning her venom on Bob, calling him a lecher, a betrayer of innocence.

Fanny had said, at that point, in a voice choked with emotion, 'Nan, dear, I hardly think all that is relevant now.'

'Huh,' Nan retaliated, 'a fat lot *you* know! You've never even been married, much less been a mother.'

Notwithstanding, despite all the hateful things that had been said, the rattling of dried bones, Nan's high-handed departure without a backward glance as she and Fanny had entered a hastily summoned taxi, Rosa knew that she had come to a wise decision in trading in her old way of life for a more hopeful, less stressful future. She could not have borne to go on living with Nan any longer. If only she didn't miss dear Fanny so much.

But times changed, and life moved on, Rosa thought, watching the gulls from her bedroom window. Besides which, that nice Herbie Barrass would be arriving later in the day, to spend the weekend with Grace and Bob.

* * *

Standing in the corridor as the train puffed past Oliver's Mount, lowering the window by means of the thick leather strap, Herbie experienced once more a marvellous sense of homecoming. Trees on the slopes of the Mount were in new leaf. Between them, he caught a glimpse of the Mere – an angler's and kiddie's paradise on the outskirts of the town he had come to know and love so well – far distanced from the grimy atmosphere of Leeds. Not that he was complaining. The bustling, smoky city of his birth had been good to him on the whole. Despite his unhappy beginning, he was doing well in his job, and he now had a nice little rented flat over a hardware shop near the city centre, plus some decent clobber, to prove it. Moreover, he was fast learning the art of cookery. Nothing fancy, of course, but he could now cook eggs and bacon without the eggs spitting fat in his eye or the bacon splintering into a dozen fragments when he stuck his fork in it. Grace would be proud of him.

Grace! The thought of seeing her again lifted his heart to the awareness of how much he owed her, how much he loved her.

Danny's wedding day had been a nightmare from start to finish, but how magnificently she had coped with it, and how lovely she looked in her simple green wool dress and matching coat, forward-tilted green felt hat, neat brown shoes and gloves.

Marriage, he reckoned, was a gamble, and it was obvious that Danny had not drawn a winning number in that particular lottery. One look at the prissy, self-conscious bride swanning down the aisle towards her bridegroom, obviously more concerned with the way she looked rather than the lifelong commitment she was about to make in the face of God and the congregation, had convinced him of that. How he had managed to hold his tongue when the parson came to the bit about anyone objecting to the marriage to speak out or shut up, he scarcely knew. He had wanted, at that moment, to shout aloud to the besotted bridegroom to get the hell out of it before it was too late.

He thought wryly, as the train juddered to a halt near the

station barrier, that, had he done so, he would probably have ended up in the psychiatric ward of the local hospital. Humping his suitcase and samples case onto the platform, he handed his ticket to the ticket-collector, stepped onto the forecourt and lifted his face to the clear, fresh sweetness of the salt-laden seaside air, anxious to get to his destination as quickly as possible. No longer a pauper, he hailed a taxi. 'Castle Road,' he told the driver.

'Certainly sir,' the man replied, tickling Herbie's sense of the ridiculous that one man should be subservient to another because of money – a half-crown fare and a tanner tip. But it wasn't all that funny, he realized, rather sad as a matter of fact. Perhaps he was getting too big for his boots? He was, after all, nowt but a state-educated lad who had struck lucky in the lottery of life, thanks to the two people on earth he loved best, Grace and Bob Kingsley.

Alighting from the taxi, he handed the driver a ten-bob note; told him to keep the change, with humility, not pride, just wanting to pass on a little of his own good luck to a fellow human being. Perhaps the man had kids. Perhaps the seven-shilling windfall would provide him, his wife and children with a blow-out fish-and-chip supper? Yeah, that would be nice, Herbie thought as the front door opened and Bob, smiling and with hand extended, welcomed him into his home.

Sitting at the dining-room table, tucking into a succulent portion of steak and kidney pie, it occurred to Herbie that his frequent visits to the house on the hill had cast him in the role of a Father Confessor, far enough away from the day-to-day lives of the Kingsley family to judge fairly, impartially, their progress or otherwise, as the case may be. A bit like King Solomon, he thought wryly, helping himself, at Grace's invitation, to more carrots and mashed potatoes.

True enough, he knew more about the state of play between the various members of the family than anyone else. Whether or not he was qualified to offer advice was a different matter entirely. He couldn't quite put his finger on what was wrong, but Grace and Bob seemed quieter than usual, vaguely worried. To his surprise, after the supper things had been cleared, Bob suggested a quiet pint at the Albion.

'Sure Grace won't object?' Herbie asked.

'It was her idea as a matter of fact,' Bob told him.

'Oh? Right. Fair enough. Lead on!'

Settled at a table in the bar-parlour, Bob opened his heart about Danny and Wilma. 'They're just not hitting it off together,' he explained. 'Grace and I are worried sick. And now there's a baby on the way . . .'

'A baby?' Herbie emitted a low whistle. 'So soon? Sorry, I just had the feeling that Wilma would want a fully furnished house, complete with nursery, before embarking on the joys of motherhood.'

'You thought right,' Bob said gloomily. 'Well, they've got a furnished house, true enough, but it doesn't belong to them. They're living in a rented place in the Old Town.' He paused to swallow a mouthful of ale. 'Worse still, Wilma doesn't want the baby, and Danny has started playing cricket again.'

Thoughtfully rubbing his chin, 'To be honest,' Herbie mused, 'I can't really blame him, can you?'

'No,' Bob admitted, 'I can't. But there's more to it than that. Wilma's parents – her mother in particular – are up in arms against Danny, and,' he grinned ruefully, 'since he happens to be our son, Grace and I have come in for our fair share of blame for the present state of affairs.'

'I'm not surprised,' Herbie conjectured, 'being the kind of people they are. No form, no breeding – a bit like a couple of broken-winded nags pulling a muck cart! Mind you, I'd rather take a couple of broken-winded horses than most human beings any day of the week.'

'So what do you think we should do about it?' Bob asked.

'In my experience,' Herbie said levelly, 'when in doubt, do nowt.' He continued as dispassionately as possible, 'Look, Bob, it's up to Danny and Wilma to sort out their own affairs now they're married and expecting! After all,

"Whom God hath joined, let no man put asunder." Start meddling, and *you'll* end up the villain of the piece. Let things ride for the time being. No use rocking the boat any further than necessary. Give the young folk time to sort out their own muddle.'

'I guess you're right,' Bob said quietly. 'Thanks, old pal, I knew I could rely on you for good advice.'

The bar-parlour was beginning to fill up now. Finishing their drinks, Bob and Herbie wended their way back home to listen to a boxing match on the wireless.

Grace had made tea and sandwiches in anticipation of their return. Glancing across at her, Herbie saw that she was knitting a matinée jacket for the baby.

There was fish for supper the next evening, Saturday, fresh haddock crisply fried in batter, served with chips and mushy peas, and lashings of bread and butter, after which he, Grace and Bob had walked down Paradise to the Foreshore for a breath of sea air.

Herbie had done well with his samples that day. Tomorrow was Sunday, a day of rest. First thing on Monday morning he would be off to Northallerton, from there to York. It struck him forcibly that, whilst his own horizons seemed to be expanding, those of his friends appeared to be dwindling into an enervating whirlpool of family strife.

He could scarcely bear to see the sad, haunted look on Grace's face as she looked out to sea, her hands gripping the iron railings, the knuckles showing white. His heart went out to her, but what could he possibly do or say to ease her pain? In any case, it was Bob who did the 'easing'. It was Bob who, releasing her grip on the railings, kissed the palms of her hands in turn; slipped his arm about her waist; brought a smile to her lips with a few whispered words in her ear.

A numbing feeling of inadequacy struck Herbie amidships at that moment. Not jealousy exactly, something far deeper, far more complex than 'the green-eyed monster', he told himself, walking a few paces ahead, trying to figure out what ailed him.

He loved Grace Kingsley, would go on loving her till the day he died, and yet . . . How long could any full-blooded member of the male sex go on living like a monk? He needed, as scorched earth needs rain, the close, warm feeling of a woman in his arms, an overwhelming tide of physical release. The trouble was, no other woman looked like Grace, no other woman possessed her simplicity and charm. So what was the answer?

At least he had her bright, shining friendship to sustain him. And he would be there, by her side, if ever she should need him. There were women a-plenty in the Red Light district of Leeds, who, for a couple of quid, would provide the arms, the body, a quick burst of physical relief. This he knew, having availed himself of a couple of quids' worth of simulated passion now and then, which had left him feeling – dirty was the operative word – as spent and useless as an ashtray full of cigarette stubs and burnt-out matches . . .

After breakfast the following morning, Rosa invited him to look at her room. 'Well, what do you think of it?' she enquired anxiously, flinging open the door.

'It's nice. Very nice indeed,' he said sincerely, understanding how much it must mean to an old lady to have her precious bits and pieces about her – her furniture, wardrobe, bed and dressing table; ornaments, silver-framed photographs, pictures and samplers.

'This is a photograph of myself and my sisters when we were young,' Rosa said, handing him the picture for closer inspection. 'Fanny was very pretty, don't you think?'

'More than pretty, I'd say. She was *beautiful*!'

Gazing at the trio of faces caught and imprisoned for all time by a long-dead artiste of flashlight photography whose head, he imagined, would have been covered with a cloth as he stared into the camera, his right arm extended in readiness to trigger the flashlight mechanism of a bygone era, Herbie thought how cruel of time to have stripped away the soft contours of youth from those faces, clustered, like flowers, above the high-necked, lace-trimmed blouses they had worn that day, in the photographer's studio, in the springtime of their lives.

'You are right, Mr Barrass,' Rosa said softly, 'Fanny was beautiful.' Her eyes filled with tears. 'Oh, I can't help wondering . . . Do you think I did the right thing in coming here to live? I miss Fanny so much. It breaks my heart to think of her all alone in that house, with only Nan for company.' Unaware of the solecism, 'I know that Nan is a much better cook than I could ever hope to be. Even so—'

'For what it's worth,' Herbie reassured her, 'I think that you took a step in the right direction when you came here to live.' He couldn't very well say that she deserved, in his opinion, a medal for bravery. Changing the subject adroitly, and turning his attention to a small vase containing a bunch of violets, 'These are pretty,' he said.

Rosa smiled, brushing aside her tears. 'Kerry gave them to me,' she told him proudly. 'She bought them especially for me. Wasn't that kind of her?' A slight pause, then, 'Has she told you that she's to be a butterfly on the Spa next month?'

'Really? No, I haven't had time to talk to her yet,' Herbie confessed, edging towards the door, knowing the time had come to leave an old lady alone with her memories: her violets . . .

Grace was in the kitchen preparing the Sunday dinner when he went downstairs. Kerry had gone to church. Bob was in the yard, tidying the shed, Jimmy upstairs in his room, Dulcie at the Pavilion.

'Don't you ever get tired of cooking?' Herbie asked, watching Grace at work, marvelling at her dexterity with the rolling-pin, the way she turned the pastry for the gooseberry pie she was making.

'No. Why?' She laughed. 'Just as well, don't you think?'

'Lots of women don't like cooking.'

'In which case, they shouldn't get married and have four children,' she commented wryly, lining a dish with pastry and deftly trimming off the surplus. When the trimming was done, she said quietly, 'Oh, you mean Wilma? Bob has told

211

you that Danny is going through a rough patch at the moment?'

'Yes. And I'm sorry, Grace, believe me.' His heart ached for her. It couldn't have been easy for her to stand by, to watch a young man in the prime of life being swallowed whole by a silly scrap of a lass intent on changing his entire personality.

He turned his attention to a few odds and ends in the sink which needed washing. 'Rosa asked me to look at her room,' he said. 'She seems much happier now than . . .' About to say, 'than she did on Danny's wedding day', he decided not to, 'than she did in South Street,' he finished the sentence.

'Yes, I suppose so,' Grace admitted, pressing the edges of the pie together and brushing the top with beaten egg, 'though I doubt my mother will ever forgive me for taking pity on poor Aunt Rosa. Oh, Herbie, I envy you at times, I really do.'

Turning away from the sink, '*You* envy *me*? In heaven's name, *why*?' he asked, disbelievingly. 'I'd have amounted to less than nothing without your help and Bob's! I came as a beggar to your door. You fed me, damn near clothed me, gave me a fresh outlook on life, and *you* envy *me*?' He was speaking quickly, hoarsely now, not stopping to think what he was saying, just wanting her to know how he felt deep inside. 'Well, let me tell you, I envy you and Bob the life you have created together, the wealth of love between you. The kind of love I've never known nor ever shall know, more's the pity!' Then, realizing that he had allowed his feelings to get out of hand, 'I'm sorry,' he murmured contritely, 'it's just that I . . . What I mean is, why should you envy a common bloke like me?'

'No need to apologize,' Grace said. 'I meant that, well, it's hard to explain exactly what I did mean. I wouldn't change my life for all the tea in China. It's just that I envy, at times, your freedom of movement, your lack of ties.'

'Go on,' he said quietly, 'you can tell me.'

'There's nothing much to tell, except . . .' Resting her hands on the table, looking dreamily into the past, 'I sometimes wish that I could go back in time to the night of the Kerry Dance.'

'The Kerry Dance?' He hadn't the faintest idea what she meant.

She continued softly, 'I was just a child at the time. My parents took me to Ireland on holiday. I was so happy there, the way children are – most children, that is – at least I like to believe so. Nothing to do with wealth, just the way children have of looking at life through untroubled eyes, certain of the future. At least, that's the way I looked at life then, jouncing along in a donkey cart, my parents beside me. We stayed at a small hotel in County Kerry.' Her voice faltered. 'It isn't really important!' Glancing at the clock on the dresser, 'Gosh, is that the time? Dinner will never be ready by one o'clock at the rate I'm going!'

Bending down, she took from the oven the joint of Sunday beef. Lifting it onto the table, she scattered about it a panful of par-boiled potatoes. The task accomplished, she returned the roasting-tin to the cooker along with the gooseberry pie, reckoning silently that when the pie was baked and the potatoes were beginning to brown, would come the time to take the pie from the oven, to relegate the roast to a lower shelf, to increase the oven temperature in readiness for the Yorkshire pudding batter.

'And then what?' Herbie insisted.

'And then what – *what*?' She looked at him in surprise, her face flushed from the heat of the oven.

'You were telling me about Ireland,' he reminded her. 'About the Kerry Dance, remember?'

'Oh, *that*!' Grace shrugged her shoulders dismissively. 'The Kerry Dance was nothing more than a dream, a childhood fantasy of mine.'

'And yet it has stayed with you all these years. I wonder why?'

Grace wrinkled her forehead. 'I've often wondered that myself,' she confessed.

'Tell me about it,' Herbie said quietly.

'There's nothing much to tell, except that the hotel we

stayed at turned out to be nothing more than a "common or garden public house", my mother's words, not mine!' She smiled reflectively. 'And, of course, she was right.

'I had a little room at the head of the stairs, but I couldn't sleep because of the laughter and chatter, the sound of music drifting up from the bar-parlour. Not that I minded. I had never heard such music before, the sound of bagpipes – Irish bagpipes.'

'And then what happened?' Herbie prompted gently.

'That's just it. I don't honestly remember,' Grace told him. 'I have the vaguest recollection of standing on tiptoe at my bedroom window, seeing a trail of lanterns twinkling like fireflies in the darkness. Then I seem to recall that someone, a young girl, came into my room, told me to get dressed; that I went with her down to the glen to watch the Kerry Dance.' She sighed deeply. 'The next morning, when I told Mother I'd seen the Kerry Dance, she told me I'd dreamt it.'

'And you believed her?'

'I *had* to believe her,' Grace said. 'After all, she was my mother. And yet . . .'

'Go on!'

'And yet my shoes were wet with dew the next morning!'

So the holier-than-thou Nan Daniel had turned a deaf ear? Herbie wondered why.

Bob came into the kitchen at that moment. 'Something smells good,' he said appreciatively, crossing to the sink to wash his hands. 'I've finished clearing the shed, by the way.'

'If you don't mind, Mr Barrass – Herbie,' Jimmy said, when the Sunday dinner had been eaten, the pots washed up and put away, 'I'd like you to come up to my room for an hour or so, if you can spare the time.'

'Sure, I'll be pleased to,' Herbie agreed, following Jimmy upstairs to his top-floor eyrie beneath the slates, in which he arrived puffing and panting from the exertion of climbing four flights of stairs.

'First of all, Mr Barrass – Herbie,' Jimmy said as his guest

214

sank down in the nearest chair, 'I'd like to give you this, the five quid you lent me ages ago, remember?'

'Of course I remember,' Herbie panted, 'but that's water under the bridge! In any case, the money I forked out, that five quid, was in the nature of a gift.'

'That's not what you said at the time,' Jimmy reminded him. 'You said, Mr Barrass – Herbie, that I could pay you back when I was rich and famous. Well, I'm not famous – not yet anyway – but I can afford to repay the money you lent me. I can't tell you how much it meant to me, Mr Barrass – Herbie.'

Herbie laughed. 'Look, Jimmy lad, for God's sake make up your mind what to call me. Frankly, I prefer Herbie.'

'Thanks – Herbie.' Jimmy sighed, deeply contented. 'The thing is, I'm going to write a book about the war, and I need your help.'

'That's a bit ambitious, isn't it?' Herbie said mildly. 'In any case, how could I help? I was nowt but a common-or-garden soldier.'

'That's the whole point,' Jimmy said eagerly, 'I want to tell the story from the viewpoint of someone who fought in the trenches. Enough has been written from the Whitehall angle, about the generals and so forth. I can research all that stuff at the public library, but that's not what I'm after.'

'Your dad fought in the trenches,' Herbie reminded him. 'Why not ask him?'

Jimmy shook his head. 'No, perhaps we're too close. Dad treats my writing as a kind of joke, though I guess he's quite pleased about it deep down. We just don't talk about it very much, that's all. He thinks writers are a bit odd.'

'So this is to be a novel, is it?' Herbie thumbed his chin thoughtfully. 'And you want me as the main character?'

'Something like that,' Jimmy acknowledged.

'Well, I dunno,' Herbie prevaricated. 'Not exactly the handsome hero type, am I?'

'I'm not looking for a handsome hero type,' Jimmy explained, 'rather an anti-hero, if you see what I mean. A real, down-to-earth character such as yourself.'

'I see. So what do you want me to do?'

'We might begin with your early life,' Jimmy suggested hopefully.

'Hmmm. Well, all right then,' Herbie conceded, 'fire away with your questions, but let's be realistic about this, shall we? You asked me up here for an hour or so, as I recall. Right? But Rome wasn't built in a day, neither was the war fought in a day. It took four bloody years to settle that argument. It'll take a lot longer than an hour or so to give you my version of that argument!'

'I don't mind how long it takes,' Jimmy assured him, finding a notepad and pencil.

Over an hour later, 'That's enough to be going on with,' Herbie decreed, getting up. It hadn't been easy for him, talking about his early life, the death of his parents, his orphanage days, and yet perhaps it had been good for him – the laying of ghosts from the past, the officials who had often struck terror into the heart of a lonely little boy.

Jimmy said respectfully, 'Thanks, Herbie – Mr Barrass. May we talk again on your next visit?'

'Sure thing,' Herbie replied, thinking what a nice lad Jimmy was, deeply touched by the return of the five quid he'd lent him ages ago. 'With one proviso. That you don't call me by my real name in this book of yours. I'd find that – embarrassing!'

Herbie walked with Kerry to the Castle after tea. It was a grim place to be, even in spring-time, he thought, squinting up at the Norman Keep, the walls of which exuded a feeling of menace, of dark deeds perpetrated there long ago. He had to admit, however, that the view from the headland was magnificent, the stiff upward climb worth the effort.

He squatted on a heap of stones to regain his breath. 'Well, Kerry love, so you're to be a butterfly, are you? Tell me about it.'

Sitting beside him, her eyes shining, she obliged. 'I asked Mum and Dad for dancing lessons as my Christmas present, and they said Yes,' she told him eagerly. 'You see, I wanted to learn to dance like Ginger Rogers in *Top Hat*.'

'And have you?'

'No, not yet.' She pulled a face. 'All I've done so far is learn how to point my feet and position my arms correctly – what my teacher calls the rudiments of ballet. When I told her I really wanted to learn tap and ballroom dancing, she just smiled and said they would come later in the curry whatsit . . . the curriculum. I had to look it up in the dictionary.'

'I guess she's right.' Herbie paused to light a much-needed Kensitas cigarette. Inhaling deeply, blowing out the smoke, 'A bit like squad drill really. When I first joined the army, I couldn't tell one foot from t'other. But it's you we're on about, not me. So what else have you done besides pointing your feet and waving your arms?'

Kerry giggled. 'I've done stretching exercises and arabesques – you know, standing still on one foot with one arm extended in front, the other arm and leg stuck out behind. I'm beginning to get the hang of it now.' Her laughter faded suddenly. 'The truth is, I'm a bit worried about being the chief butterfly on the Spa next month.' Her eyes clouded over. 'Suppose I wobble and fall over? Suppose I make a fool of myself in front of all those people?'

'Don't worry, lass, you won't,' Herbie assured her, 'you're not the kind to make a fool of herself.'

Gazing out to sea, a wistful expression grew on her tender young face, 'I did over Sid Hannay,' she reminded him.

'That you didn't!' Stubbing out his half-smoked cigarette on the grass, 'You came through that with all flags flying!' He added quietly, 'Not still worried about him, are you?'

'I guess so,' she admitted, 'you see, he's working at a bank in St Nicholas Street now he's left school, so I can't help bumping into him now and then, and it's *awful*! Pretending not to notice him. Not speaking! Oh, *Herbie*!'

'And what about *her*, that "suicide" blonde with the fog-horn voice? Is she still in the picture?'

'Oh yes. He hangs about on the corner of St Nicholas Street every evening after work, waiting for her.'

The poor little kid, Herbie thought compassionately, she had really taken her first so-called love affair to heart. He knew why. Kerry was so like her mother, all gentleness and trust, idealistic, easily hurt.

Rising to his feet, he said lightly, 'Come on, high time we were getting back home.'

As they walked together past the Norman Keep, Kerry said, 'Why does everything have to change? Why can't things stay exactly as they were before?'

'Before what?' he ventured.

'Well, you know – before Nan went to live with her sisters. Before Danny married Wilma Burton. Now everything's different. Changed. Spoilt!'

Clasping her hand, he asked, 'How old are you now, Kerry?'

'Fifteen – going on sixteen. Why?'

'What if you had stayed fourteen?'

'I couldn't have,' she said, uncertain what he was getting at. 'That's impossible.'

'When I asked you just now, you said you were fifteen going on sixteen,' he reminded her.

'Yes, I know.'

'So you'd rather be sixteen than fifteen?'

'I suppose so.' She wriggled her shoulders. 'I'd like to be older than I am right now, that's for sure.'

'Why's that?' They were walking down the steep hill now, past the green meadow where Anne Brontë was buried, hands linked, swinging arms, like father and daughter, Herbie thought.

'Mum wouldn't make me wear puffed-sleeve dresses for one thing, and socks. I hate socks, but Mum says I'm not old enough for stockings, or high-heeled shoes. It's not fair. Sid's girlfriend wears high heels.'

Herbie laughed. 'One of these days, I won't know you. You'll be so smart and grown-up you won't even speak to me.'

Deeply shocked, 'Of course I shall!'

'But you won't be my little friend Kerry any more.'

'Of course I will! I'll always be *me* on the inside, no matter how much I change on the outside!' And then she knew what he was getting at, realized what he meant. He didn't have to spell it out for her. He had taught her a lesson she would remember always, that while changes were an inevitable part of life, of growing up, people remained the same underneath, especially the people one loved. Danny, for instance.

She said breathlessly, 'Oh, Herbie, isn't this a lovely day?'

Chapter Sixteen

She fluttered into the forecourt on gossamer wings, her soft white dress lifting gently at the hemline in the light summer breeze blowing in from the sea.

Standing in the background with the other mothers, hands tightly clasped with nervous tension, Grace watched her daughter's dancing debut with mixed feelings of pride and motherly concern. Kerry, she knew, was dreading the arabesque, the finale of the dancing display when she would have to stand unwaveringly on the point of her right ballet shoe, her left leg extended, arms and hands held just so until the music ended. One quiver, a moment's panic at being the cynosure of hundreds of pairs of eyes, and all would be lost.

The Spa walks and stairways were packed with sightseers gathered there to watch the Crowning of the Rose Queen ceremony. The retiring queen, resplendent in her gold lamé gown, and her successor – a slender girl in a blue organdie crinoline – were already seated on their thrones, awaiting the transfer of the glittering paste-diamond tiara. The dancing display was in the nature of a diversion, an added attraction. The girls of Miss Williams' academy, in their floating white dresses and colourful wings, would flutter about the two queens and their retinues to the music of a Chopin Nocturne played by the town's Silver Band. On the final notes, the chorus butterflies would group together behind the solo performer, whose arabesque was meant to convey an up-lifting of the spirit, a joyous moment of release . . .

Oh, God, Grace thought, kneading her knuckles, what if . . . ?

A young man, fair-haired, standing alone among a crush of people watching the dancing display from an upper balcony, thought he recognized the chief butterfly. Her face seemed familiar, but where had he seen her before? He couldn't for the life of him remember. Such a pretty girl with shoulder-length fair hair, and how well she danced. Now, where on earth? Suddenly it came to him. Of course, she worked at that fancy-goods shop in St Nicholas Street that his mother was so fond of. She was the girl who had brought the pattern-books for his father's curtains . . .

One of the flower girls in the procession had given him a red rose earlier that afternoon, which he had accepted with a flourish. Now, on impulse, craning forward, he called 'Bravo!' and threw the rose at Kerry's feet.

Startled, Kerry looked up. The moment she dreaded was almost here. The music swelled. Tension broken, effortlessly, without thinking, she rose to the occasion. All lightness and grace, she performed a poised and perfect arabesque.

The onlookers applauded. Grace burst into tears of relief.

Ashley Hawthorn thought, I shall marry that girl one of these days.

Deeply conscious of her weight loss, newly permed hair, and the pretty cotton dress she wore, Dulcie walked along the Spa towards the Children's Corner, an area of sand littered with shallow rock-pools, close to the South Bay Bathing Pool and the Penny Tram to the South Cliff – so called because even very young children could paddle and play there in comparative safety when the tide was out.

Heart beating fast with excitement, resting her arms on the railings, she scanned the beach with eager eyes. Suddenly, she saw the tall figure of Klaus Bergmann standing near a rock-pool looking down at his daughters who, wearing rubber 'waders', and carrying small tin buckets, were apparently engaged in searching for tiny crabs and other sea creatures left stranded by the outgoing tide.

It was now or never. She had saved hard, suffered the pangs of hunger and spent good money with this moment in mind; had incurred the displeasure of the head waiter in asking for time off from work the first week in July. Not that she had cared tuppence if she'd been sacked. There were more vital issues at stake than a mere job, and if everything went according to plan, she'd soon be entering the Pavilion Hotel as a guest, not a common-or-garden waitress.

So thinking, she walked confidently down the slipway to the sands, feeling like a cross between Joan Crawford and Barbara Stanwyck, her favourite actresses, knowing that her future now depended upon her own acting ability.

Coming face to face with him, she murmured shyly, 'Why, Mr Bergmann, you're the last person I expected to meet.' Quickly turning her attention to the twins, 'Oh, how they've grown since I last saw them! You must be very proud of them.'

'Yes, indeed I am.' Bergmann frowned slightly. The girl seemed vaguely familiar, but he couldn't for the life of him remember where they had met before.

Prepared for this eventuality, with a charming smile, 'My name is Dulcie Kingsley,' she told him. 'We met at the Pavilion Hotel.'

'Ah yes, of course.' He still hadn't a clue who she was, Dulcie realized, and she wasn't about to enlighten him. She had made the all-important contact, that was enough to be going on with. She knew exactly what she wanted, that the key to this man's heart lay, not through his stomach, as the old adage suggested, but through his children.

As luck would have it, at that moment one of the twins lost her footing on a moss-covered rock, plumped down abruptly in a pool of water, and started to cry.

Seizing the heaven-sent opportunity, uncaring of the ruination of her new cotton dress, and wading into the water, Dulcie lifted up the bawling child in her arms and brought her safely to the shore.

'My dear Miss Kingsley,' Bergmann uttered as his sobbing child was restored to his care and keeping, 'how kind of you! But what about your so pretty dress?'

'Oh, never mind about that,' Dulcie murmured, 'it will

soon dry in the sun, I expect.' Now came the calculated risk, the gamble upon which her entire future may well depend. 'Well, goodbye Mr Bergmann,' she said, turning away from him.

She knew she had won when he said, 'At least allow me to buy you a cup of tea or coffee, Miss Kingsley, at the Clock Café.'

Turning slowly, she smiled and said, 'Oh, very well then, if you insist. But what about the children? What are their names, by the way?'

'The one you so bravely rescued is Heidi, her sister is Helga,' Bergmann said proudly.

By dint of painstaking, seemingly off-hand investigation, and the simple expedient of keeping her ears open, Dulcie had ascertained that Fräulein Stockmar, the plain old biddy in the camel coat and wilting feathered hat, had been disengaged as nanny to the Bergmann children. Obviously, what the twins needed most of all was not a nanny but a brand new mother, and she had made a very good step in that direction, she thought complacently, seated at a wicker table overlooking the sea, drinking coffee with their father, the two little girls, tucking into ice-cream sundaes, chattering nineteen to the dozen, calling her by her Christian name. All well and good for the time being, she considered, though she would insist upon being called Mother after the wedding . . .

'You will come down to the beach tomorrow, won't you, Miss Dulcie?' they begged her in unison when the coffee break was over.

And, 'Yes, of course,' she replied, 'if you really want me to.'

'Oh yes, *please*!' Heidi responded warmly, throwing her arms about her rescuer's neck. 'She *must*, mustn't she, Papa?'

Bergmann smiled. 'You appear to have made a great impression on my offspring,' he said calmly, 'so I take it that we shall look forward to your company again tomorrow unless, that is, you have other plans in mind?'

'No, not at all! Well, goodbye, then, for the time being. See you in the morning.'

Oh God, she thought jubilantly, wending her way back along the Spa promenade, she'd really cracked it this time. Moreover, she had actually drunk her coffee black, without sugar, had shrugged aside that plate of chocolate biscuits . . . Never mind, eh? Once married and secure, she would stuff herself to her heart's content.

Visions of roast port, thick with fat and crackling, roast beef and Yorkshire pudding, chocolate eclairs, vanilla slices, fish and chips, rose up before her as she walked homeward along the Foreshore.

'It's no use, Bob,' Grace told her husband, at bedtime, 'I can't go on like this any longer. It's high time we visited my mother and Aunt Fanny; time we called on Danny and Wilma! We can't just let things slide. That's the road to nowhere. Bob, are you *listening*?'

'Of course I'm listening.'

'Then speak to me, for heaven's sake! Say something useful!'

'Agree with you, you mean?'

'Yes, dammit! Honestly, Bob, there are times when I don't know whether to kiss you or to kill you!'

'You mean I have a choice?'

'Bob, *please!*'

'All right, I'm listening.'

'I want to make things right,' she said. 'I hate being at logger-heads, with Mother in particular. Can we go there tomorrow night?'

'We may not get a very warm welcome,' Bob said doubtfully.

'I know, and I don't care. At least we'll have tried. It's getting me down. The same applies to Wilma and Danny. The girl's our daughter-in-law when all's said and done, and she's expecting our grandchild. I want to know, to see for myself how she is. I want to see where they're living.'

'All right, love. You win.'

'Thanks, Bob.' She snuggled down beside him.

'Just a thought. Let's take Kerry with us to South Street, shall we? She's so fond of Fanny, and Fanny loves her.'

'I know, but she's just a child. I wouldn't want her to become involved in a quarrel of any kind.'

Bob said quietly, 'Kerry's young, but she's no longer a child, and we should stop treating her as such.' Remembering that February night when they had walked home together in the teeth of a gale and she had confessed her inner feelings, he added, 'The girl needs involvement in life. It's being shut out that she can't stand. She's a lot like you were at the same age.'

'Yes, I suppose you're right,' Grace smiled. 'One forgets at times what it felt like to be at the halfway stage.'

Another bright summer morning, Dulcie thought jubilantly, hurrying along to the bathroom to begin her toilette. Standing on the scales behind the door, not pressing down on them too heavily – just in case – her heart lifted to the realization that she had shed another pound in weight by the simple expedient of eating practically nothing the day before, apart from a slice of unbuttered toast, a smidgin of roast lamb and a plateful of boring lettuce leaves, tomatoes and spring onions. No pudding, no potatoes, no bread and butter. Besides which, this new perm had not gone frizzy as the last one had done, and her complexion seemed much clearer.

If only she and Mr Bergmann could be alone together today, without those demanding kids of his making a darned nuisance of themselves, preening and prancing, getting in the way of serious conversation, distracting their father's attention away from herself. But she had, at least, made her presence felt, and the cotton dress she planned to wear today was much prettier than the one she had worn yesterday . . .

'Oh, it's you!' Answering the doorbell, Nan looked askance at Grace, Bob and Kerry, standing on the pavement outside the fancy-goods shop. 'Not before time, I must say. Fanny and I might well have been dead and buried for all you cared.' Turning, she led the way upstairs, an embittered old woman relishing the thought of a continuation of the row which had erupted on Danny's wedding day, determined to have her say. There was no thought of reconciliation in mind.

Fanny was on the landing, arms outstretched in welcome, dressed in her usual clutter of scarves, bangles and beads, hair drooping from her insecurely held bun, the antithesis of her strait-laced sister, all warmth and charm. 'Oh, my dears, how pleased I am to see you,' she murmured. 'Do come into the sitting-room. Tell me, how is Rosa? Why hasn't she come with you? Is she ill?'

'No, Aunt Fanny, she's perfectly well,' Grace reassured her, 'and she sends her love.'

'And can this grown-up young lady really be Kerry? My goodness, how she's grown. She has the Mallory looks, hasn't she, Nan dear?'

Nan snorted. Seriously put out at what she saw as Fanny's treating with the enemy, she snapped, 'Never mind all that nonsense! My memory is longer than yours, apparently. Taking sides the way they have. Not even inviting us to spend Christmas Day with them.'

'Mother, that's not fair,' Grace said, deeply distressed by Nan's uncompromising attitude. 'I wrote in my card that you and Aunt Fanny would be welcome to spend Christmas with us. There was no reply.'

'Leave it, Grace love,' Bob interposed quietly. 'I told you no good would come of this. Let's go.'

'But you've only just arrived!' Fanny clasped her hands distractedly. 'I knew nothing about that invitation. Nan, why didn't you tell me?'

'That's right! Blame me!'

'No-one is blaming you, Nan dear. Please, can't we talk quietly and sensibly? What's to be gained by all this – this aggravation?' Fanny's blue eyes misted with tears. 'Why not let bygones be bygones?'

'Trust you to take the line of least resistance,' Nan exploded, goaded past bearing by her sister's weakness of

226

spirit. 'Well, I have not forgotten, if you have, the shameful events of last December!'

'What "shameful" events?' Bob demanded heatedly. 'Are you referring to the fact that we took pity on poor Aunt Rosa, or the pleasure you derived from the humiliation of your own daughter?'

'How dare you speak to me that way?' Aflame with self-righteous indignation, Nan confronted her son-in-law. 'If anyone's to blame, you are!'

'Oh please, don't! I can't bear it!' Grace covered her face with her hands.

Kerry couldn't stand it either. She had to *do* something, say something. 'What does it matter who's to blame?' she said in her clear young voice. Facing her grandmother, 'Great Aunt Fanny is right. We came because we wanted to see you, because we've missed you. Now I wish we'd stayed away.

'You've made my mother cry, and that's not fair. She's never had a nasty word to say about you, neither has my dad. I'm sorry, Nan, I suppose you think I'm too young to have feelings, that children should be seen and not heard, but you're wrong. Everyone has feelings, but not everyone makes other people miserable and unhappy!'

Turning to Grace, 'Come on, Mum,' she said, 'let's go home. We'll come back another day when Nan is feeling better.'

Fanny saw them downstairs. Nan had gone up to her room without a word following Kerry's outburst – all the more telling because she had said what she had to say calmly and clearly, not losing her temper or raising her voice. On the doorstep, Fanny kissed Grace and Bob, and hugged Kerry as if she could scarcely bear to let go of her.

On their way home, after a long silence, Grace said shakily, 'I saw some nice court shoes in Dolcis' window the other day, Kerry. And I've been thinking, it's about time you started wearing stockings.'

*   *   *

227

Mr Bergmann, Dulcie had discovered, was not German but Austrian, not that she understood the difference. All she needed to know was that he was very rich, the owner of a chain of confectioners' shops and coffee-houses in York, Grimsby, Hull, Darlington and Leeds. These facts had emerged during the time they had spent together on the beach when his children were out of earshot.

He lived on the outskirts of Leeds, he told her, with his mother and his younger brother, Franz. They, and other members of the family, had left Austria before the war. He had been 15 years old at the time. His Christian name was Klaus, and he had met and married an English girl in the summer of 1929, who had died after giving birth to the twins.

It was music to Dulcie's ears when Klaus confessed that she reminded him of his wife, and thanked her for helping to look after the twins so well. 'They have grown very attached to you this past week,' he said thoughtfully, 'which is why I have a proposition to put to you.'

They were seated in Corporation deckchairs at the time, watching the little girls building a sandcastle near the water's edge.

'Oh, really?' Dulcie's heart fluttered like the wings of a caged bird sensing freedom, wishing his proposal had happened in a less conspicuous place, under more romantic circumstances – at a candlelit table for two, for preference, with lobster thermidor and a bottle of champagne.

Of course, Klaus Bergmann was old enough to be her father, but she couldn't care less about that, and the twins were a pain in the neck. Even so, this was the moment she had been waiting for, hoping for, longing for this past week. Now, she wondered, what would she say to him when he asked her to marry him? 'This is so sudden', or 'Do you really mean it?'

He said quietly, 'I realize, of course, that you may have reservations about leaving your home, your family, that you may need time to reach a decision, but it would please me so much, the children also, if you would consider becoming their new nanny.'

228

Chapter Seventeen

Dulcie confronted her parents defiantly. Mr Bergmann had returned to Leeds on Saturday, leaving her to consider his proposition which, despite her feeling of humiliation, she had decided to accept. After all, why not? At least she would be near him, making herself an indispensable part of his life. In any case, she was sick of the Pavilion, ready to try her wings. Common sense told her that an opportunity like this was unlikely to come her way again.

Her mother was knitting bootees for Wilma's baby, her father reading the sports page of the local paper when she dropped her bombshell.

'I thought I'd better tell you,' she said coolly, 'that I'm leaving the Pavilion. I've had the offer of a good job, in Leeds, and I'm taking it!'

Grace's needles sank to her lap. Bob put down his paper. They stared up at her disbelievingly. Bob was the first to speak. 'Oh,' he said calmly, 'and I suppose it never occurred to you to talk it over with us first? To ask our advice?'

'No, not really,' Dulcie retorted. 'I'm old enough to make up my own mind!'

'Very well,' Bob conceded, keeping a tight rein for Grace's sake, realizing how upset she was, 'so what is this job? How did it come about, and what does it entail?'

'If you must know, I'm going to live with a very rich family of confectioners. I'm to be paid double what I earn as a waitress, plus my keep, with plenty of time off into the bargain,' Dulcie announced, head-in-air.

'Doing *what*?' Bob insisted.

'Looking after two six-year-old children!'

'But, Dulcie, you know nothing about children,' Grace broke in perplexedly, close to tears.

'That's not what their father thinks,' Dulcie responded sharply.

'And just who *is* their father?' Bob asked.

'His name is Bergmann. Klaus Bergmann!' Dulcie's veneer was wearing thin, her temper rising at the continued questioning: being made to feel like a naughty child, not an adult in charge of her own destiny.

'And where exactly did you meet this man?'

'At the Pavilion. He often stays there, and I met him every day last week. We went all over in his car. He took me to Filey and Whitby; treated me to lunch and tea. I had a wonderful time.'

'You were alone with him?'

'No, of course not. His children came with us,' Dulcie admitted.

'So that's why the slimming diet, the new dresses,' Grace said slowly, beginning to see the light. 'This holiday of yours with Mr Bermann was pre-arranged?'

'No it wasn't! Oh, trust you to think badly of me,' Dulcie shouted hoarsely, her temper out of control, 'you always have! You and Dad. Well, I'm sick of it. I'm taking the job I've been offered and that's that. This is my life, and I'll live it as I see fit!'

'Now you listen to me, my girl,' Bob said levelly, 'if you think that, you're wrong. I want to know more about this job you've been offered, about the family you're going to work for, make no mistake about that. If your heart is set on leaving home to live in Leeds with a family you know less than nothing about, I shall go with you to find out for myself how the land lies, and that's final.'

'If you do, I'll never speak to you again!' Turning, Dulcie fled upstairs to her room.

'I'd better go after her,' Bob said wearily, 'try to talk some sense into that silly head of hers.'

'No, love. She wouldn't even listen,' Grace advised him quietly. 'You'd be wasting your breath, the mood she's in.' She wiped the tears from her eyes. 'It's no use, Bob. Remember you told me, on Danny's wedding day, that there came a time to let go? Now the time has come to let go of Dulcie. Don't you see? Trying to hold on to her against her will isn't the answer. Dulcie has always been a law unto herself – a misfit. I've never understood why, but I know it's true.' Attempting a smile, she continued, 'One day, God willing, Dulcie will come back to us because she wants to. I'll live for that day.'

Why her son had taken such a dislike to the drawing-room curtains, Lady Hawthorn could not imagine.

'What's wrong with them?' she demanded haughtily.

'Wrong with them? They're practically threadbare, that's all.'

'Don't talk nonsense!' But the seed had been sown. After luncheon, she said off-handedly, 'Perhaps you are right about the drawing-room curtains. I'll go over to Scarborough tomorrow to see Mr Hodnot.'

'I'll come with you.' Ashley smiled engagingly.

'But you don't like shopping.'

'I know, but it will give me something to do, and I'll treat you to lunch at the Royal.'

'If only you would come to a firm decision about your future,' Frances Hawthorn murmured with a sigh. 'You've been hanging about like a ghost ever since you came down from Oxford. I wish I understood why. What is the point or purpose of all this time-wasting? Why don't you tell your father you'll take your rightful place on the board of directors, and have done with it?'

'For the simple reason,' Ashley said equably, 'that I'm not entirely certain of my ground in that direction. All I know about the building trade could be written on the back of a postage stamp.'

'Which goes to prove how foolish it was of you to have studied so hard for a degree in English Literature,' his mother reminded him.

'When I might have studied for a degree in bricklaying, you mean?' he asked, tongue-in-cheek.

Deeply affronted by her son's light-hearted remark,

231

Frances said cuttingly, 'Constructional engineering, at your father's level, has little to do with bricklaying, I assure you. He has built up a small empire here in the north of England, of which you, his son and heir, should feel proud!'

Ashley said apologetically, 'I'm sorry, Mama. Of course I'm proud of Father's achievements; his knighthood. It's just that I find myself marching to a different drum-beat. Quite honestly, I think I'd be less than useful following a star other than my own.'

'And what of all this?' she demanded, indicating the house and its contents. 'It will be yours one day, when your father and I are dead and gone.' She continued emotionally, 'Our dearest wish is to see you safely married to some nice, suitable young woman, living here in perpetuity with your wife and children.'

'I'll think about it,' he promised, wondering if his mother would consider a shop assistant as suitable. The girl he had chosen as his future wife was far too young, as yet, to be swept into a serious relationship, the reason why he had, so far, kept well away from her. It was a matter of pride not to pester the poor girl unduly, but he could, at least, make her aware of his presence.

Ashley thought she was totally enchanting. He loved everything about her, the way she moved gracefully about the shop, doing the dusting as his mother and Mr Hodnot went into a huddle over the pattern books; the pin neatness of her appearance in the plain grey skirt and white cotton blouse she was wearing, her hair caught back from her heart-shaped face with a black velvet ribbon, the youthful curve of her cheeks brushed with incredibly long black lashes at her downward glance, and she did seem to be looking down a great deal, as if modesty prevented her meeting his eyes.

Dusting as if her life depended on it, remembering her first reprimand, Mr Hodnot would probably give her the bullet if she so much as glanced at Lady Hawthorn's son, Kerry thought nervously, wishing he would stop staring at her and go away. She loved her job, and didn't want to lose it, breathed a sign of relief when the ordeal was over, when Lady Hawthorn, her son in tow, breezed out of the shop with a graciously murmured, 'Good day, Mr Hodnot. I'll expect you on Monday morning, then, to take the measurements?'

'That was most satisfactory.' Hodnot rubbed his hands together. 'Her ladyship has decided to have loose covers as well as curtains.'

A pleasant surprise lay in store for Kerry when the order was ready, even at the sacrifice of her half-day off. It had long been Hodnot's custom to take one of the girls from the sewing room as his assistant in hanging curtains and fitting loose covers, depending on the scope of the job in hand, to steady the step-ladder and hand him the tools of the trade, also to take the weight of long, heavily lined curtains from the point of contact with the rails and runners at pelmet level.

His usual helper, Mrs Frazer, had left recently to have a baby, and so he had invited Kerry to take her place. The girl had come on by leaps and bounds recently, due, no doubt, to her dancing lessons and the fact that she had graduated from flat-heeled shoes and white socks to higher heels and stockings. Also, her entire demeanour had changed subtly. In short, she was growing up in a most delightful way, Hodnot decided, thinking in terms of offering her promotion to the sewing room in due course, if the idea appealed to her, with a view to learning every aspect of the business.

The time would come when he would need a fully trained personal assistant, *au fait* with lampshade making, measuring and cutting out, as well as stock control. Someone capable of handling clients and travellers alike with charm and tact in time to come. Kerry would fill that role admirably, he considered, when she was eighteen or so. Not that he was thinking in terms of retirement. Far from it. An astute businessman, he was simply keeping a weather eye on the future.

Kerry and her employer set off for Glebe House that

Wednesday afternoon in July, in Mr Hodnot's Austin, on the back seat of which he had fussily placed Lady Hawthorn's new drawing-room curtains and loose covers to make absolutely certain they would arrive in pristine condition, immaculate and uncreased. Seated beside him as he drove from Scarborough to Malton, Kerry gazed in wonderment at the softly unfolding countryside, thrilling to the sight of lush green meadows, grazing cattle, tall trees heavy with summer foliage, little grey churches along the way. Cottage gardens were ablaze with flowers: roses, delphiniums, larkspur. She had travelled in taxis and on buses before, but this was her first experience of travel in a privately owned car, and she was loving every moment of the brand new adventure.

The sight of Glebe House in all its red-brick Victorian splendour of tall chimneys, bay windows, and imposing entrance, standing on a knoll amid an acre or so of sloping grassland and with stately elm trees bordering the curving drive to the front door, brought her to earth with a bump. It was so big, so – ugly and pretentious. But then, so was its owner, Lady Hawthorn. Kerry's heart sank to her Dolcis court shoes as Mr Hodnot applied the brake, opened the car door, and hurried up the front steps to ring the bell. But she was here to do a job of work, she told herself severely, not to criticize the house or its chatelaine.

Stepping across the threshold in the wake of her employer, holding up the curtains like a bridal train, trailing behind him to the drawing-room, Kerry glanced nervously about her, taking in the splendour of the antique furniture surrounding her, the oil-paintings on the walls, the jardinières of skilfully arranged summer flowers, the built-in showcases displaying her ladyship's collection of fine china dinner services and Meissen figurines.

She was holding onto the step-ladder with all her might as Mr Hodnot mounted it to take down the old curtains, when Lady Hawthorn swanned into the room to witness the proceedings.

'Ah, your ladyship. Good day to you. The servant told me

to make a start.' The ladder swayed slightly as Hodnot turned to converse with madam.

'You'd better let me give you a hand with those steps.' Ashley, who had followed his mother into the room, moved forward swiftly to help steady the ladder. Kerry blushed to the roots of her hair. 'There's no need, thank you, I can manage.'

Hodnot said, 'This is my assistant, Miss Kingsley.'

'Quite so,' Lady Hawthorn said dismissively, turning her attention to the matter in hand. 'Now, Mr Hodnot, you will take care not to . . .'

Kerry missed the drift of the conversation as Ashley murmured, *sotto-voce*, 'I've been longing to meet you, Miss Kingsley.'

'Have you?' Her blush deepened. She didn't know what else to say to him except, 'There's no need, really . . .' She meant his holding the step-ladder. 'Please! Mr Hodnot will be cross with me.'

'Of course. I understand.' The last thing he wanted was to embarrass the girl. But the expression of relief on her flower-petal face, as he moved away from the ladder, convinced him that he had made a favourable impression on her. Hopefully a lasting impression to stand him in good stead at their future meetings, because, quite simply, they *would* meet again, and quite soon, he decided.

Tears streamed down Kerry's cheeks when she knew that Dulcie was going away from her, leaving home to live with strangers. Dulcie could be haughty, difficult, even hostile at times, but she couldn't bear the thought of losing her. 'Oh please, Dulcie, don't go,' she begged her, but to no avail.

'Anyone would think I was going to the moon,' Dulcie said coolly, packing her suitcase. Then, irritably, 'Oh, for heaven's sake, Kerry, stop snivelling. It isn't the end of the world.'

But it was, so far as Kerry was concerned. Another bewildering change in the pattern of the old way of life she had known and loved, so that nothing seemed secure and stable any more, herself least of all.

'I thought you were happy at the Pavilion,' she said wistfully.

'You thought wrong, then! I hated being ordered about as if I was a servant.'

'But you were,' Kerry said heedlessly, speaking the truth as she saw it. 'What's wrong with that? We all have to do as we're told when it comes to earning a living.'

'You're weak-kneed, that's your trouble,' Dulcie said scornfully. 'You have no ambition. You'll just stay here in Scarborough and rot.' Closing the lid of the suitcase, 'You think you are different, better than most, but you're wrong!'

'*Dulcie!*' Kerry stared at her sister disbelievingly. 'How could you say such a thing?'

'Because it's the truth. You've been spoilt rotten all the days of your life. But just you wait and see. You'll end up marrying some chinless wonder with a nice steady job, living in a two-up, two-down house in a back street, with a couple of bawling kids to take care of! What price then all your fancy, romantic ideas? Look at Danny, if you don't believe me. He had fancy ideas, too, and where did they get *him*?'

Weak-kneed? Lacking ambition? A snob? Spoilt rotten? Was she really all those things Kerry wondered. Too upset to reply, she left the room abruptly, sped downstairs to the hall, opened the front door and ran out of the house, crying as if her heart would break. Deeply distressed and in need of solitude, she came to the broad meadow overlooking the sea, in which the authoress Anne Brontë lay buried. As she stood there, gazing out to sea, the hardest thing of all to bear was the knowledge that Dulcie had never really loved her.

Evening shadows had deepened to a soft, translucent twilight when she returned home.

'Kerry, love, where on earth have you been?' Grace asked with concern when she entered the dining-room. 'Supper's nearly over. I put your plate in the oven to keep hot.'

'Thanks, Mum. I've been for a walk, that's all. Sorry I'm late.'

236

'Is anything the matter?'

Glancing at Dulcie across the table, 'No,' Kerry said quietly, 'I just wanted to look at the sea – and the stars.'

'That's my girl!' Jimmy grinned approvingly. 'As Keats had it: "Magic casements, opening on the foam of" – I forget the rest.'

Kerry quoted softly, ' "Charmed magic casements, opening on the foam of perilous seas, in faery lands forlorn." '

Rising quickly to her feet, 'I don't want any pudding,' Dulcie announced, 'I'm going up to my room to finish packing.'

Grace and Bob exchanged glances. Their wayward elder daughter had looked daggers when her father said he would go to Leeds with her to see her settled.

And what had Dulcie said to upset Kerry? Something had gone wrong between the pair of them, this much was obvious, hence the stricken look on Kerry's face. Despite her concern for Dulcie's welfare, Grace could not help thinking that life would be less stressful without her. Poor Dulcie had always been her own worst enemy in holding at bay the love of her family, her own in particular. Even so, she must make an attempt at reconciliation.

The girl was in bed when Grace went up to her room, feigning sleep. 'Dulcie,' Grace said quietly. No response. Looking down, she saw, not the face of a wilful young woman, but that of a beloved child whom she had lost somewhere along the way. Now the time had come to let the girl make her own way in life. Smoothing the pillows, bending down to kiss her forehead, 'Good night, my love,' Grace whispered, 'God bless you.'

Leaving the room, she closed the door quietly behind her.

Kerry went up to Jimmy's room after supper, in need of sanctuary.

'What's up, kiddo?' He spoke light-heartedly. 'Has Dulcie said something to upset you?'

'Am I really spoilt rotten?' she faltered.

'That damned lass wants her neck wringing,' Jimmy said

angrily. 'Just as well she's off to Leeds first thing in the morning, otherwise I'd give her a piece of my mind. What else did she say?'

'That I'd end up married to a chinless wonder with a couple of bawling kids to take care of.' Kerry felt in her pocket for a hanky. 'It was the "chinless wonder" bit that got me. Why "chinless"?'

'Typical,' Jimmy muttered savagely, pacing the room. 'Trust Dulcie to put the boot in. I've never understood what's wrong with that lass. In any case,' he added grimly, 'she hasn't got her own cake baked yet! I wouldn't mind betting she'll come down to earth with a wallop one of these days when she finds herself lumbered with a couple of bawling kids to look after, and Dulcie knows as much about children as I know about deep-sea fishing!' He snorted derisively, 'She'll end up wishing she'd stuck to a job she knows summat about.'

'I'll miss her,' Kerry said simply. 'With Danny gone and now Dulcie, there'll only be the two of us left at home.'

'Yeah, well,' Jimmy conceded, 'but Danny's only a stone's throw away, and Leeds isn't that far off. Herbie lives there, remember, and he's always popping up out of the blue.' He added, consolingly, 'Try to look on the bright side. At least Dulcie will have a friend in the wicked city.'

Kerry sighed deeply. 'Dulcie doesn't like Herbie,' she said wistfully, 'she told me so. She thinks he's common, a sponger. She hasn't a good word to say for him.'

'The truth is, Dulcie hasn't a good word to say about anyone,' Jimmy responded darkly, 'not even her own family.'

The Bergmann residence certainly looked imposing, Bob reckoned, as the taxi swung between the gateposts and drew up at the main entrance, but one could not tell a book from its cover. He wanted to know exactly what his daughter's duties entailed, to see for himself her future accommodation, to speak personally to this Klaus Bergmann who had lured Dulcie away from home to act as nursemaid to his children.

He was, of course, prejudiced. He knew that. Haunted by his memories of trench warfare, he mistrusted foreigners in general, Germans in particular. And if he suspected, for one moment, that all was not as it seemed on the surface, he would not hesitate to bundle his recalcitrant daughter on the next train to Scarborough, whether she liked it or not.

An elderly, po-faced English butler answered the door. 'Frau Bergmann and Mr Klaus are in the drawing-room,' he said stiffly, leading the way.

Stiffness was the operative word, Bob thought, entering the drawing-room. Stiffness allied to coldness. He shivered slightly despite the warmth of the world outside, bathed in July sunshine. In this magnificently furnished room, the blinds were half lowered to protect the fading influence of strong sunlight on the velvet-covered armchairs and sofa grouped about the fireplace, the many items of heavyweight antique furniture lining the walls. Above all, one felt, to shade the features of Frau Bergmann sitting upright in a wing chair with its back to the light.

Klaus Bergmann rose quickly to his feet when Dulcie and her escort were shown into the room. 'This is my father,' she muttered ungraciously.

Shaking hands, 'Of course. How kind of you to come. May I introduce you to my mother? Mama, this is the young lady I've engaged as the children's new nursemaid, and her father, Mr Kingsley.'

The old woman in the wing chair inclined her head in acknowledgement, but did not speak. Bob said easily, 'I hope I'm not intruding?'

Bergmann smiled. 'Of course not. Naturally you wished to see your daughter settled in her new surroundings. Please, sit down.' He indicated the sofa. 'I understand your concern. I, too, am a father.'

'Thank you.' Bob seated himself next to Dulcie. 'This is the first time she has been away from home, you see. And she *is* very young.' The man must be about his own age, Bob reckoned, perhaps a little older. He was certainly good looking, obviously wealthy and successful, a man of the world, possessed of a certain patina and polish common to rich men the world over. Despite the greyness of his hair, his eyebrows, dark in colour, were boldly etched above his curiously clear grey-blue eyes. In his case, Bob thought, age had not withered nor the years condemned. Little wonder, he realized, with a sinking of the heart, that Dulcie had walked in where angels feared to tread. Hadn't she the sense she was born with? Apparently not. Glancing sideways, he saw that she was gaping at Bergmann, open-mouthed with admiration. At least he hoped it was just admiration, nothing more serious than that.

Frau Bergmann broke the silence unexpectedly. In a clear, ringing voice, she said, 'I imagine, Mr Kingsley, you came here, uninvited, to satisfy your curiosity? No doubt you fought in the war? Well, we are Austrian, not German! Confectioners, not warmongers. As for your daughter, nurse-maids are ten a penny. I suggest you take her back home with you, where she belongs.'

The twins burst into the room at that moment. Making a beeline for Dulcie, tugging at her hands, they begged her to play games with them upstairs in the nursery.

'Enough, children!' Bergmann spoke to them severely. 'Go into the garden and play by yourselves for a while. Such deplorable manners.'

When they had gone, 'Come on Dulcie,' Bob said, getting up, 'we're wasting time here. We'd best be getting back to the station.' He nodded briefly to the old woman in the wing chair.

In the hall, 'I beg you to reconsider, Mr Kingsley,' Klaus said, 'to remember that my mother is a very old lady whose roots are deeply buried in the past, who hated the Germans as much as you must have done during the war. But you saw for yourself how fond my children are of your daughter.'

'Well, yes,' Bob admitted.

'And they will be starting school in September,' Bergmann went on, 'a kindergarten, of course, within walking distance of the house.'

'I see. So why a nursemaid?'

240

'If you would care to come up with me to the nursery suite on the top floor, I could possibly explain the situation more clearly to you there,' Klaus said, leading the way.

Following in their wake, seething beneath her hair, damn it all, Dulcie thought bitterly, this was *her* future at stake, and so far no-one had consulted her, had asked her a single question about the way *she* felt. Nothing at all to do with her father or that fat old bitch in the drawing-room.

Opening the door of the nursery suite, Bergmann said, 'As you can see, it's an entirely self-contained unit comprising a nicely furnished sitting-room, a kitchen and two bedrooms. And your daughter's duties would not be too arduous, I assure you.'

'What exactly do you mean by "not too arduous"?' Bob demurred.

'Simply a little plain cooking. Nursery fare, you understand? Washing and ironing the children's clothes, making sure that they receive a sufficient amount of exercise and fresh air; putting them to bed early.' He continued urbanely, 'She would naturally be allowed an adequate amount of time off to follow her own pursuits. On Saturday and Sunday evenings, for example, the children are allowed to join the family in the drawing-room, after nursery tea.'

'You wouldn't see much of them otherwise, I suppose?' Bob remarked, feeling sorry for the poor little devils.

'Unfortunately not,' Bergmann conceded, 'which is why I need someone reliable to look after them during my absence on various trips connected with the running of my business concerns both here and abroad. That was the reason I chose your daughter as their companion. You understand, Mr Kingsley?'

Mr Kingsley understood only too well. He said, 'In which case it's up to Dulcie to decide.' Frankly, he couldn't begin to envisage his temperamental elder daughter as a nursemaid, cooking, washing and ironing, incarcerated here in the nursery suite of a posh house in Leeds with a couple of demanding kids as her sole companions, but if this was what Dulcie wanted, what right had he to stand in her way?

Champing at the bit, Dulcie wished that her father would simply go away. So far he had done all the talking. She had not uttered a word – as if she had been struck dumb or stupid. As if she were a child incapable of making an entry into a new way of life. Had it not been for her father's interference, she thought, when he had gone, that old cow downstairs would not have uttered the words 'Nursemaids are ten a penny'. Well, she'd show the old cow that she was not some namby-pamby kid but a force to be reckoned with. Sooner or later, her day would come. She looked forward to that day. Oh God, how much she looked forward to that day.

Chapter Eighteen

Red leather cracked smartly against Danny's cricket bat. The ball lofted skyward. One breathless moment as a member of the opposing team hovered for the catch, then all was well. The ball flew unimpeded to the boundary. Danny raised his bat in acknowledgement of the applause from the spectators.

'Danny, you were marvellous!' Meg Jenkins linked arms with him as they strolled away from the ground to the bus-stop, her face aglow; her penny-gold hair was tangled with the sunlight of a perfect summer afternoon, her breasts taut against the bodice of the blue cotton dress she was wearing.

She resembled, Danny thought, a sun-warmed peach ripe for the plucking and wondered why he had not realized, at the time of their brief flirtation two years ago, how lovely, how desirable she was. He had not been in love with her then, but he was now. Head over heels in love with her. She with him.

The beginning of this new romance had happened that day in May when they had bumped into each other in St Nicholas Street. Thereafter, they had taken to walking through the gardens to the Foreshore together, taking care to bypass Princess Street in case Wilma happened to be looking out of the window.

Conscience-stricken at the time, 'This isn't right, Danny,' Meg told him.

'Why? We're doing nothing wrong!'

'Then why are we hiding?'

'We're not!'

'Oh, come off it, love. We are, and you know it.'

'Only because Wilma might put two and two together and

come up with the wrong answer,' he'd said desperately, 'the state she's in!'

'Pregnant, you mean? Expecting your child?'

'Well, yes, but it isn't as simple and clear-cut as that. Meg, I need someone to talk to. I'll go off my head otherwise.'

'Sorry, Danny, nothing doing. You're a married man now. You have no right to—'

'*Please*, Meg! Say you'll meet me tonight on the Foreshore, near the Penny Tram. I'll be there about eight. Don't let me down. I need you.'

Temptation proved too strong to resist. Danny needed her, and warm-hearted Meg must go to him. Old feelings could not be put aside so easily, she had discovered. The day he was married, she had gone to work red-eyed with crying, pretending she had a cold, her mind in a turmoil as she imagined the bride and groom exchanging vows, gazing into each other's eyes, setting off on their honeymoon together amid swirls of confetti. Lying in bed that night, she had imagined them lying together in each other's arms, making love, wishing that she was the one in his arms.

Hardest of all to bear was the thought that he now belonged irrevocably to someone else. Brought up to believe in the sanctity of marriage, the last thing she wanted was to come between husband and wife, and yet she was powerless to deny his cry for help. And so, telling her parents she was going out for a breath of fresh air, she had hurried along the Foreshore to the tramway. She had known, by her response to the expression of relief in his eyes, the way he held out his hands to her, that she still loved him, and always would.

Walking along the sands together near the water's edge, and watching the twilight deepening over the sea, the emergence of the first stars in an aquamarine sky, she listened in complete silence as he told her, haltingly, emotionally, that his marriage was a sham, and why. 'The truth is,' he ended bitterly, 'I married the wrong girl, and I don't know what the hell to do about it.'

Breaking her silence as they turned and walked back the

way they had come, Meg said quietly, compassionately, 'There's nothing you *can* do about it now, Danny. You married for better or for worse, remember? As I see it, you owe it to Wilma to stand by her – especially now that she is carrying your child.'

'A child she never wanted in the first place,' he reminded her.

'Even so, Danny, you are the child's father! I'm sorry, but what more can I possibly say?'

'Nothing, I suppose,' he murmured, close to tears. 'You are quite right, of course. It's just that I haven't the strength to face this alone, the reason why I needed to see you tonight, to talk to you . . . I'm sorry Meg, but you see, I wish it was you I'd married, not Wilma.'

'Are you out of your mind?' She stared at him disbelievingly. 'What kind of a girl do you take me for?' She was deeply angry. 'You made it clear enough two summers ago that it wasn't me you wanted. Now here you are saying the exact opposite. What a waste of breath!' Her anger had to do with frustration, her own vulnerability in face of this bewildering turn of events, uncertainty how to handle the situation. 'I shouldn't have come,' she said sharply, 'it wasn't fair of you to ask me.'

'I know. I'm sorry. It's just that I . . . Oh, what's the use?'

It was almost dark now. The sand felt cold beneath their feet. Shore lights blossomed against the dusk. Meg's anger faded. Memories of other summer nights invaded her mind: dancing at the Olympia Ballroom, Danny's arm about her waist; walking with him past the Futurist cinema, the ice-cream parlours and fish-and-chip restaurants; good night kisses on the doorstep of her home in Paradise . . . A Paradise Lost so far as she was concerned, when she realized that Danny was not in love with her. And now . . .

Clasping his arm as they walked up a slipway to the Foreshore, she said quietly, 'If you need a friend, you can count on me. But that's all I can ever be to you, just a friend. You understand?'

'Yes, of course.' But they were standing far too close,

their hearts beating much too fast. Next thing she knew, his arms were about her, his lips were on hers, and there she was, lost in the magic of his embrace.

Meg had never meant it to happen, this resurrection of an old romance – new in the sense that she and Danny were much closer than they had ever been before, because he needed her now as he had never done before. Even so, she had felt conscience-stricken at first at their secret meetings, whenever they could snatch a blissful hour or so together without creating undue suspicion in the minds of her parents or Danny's wife.

Truth to tell, she felt sorry for the lass, although they had never met. Possibly what Danny had told her, that he and Wilma occupied separate bedrooms, that they had not slept together, in the true sense of the word, since their honeymoon débâcle, was the gospel truth, but there were two sides to every question and, despite her own new-found happiness in Danny's company, she could not help wondering what Wilma's reaction would be if she knew that she, Meg, had begun going with him to country cricket matches on Sunday afternoons; sitting on the sidelines, to all intents and purposes an innocent spectator. In reality, much more than that, a woman deeply in love with the captain of the Scoresby team.

The team travelled by charabanc to the various country venues, accompanied by wives or lady friends, a source of embarrassment for Meg. Danny's team-mates, who had never set eyes on Wilma, called her Mrs Kingsley. When word got around that she was not his wife, she was given the cold shoulder by the other women.

Danny told her not to worry.

'But what if Wilma finds out?'

'So what if she does?'

'Danny, that's cruel.'

He failed to catch the drift of her argument. 'Cruel? In what way is it cruel? Wilma hates cricket. You enjoy it.'

'For heaven's sake, Danny, it's not cricket I'm on about!'

'Isn't it? I thought it was.'

Was he being deliberately obtuse, or didn't he care if Wilma found out about their friendship?

He said with a sigh, 'All right, love, you win. If it will set your mind at rest I'll tell Wilma about us.'

'No, Danny. You mustn't do that. Not in her condition.'

'Then what exactly do you want me to do? You can't have it both ways.'

'I know,' Meg said bleakly, 'which is why I can't go on seeing you. I'm sorry, Danny, but I *can't*!'

They were on the beach at the time, against a backdrop of indigo sea edged with rippling white wavelets washing in on the sand, the coloured lights of the Foreshore reflected in the deep water of the South Bay.

'You don't mean that?' he said hoarsely. Clasping her hands, 'I love you, Meg, and you love me. That's true, isn't it?'

'You know it is, but there's no future for us, my darling. As things stand, we haven't done anything wrong. You haven't been physically unfaithful to Wilma. But how long will that last if we go on seeing each other, feeling the way we do?' Pulling away from him, she ran up a slipway to the promenade. Blinded with tears, she bumped into people unseeingly, knowing that Danny was close behind her, wanting desperately to get home before he caught up with her.

Breathless, panting with exertion, she ran into the house and slammed the door. Standing with her back to it, she heard him calling to her, 'Please, Meg. We can't leave things like this. For God's sake, Meg, open the door!'

'No, Danny. Go away and leave me alone.' Stumbling upstairs to her room, she flung herself on the bed, crying as if her heart would break.

Turning away, Danny walked unsteadily towards the Golden Ball pub on the Foreshore where he drank, in quick succession, three double whiskies, his cricketing triumph forgotten – that proud moment when he had belted the ball to the boundary in the final over.

At nine o'clock he left the pub to walk even more unsteadily towards Princess Street. More than a little drunk, he remembered his stag night with his pals. He had been a happy man that night, looking forward to his honeymoon. Now all his hopes and dreams had ended in despair. Just as long as Wilma had gone to bed early, he thought. He couldn't stand another row, not tonight.

Opening the front door, stepping into the parlour, he saw, with a sick feeling in the pit of his stomach, that Wilma had company. His parents, with Kerry and Jimmy, were seated about the room, drinking the tea she had made for them.

'Hello, son,' Bob said warmly, 'we'd almost given up hope of seeing you.'

Trying hard not to slur his words, to appear normal, smiling foolishly, he said slowly and carefully, 'Well, what a surprise.' Walking forward was a different matter entirely, and so he stood, framed in the doorway, not daring to move lest he fell flat on his face.

Bob and Grace exchanged worried glances, Kerry put down her cup of tea, untasted, knowing that something was wrong with Danny, but what? Then Jimmy, rising easily from his chair near the fireplace, took charge of the situation. 'Come on, old sport,' he said cheerfully, grasping his brother firmly by the elbow, 'bed's the best place for you, my lad!'

After Jimmy had guided Danny up the narrow stairs to his bed in the box-room, Wilma, now seven months pregnant and bearing no resemblance whatever to the band-box-neat, self-contained young woman who had picked over the lettuce leaves last spring, cried shrilly, 'Well, I hope you're satisfied! Now you've seen for yourselves what I have to put up with from your precious son!' Rounding fiercely on his parents, 'The lot of you, clear out of my house. I didn't invite you here – and you can take that with you!' She pointed a shaking finger at the parcel of baby clothes Grace had brought for her.

Kerry felt stunned, with no clear idea of what was happening. 'Is Danny poorly?' she faltered as her mother and father stood up.

'Ha, that's rich!' Wilma began to laugh hysterically. 'Poorly? No, Miss Prim and Proper, Danny isn't poorly, he's—'

'That's enough, Wilma!' Grace's cool, clear tone of voice silenced the outburst. The girl stared at her as if she had received a slap on the face, then burst into tears. Grace continued calmly, 'And you can stop that, too. Whether you like it or not, you have the baby to think of now.'

'Oh yes,' Wilma flung back at her defiantly, 'and suppose you tell that to the father?'

'You needn't worry on that score,' Bob said grimly, 'he'll hear from me later. On that you may depend.'

Jimmy came downstairs at that moment. 'I've put him to bed,' he said. 'He'll be OK in the morning.'

'We're leaving now, son,' Bob told him. Kerry had risen to her feet. Her face was chalk-white, lips trembling. Placing a comforting arm about her shoulders, Bob said, 'Come on, love, there's nothing for you to worry about.'

But there *was*. It was something she didn't understand, to do with growing up, something veiled and unpleasant, beyond her power of comprehension.

Walking up Paradise to the house on the hill, there was more to growing up than wearing stockings, Kerry realized. Once more came the feeling that her safe, secure world of childhood was crumbling beneath her feet like dust.

Leaving the shop for her dinner break, Kerry walked along St Nicholas Street to the gardens to eat the sandwiches her mother had put up for her early that morning.

She had just settled herself on a seat overlooking the sea and bitten into a sandwich when Ashley Hawthorn walked jauntily along the path towards her. 'Mind if I join you?' he asked brightly.

Too young to administer a verbal *coup de grâce*, too innocent to see that this seemingly chance meeting had been carefully planned, 'No,' Kerry said politely. 'Would you like a sandwich?'

'I have a much better idea,' Ashley said engagingly. 'I'll treat you to lunch at the Royal Hotel.'

'No thanks, I'm quite all right where I am,' she replied stiffly, 'but you go, if you want to.'

Sitting down on the seat beside her, 'I'm sorry,' he said, 'I just didn't want to eat your food.'

'Oh, that's OK,' she said innocently, 'Mum always makes me more sandwiches than I can manage. I usually feed the leftovers to the birds.' She added quickly, 'Not that I *tell* her, I wouldn't want to hurt her feelings.'

'What a kind girl you are,' he said quietly, sincerely. Then, hesitantly, 'I meant what I said the other day, you know, when you came with Mr Hodnot to hang the drawing-room curtains. You see, I was on the Spa the day of the Rose Queen ceremony. I saw you dance. I threw you a rose.'

'You *did*?' Colouring to the roots of her hair, she dare not confess that she had picked up that rose afterwards, that it now lay pressed within the pages of *Palgrave's Golden Treasury*.

'You dance beautifully,' he said softly, thinking how pretty she was, how desirable, how tender, how sweet, how young, albeit with a mind of her own. He felt pleased, deep down, that she had not accepted his luncheon invitation as most other girls of his acquaintance would have done, knowing he was financially well-heeled, eager to make inroads on a four-course meal at his expense. But this girl was different, preferring a packet full of home-made ham sandwiches to a blow-out meal at one of the most prestigious hotels in town.

'Well, do you want a sandwich or not?' she asked him, wishing he would stop staring at her, remembering Mr Hodnot's words of warning: 'Sir Charles and Lady Hawthorn are rich people. They live in a different world from us.'

Taking a sandwich, 'Won't you tell me your Christian name?' Ashley begged her.

'It's Kerry,' she replied, getting up, brushing the crumbs from her skirt. 'Now, if you'll excuse me, I must go back to work.'

'So soon? But I haven't finished my sandwich!' With his most charming smile, 'In any case, I'm sure that Mr Hodnot would forgive your being a few minutes late if you told him it was my fault.'

'No, he wouldn't! Likely as not, he'd give me the sack,' Kerry blurted, in a fluster.

Ashley stood up, holding his sandwich. Utterly bewildered, 'But *why*?' he asked in amazement. 'What has he got against me, for heaven's sake?'

'Nothing that I know of,' Kerry said miserably, unable to cope with the situation, 'except that your mother is a customer of his, and . . . '

Light dawned. 'Oh, I get it,' Ashley said quietly, deeply aware of Kerry's dilemma, loving her youth and innocence, her lack of sophistication. 'In that case, of course you must go now.' He added, in all humility, 'Thank you for sharing your lunch with me. Will you tell your mother it's the nicest ham sandwich I've ever tasted?'

Kerry smiled at him, thinking how nice he was, and how handsome. Remembering the rose, brown and scentless now, pressed in the pages of Palgrave, she said shyly, 'You'd best finish eating it then, hadn't you?'

'Before you go, please may I see you again tomorrow? Same time, same place?' He put his question light-heartedly. 'You see, I'm on holiday at the moment. That is, I've come down from Oxford for good, and I'm at a bit of a loose end – trying to decide what to do next. It would help to talk about it to someone outside the family. What I mean is, from an unbiased viewpoint. It would help me a great deal.'

'You mean – *me*?' Kerry looked as doubtful as she felt. She knew about Oxford, the City of Dreaming Spires, that only clever people went to college there. How could she, a poorly educated girl possibly advise an Oxford graduate? It didn't make sense. On the other hand, she couldn't help liking Ashley Hawthorn despite his Oxford accent, expensive clothes, and his rich family background so far removed from her own simple lifestyle. Not that she would trade places with him for all the tea in China. She had a home, all he had was a posh house filled with antique furniture and oil-paintings.

Feeling suddenly sorry for him and remembering the rose, 'Oh, all right then,' she said reluctantly, moving away from him, 'unless it's raining.'

Watching her go, Ashley prayed for a fine day tomorrow, as he had seldom prayed for anything in his life before – except the love of his parents. Just – love.

The Kingsley family had just finished supper, Grace was in the kitchen starting the washing up, Bob in the back room reading the evening paper. Rosa and Jimmy were upstairs in their rooms when the doorbell rang.

'I'll answer it,' Kerry said, putting down her tea-towel, since her mother's hands were covered in soapsuds.

'If it's the Salvation Army man come to collect his donation,' Grace called after her, 'the money's in an envelope on the hall table.'

But it wasn't the Salvation Army man. Opening the door, Kerry came face to face with Wilma's parents, grim-faced, unsmiling.

'We've come to see your mother and father,' Mrs Burton announced, pushing past Kerry, 'so you'd best tell them we're here, and we won't take no for an answer!'

Grace appeared in the hall, drying her hands. 'Go up to your room, Kerry,' she said quietly. Facing the Burtons, 'Come through to the back room,' she continued levelly, leading the way and closing the door firmly behind them when they had entered.

'Well, this is a fine kettle of fish, I must say!' Mrs Burton declared angrily, glaring at Bob, who had risen hastily to his feet at the Burtons' intrusion into his special sanctuary, scattering the pages of his newspaper as he did so. 'But you needn't think you'll get away with it. No sir! If you don't make that misbegotten son of yours toe the line, then *we* will. Ain't that so, Arthur?'

The male Burton nodded his assent, then, 'Too true,'

he bellowed, 'he wants locking up, the way he's treated our lass!'

'Be quiet, Arthur! Let me do the talking,' his wife advised him.

Grace entered the arena. Standing tall and proud, she said, 'In case you've forgotten, Danny and Wilma married for better or for worse. There have been faults on both sides, I dare say.'

'If you are in – intimidating that we shouldn't interfere,' Mabel spat forth in high dudgeon, 'a bit like the pot calling the kettle black, ain't it? Oh yes,' with an almighty sniff, 'Wilma told me how you'd stuck your noses in where they weren't wanted on Sunday night, without so much as a by your leave. And that's not *all* she told me. Well, all I can say is, you saw with your own eyes, the state your son was in when he came home. So don't come the high and mighty with me, Grace Kingsley. Drunk, he was! So drunk he had to be put to bed by his brother. And you dare stand there and tell me there have been faults on both sides? Well, that's a damned lie, and you know it.

'My poor little girl married that swine of a man in good faith, him having a good job in the Town Hall and all. And what did he do? Got her in the family way before they'd even begun saving for a place of their own. Now the poor kid's alone most of the time while he's off playing cricket – and not just cricket, so I've heard. Playing fast and loose with another woman, more like.'

Deeply angry, eyes flashing fire, 'That "swine of a man" as you call him, happens to be my son! As for Wilma's baby, why the sense of outrage? Unless you knew all along that the last thing Wilma wanted was motherhood. But you *did* know, didn't you? All Wilma wanted was a wedding ring on her finger and a husband with a good steady job. In short, she wanted my son. What she did not want, at any price, was to have a child by him!' Grace reminded her.

'Now you listen to me, my lady—' Mabel burst forth.

'No! You listen to me for a change, Mrs Burton!' Standing her ground, 'The truth of the matter is, my son was rushed into marriage by yourself and Wilma. Whose idea was that winter wedding? Certainly not Danny's. Now here you are, bleating because they hadn't saved up enough money for a home of their own. But you didn't really want that either, did you? You wanted Wilma at home with you, my son as a paying lodger beneath your roof.'

'If you've quite finished,' Mabel began.

'*Finished?* I've scarcely started!' In a voice as clear and cold as ice crystals, Grace continued, 'From my point of view, marriage is a matter of give and take. You referred to my son's return to cricket – a game he has always loved – which he gave up to please your daughter.'

Seizing the opportunity, 'Oh, gave it up, did he?' Mabel smirked. 'Can't say I'd noticed! Seems to me he took it up again in a hurry when he knew the fix my poor little girl was in!'

'And why do you suppose he did that?' Grace continued relentlessly.

'You tell me.'

'Very well then, I will. Because Danny wanted a wife, not a keeper. Because he's a man, not a cipher. Ask yourself this question, Mrs Burton, how did you imagine any full-blooded young man would react to finding himself trapped in a marriage of convenience?

'And if listening to gossip, as I'm sure you do – if what you say about Danny having turned to another woman for sympathy and understanding is true – perhaps the time has come for you and your daughter to ask yourselves why.'

'Now you listen to me,' Mabel reiterated defensively, but Grace held the floor space between them.

'Just one thing more,' she said coldly. 'As I recall, you came here tonight complaining bitterly that my husband and I had "stuck our noses in where they weren't wanted, without so much as a by your leave". The same applies to you and your husband, wouldn't you say? Now I want you to go. My husband will show you out.'

'You haven't heard the last of this, my lady!' Mabel

Burton flung back at her over her shoulder. 'Oh, come *on*, Arthur. A fat lot of help you were!'

Grace heard the closing of the front door as one in a dream. When Bob returned, she burst into tears.

Taking her in his arms, understanding what it had cost her to confront the awesome and awful Mabel Burton, 'I'm so proud of you, my love,' he murmured against her hair. 'You were magnificent!' Smiling tenderly, he handed her a clean hanky. 'Come on now, blow your nose, dry your eyes, and sit down. I'll put the kettle on. What you need is a strong cup of tea!'

In the kitchen, waiting for the kettle to boil, Bob remembered how he and Grace had struggled together to create this home for their children, every item of which had been bought and paid for, by one means or another, because of their belief in family life.

First had come the Clothing Club cards, sixpence a week contributions to ensure that the kids, come Christmas, would have toys and sweets in their stockings. Later, when his business had become more established, their weekly visits to the saleroom to bid for items of furniture going for a song. The dining-room table, chairs and sideboard, had, for example, been long cared for by other hands than theirs, so had the furniture for the bedrooms and front room.

When he returned with the tea, Grace asked, 'What Mrs Burton implied about Danny and another woman, you don't think it's possible, do you?'

'I honestly don't know, love. But I'll make it my business to find out,' Bob assured her. 'Danny's bound to turn up here sooner or later, and when he does . . .'

'You won't be too hard on him, will you?' Grace enquired anxiously. 'No use making things worse, they're bad enough already.' Tears were close to the surface. 'Oh, Bob, what's happening to us? What's gone wrong, and why? *Why?*'

'It's to do with growing up, I reckon,' Bob said. 'You know, the younger generation wanting to try their own wings. All we can do is stand by to pick up the pieces if they find they can't fly after all.'

Chapter Nineteen

'Look, Danny, all I'm saying is—'

'I know what you're saying, but it's none of your business, is it?' Danny retorted. 'It's up to me and Wilma to sort out our problems.'

'Then you'd better tell her parents the same thing!' Bob hadn't meant to come the heavy-handed father, now the gloves were off. 'Coming here the way they did, upsetting your mother, spreading gossip—'

Danny's face paled suddenly beneath his tan. 'I don't know what you mean,' he interrupted. 'What gossip?'

'About you and another woman. But you *do* know, don't you? My God, son, are you completely mad or just plain stupid?'

'I haven't been unfaithful to Wilma, if that's what you're thinking,' Danny uttered defensively. 'It's just that I needed someone to talk to.' Then, his defences down, 'I'm sorry, Dad. I never meant it to happen. In any case, it's all over now. She – the girl I'm fond of – doesn't want anything more to do with me. Can't say I blame her.' He added bitterly, 'She gave me the brush-off last Sunday night. I – I stopped off at a pub on the way home; had a drop too much to drink. Well, now you know.'

'All right, son, I believe you,' Bob said quietly. 'The thing is, what are you going to do next?'

'I don't honestly know,' Danny confessed. 'The way things stand, I can't let the team down, but the cricket season should be over before the baby's born.'

'And if Wilma asks you not to play next season?'

'I'll cross that bridge when I come to it. I'm not making any promises I can't keep.'

Bob said sharply, 'Perhaps you should remember your

promise to love and to cherish until death do us part.'

The confrontation was taking place in the front room. As hungry as a wolf, Danny had come home to assuage his appetite for his mother's cooking – shepherd's pie, rissoles, bangers and mash – he couldn't care less about the menu as long as the food was plentiful, hot, and served with love.

Love! Wilma had never loved him, he knew that now. She couldn't even be bothered to cook for him. He said dully, 'Wilma made promises too.'

'I know, son. But two wrongs don't make a right,' Bob reminded him. 'You spoke of sorting out your problems. That won't happen unless you and Wilma talk things over quietly and sensibly.'

'A fat chance of that,' Danny sighed. 'She's not talking to me at all at the moment.' His shoulders drooped despondently. 'She may never speak to me again if she finds out about . . . Well, you know what.'

Grace popped her head round the door. 'Supper's on the table,' she said brightly. 'Are you coming, or not?'

'Sure thing,' Bob returned her smile. 'Come on, son,' laying a comforting arm about Danny's shoulders, 'you'll feel a lot better with a hot meal inside you.'

Seated at the dining table, tucking into a plateful of sausages, mashed potatoes and onion gravy, Danny glanced across at his mother, busily engaged in handing round the accompanying carrots and cauliflower, and realized what a fool he had been to turn his back on so much love – and for what? At best the fulfilment of a sexual desire which he now knew, to his cost, had nothing whatever to do with real love at all.

Jimmy collared him after supper. 'You really go into the mire feet first, don't you?' he said impatiently. 'What the hell were you playing at, coming home the state you were in last Sunday night?'

Flumping down on Jimmy's bed, 'Oh, don't you start,' Danny groaned, 'Dad's already had a go at me!'

'I'm not surprised! You'd have fallen flat on your face if I hadn't hauled you upstairs pretty damn quick.'

'I know. Thanks, Jimmy.'

'I should think so, too! What a carry-on. I had to undress you and stuff you into your pyjamas. There you were, flopping about like a rag doll, muttering on about Meg Jenkins. Yeah, you may well look surprised. Come on, Danny, I wasn't born yesterday. What the dickens have you been up to? You and Meg Jenkins?'

'*Nothing!*' Aware that he had spoken too quickly, too vehemently, Danny responded, 'Nothing I'm ashamed of, that is. I happen to be in love with her.'

'Oh, that's great, isn't it?' Jimmy returned sharply. 'A pregnant wife on one hand, a mistress on the other! Have you a death-wish or what?'

'How should I know? It just – happened – that's all. I didn't want it to happen, I didn't even realize myself what was happening until it was too late. I guess I just needed someone to talk to at first—'

'All right. No need to go on. I get the picture,' Jimmy said brusquely. 'In any case, I'm your brother, not your keeper. But let's get one thing straight, shall we? I never cared much for the lass you married, as you well know. But she was your choice, remember?'

'Go on, rub it in,' Danny said bitterly.

'Don't worry, I intend to.' Pacing the room, Jimmy spoke his mind in no uncertain manner. 'I happen to know that those benighted in-laws of yours gave Mum a hell of a roasting the other night. At least the dreadful Mabel tried to, but she didn't succeed. Mother saw to that. God, she was magnificent – a kind of avenging angel. I know, because I was in the hall at the time, eavesdropping.

'Now, as I see it, Mother and Dad have had enough to put up with recently, with Nan, the great aunts and Dulcie to worry about, let alone *you*!' Drawing in a deep breath, fists clenched, he continued, 'So, Danny, I'm warning you: give Mum and Dad more grief, more trouble, and you'll have me to answer to, OK?'

Danny knew that Jimmy meant what he said. Deeply regretting the loss of the old affectionate rib-punching tussles of long ago, he got up from the bed and said wryly, repeating the words of a worn-out catchphrase, 'You and whose army?'

There came a brief knock at the door. Breathlessly, Kerry entered the room. 'Oh, Danny!' she cried, catapulting herself into his arms, 'I've been so worried about you. Are you better now? You seemed so poorly last Sunday night, I didn't sleep a wink!'

Holding her close, he said jerkily, close to tears, 'Not to worry, Kerry love. It was a kind of fever, I guess.' Seeking his brother's eyes, 'That's right, isn't it, Jimmy?'

Relaxing his hands, loving Danny so much, 'Yeah,' Jimmy agreed. 'He'll be as right as rain from now on, you'll see.'

'It's like this, Kerry,' Ashley explained, so deeply aware of her flower-petal face, her grey-blue eyes fixed upon him, that he almost forgot what he was about to say. 'My parents want me to enter the family business, but I'm not in the least bit interested.'

'Oh? Have you told them?' She opened her packet of sandwiches.

'No, not yet. I'm still thinking about it.'

'Would you like one?' she asked offering him the packet. 'They're egg and cress.' Sensing his hesitation, 'Oh, go on,' she said, 'there's enough for two.' Then, colouring up, 'What I mean is, there's an excellent sufficiency.'

Ashley chuckled. 'Have I said something funny?' Kerry demanded, up in arms at his laughter, wishing he would go away and leave her in peace. They belonged, after all, to different worlds. He was an Oxford graduate. She had left school at 14. He was rich, she was earning 10 shillings a week.

'No, not at all. It's just that I have the feeling there's a kind of barrier between us.'

'So there is,' she said stiffly, worried sick that she would make a gulping sound swallowing the first bite of her egg-and-cress sandwich.

'But *why*, Kerry? I wish you'd tell me.'

Easing egg and cress carefully past her gullet, remembering her mother's edict that it was a sign of bad manners to speak with one's mouth full, she made no reply. She couldn't.

'Are you – frightened of me? Is that it?' Ashley continued seriously. 'If so, there's really no need. The last thing on my mind is to hurt or embarrass you in any way. You must believe that. Please say that you believe it.'

Her mouth clear of obstruction, 'I can't see that it makes much difference one way or the other,' she said primly.

'Not to you, perhaps, but it does to me.' Gaining control of her hands, he continued, 'You see, Kerry, I think you are the loveliest girl in the world.'

'You *do*?' The packet of sandwiches slipped off her lap unnoticed. She stared at him disbelievingly. 'But that's daft!' Out of her depth, she rose quickly to her feet. 'Oh, just go away and leave me alone,' she cried in alarm. Turning away from him, she hurried back to the safety of the shop.

Staring at her reflection in the cloakroom mirror, she tidied her hair, aware of a hunger pain in her stomach, and regretting the waste of her lunchtime sandwiches, from now on, Kerry thought, she would eat her lunch in the work-room, forgo the benison of fresh air and sunshine. Anything, just so long as she steered clear of Ashley Hawthorn.

The first thing she would do when she went home was get rid of that faded rose in her *Palgrave's Treasury*. Perhaps she *was* frightened of Ashley Hawthorn; scared of the way he had looked at her so intently, making her feel flustered, unsure of herself, robbing her of spontaneity.

Come to think of it, she had never felt entirely at ease with Sid Hannay either: a bit tongue-tied and foolish because of his superior education, the panache with which he had worn his High School blazer. But Danny had gone to the High School, and she had no trouble conversing with him.

Weighing up the pros and cons as she went into the shop to pick up her duster, she realized that Jimmy had also left school at 14, and he was much cleverer than Danny. So perhaps she was afraid of Ashley Hawthorn because he was rich, his father a baronet, his mother a lady. But what constituted a lady? Plenty of money? Fine clothes? A posh accent? Her way of speaking down to people less rich and influential than herself?

Dusting a cut-glass vase, Kerry reached the conclusion that her mother, rich in compassion, despite her work-worn hands, her lack of money and fine clothes, was every bit as good as, if not better than, Lady Hawthorn.

At least Grandma Daniel had got something right, Kerry conjectured, in choosing her mother's Christian name. The word grace, she knew – because she had looked it up in Jimmy's dictionary – meant a pleasing quality, attractiveness and charm, ease and refinement of movement, a regenerating, inspiring and strengthening influence. Hawthorn, on the other hand, referred to a thorny shrub or small tree. That figured!

But why worry? Surely, from now on, Ashley Hawthorn would leave her alone to get on with her own life in her own way? She had, after all, given him the brush-off in no uncertain terms. Of course he was very handsome, and she couldn't help feeling a bit sorry for him . . . and he had very nice hands, warm and strong. Even so, she'd rather have a far-distanced, silver-screen romantic hero than a real one any day of the week. Her latest heart-throb was Robert Donat, seen recently in *The 39 Steps* at the Capitol Cinema.

Growing up, she reckoned, was not simply a matter of adding an extra half inch to one's stature between birthdays. There was far more to it than that.

When the shop closed, she said good night to the other girls and Mr Hodnot, and walked quickly along St Nicholas Street, giving a quick glance over her shoulder to make sure that Ashley Hawthorn wasn't lurking in a doorway.

Her heart sank when she noticed Sid Hannay standing on the pavement outside Boots the Chemists. Lifting her chin, she sailed past him, her heart thumping wildly as it always did on these occasions, hating the pretence of not knowing him. But what else could she do? At least she had graduated from flat shoes and ankle-socks, she consoled herself. By the same token, Sid had graduated from his High School uniform to a navy-blue suit, a starched collar and a striped tie. Moreover, he was beginning to fill out, to lose that gangling, unfinished look common to schoolboys and young horses.

As Kerry passed by, apparently absorbed in the buildings on the other side of the road, Sid's thoughts ran much along the same lines. The soppy, wide-eyed kid he'd once treated to an ice-cream cornet because she was pretty and he had wanted to impress her with his superior intellect, incidentally to make another girl jealous, was no longer wide-eyed or, apparently, soppy – especially not about him.

Now here she was, pin-neat and self-composed, not merely pretty but beautiful, possessed of a certain elegance – a bit like a ballerina. And those legs of hers! He couldn't help himself. At the moment of passing he said awkwardly, 'Hello, Kerry.'

She turned her head, with a cool glance in his direction. 'Do I know you?' she murmured, and walked on, head in air, thinking that she was, perhaps, beginning to grow up a bit after all. On the other hand, if growing up had to do with growing a kind of shell against the slings and arrows of life, she would far rather cling to the simple, uncomplicated joys of childhood, flat shoes, ankle-socks and all.

Entering the house on the hill, Kerry wondered if she should tell her parents about Ashley Hawthorn. But what was there to tell? Besides, they had enough on their plates to worry about without her adding to their troubles. She would simply get rid of that silly, faded rose that he had thrown at her feet, eat her supper and have an early night – although the bedroom she had once shared with her sister seemed cold and lonely now, without Dulcie.

The rose! She could easily nip out with it to the dustbin or, more romantically, throw it into the sea at sunset: a symbolic gesture of release. From what, she wasn't entirely sure.

After supper, she came downstairs, the rose in her cardigan pocket. Popping her head round the door, 'I'm just going out for a walk,' she told Grace and Bob. 'I shan't be long.'

'Where are you going?' Grace asked.

'Just as far as the seafront and back.'

'Mind if I come with you? I could do with a breath of air.' Jimmy had appeared in the hall behind her. 'Who knows? I might treat you to a knickerbocker glory if you play your cards right!'

They walked down the front steps together. Kerry seemed unusually quiet, Jimmy thought. Perhaps she had a secret rendezvous and his company was unwelcome? When he asked her, 'Don't talk so daft,' she said haughtily, all edges and corners. 'Men. *Ugh*!'

Before very long, he had winkled from her the saga of Ashley Hawthorn. With a deep-throated chuckle, 'Good for you, kiddo,' he said admiringly. 'It isn't every day that a filthy-rich Oxford graduate is given the brush-off by a member of the bourgeoisie!'

The ice broken, she went on to confide in Jimmy about the rose, and lots of other things, too: the way she had given Sid Hannay the cold shoulder earlier that evening. She spilled out her thoughts and feelings as she had seldom done before, glad of her brother's quick, intelligent understanding of her mixed and muddled emotional problems which, indeed, he appeared to understand far better than she did.

Halfway along the Lighthouse Pier, Jimmy suggested, 'Might as well ditch that rose now. This seems as good a place as any.' He added, 'I won't look if you don't want me to.'

The sea below was full and deep, as calm as a millpond. There were slow-moving ships on the horizon; lights reflected in the water; a slip of a moon, a sprinkling of stars. True, there were people about, lots of people: couples strolled along hand-in-hand, parents with small, tired children in tow, passengers about to disembark from the pleasure-steamers hawsered alongside the quay. There were sounds, too: of laughter, the rattle of chains, hoarse shouts of ships' crews as gangplanks were manoeuvred into position. No-one would even notice the figure of a young girl throwing some unidentifiable object into the sea.

Even so, when the moment came, holding the poor, crushed rose in her hand, Kerry knew that she could not bear to part with it; she remembered, with a little lifting of the heart, that afternoon on the Spa, a perfectly poised arabesque, the breaking of her nervous tension as the flower landed at her feet and she had looked up in surprise, wondering who had thrown it. Picking it up afterwards, she took it home with her, pressed it in the pages of her *Palgrave's Golden Treasury* as a kind of talisman, a good-luck charm.

'Well?' Jimmy asked her when she returned to his side, 'Ready for that knickerbocker glory now?'

She said, shame-facedly, 'About the rose. I didn't throw it away after all. It's still here, in my pocket.'

'I figured it might be,' Jimmy replied off-handedly. He added intuitively, 'This Ashley Hawthorn. I think you like him more than you realize, more than you are prepared to admit. Come on now, be honest.'

'I like him well enough,' Kerry confessed miserably, 'but . . . Oh, what's the use? I can't be myself with him. I couldn't even swallow naturally with him staring at me so hard. I very nearly choked on that egg-and-cress sandwich!'

'Men have a way of staring at pretty girls,' Jimmy said easily, linking her arm, drawing her towards Jaconelli's Ice-Cream Parlour.

'*You* don't stare at girls,' Kerry stated flatly. 'I've often wondered why. Don't you *like* girls?'

'Not much,' he admitted. 'Not the ones I've clapped eyes on so far, anyway, which is why I steer clear of them. I'd rather be a writer than a Romeo any day of the week. I thought you knew that!'

'Yes, I do,' Kerry responded warmly, 'of course I do. But just what kind of girl are you looking for?'

'I'm not quite sure,' he said mistily, gazing into an unknown future. 'Someone tall and graceful; not necessarily beautiful, but clever, with a great sense of humour. A fellow writer, perhaps, or an artist. How the hell should *I* know?' He added defiantly, 'Well, do you want a knickerbocker glory or not?'

'Yes, Jimmy,' Kerry said meekly, glad of the new, potent understanding between them, far deeper now than ever before, as if they had suddenly grown up together within the space of an hour.

Now that his mother-in-law had got wind of his friendship with Meg Jenkins, Danny was filled with a deep sense of foreboding. Wilma and her mother were in close contact most days, he knew. How long would it be before Mabel Burton felt it her duty to divulge that juicy item of gossip?

He hadn't long to wait to find out. Coming home from work one afternoon, he found Wilma in bed, hunched beneath the bedclothes, red-eyed with weeping.

No need to ask what was wrong. Sitting bolt upright, she cried hysterically, 'Get out! I want you out of my room, out of this house right now, you rotten, two-timing beast!'

'What has your mother been saying?' he demanded, shocked at the outburst, his wife's hysteria.

'You dare to stand there and ask me that? And you can take that idiotic look off your face. I know damn well you've been having an affair behind my back. Did you really think I wouldn't find out about it?'

Sitting on the edge of the bed, holding her wrists, he said, 'Let's get this straight, shall we? I haven't been having an affair, as you call it. I've done nothing wrong. Nothing I'm ashamed of.'

'Oh, you would say that, wouldn't you? Trying to make out my mother's a liar. And let go of my wrists, you're hurting me!'

'I'm not letting go until you calm down, until you listen to what I have to say. Your mother got her facts wrong, that's all.'

Working herself into a frenzy, struggling to free herself, she sobbed wildly, 'You *have* been seeing someone, I can tell by your face; the way you've been treating me lately. Leaving me on my own, going off with your so-called cricketing friends! Ha, do you think I'm blind or just stupid?'

'Stop it, Wilma! Stop it, I say!' Afraid that she would bring on a fit or a miscarriage, he struck her across the cheek with the flat of his hand. It was no more than a light slap, but the effect was electrifying. Wilma stopped crying and struggling. Her eyes opened wide. 'You hit me,' she said childishly.

'Yes, I know love, and I'm sorry. I thought you'd harm yourself and the baby.'

'A fat lot you'd care.'

'Of course I care.'

She had started to cry again, but quietly this time, like a little girl. Strangely moved by her tears, her wretched appearance, swollen body and eyelids, he put his arms about her and held her close, remembering all that she had once meant to him.

He said quietly, 'You have my word that I have never been unfaithful to you.'

'But you do want to leave me, don't you?'

'No. I want to stay here with you. It was you who told me to get out.'

'Did I?' she said childishly, 'I don't remember.'

He knew she was telling the truth, that she had forgotten what she said or did at the height of her hysteria.

She said wearily, 'I'm so tired. I want to go to sleep now.'

Sleep, he knew, would be the best thing for her. Straightening the bed, plumping up the pillows, he eased her into a comfortable position, and made certain that she was fast asleep before quitting the room.

Downstairs he paced the living-room; all this was his fault, he thought bitterly, and yet Meg Jenkins' friendship and understanding had meant so much to him. But he knew, deep down, that given the chance, he would have made love to her. It had taken a girl of Meg's calibre to put an end to their 'affair' before it got out of hand. And then what? The answer came clear and simple, he would not have been able to give Wilma his word of honour that he had never been unfaithful to her.

Sitting down suddenly in a rented armchair, covering his face with his hands, he thought what a bloody awful mess he had made of his life so far. Memory drew him back to the first night of his honeymoon in that God-awful hotel in the Lake District. If only he'd possessed enough wisdom to hold back until Wilma was ready to have him make love to her, how differently everything might have turned out. If only he had worn a sheath. But no. Wanting her so much, he had taken her against her will. Now he was paying the full price for that act of sheer folly.

What next? he wondered. Where would he and Wilma go from here? One good thing about rented accommodation was that there were no strings attached. If Wilma decided to go home to her parents, all he'd have to do was give the landlord a week's notice.

He was sitting alone in the dark when he heard Wilma calling to him from the room above. Hurrying upstairs, 'Yes, love, what is it?' he asked, opening the door.

She said weakly, 'I've had such an awful dream. I dreamt I was alone in the house. All alone in the dark.'

Switching on the bedside lamp, holding her shaking body in his arms, 'It was just a nightmare, love,' he told her. 'I'm here. I promise I'll stay with you for as long as you want me to.'

'Yes, Danny,' she whispered, 'I do want you to stay with me.'

Chapter Twenty

Dulcie was slowly beginning to get the hang of her new job. It was less of a doddle than she had imagined it would be. That first morning, faced with a packet of Scott's porridge oats, a double boiler and a pint of milk, she had been obliged to read the instructions on the box before embarking on the risky business of providing the twins' breakfast.

It was Heidi who told her patronizingly, 'No, silly! The oats go in the *top* pan not the bottom. Even Fräulein Stockmar knew *that*!'

Washing and ironing the twins' clothes had posed an even greater problem. Thank God there was no-one to see her Titanic struggle to quell the rising tide of bubbles in the sink from her over-lavish use of Lux soap flakes, her desperate pulling-out of the plug as the bubbles cascaded onto the floor. As for the ironing! How was it possible for any iron to leave behind more creases than had been there in the first place? At that point, it had occurred to her to connect the plug to the electricity supply.

It had been hard for her, at first, to come to terms with the loneliness of her top-floor eyrie after the constant rush and bustle of the Pavilion Hotel. Even so, her weekly wage-packet would more than compensate for the lack of companionship. In a sense, she was the monarch of all she surveyed, in no way comparable to the servants who occupied the jutting west wing of the house adjacent to the kitchen, the pantries and fuel-stores – the cook-housekeeper, the butler, the house and kitchenmaids – all of whom she regarded as her inferiors.

She, after all, was in sole charge of a new generation of Bergmanns, responsible for their well-being, the food they ate, their appearance, their manners. Besides which, she was a quick learner, an opportunist with an eye to the future – hopefully as the future mistress of the Bergmann mansion – all those spacious, elegantly furnished rooms, that broad, red-carpeted staircase dappled with prisms of light from the stained-glass landing window.

Miraculously, weight was falling from her quite rapidly now, due mainly to an enforced nursery diet of porridge, steamed fish, eggs and vegetables, according to the wishes of the twins' father. Klaus Bergmann preferred his daughters to eat fresh fruit rather than sweets or chocolates. No wonder her figure was fast assuming hour-glass proportions. Thankfully, she coped quite well with the preparation and cooking of such innocuous fare in the small nursery kitchen.

Above all, she wanted to present a picture of smiling efficiency when Bergmann appeared to say good night to the children, which was not as often as she would have wished. Sometimes he would be away from home for days at a time on extended business trips, and she would find herself willing away the hours until his return, knowing that his first priority would be an affectionate reunion with his offspring, followed by in-depth conversation with herself regarding their well-being and general behaviour.

On one such occasion he had said, with a smile, 'I congratulate you, Dulcie, on the obvious care and attention you have given to this new job of yours. It can't have been easy for you, which is all the more reason for congratulation.' He went on, 'You must feel isolated at times. The house has been quiet recently. That will change when my brother returns. Franz is what I think is called a live wire, fond of company. Soon there will be week-end house parties, laughter, music, people coming and going; also the children will become over-excited, a little naughty perhaps. Will this worry you unduly, make your work harder?'

'No, I don't think so.'

'You mustn't let my brother and his friends spoil them too much. Remember that you are in charge up here. Are you comfortable, by the way?'

'Oh yes. Very. I love my room.'

'That is good.'

When he had gone, she hugged herself with delight. He had called her Dulcie. Not *Miss* Dulcie or Miss Kingsley, but Dulcie! Lying awake till the early hours, too excited to sleep, she mulled over their conversation, reading hidden meanings into every sentence he had uttered, remembering his smile, the warmth of his voice, the way he had looked at her – appreciatively, admiringly – and why not? He must have noticed how trim and neat she appeared in her navy-blue skirt and crisp white blouse.

When sleep overcame her at two o'clock in the morning, she had already planned, to the smallest detail, her wedding dress and accessories. White silk, she decided, she would wear a gown of pure white silk. Not satin. She hated satin: such stiff, ugly material. And she would carry a bouquet of orchids. Pale pink orchids . . . Roses were so common.

That fat old cow, Frau Bergmann, hated her guts, of course. Dulcie had realized that from the outset, and the feeling was mutual. Jealousy pure and simple, from the old woman's viewpoint, because she knew deep down that her grandchildren's nanny would one day become the mistress of the house. Ah, bliss, to have so many servants at her beck and call, to spend her days planning intimate dinner parties, giving instructions to the cook . . . Mmmmm. Dulcie fell asleep with her mouth open. Then, very gently at first, she began to snore.

The following Saturday afternoon, seated at a table in a Bergmann café overlooking the Headrow, she was tucking into a vanilla slice, several bags of shopping stacked up beside her chair, when she looked up in surprise at the mention of her name.

'Hello, Dulcie. Mind if I join you?' Slipping into the seat opposite, 'Been shopping, have you?' Herbie Barrass enquired mildly.

'What does it look like?' Dulcie's hackles rose at the sight of him. 'In any case, what business is it of yours?' She added venomously, 'I suppose you're here to spy on me?'

270

'Spy on you?' He mopped the perspiration from his forehead with the back of his hand. 'Am I hell as like! I call in here most Saturday afternoons to pick up my bread order. I live just round the corner. Nowt sinister in that, is there?'

'I suppose not,' she said grudgingly. 'In any case it doesn't matter much. I've almost finished my tea. You can have the table to yourself then.'

'Look, Dulcie love,' he said awkwardly, 'I know we've never exactly hit it off together, but surely we can spend the next five minutes without your turning nasty with me? What's eating you anyway? Is it the cut of my jib you don't like, or the fact that I'm breathing in my fair share of oxygen? I wish I knew.'

Suddenly, a handsome young man strode purposefully past the tables to the bread and confectionery counter at the far end of the premises, behind which he was greeted with enthusiasm by the assistants, the most senior of whom cried out gleefully, 'Oh, Mr Franz, how lovely it is to see you again! Welcome home!'

Agog with curiosity, and craning her neck to catch a closer look at the centre of attention, it seemed to Dulcie that she was glimpsing a mirror-image of the Klaus Bergmann of 15 years ago, before the mantle of middle age had settled on his shoulders.

Franz Bergmann's hair was dark, his skin tanned, emphasizing the brilliance of his smile, the blueness of his eyes. He was leaner, more muscular than his brother, seemingly less inhibited, evident by his informal approach to the assistants, his laughing response to their light-hearted repartee.

Uplifted by the thought that soon she would be meeting the handsome stranger face-to-face, she was inordinately pleased that she had kept, albeit unwillingly at times, to her diet. She actually smiled at Herbie, thinking not of him but of the smart new clothes and the various items of make-up in her shopping bags, on which she had blown her first month's salary.

Hurriedly settling her bill when the waitress came to the

271

table, she picked up her shopping. 'Must be going now,' she said airily, 'I have a hair appointment in twenty minutes.'

Mystified by her sudden change of attitude, half rising to his feet, 'Yeah, fine, Dulcie,' he murmured. 'By the way, I'm going to Scarborough next weekend. Any message?'

'Huh? Oh yes, tell Mum and Dad I'm fine!' And then she was gone.

Sitting down, Herbie thought the girl certainly looked fine. Even so, he'd have felt happier had she said, 'Oh yes, give Mum and Dad my love.' But then she was, at heart, a selfish little beast, and it would take more than the loss of a stone and a half in weight, a couple of bags of shopping and a visit to a hairdressing salon to change that basic flaw in her character.

It had been a long, hot summer. Now the stultifying heat of August had given way to the gentler warmth of September. Herbie noticed, as the train slid past Oliver's Mount, that the burgeoning trees of summer seemed sadder and much wiser now. Nature's reflection on the human condition, he reckoned. Perhaps he, too, had reached the point of no return to a spring-time blossoming?

Hiring a taxi in the station forecourt, he was deep in thought as it sped towards Castle Road. On this his fiftieth birthday, he wondered what had he to look forward to except his old-age pension? What had he to look back on apart from his 'glory' days in the Green Howards during the war, a string of abortive sexual encounters that had meant less than nothing to him, a mental love affair which could never come to fruition?

On this, his half-century watermark, he deeply regretted his lack of family life, a wife, a woman to call his own, and children. Aw, what the hell? Laugh and the world laughs with you, cry and you cry alone.

Alighting from the taxi, a smile soldered to his lips when Bob opened the front door, he said blithely, 'Well, here I am again, as large as life and twice as ugly,' and bundled his cases into the hall.

He had sensed at once a subtle lightening of the atmosphere so far as his friends were concerned. He understood why, when Bob told him that Danny and Wilma had patched up their marriage.

'It's a weight off our minds, I can tell you,' Bob said over a pint at the Albion. 'We'd almost given up hope of a reconciliation. Now they're starting to visit again. They're coming to supper tomorrow night, as a matter of fact.' Pausing to swallow a mouthful of best bitter, he went on, 'It's what you might call an uneasy truce, but, in political parlance, the deadlock has been broken and talks are under way.' Then, with concern, 'Are you all right, Herbie? You seem a bit under the weather.'

'Eh? Oh yeah, I'm fine. It's just that—'

'Well, go on. Spit it out!'

'I have a gut feeling we'll soon be back in uniform, the way things are going in Germany and Italy right now.'

'You're not serious?'

'Oh, I'm serious right enough. There's trouble brewing, mark my words. I wouldn't trust that Hitler and Mussolini as far as I could throw them.' Herbie sighed deeply, 'And now the old King's dead and gone, I dain't see that fakey son of his as much of a monarch – more of a womanizer. Him an' that American girlfriend of his. What's her name? Wallis Simpson. Nice going's on, I must say. The King of England mucking about with a married woman. Well, no good will come of it, you wait and see.'

'I'm sorry, Herbie. I had no idea you felt this way,' Bob murmured apologetically, surprised at his friend's intensity of feeling in matters political. 'But surely you can't believe that the likes of you and me would be called on to fight another war?' He frowned, out of his depth. 'We're too old, for starters. War is a young man's game.'

'Yeah, men about Danny and Jimmy's age, I reckon,' Herbie reminded him. Then, thrusting aside his fiftieth birthday blues, he said, 'Oh, take no notice of me. I'm getting queer in my old age. So Danny and Wilma are back together again? That's great news! Tell me more.'

'There's nothing much more to tell,' Bob said dully. 'In any case, it doesn't seem all that important now.' Deeply shaken, and meeting Herbie's eyes across the table, he said, 'You meant what you said just now, didn't you? You really do believe there's another war in the offing?'

'Yeah,' Herbie prevaricated, 'but I could be wrong. In any case, why worry? Sup up and I'll order us another round of drinks.' Frankly, he'd surprised himself. He hadn't meant to spout all that doom and gloom stuff about war, to upset Bob the way he had done. 'Look, mate,' he added by way of apology, 'the fact is, I've just hit the half-century mark and I don't much like it.' He grinned awkwardly, 'By the way, I bumped into Dulcie the other day.'

'You did?' Bob's face brightened. 'How was she?'

'Fine, just fine!' Romancing, 'We had a nice little chat over a cuppa. Very smart she looked, too.'

'Did she say anything about Grace and me?'

Continuing his fairy story, 'Sure thing,' Herbie enthused, 'she said she's missing her mother's cooking, and when I told her I was coming to see you, she asked me to give you her love.'

When Ashley told his parents that he had finally decided to enter the family business, Lady Hawthorn lost no time in organizing a celebration party in her son's honour, making certain that the guest list included friends with daughters of a marriageable age.

In her element, she handed her cook a buffet-menu a yard long, inclusive of such delicacies as oyster patties, poached salmon, asparagus tips with hollandaise sauce, cold roast pheasant, and chicken in aspic, not to mention a bewildering variety of cold sweets.

On the morning of the party, a florist's van delivered a veritable wealth of flowers: delphiniums, lupins, carnations, long-stemmed roses, arum lilies and gypsophila. Her ladyship, a stalwart of the Malton Flower Club, left the arrangement of these to the small army of female helpers, gleaned from the Flower Club ranks, on whom she could rely to fill the cut-glass vases and the important alabaster jardinières to the best possible advantage. After all, it was no use owning a dog and barking one's self, she thought, slipping away to have her hair done, her fingernails manicured at Maison Marcel's, her York beauty parlour.

That evening, alone in his room, dressing slowly, unenthusiastically for the party in his honour, Ashley Hawthorn's every thought was centred, not on the feast or the flowers, but on the face of one girl. A girl called Kerry Kingsley.

God, what a fool he'd been, he considered, battling with his bow-tie, in taking his fences too fast, frightening the poor kid with his intensity of feeling towards her. No wonder she had run away from him in such a hurry in view of his insensitive response to her 'excellent sufficiency' remark. How deeply hurt she must have felt by his ripple of laughter which she must have construed, not as appreciation of her naïvety, but rather as a condemnation of it.

His mother had really gone to town on this party. Going downstairs, the place resembled a cross between Kew Gardens and a funeral parlour, he thought, catching sight of the floral arrangements, a whiff of the arum lilies. He dreaded the evening of enforced gaiety ahead of him as much as he dreaded his inculcation into his father's business concerns. He wondered what his parents would say if they knew his decision to join the firm had nothing to do with temptingly dangled carrots of inheritance, power or position, but everything to do with being in love, wanting to stay close to Kerry. To this end, he had turned down a teaching post at a public school near Cambridge.

The guests were beginning to arrive. Joining the welcoming committee, his father stiffly resplendent in starched shirt and bow-tie regalia, his mother dressed to the nines in lilac-and-silver brocade, Ashley groaned inwardly at the sight of so many well-heeled middle-aged couples accompanied by their female offspring. He knew, of course, why they had come, all a-flutter, dressed mainly in pink, green, blue and white frocks embellished with girlish ribbons and bows. His mother, he thought, possessed the subtlety of a dreadnought.

Even so, courtesy demanded a show of interest in the bevy of girls clamouring for his attention. Making certain they had enough to eat and drink, he found himself saying, 'Yes, I'm looking forward to joining my father . . .'; 'Yes, I do miss Oxford . . .'; 'Tennis? No, I'm not a very good player, I'm afraid . . .'; 'Oh yes, I enjoy listening to music . . . My favourite composer? Johann Sebastian Bach, that great master of contrapuntal music, you know? I particularly admire his . . .'; 'The cinema? No, not really, such a waste of time, don't you think? . . .'; 'Poetry? Ah yes, John Milton stands supreme, of course, in that particular field . . .' and so on.

He thought afterwards, while undressing in the blissful privacy of his bedroom, how puzzled his mother would be by her younger guests' primly uttered farewells when the party was over. His fault entirely. On the other hand, had he told Fiona Emblow that he had, by the merest fluke, beaten the reigning Wimbledon champion, Fred Perry, 6-4, 6-4, at a private match in Oxford last year, the toothy Fiona would have claimed him as her own.

By the same token, had he admitted to Alison Begley that his favourite composer was George Gershwin, to Lucille Grayson that he adored the cinema, particularly light-hearted musicals, or had he dared to tell the plumply breathless Elizabeth Entwistle that he loved, above all, the poetry of Elizabeth Barrett Browning, he'd have sunk without trace in a flummery of bows, bangles and beads. Instead of which, he thought guiltily, he had gone to considerable lengths to impart the impression of himself as a 'culture vulture', a 'stuffed shirt' or whatever, as a matter of survival in a world of predatory females intent upon marrying into the Hawthorn family.

Getting into bed, it occurred to him that the girl he really wanted didn't give a damn for his wealth or his position in society. More to the point, and to his chagrin, she appeared

276

not to give a damn about him at all. He couldn't help wondering about her deep-seated antipathy towards him. Did she regard herself as his inferior? Was that it?

He lay awake until dawn; fell asleep at last, the question uppermost in his mind dissolving into dreams of a sylph-like girl in a white ballet dress, running away from him into a cloud-bank of mist.

Something was wrong with Fanny. Her sister had not been herself since that visit from Grace, Bob and Kerry, Nan thought, although the subject had never been raised or even mentioned after their departure. Not that she could pinpoint what ailed Fanny. She looked and behaved much the same as before, but something was missing. Perhaps she was getting deaf? Yes, that would account for the fact that she seemed not to catch the drift of a conversation, the faraway look on her face as she stitched away at her embroidery.

She had, moreover, taken to switching on the wireless set when she came upstairs from the shop at tea-time, a new-fangled habit which Nan found intensely irritating.

More disturbingly, last Saturday evening Fanny had sat with her ear glued to the wireless listening to a full-length performance of *The Chocolate Soldier*, a beatific smile on her face, occasionally breaking into song with the tenor Jan Van der Gucht, singing the words of the waltz: 'Come, come, I love you only, my heart is true. Come, come, my life is lonely, I long for you . . .'

'Really, Fanny! *Must* you do that?'

'Hmmm? Did you say something, Nan dear?'

'I wish you'd switch that thing off. You've hardly spoken a word to me all day.'

'Haven't I?' With a distant smile, an expression of wide-eyed innocence, she added, 'I'm sorry, dear, I thought you liked music. Remember Uncle Ambrose and his violin?' But the wireless had not been switched off and Nan, in high dudgeon, had stalked upstairs to her bedroom, leaving Fanny to make her own cocoa, and serve her right! If she was being given the silent treatment on purpose, well, two could play that game, Nan thought mutinously.

Tossing and turning in bed, the thought occurred that she knew little or nothing about Fanny's life in London during the war. Who, for instance, had given her that black sealskin cape she had worn at Danny's wedding? Some man or other she'd be bound! It was scarcely likely that Fanny would have been able to afford a garment of that quality from her own pocket.

The worm having entered the apple, and overwhelmed with jealousy, bitterly resentful of Fanny's withdrawal, Nan decided to find out the truth for herself. How this might be accomplished, she had no clear idea. Fanny regarded her bedroom as sacrosanct, preferring to make her own bed and seeing to the dusting and polishing herself.

The more she thought about it, the more curious Fanny's behaviour had been of late. Secretive was the word. Not that she had ever been entirely forthcoming. Nan had felt more than a little surprised that long-gone Sunday, when Fanny had suggested putting in a good word for Kerry with Mr Hodnot. Surprised and aggrieved, until that day, Nan had no inkling that Fanny even *knew* the man. Now Fanny had taken to writing letters in the privacy of her room and walking along to the pillar-box on the corner to post them. This Nan knew for a fact because she had watched her from the drawing-room window.

Habitually, the postman delivered mail addressed to Fanny at No. 27 South Street through the shop letterbox and other missives to No. 27A, the house address, which meant that she, Nan, had no access to her sister's personal correspondence. What this comprised apart from the bills which flopped through the shop letterbox, Nan had no idea. By the same token, infrequent mail addressed to Mrs Nancy Daniel found its way through the house letterbox – the reason why she had been able to smuggle Grace's Christmas card upstairs without Fanny's knowledge, without her seeing the Christmas Day invitation contained within that card.

Choosing her time carefully, Nan entered Fanny's

278

bedroom after breakfast the next day. Closing the door quietly behind her, heart hammering, she crossed over to the wardrobe, a towering mahogany edifice that had once graced their parents' room in their childhood home, along with the Victorian dressing table, marble-topped wash-stand, chest-of-drawers, and the bed itself, brass-railed with gleaming 'pineapple' embellishments.

Opening the wardrobe doors, Nan drew in a deep breath of amazement at the bewildering variety of clothes it contained, none of which, apart from the sealskin cape, she had ever seen before. There were exquisitely beaded evening gowns on padded hangers adorned with muslin bags of fresh lavender, daytime coats and costumes of World War vintage. Apart from the sealskin cape, a musquash fur coat, an ermine stole. On the floor of the wardrobe, shoes of every description: polished brogues, diamanté-studded dance shoes, sandals, court shoes, padded slippers, feather-trimmed mules. Each pair was fitted with stretchers to maintain its shape, although the feet which had once slipped, with ease, into those shoes, were misshapen now with age and avoirdupois. Gazing at the spectacular evening gowns, Nan could scarcely credit that Fanny had kept these reminders of the way she used to look in the heyday of her youth and beauty.

Riddled with guilt, yet determined to discover more about her sister's secret life, Nan opened Fanny's desk, a French escritoire totally out of character with the rest of the furniture, and purchased, if memory served her correctly, at a country-house sale shortly after the war. Frankly, she had never understood Fanny's desire to possess such a ridiculous, ornate piece of furniture. Now, prying into its secrets, Nan wondered if she had ever understood Fanny at all.

A bundle of letters tied with blue ribbon, penned to 'My dearest darling Fran', and signed 'Yours ever devotedly, James', were obviously those of a lover to his mistress. Sick with disgust, eaten up with jealousy, and with shaking fingers, Nan re-tied the bundle, which she thrust back from whence it came. But worse, much worse was to come . . .

279

The next letter she opened read, simply, 'Dearest Sister, Thank you so much for your continuing love and support. I am happy enough in my new life, thanks to the generosity and kindness of dear Grace and Bob who realized that I could not have borne to live under the same roof as Nan a moment longer. Even so, my darling Fanny, I miss you more than words can say. We were so happy together, you and I, until Nan came to live with us, until I reached the sad conclusion that I was no longer a necessary part of your life or hers. Or so I thought, until the arrival of your loving letters to me. Letters I shall keep and treasure all the days of my life as an assurance of your undying affection for, Your ever loving sister, Rosa.'

So that was the way of it! Nan sat down abruptly. She was trembling so violently that her legs felt like water. To think that Fanny, of all people, had betrayed her in such a way was more than she could bear. As for Rosa! The words, 'We were so happy together, you and I, until Nan came to live with us,' burned into her brain. Happy? How could Fanny have been happy with that snivelling, inept fool Rosa for company? Rosa, who couldn't even boil an egg properly. Rosa the pathetic, the ridiculous, who had nevertheless succeeded in causing a rift between herself and Fanny. Well, she'd see about that . . .

Rising unsteadily to her feet, she closed the lid of the escritoire; the sooner she tackled Fanny, the better, Nan decided. Bristling with self-righteous indignation, she quit her sister's bedroom intent on going downstairs to the shop to speak her mind. Her hand on the banister, Nan realized, with a jolt akin to a mild electric shock, that a confrontation with Fanny over her letters to Rosa was impossible in the circumstances of her own underhand meddling with the contents of her sister's desk.

Burdened with an intolerable weight of anger and guilt combined, Nan began to see that she had become the victim of her own deceit.

*　　*　　*

She was to play the part of Light in her dancing mistress's production of *The Bluebird* at Christmas, Kerry told Herbie. Discerning an air of wistfulness about her, he asked her about Sid Hannay, probing the old wound delicately. 'Oh, I don't go in for that kind of stuff now,' she said with a sigh.

'What kind of stuff?'

'Falling in love. Look what happened to Juliet.'

'Juliet who?' Herbie asked innocently.

Danny helped his wife up the front steps as though he were handling a Ming dynasty vase likely to shatter at any moment. 'Sure you're feeling all right?' he ventured.

'For heaven's sake, stop fussing!'

Despite the patching up of their marriage, pockets of resistance remained so far as Wilma was concerned. In her present predicament, she could scarcely be expected to forgive and forget, as easily as all that, the misery of the past months. A harsh exchange of words with her mother, when she told her that she had decided to stay with Danny for the sake of the baby, had done nothing to add to her peace of mind. And yet, that time in the bedroom when Danny had begged to be given a second chance, she had experienced a feeling akin to that of their first meeting in the Olympia Ballroom, the way she had felt afterwards, in that dark shelter in the St Nicholas Gardens, at their first kiss.

Mabel Burton had condemned her daughter's decision to stay with Danny as 'the road to nowhere'. Even so, Wilma had sensed her mother's underlying relief that her snug little parlour would not be filled with clothes-horses of damp nappies drying in front of the fire, her father's off-duty periods interrupted with the fretful sounds emanating from a newly-born infant.

At that particular crossroads in her life, having weighed up the pros and cons, Wilma had reached the firm conclusion that staying with Danny was a far better option than returning to the house in Aberdeen Terrace. Danny, when all was said and done, had a good job at the Town Hall – and she still had her pride to consider. The thought of the scandal connected with the failure of her marriage was unbearable if she went back to her parents in this, the final month of her pregnancy.

Opening the door, Grace's heart went out to the girl. Shocked by her unkempt appearance, the purple shadows under her eyes, lack-lustre hair, hitched-up skirt and awkwardly splayed legs, she said gently, 'Come in.' She looked so young and vulnerable, completely different from the self-assured young madam of that fraught party, when she had managed to discover the one and only bone in two tins of Jumbo salmon.

This time, Grace had made no special preparation. The dining table was set with its usual complement of everyday china. It would be kinder to welcome Wilma as a member of the family rather than a guest, she thought, and Bob agreed with her. They were simply thankful that their son and his wife had decided to stay together. How that decision had been reached, they had no idea, nor did they intend to pry into the whys and wherefores. The past was over and done with. All that mattered now was the future.

Dishing up the food in the kitchen, and putting herself in Wilma's place, Grace remembered the way she had felt in the final stages of her first pregnancy – lost, lonely and frightened, scared stiff of the ordeal of childbirth. Of course the circumstances had been vastly different in her case, with Bob far away from her in France, fighting for his country, and faced, as she had been at the time of her confinement, with the cold indifference of her mother, the lack of warmth and understanding on the part of her father.

Wilma's child, she consoled herself, bustling the food through to the dining-room, would at least find its way into the world under less stressful circumstances than the child's father had done.

'Allow me, madame,' Herbie said, with mock gallantry, assuming a phoney French accent, smiling, tongue-in-cheek, as he opened the dining-room door for her. 'Ah, what have we here?' Examining the tray she was carrying, 'Quails' eggs in aspic, frogs' legs au gratin, et, je mean aussi, les escargots fresh from le jardin!'

Grace burst out laughing, 'In other words, bangers and mash!'

'Yeah, well,' Herbie retorted merrily, 'so ze sooner nous get stuck into 'em, the better!'

Glad of his presence at the table as she set forth the dishes of sausages and vegetables, the sauce-boats of onion gravy, Grace knew that she could rely on Herbie to relax the tension of this family reunion, just as he had relaxed, with his innate charm, so many other fraught family occasions. Dear Herbie, a friend worth his weight in gold. A friend in a million . . .

The crisis happened with startling suddenness. Silent throughout the meal, on her way to the front room for coffee, Wilma sank to her knees. Face ashen, whimpering with pain, 'Oh, God, it's started. The baby. Help me, Danny! Don't just stand there! Help me!'

'It's all right, darling.' Kneeling beside his wife, he attempted to lift her.

Perversely, Wilma groaned, 'Oh, don't. You're hurting me.'

'All right, Danny,' Grace said quietly, 'I'll see to her. The best thing you can do is ring for the doctor. Try his home number. Tell him it's urgent.'

'Yes, Ma.' Easier said than done, his hands were shaking so much that he could scarcely turn the pages of the telephone directory.

'We must get her upstairs to bed as quickly as possible,' Grace said urgently, supporting Wilma. 'The baby's on its way.'

'Here, let me!' Bending down, Herbie lifted the weeping girl in his arms. 'Which room?'

'Danny's room.'

'I'll open the door for you,' Bob said hoarsely, leading the way, feeling as useless as a spare bridegroom at a wedding.

In retrospect, Grace would never forget the events of that traumatic Sunday evening, the way Herbie had taken charge of the situation by reason of his army medical training, and something more. Obviously, she thought, this was not the first time that he had attended a woman in childbirth. How else would he have known exactly what to do?

'Yeah, well,' he admitted awkwardly, when she asked him, 'war or no war, we, my mates an' me, did us best to help out in an emergency. There weren't many doctors at hand, you see, when it came to helping women in – distress. What I mean it, we couldn't very well have left 'em alone, to let nature take its course, now could we?'

Herbie's gentleness and compassion towards Wilma, as the girl lay turning and tossing on her bed of pain, whimpering that she was dying and nobody cared, his soothing words of comfort throughout her ordeal, allied to his strength of purpose, his expertise at the various stages leading up to the emergence of the baby's head, had touched Grace to discover that her feeling of friendship towards him had deepened into love. Oh, it was nothing whatever to do with physical desire, simply a tremendous sensation of warmth, of joy in his company, a different dimension of loving, perhaps? A dimension that she had never known or even realized existed, before tonight, until she had glimpsed, beneath the rough exterior, the kindness, the gentleness, the true nature of the man.

Later dawned the knowledge that Herbie loved her, too. Not that this distressed or upset her in any way. How could it? This was the kind of love which demanded nothing in return, simply the perception of its existence based on mutual respect and understanding, tinged with something deeper by far, a kind of awareness of each other's needs – as if they were brother and sister, linked by a long lineage of love.

PART THREE

Chapter Twenty-one

The town was seething with summer visitors. Hurrying down Westborough towards the shop, it seemed to Kerry that the main street was akin to a race-course, with strolling visitors being overtaken by those anxious to get where they were going on time, and she must be back at work by two o'clock.

In her lunch hour, she had been to Rowntrees department store to buy a pair of silk stockings, after which she had eaten her sandwiches in the Londesborough Lodge Gardens. On a bench overlooking the lily-pond, her face turned to the sun, and blissfully aware of the beauty of life, she saw it as a bright kaleidoscope of ever-changing patterns, each lovelier than the last. But she must not lose track of time. At ten minutes to two by the gold-plated watch on her wrist – a seventeenth-birthday present from her parents – she walked up York Place, beneath Rowntrees arcade, and sped down Westborough, lithe and young and so pretty that people turned to look at her as she passed by.

Tall, as slender as a birch sapling, fair hair tied back with a broad, black velvet ribbon, wearing a crisp, white blouse and a smart, grey tailored skirt, her face aglow, she resembled a thoroughbred filly, full of life and vitality.

Mr Hodnot smiled as she entered the shop. Remembering the bright-eyed 14-year-old girl he had taken on as a dogsbody three years ago at Fanny Mallory's request, he could scarcely equate this smart, competent young lady with the incompetent, albeit willing little lass who had once ended up with more straw in her hair than she had managed to sweep up from the stock-room floor.

The time had come, he reckoned, to offer Kerry the job as his personal assistant, with a commensurate rise in salary. He wasn't getting any younger, worse luck. Besides which,

Kerry knew the shop side of the business like the back of her hand: the customers, representatives, and his staff of backroom workers liked her, and why not? She was smart, intelligent, lovely to look at, and more besides: compassionate, funny and possessed of the gift of happiness.

'Come through to my office, Miss Kingsley,' he said. 'I want a word with you.'

Kerry's heart sank. What had she done wrong? Recently, her mother had played war with her for wearing cheap make-up. 'Now just go upstairs and wash that stuff off your face at once, do you hear me?' Grace admonished her sharply. 'You'll ruin your skin!' Kerry had fled to the bathroom, accepting her mother's authority without question.

Later, 'Look, love,' Grace said gently, 'it's only natural that you should want to be like other girls of your age. The thing is, when you start wearing make-up, make sure you choose the right colours, and buy the best that you can afford. All right?'

'Yes, Mum.'

On her seventeenth birthday, she had discovered, among her presents, a pot of Rose Laird tinted foundation cream and a pale pink lipstick.

Now Mr Hodnot was saying that he had decided to promote her, to teach her the intricacies of the soft-furnishing side of the business, if the idea appealed to her. In other words, she would assume the role of his personal aide at an increased wage of 25 shillings a week.

'Well, Kerry, what's the matter?' He stared at her in surprise. 'I thought you'd jump at the chance.'

'I would. That is, I wish I could. And thank you Mr Hodnot, but—'

'But what?'

She had to be entirely honest. 'I – I can't do sums to save my life!'

Hodnot chuckled. 'Oh, is *that* all? Not to worry, my dear, I'll teach you everything you need to know. In any case, it is not my intention to throw you in at the deep end. Also, under my tuition, you will learn all there is to know about book-keeping and stock control.'

'Book-keeping? Oh, I don't know, Mr Hodnot. I mean, you wouldn't want to go bust, would you?'

'The trouble with you, Kerry,' he said, 'is that you haven't yet realized your full potential. But,' he sighed deeply, 'I have no wish to offer you this promotion unless you feel that it is well within your scope. I think it is, but perhaps you would prefer to discuss the matter first with your parents?'

'What about the shop?' she asked him.

'Ah, well, I should naturally appoint a new assistant to take your place,' he said carefully, 'to attend to the dusting and sweep up the stock-room. Why? Is that a problem?'

'No, not really. It's just that I love the shop,' Kerry replied wistfully, 'and I wouldn't want to lose touch with it.'

Quickly making up his mind, 'No reason why you should,' Hodnot assured her. 'As my second in command, you would be expected to keep a close eye on the shop and the stock-room.' In other words, the poor lass would more than earn her increment, he thought compassionately, if she wished to burden herself with more duties than were strictly necessary. But this was no ordinary lass, he considered. Otherwise, he would never have contemplated offering her promotion in the first place.

To his intense relief, and smiling like a sunburst, Kerry accepted his offer.

Even so, smiling, 'Are you quite sure,' he enquired cannily, 'that you would rather not talk this over first with your parents before reaching a firm decision?'

'No, I don't think so.' She added breathlessly, 'I can't wait to see their faces when I tell them that from now on I'll be earning twenty-five shillings a week!'

It wasn't the money she coveted, far from it; rather the sublime, uplifting feeling that she could now begin to repay her parents for the dancing lessons, the ballet shoes, tulle and trimmings, and so much more. Soon, perhaps, she would be able to afford a new hat for her mother. Come Christmas, decent presents for all the family – a book of poems for Jimmy, a silk scarf for Aunt Rosa, a handbag for Mum, a new wallet for her father, a bottle of perfume for Wilma, a tie for Danny, a special toy for her precious nephew, William. As for Dulcie, who knew what that long-lost sister of hers would want?

But why think of Christmas in this burgeoning, blossoming month of June, with a cloudless sky above, the town alive with visitors, and the opening night of the Bouquets' Concert Party on the Spa to look forward to?

So elated was Kerry that, bumping into Sid Hannay on her way home, she actually smiled and said hello. Why waste time harbouring grudges? In any case, he had lost his power to hurt her. Now it seemed ludicrous that he had ever possessed that ability. Walking on air, he had, at least, taught her a lesson worth remembering, she thought. Never again would she let her heart rule her head.

It was a perfect summer evening. Kerry and her friend Betty, one of the girls from Miss Williams's dancing academy, walked along the Spa peninsula together, chatting and laughing. Both wore pretty summer dresses, silk stockings and high-heeled sandals. The world was their oyster.

Betty, as dark as Kerry was fair, had been given complimentary tickets for the show. People were flocking towards the theatre. Excitement was in the air. Once in a while, Kerry thought, came moments of supreme happiness impossible to analyse or forget, moments which remained trapped for ever in the heart and mind for no particular reason other than the realization of happiness itself. Wherein the magic lay, she had no idea. The sound of the sea, perhaps, the colour of the sky, a trick of light on water, the scent of summer-time, the feel of silk stockings against a softly swishing cotton skirt, a lace-edged petticoat? A feeling of utter security, of well-being, with something nice to look forward to?

She imagined, as they entered the theatre, all the little milestones of happiness she had known so far as the connecting links between the past and the future; small stepping stones of joy as bright and unchanging as the stars in the Milky Way.

There was a buzz, a hum of anticipation from the audience awaiting the parting of the red velvet curtains, a ripple of applause when the orchestra struck up the overture, a moment's silence preceding an outburst of clapping when the curtains parted to reveal the various members of the Bouquets' Concert Party in Victorian dress. The men, in top hats, cutaway coats and tightly fitting trousers, were guiding their crinolined female partners across the stage singing 'Lovely to Look At', whereupon the ladies of the chorus snapped open and twirled their multi-coloured parasols in a dipping, swaying movement reminiscent of a Busby Berkeley musical.

Enchanted, Kerry clapped until her hands ached. The dresses were lovely, the choreography delightful. She longed to be up there on the stage, twirling a parasol. Dancing had become an all-important factor of her life. A week from now, she and Betty would take part in the Crowning of the Rose Queen ceremony, when they would perform a *pas-de-deux* to the music of Tchaikovsky's *Nutcracker Suite*.

During the comedian's solo performance, her mind strayed to her first Rose Queen appearance, that nervously anticipated arabesque, the throwing of a rose, and inescapably to Ashley Hawthorn. What had become of him, she wondered. Had he gone into his father's business? Water under the bridge now. She hadn't laid eyes on him since the day she had almost choked on an egg-and-cress sandwich. Nor, come to think of it, had his mother patronized the shop recently.

During the interval, she and Betty strolled along the balcony overlooking the bay. The sky was dark now, pinpricked with stars. 'Ooh, isn't it romantic?' Betty sighed deeply. 'Aren't we lucky to have seats near the front?' She giggled. 'I'll swear that handsome dark-haired bloke was looking right at me during the last scene.' She consulted the programme. 'His name's Rory Traherne. Look, there's a photograph of him.' A squeal of excitement, 'He's on next! It says here he's the natural successor of Count John McCormack, whoever *he* was. I've never heard of him, have you?' She gave Kerry a nudge. 'Are you listening?'

'Hmm? Oh yes.' Kerry had been star-gazing, remembering the words of a favourite poem: 'She walks in beauty, like the night of cloudless climes and starry skies . . .' 'Count John McCormack was a famous Irish tenor. We have a gramophone record of him at home singing "I'll take you home again, Kathleen".'

'Oh, trust *you* to know, Miss Clever Clogs,' Betty laughed.

'Well, you *did* ask.'

'Come on, let's get back to our seats.'

The house lights dimmed, the curtains parted to reveal a backdrop of a larger-than-life shamrock. The chorus girls, in green-and-white, short-skirted dresses, performed a lively jig to the music of 'The Irish Washerwoman' with their male counterparts. The audience clapped in rhythm; the girls' shamrock-patterned skirts billowed about their legs as they danced. The applause rose to a crescendo as they took their bows and ran breathlessly to the wings, leaving the stage empty momentarily – a production ploy to give the audience time to settle down in anticipation of the next act: the Irish tenor, Rory Traherne.

Imperceptibly, the stage lights dimmed, and a spotlight was turned, full-beam, on the figure of a tall, dark-haired, handsome young man in evening dress. Standing centre-stage, relaxed and smiling with more than a smidgin of Irish charm, his offering of the heart-rending ballad *Macushla* had the ladies of the audience taking out their handkerchiefs to dry their eyes.

It was a desperately sad song concerning the emotions of a lover lamenting the death of his beloved.

One might have heard a pin drop in the theatre. Betty was leaning forward in her seat, clutching her handkerchief. The man certainly could sing, Kerry thought, and the song was guaranteed to award the singer a storm of applause at its conclusion.

Now the singer was begging his lost love to wake from her sleep of death, to stay with him for ever.

The last, lingering high note – a pearl of perfection – slowly faded away into silence before the applause began.

'Oh, God, wasn't that simply marvellous?' Betty gulped, drying her eyes with her hanky. 'And did you notice the way his eyes were fixed on me the whole time?' She added breathlessly, 'I've simply got to meet him! We'll go to his dressing-room after the show.' Anxiously, 'You will come with me, won't you?'

'Not on your life!' Kerry responded sharply. 'You go if you want to. I'll go home.' She wouldn't be seen dead hanging about backstage, not for all the tea in China!

Predictably, the tenor's next number was on a much lighter note. The audience tapped their feet to the catchy tune of ' "Has Anyone Here Seen Kelly? . . . Kelly from the Isle of Man",' they roared in unison, to Betty's disgust, who felt that her romantic liaison with Rory Traherne had somehow been shattered by his rendition of a comic song so out of keeping with his true character. Frankly, she hated the sight of him prancing about on stage, conducting the audience in a silly song when, above all, she wished him to sing another romantic ballad directed towards herself.

She was, after all, a very pretty girl, and she knew it. Dark-eyed, with a mop of curly dark brown hair, a slender figure which went in and out in all the right places, unlike her friend Kerry, who had no bust to speak of, and not much of a bum either, come to think of it.

As the stage lights dimmed once more, the tenor stepped into the spotlight. 'And now, ladies and gentlemen,' he said in his rich-as-cream Irish accent, 'I'd like to sing you a song reminiscent of my childhood way back in the land of my birth, a song dear to my heart. "The Kerry Dance".' He began to sing softly,

' "Oh the days of the Kerry dancing,
Oh the ring of the piper's tune;

Oh for one of those days of gladness,
Gone, alas, like our youth, too soon".'

The Kerry Dance? Never before had Kerry realized that such a song, such a dance existed. *Her* dance! *Her* song! Her heart melted suddenly towards the singer. Her head ceased, in a moment, to rule her heart. Gazing up at the stage, she knew that she had fallen under the spell of the handsome Rory Traherne.

' "When the boys began to gather
In the glen of a summer night,
And the Kerry piper's tuning
Made us laugh with wild delight . . .".'

His eyes were as blue as a summer sky, lashes black as soot. His dark hair fell forward a little onto his forehead. His lips parted to reveal perfect teeth. His evening dress-suit fitted to perfection his lithe, broad-shouldered body. He used his hands and arms to great effect, gracefully, expressively. He sang from the heart, imbued with the gift of making every woman feel that he was singing to her alone.

' "Oh to think of it, oh to dream of it,
Fills my heart with tears . . . ".'

The words of the song painted a picture of soft summer darkness, lantern glow, happy smiling faces long gone and forgotten.

' "Silent now is the dark and lonely glen,
Where the glad, bright laugh will echo ne'er again . . .".'

Kerry's eyes filled with tears.

' "Oh the days of the Kerry dancing,
Oh the ring of the piper's tune.

Oh for one of those hours of gladness,
Gone, alas, like our youth too soon".'

The last note, high, soft and clear, faded imperceptibly into silence. The singer bowed his head. He's crying, Kerry thought tenderly, he really is crying. Her heart went out to him. How lonely he must feel far away from his native Ireland, his own kith and kin. Just as lost and lonely as she would feel parted from her family, in some far-off country, among strangers. How dreadful that would be.

Her thoughts far distanced from the present, she scarcely saw or heard the rest of the show: the dance routines, the second solo appearance of the comedian, the sketches, the soprano.

Thankfully, Betty appeared not to have noticed. The minute they were outside, 'Come on,' she said, 'let's go round to the stage door.'

Kerry demurred. Never one to follow the crowd, she couldn't bear the thought of standing there like a star-struck ninny, tongue-tied into the bargain. Betty had no such inhibitions. Grabbing Kerry's elbow, she hustled her along the balcony to the stage entrance.

'Betty, we can't just barge in,' she said helplessly.

'Don't talk so daft! I'm going to ask him to sign the programme, what's wrong with that?'

Everything was wrong with it, in Kerry's opinion. She hated the obvious. Admiring Rory Traherne from a distance was one thing, begging his autograph a different matter entirely. The magic lay in the misty shadowland between dreams and reality. 'I really don't want to,' she said decisively. 'You go, I'll wait here.'

'Oh, please yourself then!'

When Betty had gone, Kerry leaned her arms on the balustrade. Hands clasped, looking out to sea, scarcely aware of the voices, the laughter, the footsteps of the theatre audience making their way homeward along the gas-lit paths into town, she listened to the music of the sea washing up on the rocks below, remembering the haunting words of 'The Kerry Dance' . . .

Shivering slightly, she turned away from the balustrade. Glancing at her watch, she realized that Betty had been gone for twenty minutes or more. Five seconds later, she reappeared in the company of Rory Traherne. The pair of them were laughing together like old friends, he still wearing the tight Victorian trousers, frilled shirt and waistcoat he had worn in the finale, having shed the cutaway coat for comfort, Kerry imagined.

'Just coming!' Betty called out to her. Then, with a flirtatious upward glance at her companion, 'Thanks ever so much for the autograph, Rory,' she said breathlessly. 'It was so lovely meeting you.' She added, less enthusiastically, 'Gotta go now, I'm afraid. My friend is waiting for me.'

Moving forward, Rory Traherne said smoothly, 'You might at least introduce us.'

'Yeah. Well, this is my friend, Kerry Kingsley. We're both dancers, you know. As a matter of fact we'll be dancing together next week at the Crowning of the Rose Queen ceremony . . .'

Her voice drifted away into silence as, holding her hand, Rory Traherne said, 'Hello, Kerry. Did you enjoy the show?'

'Yes, very much indeed, thank you.' Shyness made her sound prim, at times.

'And to think, there I was singing "The Kerry Dance", and there you were in the audience all the time. How's that for a coincidence?' He had a pleasant laugh, soft and rich, a firm handclasp. His frilled shirt shone white in the darkness of a summer night that was not really dark at all, just shadowy, dim, warm, threaded with starshine and the twinkling lights of the promenade reflected in the deep, dark water below. 'Tell me, Kerry, which part of Ireland are you from?'

'Oh, I'm not Irish. I was born here, in Scarborough. I've never even been to Ireland.'

'Then how come the name Kerry?'

'That was my mother's idea. She spent a holiday in Ireland

once. But that was a long time ago. She was just a child at the time.'

'It must have made a deep impression on her then, to be sure,' he said softly.

'Yes, I suppose it must have.' His hair reminded her of Danny's. She smiled.

Betty said sharply, her nose out of joint, 'It's time we were going! It's getting late. Come on, Kerry.'

'If you are going into town, I'll walk with you,' Rory said easily. 'Just give me a minute to get out of this gear, otherwise the wardrobe mistress will play merry hell with me.'

When he had gone, knowing that Betty was feeling put out, and why, Kerry said, 'If you don't mind, I'll make myself scarce. After all, two's company. In any case, I'll get home much quicker on my own.'

'That's true enough, I suppose,' Betty agreed. 'You'd better be going then, hadn't you?' The sooner the better from her point of view. 'Good night, Kerry. See you at rehearsal on Monday.'

'Good night, Betty.'

Emerging from the theatre by the stage door, 'Where's your friend?' Rory wanted to know.

'Kerry? Oh, she couldn't be bothered to wait any longer.'

Chapter Twenty-two

Dulcie's visits to Scarborough had been few and far between since joining the Bergmann household, and on those widely spaced occasions when she had turned up, she behaved as a guest rather than a member of the family, to her mother's distress. Not that Grace could fault the girl's appearance, rather she could not equate the much slimmer, well dressed stranger, picky about her food, with the old, well upholstered Dulcie who had greedily gobbled up everything set before her, and more besides.

Despite their former uneasy relationship, Dulcie's outbursts of temper, her general air of dissatisfaction with her looks, her hair, her figure, linked to a deep-seated inferiority complex, Grace could better have borne Dulcie's censure than her silence, the feeling that the girl had not wanted to come home at all. And, of course, she was right . . .

According to his brother's prediction, Franz Bergmann's return from a business trip to America had added a bright new dimension to life at the family home in Leeds. Unlike Klaus, Franz, the younger brother, adored company, music, laughter, parties, gaiety. Soon the house had been filled with his vital, overwhelming presence. Even the old girl, his mother, more relaxed in the charm of his company, had seemed far less formidable. As for the twins . . .

Never would Dulcie forget the way Franz had entered the nursery quarters on the night of his arrival, when the children were tucked up in bed; waking them, to shower them with gifts of chocolates, toys, making them wild with excitement.

She knew him by sight of course, because she had seen him that afternoon in the café overlooking the Headrow. Even so, standing on her dignity as the children's nanny, owing allegiance to their father, she said coldly, heart thumping beneath or above her ribs – she couldn't decide which since her whole body seemed to be thumping and bumping madly at the time – 'I am in charge here! The twins are *my* responsibility. You had no right to disturb them.'

'Yes,' he murmured contritely, 'I'm so sorry, Miss . . .'

'Kingsley,' she supplied. 'Dulcie Kingsley.'

'Ah yes, Miss Kingsley,' he said, taking in at a glance her generously proportioned bosom, neatly controlled waistline and her delightfully plump thighs, 'Well, what more can I possibly ask than your pardon for this intrusion? My only plea is that I could not bear to be separated from the twins a moment longer.'

He turned at the door, his hand on the knob, 'I realize, of course, that I shall not be welcome here in future. So be it.' He smiled charmingly, 'Well, good night, Miss Kingsley. Sleep well.'

'No, I didn't mean that. Their father said they mustn't be given sweets, and they mustn't get spoilt and over-excited.'

Franz laughed, 'And you felt it your duty to protect them from their over-indulgent uncle?' He looked at her with considerable amusement. 'Does this mean that you will allow me to come here again – if I promise to behave?'

'Yes. Come as often as you like, but no more sweets.'

It seemed that an unspoken message had passed between them. Nothing whatever to do with the children, everything to do with physical awareness between an attractive, arrogant man and a susceptible, emotionally insecure girl in desperate need of fulfilment.

Jealousy had eaten deeply into Dulcie at first. Alone in her eyrie, apart from the twins asleep in the adjoining room, catching the sounds of music and laughter when a party was in progress down below, she pondered bitterly the unfairness of her role in life. Dinner parties were bad enough. Even worse those weekend house-parties when, standing remote and shadowy on the top-floor landing, she watched, sick at heart, the emergence of elegantly dressed guests from their rooms at the sounding of the dinner-gong, hating the sound of their laughter. Hating, above all, the many, apparently unmarried women friends of Franz Bergmann, mainly tall and slender, dressed in the height of fashion, loaded with expensive jewellery, and smelling divinely of Jean Patou perfume.

On one such evening, when the dining-room doors had been closed behind the influx of weekend guests, deliberately, wantonly, she had flushed away the entire contents of a bottle of 'Soir de Paris' scent purchased in Schofield's the day before.

Never again, she thought mutinously, would she demean herself by wearing anything other than Jean Patou perfume, Chanel No. 5, or Worth's 'Je Reviens'.

Later that night, aroused by a light, insistent tapping on the door, thinking one of the twins wanted a drink of water, she got out of bed. 'Coming!' she called wearily.

'Sshhh!' Franz Bergmann raised a warning finger to his lips. 'May I come in?'

'What time is it?'

'Rather late, I'm afraid.'

'What do you want?'

'Don't you know? Can't you guess?'

He was not drunk, she realized, nor was he entirely sober. She stared at him, not knowing what to say, how to handle the situation. A world of difference lay between dreams and reality. It was one thing to imagine losing her virginity. Now she felt more inclined to hang on to it. In any case, this was not the kind of seduction scene she had long envisaged, with soft music, candlelight and wine, herself in a white chiffon nightdress in some lavishly appointed hotel bedroom, her lover, in a kind of Noel Coward dressing-gown, plying her with champagne. All this leading up to an exquisite moment of surrender on a feather mattress.

'Oh, I can guess right enough,' she said sarcastically, feeling foolish in her white cotton nightgown, the front of her hair done up in Dinkie curlers. 'Well, you can just leave me alone.' Her eyes filled with tears of frustration. 'I don't suppose you care tuppence that I might lose my job?'

'Would you care if you did?' He smiled down at her from his great height, amused and intrigued by her naïvety.

'Of course I'd care! I have my living to earn.'

'There are other jobs,' he reminded her.

'That's as may be, but I happen to like the one I've got, ta very much!'

'And if I told you that I could offer you something far better? What would you say to that, Miss Kingsley?' he asked, tongue-in-cheek.

'I'd want to know what it was, for a start,' she replied tartly. 'Well, are you going or not?'

Sniffing the air, playing cat and mouse with her, 'There's a strong smell of scent in here,' he remarked lightly, ' "Soir de Paris", unless I'm much mistaken? Tell me, Dulcie, are you fond of that particular fragrance?'

'What do you think?'

'Since you ask, I think you're not entirely satisfied with the way things are. Despite your stalwart defence of your job a moment ago, it's not really what you want, is it?' He chuckled softly, 'Unless you imagine something far better for yourself if you play your cards right.'

'I don't know what you mean,' she said sharply.

'Of course you do. Just as you know why I came here tonight. You're quite delectable, Dulcie.' He took in the generous curves of her young body beneath the thin cotton nightgown. 'You'd look even more so dressed in the height of fashion, a fur stole about your shoulders, flashing diamonds.' He laid his hands on her shoulders as he spoke. 'Just think of it, Dulcie. But then, you have thought of it many a time, haven't you?'

'I don't know what you mean,' she reiterated, but with less conviction. 'Why don't you stop beating about the bush? It's late, and I'm tired. And you can stop pawing me, I don't like it. If you think I'm going to lie down and let you . . . Well, you've got another think coming, that's all!'

He smiled ruefully, 'Can't say I blame you. After all, where would you be robbed of your Ace of Hearts? Brother

301

Klaus would certainly turn his back on, shall we say "damaged" goods?'

'Why, you odious—' Inflamed with anger, she raised clenched fists against him.

He clasped her wrists before the blows aimed at his chest could find their target. 'All right, you've made your point, Miss Kingsley,' he said calmly. 'I apologize. You must make allowances. I drank more than I should have done earlier on this evening. I simply thought—'

'Oh, I know what you thought,' Dulcie said caustically, 'that you'd chance your luck with a servant. Huh! Why was that, I wonder? Did those fakey women friends of yours give you the cold shoulder when they saw the state you were in?'

'Something like that,' he admitted, holding onto her wrists. 'But there was more to it than that.' Drawing her closer, 'I wanted sex, but not the boudoir kind, if that makes sense?' He looked down at her, a strange look on his face. Her heart lurched suddenly. He said, 'Frankly, I wanted *you*, Dulcie. You and only you. I thought that you wanted me too. All the signs and signals were there. Apparently, I was mistaken. I'm sorry.' Briefly, he kissed the palms of her unclenched hands. Then, 'Good night, Dulcie,' he said quietly, turning away from her.

In a ferment of indecision, and recalling his offer of 'something far better', his veiled references to clothes, furs and jewellery, she was avid to know more. Overwhelmed by his looks, his charisma, his reference to the undeniable sexual urge and desire between them, she knew that to let go of him, without a word of encouragement, might be tantamount to cutting off her nose to spite her face. Thinking quickly, 'You might at least tell me about – you know – the job you mentioned,' she said coolly.

Jimmy's novel about the 1914–18 war was nearing completion. Writing it, he could not help thinking that history was about to repeat itself in the emergence of two present-day dictators – the German Chancellor, Adolf Hitler, and his Italian sidekick, Mussolini, whose sights were set on

302

world domination as surely as Kaiser Bill's and his alter-ego, General von Hindenberg's had been in the winter of 1914.

The trouble was, in this gloriously lazy summer-time of 1938, intent on sunning themselves on the beaches of holiday resorts from Bournemouth to Morecambe, from Land's End to John o' Groats, the British public had turned a blind eye to the ever-present danger of a second world war.

Pounding away at his typewriter in his room beneath the stars, Jimmy paused now and then to reflect on Hitler's annexation of Austria, the pledge of everlasting friendship between Hitler and Mussolini, in Rome on 7 May little more than a month ago. And here was he writing his tentatively named novel, *Remembrance*, based on the assumption that never again, under any circumstances whatsoever, would mankind endure a second conflict, a blood-letting in any way comparable to the first. Now he was not so sure. A seriously-minded young man, it occurred to him, finishing the last chapter of his book, that if perchance some publisher or other made him an offer, in the event of a second world war, *Remembrance* would defeat its own purpose.

He had talked long and earnestly to Herbie during their question-and-answer sessions about the worrying European situation, finding little or no comfort in Herbie's pessimism, his view that a second conflagration was simply a matter of time. There had already been violent scenes in Leeds city centre, the stoning of shop windows, hostility against those of German, Italian or Jewish descent, public meetings in support of Sir Oswald Mosley's Fascist organization; the spouting of hot air, the painting of slogans on walls, particularly in the Chapeltown area, with its largely Jewish community.

'It's all bad news in my opinion,' Herbie said heavily. 'I just hope and pray that the bloody Whitehall politicians will come to their senses before it's too late. But Neville Chamberlain's a doddering incompetent, in my view. No match for the likes of Hitler and Mussolini.'

Deeply troubled, Jimmy said, 'If and when it does happen, Danny and I will have to go, that much is certain.'

'Yeah.' Herbie grinned awkwardly, 'Me too. And before you start telling me I'm too old, all I can say is, they'll need older men, experienced old sweats like me to teach kids like you!'

'You mean you'd give up your job, your home, your security?'

'Let's face it, son,' Herbie chuckled, 'who in the hell would want celanese nightgowns and petticoats? As for my home, a small furnished flat off the Headrow scarcely constitutes a real home. It's just a place to go back to after slogging my guts out, somewhere to sleep and cook myself summat to eat. And security's just a word to me, always has been: an unattainable chunk of pie in the sky. So now you know.'

Jimmy pursued the subject. 'I'd plump for the Navy,' he confessed. 'I couldn't stand the Army: squad drill and all that stuff. Given the choice, I'd rather drown than be shot at. Face-to-face, that is. "The boy stood on the burning deck", and all that jazz.'

'What about Danny?'

'Oh, he'd go for the Air Force any day of the week. He's always had his head in the clouds anyway, the silly mutt.'

'What about his wife and child?' Herbie ventured.

Jimmy shrugged briefly. 'He adores the kid, of course. As for Wilma . . . He married the wrong girl, that's all. I tried to warn him, but he wouldn't listen. And yet, you know, after William was born, when Mum and Dad persuaded them to stay here for a while until Wilma regained her strength . . . she nearly died, didn't she? I mean, you should know. You were here at the time. Well, I thought, we all did, that Danny and Wilma had drawn closer together somehow.

'Then, six months later, there she was, chivvying Danny to find a place of their own to live, to stump up the money for a mortgage and furniture on the never-never! Now look at him, struggling to make ends meet in a terrace-house in Norwood Street with a shrew of a wife who would rather spend her time planning little supper parties for her friends than read her son a bedtime story!'

The minute Danny had received a rise in salary, promotion to deputy head of the accounts department at the Town Hall, Wilma began harping on the old theme of finding a place of their own to live. In two shakes, she had inveigled him into a frenzy of spending, entailing almost the full amount of his increment, presenting him with a precisely worked-out budget inclusive of mortgage repayments, instalments on furniture at so much per month, heating, lighting and food, backed up by her strong argument that a man in his position had a duty to perform in providing a secure home for his wife and child.

Unwilling to shake the foundations of their tentative relationship, to cross Wilma who had very nearly died in giving birth to their son, and faced with the fact that they could not continue living with his parents indefinitely, Danny had accepted his wife's ultimatum. He had shouldered his burden of debt and guilt with the fortitude of poor old Christian in John Bunyan's *Pilgrim's Progress*, faced with his own Slough of Despond.

Bedroom furniture, a lounge suite, tables, chairs, a kitchen cabinet, gas-cooker, pots and pans, carpets and curtains, a new cot for William – all these were essential. But a fancy china-cabinet, coffee-table, mirrors, pictures and ornaments for the front room were, in Danny's opinion, not merely superfluous, but a wicked waste of money.

'Oh well, if you don't want a nice home, I *do*!'

'We *have* a nice home, Wilma. All I'm saying is, we can't afford luxuries. Not yet, anyway. That hearthrug, for instance, and that standard lamp—'

'What's wrong with them?' she demanded in a voice pitched high with anger.

'Nothing's *wrong* with them exactly. It's just that we could have done without them for the time being.'

'Not if we intend to entertain our friends,' she reminded him sharply. 'And if you think I'm inviting them round to a half-furnished house, you have another think coming, that's all!'

At that moment, his father's words 'Marriage costs money', uttered on the eve of his engagement, struck Danny forcibly amidships. He had lightly dismissed those words as nonsensical at the time. Supremely self-confident and ablaze with the arrogance of youth, he thought he knew it all, but he had learned too late that everything his father had tried to tell him that night was true.

When his own son William had grown to manhood, would the boy, inflamed with a similar arrogance, as lightly dismiss his own counsel, he wondered. A moot point, inarguable, undebatable at this moment. In the event, Danny realized, his own father had spoken from his experience of a rock-solid marriage founded on love and trust – old-fashioned values underlying the joining together of two people in the holy estate of matrimony. They were scarcely applicable in his and Wilma's case, whose marriage had borne the hallmarks of failure from the beginning.

Norwood Street, Grace thought, inspecting her son's new home when the mortgage had been arranged and the house was ready for Danny, Wilma and William to move into.

'Well, what do you think of it, Ma?' Danny asked her.

'It's lovely. Really nice.' Standing in the hall, she enthused, 'Oh, what a pretty door.' Feasting her eyes on the richly coloured stained glass dappling the staircase with multi-coloured prisms of blue, red and green light, 'How strange,' she recalled, 'your father and I started our married life in the street next to this: Roscoe Street, a stone's throw away. There was a glass-panelled vestibule door similar to this. Of course you wouldn't remember, but you loved those coloured lights. I expect William will like these just as much.'

She thought fondly of her grandson, who closely resembled his father, who looked much as he had done at the same age. 'I'll miss you when you leave Castle Road,' she said simply.

'I know, Mum, but we couldn't have gone on living with you and Dad indefinitely.'

'I wouldn't have minded.' But she knew that what he said was true. Wilma and she would never see eye to eye in a thousand years. There had been no softening of the girl's attitude towards herself and Bob except, perhaps, in the days following the birth of her baby when, too ill and frightened to do otherwise, she had lain uncomplainingly against her pillows, desperately afraid of being left alone in a strange room.

Then, clinging weakly to Grace's hand, 'I'm not going to die, am I?' she had whispered.

'No, of course not,' Grace told her gently. 'You'll soon be well and strong again, able to look after the baby yourself. Just bear that in mind, and stop thinking about dying.'

'I want my mother,' she uttered fretfully.

'Yes, of course you do, and she will be here soon, I promise.'

Patching up her quarrel with Mabel Burton hadn't been easy, Grace recollected, in view of the woman's hostility when she had come to see her daughter. Swallowing her pride, she took the bull by the horns. 'Look here, Mrs Burton,' Grace said quietly, 'the past is over and done with. All that matters now is the future. The last thing Wilma needs right now is tension. She is still extremely poorly—'

'Oh? And who are you to tell me how to handle my poor little girl?' She bridled with indignation. 'If she had listened to me, she'd have given birth at home, where she belongs. But no, she chose to stay with that feckless son of yours. *Why*, God only knows. Now she's here with you when she should be at home with me, her own flesh and blood.'

'That's as may be,' Grace conceded. 'The fact remains that Wilma was here with her husband when the baby started coming. I'd have thought that any mother would be glad, not sorry, that a young couple had decided to give their marriage a second chance of success. But possibly you are not that unselfish?'

They were standing in the hall at the time, Grace at the

foot of the stairs, barring the way upstairs until Mabel Burton had calmed down before bursting into Wilma's sick-room like an avenging angel. She said calmly, 'If you really love your daughter, and I'm sure you do, as much as I love my son, you'll go up to her room quietly and peaceably. *Please*, Mabel, I beg of you. There is far more at stake here than old resentments, old quarrels that are best gone and forgotten. There is a new life to think of now.'

'Very well then, I accept your apology,' Mabel muttered ungraciously. 'Now, may I see my daughter?'

'Yes, of course.' Stepping aside, unaware of having made an apology, Grace murmured, 'Her room is the second door on the right on the first landing.'

But all that had happened in the September of 1936. Now, in this summer-time of 1938, William, a sturdy toddler, had become the apple of his grandparents' eye; a bridge over the troubled water of his parents' far from stable marriage, as shaky still as it had been in the Princess Street days.

Grace knew why. Bogged down with a burden of debt, Danny had become a pale shadow of his former self, a nervous, irritable individual unequal to the demands made on him by a spendthrift wife. Wilma seemed intent on squandering every penny of his income on new clothes for herself, unnecessary items of furniture for their home, determined to further his career with an endless series of intimate supper and dinner parties totally out of keeping with their limited income.

On the other hand, Grace consoled herself, Kerry was now earning 25 shillings a week, Jimmy's novel was nearing completion, Aunt Rosa was well and happy. On the debit side, she could not help worrying that the breach between herself and Nan had never been healed to her satisfaction, and that Dulcie had seemingly been swallowed up by her new life in Leeds.

She would sleep, then, in the warmth and safety of her husband's arms, until the light of a new day filtered between the drawn curtains of their room.

Chapter Twenty-three

'I'm not sure about that costume,' Grace demurred, assessing her daughter's appearance. 'It's a bit revealing, isn't it?'

'I'm supposed to be a man,' Kerry reminded her, 'a kind of female Nijinsky.'

'I know, but couldn't Miss Williams have asked one of the boys?'

'Which one? We've only got two. Bertie Bowes is as fat as butter, and Peter Pan is only fourteen.'

'*Peter Pan?*'

'Well, his name's Potts, but everyone calls him Peter Pan. Miss Williams chose me 'cos I'm tall and skinny, with long legs.'

'It's the legs I'm worried about,' Grace said. 'Couldn't you pull your tunic down a bit?'

'Don't worry, Mum,' Kerry responded cheerfully. 'In this outfit, everyone will think I'm a boy.'

'I very much doubt it,' Grace said, thinking that no-one in their right senses could ever mistake Kerry for a boy. Despite the ballet tights and the short red velvet tunic, her scraped-back hair and the plumed red velvet cap which covered it, there could be no question of her daughter's femininity.

Kerry said patiently, understandingly, 'Look, Mum, a *pas-de-deux* has to do with a male and a female partnership. Miss Williams chose me as the male because, well, let's face it, Betty's bust is too big and she's much shorter than I am. Just think how ridiculous it would look the other way round.' She giggled suddenly. 'Honestly, Mum, can you imagine how daft poor Betty would look, her tunic halfway down her legs, pursuing a female partner a good six inches taller than herself?'

'Oh, well, have it your own way. Just remember to pull your tunic down a bit, that's all!'

The day of the Rose Queen ceremony dawned fair and clear. Joining the throng of spectators, Rory Traherne, dressed casually in a lightweight summer shirt and trousers, watched the proceedings. Just his luck, he thought wryly, to have lumbered himself, on the opening night of the show, with Betty, when it was the other girl, Kerry, who had made the far deeper impression. Experience had taught him that summer seasons in seaside towns yielded an annual crop of ardent hangers-on. Not that he was averse to admiration, far from it. But girls of Betty's ilk, clinging like leeches, being overly possessive, were a liability rather than an asset. That first night, for instance, while escorting Betty, he wondered what had become of Kerry, the girl he had really wanted to take home?

Thankfully, the chatterbox Betty had referred, *ad nauseam*, to her role as a dancer at the Rose Queen ceremony, forgetting she had previously mentioned that she and Kerry would be dancing together. But he hadn't forgotten, and it was Kerry he desperately wanted to see again.

Standing on the edge of the crowd, he viewed with a jaundiced eye Miss Williams' *corps de ballet*, girls of all shapes and sizes in white tulle dresses, dancing to the music of *The Nutcracker Suite*.

Then came the *pas-de-deux*. Betty and Kerry entered the arena. He had eyes only for Kerry in her red velvet tunic. Her long slim legs, encased in flesh-coloured tights, were a joy to behold, a poem of fluidity and grace linked to superb muscle control, a kind of springy *joie-de-vivre* which took his breath away. My God, he thought, here was a real dancer, a potential ballerina worthy of Covent Garden. Feasting his eyes on her form and face – that lovely face of hers first seen by starlight – he experienced the old familiar arousal of his male instincts at the sight of a beautiful, desirable young woman.

Betty's performance passed unnoticed. His every thought

was centred on Kerry, the summer season ahead of him: the long days and the summer nights made for romance. The wooing and winning of so lovely a girl, the beginning of a new affair of the heart that would be more meaningful than all the rest put together.

A bitter feeling of betrayal had marked Dulcie's departure from the Bergmann household.

Thank God she'd had the common sense to accept Franz Bergmann's offer of employment as the manageress of the Headrow café. It was a matter of self-preservation when she had seen which way the wind was blowing . . . certainly not in her direction at the time.

She would never forget or forgive the humiliation of entering the drawing-room one Sunday afternoon to find a fashionably dressed young woman taking tea there with Klaus and his mother, the latter of whom was chatting amiably to the younger woman. She was slender, with fair hair, a pale complexion devoid of make-up, and large white teeth in what seemed, to Dulcie, a disproportionately large mouth.

When the twins had rushed past her to clamour about their father, 'Oh, aren't they absolute darlings?' the mouth had uttered ecstatically, and Dulcie had known, by the triumphant look on Frau Bergmann's face, that her dream of one day becoming the mistress of the house had turned to dust beneath her feet. The young woman with all the teeth was destined to become Mrs Klaus Bergmann.

Worst of all to bear had been Frau Bergmann's abrupt gesture of dismissal, the expression of triumph allied to hatred in the old woman's eyes.

How she had managed to quit the room with dignity, Dulcie would never know. Upstairs in the nursery, she had burst into floods of tears. When the tears ran out, coming to terms with reality, Dulcie thought mutinously that Frau Bergmann thought she had won. But she hadn't – not by a long chalk! She would teach the silly old woman a lesson worth remembering.

*   *   *

Franz had been apologetic about the state of the maisonette above the Headrow café when he had first taken her there to look over it. 'But not to worry,' he said urbanely, 'just tell me what you want and I'll see that it's done. Money no object!'

And so, at his expense, Dulcie had swanned round the shops choosing the paint and the wallpaper, the colour schemes she had envisaged in her future home.

For the first time in her life she could choose a background to reflect her own personality. Strong colours; dramatic wallpaper – deep crimson heavily embossed with gold fleur-de-lys. No rosebuds or sweetpeas of the kind favoured by her mother. She had not yet become Franz's mistress, nor would she until she was ready, until her new home was fit to move into.

Money no object. Those words had sounded as music to her ears. The decorating completed, she went to town to choose everything her heart desired. In the city's most prestigious store, she chose the carpets, curtains and furniture she wanted. Franz watched, with tolerant amusement, Dulcie's attempts at self-expression in the selection of colours, fabrics and floor covering. The girl had been hurt, and he was prepared to wait until the dust, metaphorically speaking, had settled, from his viewpoint as well as hers.

There had been an ugly scene in the drawing-room when he had broken the news that he had offered Dulcie the job as manageress of the Headrow café.

'You have done *what*?' Frau Bergmann had regarded him coldly from beneath hooded eyelids, and yet he had known by the clenching and unclenching of her knotted hands on the arms of her chair, the extent of her anger.

'Why not? After all, the property belongs to me, and Dulcie is a free agent.' Trying the charming, light-hearted approach, 'Come now, Mother, be reasonable. The girl needed a job, I needed someone I could trust to manage the shop—'

'*Trust!*' The old woman's anger burst forth explosively.

Rising from her chair, prodding the carpet with her silver-knobbed walking stick, each jab underlined her sense of outrage. 'You dare to stand there and tell me that you trust that – that common, scheming little baggage?'

'I was simply taking my cue from brother Klaus,' Franz reminded her, 'who, as I recall, entrusted Miss Kingsley with the responsibility of looking after the twins.' Refusing to be brow-beaten or intimidated, his own anger began to rise. 'A task she performed quite admirably in his opinion – or so he told me when I returned home from America.'

'Pah!' The old woman snorted contemptuously, beating a tattoo on the carpet. 'Miss Kingsley's interest lay, not in the twins, but their father! I knew it the minute I laid eyes on her. It was this house she wanted, a rich husband. I have met her kind before. Need I remind you that she was quick to hand in her notice when she realized that Klaus had become engaged to marry Fräulein Constanz?'

Drawing herself painfully, arthritically to her full height, Frau Bergmann continued contemptuously, 'Now, robbed of the older brother, her sights are set on the younger!' A pregnant pause, then, 'Tell me, Franz are you really so blind or so stupid that you cannot see what she is up to?'

'You underrate my intelligence, Mother,' Franz replied coolly, 'but then, you always have. Now, if you'll excuse me, I have other matters to attend to.'

Crossing the room, and turning to face his mother, his hand on the doorknob, he said hoarsely, 'I know that the estimable Klaus has always been your favourite son, and that you have always regarded me as a kind of joker in a pack of playing cards, that you deeply resented the fact that Father willed the Headrow premises to me, not Klaus. Well, hard luck. Unlike Klaus, I am not prepared to make a lasting commitment to any one woman. I happen to believe that life is for the living, for the pursuit of pleasure. After all, who knows what tomorrow may bring?'

At last, Dulcie had everything she had ever wanted from life: money to squander at will, a home of her own, a prestigious job, a rich admirer. What had she to lose apart from her virginity?

The more she saw of Franz Bergmann, the more she liked him. He was fun to be with, handsome beyond belief, generous to boot, a real gentleman, unlike his stuffy elder brother Klaus, who had simply used her for his own ends. She could see that quite clearly now. All that stuff and nonsense at the Children's Corner, for instance, when all he had really wanted was a nanny, not a wife.

Well, now that she had her place in the sun, a rich, ardent admirer, the rest was up to her. She and Franz were two of a kind, her common sense told her, intent on the good things of life: money, pleasure, possessions. She couldn't care less about the ethics of the affair. He wanted her, she wanted him, it was as simple as that. He wanted physical satisfaction, she wanted money, fine clothes, jewellery and French perfume, fine food, too, served in expensive restaurants. That was a far-distanced dream nowadays, since the alluring curves of her body had been achieved, and might reasonably be maintained only by a constant, boring diet of lettuce leaves, grilled fish, and broiled chicken; boiled vegetables, and fresh fruit. Even so, she still desired roast beef and Yorkshire puddings, mashed potatoes smothered in gravy, roast pork thick with crackling, steak and kidney pie, fish and chips, and knickerbocker glories piled high with whipped cream and crowned with a scattering of pistachio nuts.

But the old, fat Dulcie, the Pavilion Hotel waitress, had whistled down the wind long ago, thank God. Now, standing on the threshold of a new, infinitely more rewarding life than she had ever known before, she knew that it was simply a matter of time before she and Franz Bergmann became lovers . . .

When Kerry had changed from her tunic, tights and velvet cap into a lightweight summer dress, silk stockings and straw hat trimmed with a multi-coloured chiffon scarf, a figure moved swiftly forward to claim her attention, linking his arm in hers as she emerged from the makeshift dressing-room adjacent to the Spa forecourt.

'Don't talk, just walk,' Rory Traherne advised her in his rich as cream Irish accent, 'otherwise we'll not have a moment alone together.'

Taken by surprise, 'Here, hang on just a minute,' she said, half laughing, half serious, as he hustled down a flight of worn steps to the beach below, 'just what do you think you're doing? I promised to meet Betty after the show!'

'Never mind about Betty,' he chuckled as the sand bit into their shoes, 'just concentrate on me, Kerry my love.' He began to sing softly,

'"Oh the days of the Kerry dancing,
Oh the ring of the piper's tune.
Oh for one of those hours of gladness,
Gone, alas, like our youth, too soon".'

'Know what? You're barmy,' she said equably, a happy young girl in the company of a handsome young man on a lovely summer day with a blue sky above, the feel of sand beneath her shoes, the sound of the sea washing in on the shore, the crying of seagulls overhead; hearing, in the far distance, the Town Band playing, 'Land of Hope and Glory'.

'Come on, run!' he adjured her, clasping her hand. 'I'm barmy, so what? I'll race you to that ice-cream stall over yonder. Ready, steady – *go!*'

Standing near the sea wall, looking down, Ashley Hawthorn watched the couple on the beach below, saw the laughing Kerry running hand-in-hand with the tall, good-looking man, filled with the exuberance of youth, snatching off her hat, the breeze lifting her cloud of golden hair.

Marking the date of the Rose Queen ceremony on the calendar, he had moved heaven and earth to be in Scarborough on that particular date, in the hope of seeing her again. And he had seen her, dancing divinely; had pushed his way through the crowds thronging the forecourt to get to her – too late. The other man had already claimed her attention. A chance meeting, he felt sure, seeing her look of surprise. Then the other man had seized her arm and hurried her away along the promenade and down the steps to the beach.

Now all he could do was stand there and watch the pair of them running and laughing together on this wine-sweet summer afternoon, deeply regretting that he was not the man by her side, thinking bitterly that he might have been had he not been so easily put off by her girlish rejection of him that day in the St Nicholas Gardens, her startled-fawn expression when he told her how lovely she was.

Absorption into his father's business had convinced Ashley that he was something of a square peg in a round hole. Thankfully, the 'old man' had landed him with the responsible, at times boring job, as a liaison officer in charge of wining and dining potential investors in the Hawthorn 'empire', which meant that he had had to do a certain amount of homework beforehand, to become *au fait* with the building trade in general, in order to convince those investors that they were not about to part with their money unwisely.

But was this entirely true? Delving into the records of the firm's business dealings of the past, it struck him as odd that certain invoices for goods delivered did not match entirely with the goods ordered. These discrepancies worried Ashley a great deal. Was his father's 'empire' as sound as he had supposed it to be, or not?

If not, what then? There could be only one answer to that question. If those discrepancies were discovered by an outsider, a government investigator, for instance, the Hawthorn 'empire' might well cease to exist.

Meanwhile, his mother had continued to throw dinner and supper parties with a view to ensnaring him into matrimony. There was, in the Vale of York area, a seemingly inexhaustible supply of young women ready and willing to say 'Yes' at the drop of a hat. Girls of all shapes and sizes; daughters of wealthy parents, determined to hitch their wagons to his particular star, whom he had treated with courtesy, nothing more, to her ladyship's disgust.

One evening, rounding on him fiercely after an abortive supper party during which he had paid scant attention to the slim, reasonably attractive offspring of a local MP and his wife, 'I wish I knew what is wrong with you, Ashley,' his mother said forcibly. 'Here you are, a good-looking young man, in the prime of life, who should be thinking in terms of settling down. Heaven knows I've done my best to introduce you to gals of your own age and social standing who would fit into our family circle. Take Celia Mountjoy, for instance,' – referring to the MP's daughter – 'who would make you a charming wife, given the slightest encouragement.'

'I'm sorry, Mother, but has it ever occurred to you that I might prefer to do my own choosing? That if and when I marry it will be for love, and no other reason, whether or not the girl of my choice is acceptable to you and father?'

Brave words. Now, turning away from the sea wall, walking dejectedly the uphill paths to the Esplanade where he had parked his car, it seemed to Ashley that the girl he loved was as far distanced from him as the sun, moon and stars.

'It's a crying shame, so it is, that you were not the one being crowned the Rose Queen of Scarborough this afternoon,' Rory told Kerry when, out of breath, they had stopped running. Taking in her flushed, wild-rose complexion, sparkling blue-grey eyes and her breeze-winnowed hair, 'I mean what I say! It should have been you, mavourneen, wearing that crown, walking down that long flight of steps, your arms filled with roses.'

Impervious to his blarney, screwing up her eyes against the sun, swinging her straw hat by its chiffon streamers, a young girl in love with life, aware of the creaming in of the sea on the shore, the blue sky above, commanding this sublime moment of happiness, she said laughingly, 'What about that ice-cream you promised me?'

Glancing at his watch, he muttered apologetically, 'Faith! I'd forgotten entirely, so I did! Here I am when I should be back there, in the theatre, rehearsing a new number for tonight's show!'

'You'd best be off then, hadn't you?' Kerry said light-heartedly, refusing to let her heart rule her head.

He said gruffly, drawing her closer, gazing at her lovely, laughing face upturned to his, 'Promise me you'll be there tonight? I'll leave a ticket at the box-office for you. A front row seat. Promise?'

'I'm not sure,' she demurred.

'*Promise?*'

'Oh, all right then, if you really want me to.'

'And that's not all. Promise you'll wait for me after the show? Come round to the stage-door?'

'I'd rather not, if you don't mind. Come to the stage-door, that is.'

'No? Well, it's up to you. But promise you'll wait for me.'

'Yes, all right, I'll wait for you.'

''Bye for now then. Don't forget!'

Watching his receding figure hurrying back the way they had come, what was happening to her? Kerry wondered. Why the feeling that her heart had wings? Why the added shine and lustre to this already perfect summer afternoon? Why did the sky suddenly seem much bluer, the waves frilling the sand much creamier than before? Why had her head ceased suddenly to rule her wildly beating heart?

The girl in the box-office glanced curiously at Kerry when she asked if there was a ticket in her name, and she flushed slightly as she accepted it. Perhaps Rory Traherne made a habit of leaving complimentary tickets for his admirers? Truth to tell, she felt guilty that she had given Betty the slip after the *pas-de-deux*. Not intentionally. Even so, Betty would be put out if she knew why. More so if she found out that Rory had not wanted her company.

Half wishing she had not come to the theatre after all, and feeling conspicuous, Kerry found her seat in the front row. And yet a tingling feeling of excitement swept through her as the orchestra struck up, the lights dimmed and the red velvet curtains parted to reveal the opening number of the show, the Bouquets' Concert Party in Victorian costume, the girls with their parasols, the men singing 'Lovely to Look At'.

With Betty, on the opening night of the show, she had scarcely noticed Rory Traherne. Now, to her chagrin, she could scarcely take her eyes off him. Moreover, to her surprise, she actually felt a little bit jealous of his partner in the ensemble, a pretty, dark-haired chorus girl twirling her parasol.

The thought occurred that she could slip away, unnoticed, during the interval. And yes, she thought, she would do just that: put an end to this nonsense; walk home alone along the Foreshore; tell her mother she was tired, and have an early night. She was, after all, a responsible young adult with a good job, and no great opinion of the male sex in general, apart from her father, and her two brothers. And yet she longed to hear the words of 'The Kerry Dance' once more. *Her* song.

There had been a change in the programme, she realized when, after the 'Irish Washerwoman' jig, Rory came on stage to sing, without preamble, the simple, ballad, 'Macushla'.

When the applause had died away, standing in a much softer spotlight than he had done on the first night of the show, Rory thanked the audience, then he said quietly, 'And now, ladies and gentlemen, for a very special lady in the audience tonight, a song dear to my heart, "The Kerry Dance".'

Listening to the words, the haunting tune, Kerry's eyes filled with tears. Gazing up at the stage, she knew that Rory Traherne was singing for her alone, as if she were the only person present in that darkened auditorium:

'Oh for one of those hours of gladness,
Gone, alas, like our youth, too soon.'

The words struck a chord in her heart. After all, how

319

fleeting were the golden days of youth. Growing old, how long would the magic of seemingly endless summer days and moonlit nights last? And what price a human heart unwilling to take a chance on love?

Rory's final song said it all so far as she was concerned: 'Love Walked In' . . .

After the show, she was standing near the railings, watching the play of moonlight on the sea when, at long last, he came to her. 'Oh, Rory,' was all she could say. Then suddenly she was in his arms, lost in the magic of his kiss, the strength and warmth of his virile young body against hers, knowing that she was marvellously, deeply in love at last, witnessed by the moon and stars above, the music of the sea on the rocks below.

Chapter Twenty-four

The new King, George VI, had been crowned in the spring-time of the previous year. Few people regretted the abdication of the emotionally tortured Edward VIII, the uncrowned monarch who had renounced his throne for love, and yet Ashley Hawthorn harboured a strong feeling of sympathy for the man whose overwhelming love for one woman had far outweighed all else. Watching newsreel pictures of Edward making his abdication speech from Windsor Castle, his subsequent departure to France to marry Wallis Simpson, Ashley thought compassionately that there was a man who knew his own mind. Contrary to popular belief, a strong man, not a weakling. It must have taken a great deal of courage to fly in the face of his family's condemnation, let alone that of an entire nation, to marry the woman he loved.

Now, here was he, a man in love, lacking the courage to straighten out the mess he was making of his life. The building trade was not for him. He had known that from the outset. 'Constructional engineering', as his mother would have it. But then, his mother was a snob at heart, never one to call a spade a spade. Worse still, Ashley suspected that his father, an astute businessman, was cutting corners to build new houses; using sub-standard bricks and mortar to increase his profit-margin. Or perhaps he was wrong? He hoped to God that he *was* wrong.

So where exactly did that leave him? The heir apparent of, not a throne or an empire, but a far less spectacular building firm based in the north-east of England; lacking the courage to either confront his father or to ask the girl he loved to marry him.

Walking up the sloping paths to the Esplanade on the day

of the crowning of the Rose Queen ceremony, he knew that he must see Kerry again, and the sooner the better. How to approach her, he had not the foggiest idea, until . . .

Driving into town, entering a florist's, he ordered a dozen long-stemmed red roses to be delivered to Mr Hodnot's shop in St Nicholas Street the following morning. The attached card read, 'The Royal Hotel, one o'clock? *Please* come! A.H.'.

He walked forward to greet her. Smiling, he said, 'I'm so pleased you came. I wondered if you would care to have lunch with me?' Sensing her hesitation, 'Or somewhere else, if you'd prefer?'

'I don't understand. The flowers are lovely, but why did you send them? Why this sudden invitation?'

'Perhaps I felt that I owed you an apology and an explanation. The last time we met, I'm afraid you gained a wrong impression of me.'

'But that was ages ago.'

'Even so, I've never stopped thinking about you. Please, Kerry, I'd really like to talk to you.'

'Oh, all right, then. But not here. I'm in my working clothes.'

He knew what she meant. The Royal catered for an uppercrust clientèle, mainly elderly couples, the women largely over-dressed and overfed, wearing too much jewellery. Useless to tell Kerry that she, in her plain grey skirt and pristine white blouse, outshone them all. She would not believe him, and he had no wish to embarrass the girl.

'You lead the way,' he said quietly, 'I'll follow.'

'There's a café round the corner in Huntriss Row,' she said, 'where they serve things on toast. You know, baked beans and poached eggs. It will be pretty crowded, I expect, at this time of day, but I dare say there'll be room upstairs.'

She was speaking quickly, nervously, and he guessed why. The poor kid was ill-at-ease in his company, uncertain of his motives.

'I have a much better idea,' he said. 'Let's take the Penny

Tram to the Foreshore and buy a couple of ice-cream cornets. It seems such a pity to waste time indoors on a day like this.'

'Really? Oh yes, I'd like that!' Kerry breathed a sigh of relief. Frankly, she had hated the thought of sitting opposite Ashley Hawthorn at a tile-topped table, toying with a plate of baked beans on toast, his eyes upon her all the time, and she trying not to blush; attempting to make polite conversation, worrying, at the same time, that she might have trouble swallowing the toast.

In the lift, he said, 'I was on the Spa yesterday. You're a very good dancer. Have you ever thought of taking it up professionally?'

'No, not really. Well, not seriously. Mum would have a fit. Besides, Mr Hodnot has promoted me as his personal assistant. Dancing's just a hobby.'

The beach was alive with visitors. Small children were paddling, their screams of delight as the waves lapped their feet sounded high and clear in the warm air. There were patiently plodding donkeys, ice-cream stalls; pleasure boats in the bay, a cluster of green canvas bathing tents beneath the Gala Land rotunda. Kerry smiled, thinking of Rory Traherne, remembering that he had walked her home this way the night before. The sea had been dark then, threaded with silver ribbons of moonlight, full, deep and mysterious, shore-lights gleaming on wet sand.

'You look happy,' Ashley remarked.

'Do I? Well, yes, I suppose I am,' she said dreamily. 'Aren't you?'

'I am now.'

'Why now, especially?' In all innocence.

'Because I'm with you.' He had to say it, 'Because I – love you.'

Her footsteps faltered suddenly. She looked up at him, eyes wide with surprise and something more – disbelief. 'But that's not possible!' She had been about to say, 'Plain daft.' 'We scarcely know each other! Besides—'

'I know what you're thinking,' he said urgently, 'but

you're wrong. I know I'm a bit older than you, that my parents are well off, but what difference does that make? Money means less than nothing to me. Love is all that matters in the long run. Love and – happiness.'

Taking her hand, he drew her towards a bench beneath the St Nicholas Gardens' arcade, 'Please listen to me, Kerry. I fell in love with you the first moment I saw you. When my mother and I came to the shop to choose curtain material, remember?'

'Yes, of course I remember,' she said dully, 'but—'

'Please hear me out,' he interrupted gently. 'The truth is, you've never been out of my mind for a moment since our last meeting. That's why I sent you the flowers, why I needed to talk to you, to tell you how I feel.'

'I'd far rather you didn't,' she said miserably. 'It isn't that I don't like you. I do. I've often wondered about you – if you went into the family business. As a matter of fact, I've still got that rose you threw me. Somehow, I couldn't bear to part with it, but I'm not in love with you. In any case . . .' Words failed her.

'In any case what?' he prompted her gently.

'Oh, you *know*!'

'Please, Kerry, I'd rather you told me,' he persisted gently, keeping tight hold of her hands.

'Well, if you must know, I don't belong in your world! I've seen where you live and I didn't like it. All those big rooms and those oil-paintings on the walls . . . ' Drawing in a deep breath. 'You said that money doesn't matter, but it does to me. The fact is, I'd hate to live in a house like yours. I'd shrivel up and die in a house like that. I'd rather be poor all the days of my life than live in such a house.'

'And what if I told you that I don't like it much either?'

'I don't know. But then I'm not as clever as you are.' Withdrawing her hands, 'Oh, come on, let's go! What's the use of talking?'

'Kerry,' he said bleakly as she rose to her feet, 'please let me explain. I went into the family business as a matter of loyalty to my father. I'm living at home because I have to, for the time being at least. Kerry! Please come back!' But she was hurrying away from him, intent on catching the next tram into town.

He caught up with her at the ticket barrier. The tram doors opened, then closed. Standing beside her as the lift rose to its destination, sensing her withdrawal, he murmured hoarsely, 'I really do love you, you know!'

The tram doors opened, then came the clicking of the turnstile as the passengers filed out, one by one, into the heart of the town centre, adjacent to St Nicholas Street and the Royal Hotel.

Facing him, 'Yes, I believe you,' Kerry responded quietly, 'but it's no use. I'm sorry, Ashley, I do like you a great deal. I just happen to be in love with someone else!' Turning away from him, she hurried along St Nicholas Street to her place of employment where, in the safety of the cloakroom, she dried her eyes on the roller towel behind the door. Why she was crying, she had no idea, except, perhaps, that she had retained one poor, withered rose – the rose that Ashley had thrown to her two summers ago – within the pages of her *Palgrave's Golden Treasury*.

And perhaps her feelings for him ran deeper than she realized? Even so, the barrier between them remained insurmountable. Besides which, she was head over heels in love with an Irish tenor . . .

A side door adjacent to the café led to a narrow staircase. The landing opened onto a sizeable kitchen, dining-room, and a large drawing-room, Victorian in character, with a high ceiling rosette, deep skirting boards, and picture mouldings. On the upper landing were two bedrooms and a bathroom.

During the refurbishment of her new home, Dulcie had been staying at a hotel near the city centre, an experience which she had enjoyed to the full, at Franz Bergmann's expense, of course. How she had loved playing the lady; ringing up room service, demanding breakfast in bed; swanning out at midday to have her hair done. Sauntering along the Headrow, dressed to kill: she would return to the hotel in time for afternoon tea, and revel in the red-plush, potted-palm elegance of the lounge, the tinkling of silver-plated spoons against Chinese Rose tea-cups and saucers, ordering Earl Grey rather than China tea, nibbling thinly cut cucumber sandwiches.

Deriving equal pleasure from the situation, Franz fancied himself in the role of a latter-day Pygmalion to Dulcie's Galatea. It pleased him to indulge her, to watch her greedy little eyes light up when he handed her a giant-size package of French perfume, an item of jewellery, a Schofields' carrier-bag containing a selection of silk and lace lingerie, or whatever.

Curiously, it was this greed of hers, her basic coarseness which most attracted him. She, too, was a go-getter, a survivor. These qualities, if they could be regarded as such, were common ground. The younger son of the Bergmann family, he had lived in the shadow of his brother, the estimable Klaus. Not that he had appeared to do so. His natural charm and ebullience had stood him in good stead throughout his life so far.

Klaus had always been his mother's favourite son, Franz knew that. On the other hand, he had been his father's favourite, and the old man had made certain that, after his death, a percentage of the profits from his manifold businesses should accrue to his younger son. Moreover, he had willed to him absolutely the Headrow café and bakery – the most lucrative of his assets, to the disgust of his mother, who felt that Klaus should have been awarded that particular plum.

And so a certain coolness had sprung up between himself, Klaus, and the old lady since the reading of his father's will: nothing substantial or immediate, until that day in the drawing-room when he had confessed to offering Dulcie the job as manageress of the Headrow café.

He had known, deep down, that what his mother said was true, that Dulcie had had her sights set on Klaus as a husband. More power to her elbow! And perhaps she was, as his mother had suggested, 'a common, scheming little baggage'.

Even so, he had reason to admire the girl's guts and determination, her ability to hold down a difficult job in the face of the old girl's dislike of her. Moreover, Klaus had praised to the skies her handling of the twins, her dedication to duty, her patience and forbearance; not knowing, not even suspecting the underlying main reason why Dulcie had cared for the twins so assiduously. But then, the dull, estimable Klaus, despite his good looks, possessed a wooden heart totally devoid of romance – witness his former wife, a fat, 'jolly hockey sticks' English girl with buck teeth, his present fiancée, as plain as the proverbial pikestaff.

Dulcie, on the other hand, earthy, greedy, difficult to handle, who had sent him away with a flea in his ear that night in the nursery, had proved a challenge difficult to resist. Standing there, her hair done up in curlers, she had told him to get lost in no uncertain terms. She had, moreover, threatened him with physical violence if he did not leave her alone. And yet, cunningly, indicative of a good, common-sense head on her shoulders, she had wanted to know more about the job he had in mind for her before closing the door firmly behind him.

Now he wanted her as he had never wanted any woman before, and he intended to have her. The time was almost at hand. The maisonette was ready for her to move into – and the piper must be paid. Dulcie knew that as well as he did.

She had set the dining-room table with a pristine white cloth, a centrepiece of red dahlias – the first of the autumn flowers – a reminder that summer was almost over. And yet the weather remained stultifyingly hot and humid, the reason why she had chosen cold food: smoked salmon, melon, cold chicken and salad, fresh fruit and ice-cream for this, the first ever meal in her new home.

Looking anxiously at the carriage-clock on the mantelpiece, rearranging a fork here, a spoon there, smoothing the folds of the full-skirted, red velvet hostess gown Franz had given her to mark the occasion, he would be here in ten minutes or less, she thought distractedly. And then what? Momentarily, awaiting the ringing of the doorbell, she remembered another supper table, long ago, her mother handing round the tureens of vegetables, plates piled high with home-cooked food, a happy, smiling face beneath a crown of light brown hair, and knew, beyond a shadow of doubt, that she had exchanged gold for dross. Too late now. The die was cast. The past over and done with. She, Dulcie Kingsley, had all she had ever wanted from life firmly within her grasp. She'd be a fool to turn back now.

When the doorbell rang, she walked firmly, upright, down the stairs, her red velvet hostess gown swishing softly about her ankles, to welcome her lover.

Chapter Twenty-five

Every hour, every minute of that summer would remain with Kerry for ever, the bittersweetness of her first real love affair; that deep awareness of another person, the way he looked, moved and laughed. She would find herself willing away time until their next meeting, day-dreaming when she should have been working, remembering his every word, wondering if he really meant what he said when he told her how much he loved her? Then she would find herself dreading the end of summer-time, when the shore lights would be extinguished and the winter seas came crashing in on the rocks beneath the Spa wall.

Needing to confide in someone, she chose Jimmy as her confidant. Perched on the end of his bed, she confessed that she had fallen deeply in love with Rory Traherne.

'I've been wondering what was up with you,' Jimmy said matter-of-factly. 'So have Mum and Dad. There's been no keeping track of you lately. All those mysterious late-night excursions of yours. Well, just watch it, kiddo. Don't do anything daft.'

'I don't know what you mean!' She wished that she had not confided in her brother after all.

'That's just it, Kerry. Talk about Innocents Abroad. Just you be careful, that's all. I mean, what do you know about this man? Apart from what he's told you, that is?'

'Well, if that's your attitude—'

'Look, kiddo, all I'm saying is, men don't go in for the moonlight and romance nonsense as a rule. There's usually an ulterior motive.'

'What ulterior motive?'

'Oh, come on, love, you can't be as innocent as all that!' But he knew, deep down, that she was. And it was this crystal clear innocence of hers which could be her undoing. He wondered if their mother had ever told her the facts of life? Most probably she had, in a roundabout way. Whether or not Kerry had taken them in was a different matter entirely.

Pacing the room, he said haltingly, 'You see, Kerry love, men are – well, *men*! What I mean is, they get – wound-up – kissing a girl.' This wasn't the doddle he thought it would be. 'What I'm trying to say is, real life isn't like the cinema. Have you ever stopped to think what happens after the fadeout kiss?'

'I expect the director calls "cut", and everyone goes home,' Kerry said mildly.

'Exactly! And there you have it in a nutshell,' Jimmy expostulated. 'Everyone goes home! But real life isn't like that. There's no director to call "cut", for one thing. Then things begin to get out of hand. Next thing you know, the man takes advantage of the girl, and . . . ' he sat down abruptly, 'well, I just don't want anyone to take advantage of you, that's all.'

Perched beside him on the bed, 'Rory isn't like that,' she said quietly. 'He really loves me, and I love him. Oh, Jimmy, he's such fun to be with, so thoughtful and – tender.' Glowingly, 'I have the feeling he's going to ask me to marry him.'

'And if he did, would you say Yes?'

'Of course.'

'Even if it meant leaving home? Going to Ireland or wherever, to live? Or just following him from place to place during the summer-time?'

'Yes. Why not?'

In a turmoil, 'Oh, grow up, Kerry,' Jimmy said savagely, springing to his feet. 'The man is, presumably, a Catholic, so what if you found yourself living in Ireland with a brood of kids to bring up on your own while young feller-me-lad was in England? In Scarborough, Eastbourne, Skegness, or wherever?'

'I thought that you, above all people, would understand

how I feel.' Kerry crossed to the door. 'I know you think I'm letting my heart rule my head, but that's what love is all about, isn't it? Knowing when someone is right for you, no matter what the future may bring?'

'In that case, why all the secrecy?' Jimmy stood his ground. 'Why not bring him home to meet Mum and Dad?'

'Because – oh, how can I explain? Because Rory isn't the kind of person to make polite conversation over afternoon tea. And because, well, I'd hate him to think that I have designs on him! Because,' she faced Jimmy appealingly, 'our love-affair is so special, no – wonderful, I couldn't bear to have it spoilt in any way.'

'OK, Kerry, you win,' he said harshly, turning his back on her to hide his emotion. 'Just you take care, that's all.'

'I'm sorry, Jimmy, I didn't mean to upset you.'

'Upset? Who the hell's upset?'

When she had gone, he rooted in the top drawer of his desk for the completed manuscript of his novel. Riffling through the pages, it was utter and complete rubbish, he decided, the kind of stuff a schoolboy might have written: lacking in depth, breadth and substance, shallow, inconsequential. The reasons why this was so, he reckoned, had to do with this house, this room, his comfortable existence, his lack of experience of life beyond these four walls.

Lying flat on his back, staring up at the ceiling, the old patterns of light emerged; a trace of moonlight, the distant, effulgent glimmer of a gas lamp in the street below, each as familiar to him as his own two hands; part and parcel of his past, his development from the gangling youth he once was to the man he now knew himself to be. Closing his eyes to the moonlight, the gaslight on the ceiling of his room, he knew the time had come to leave behind him all the old familiar and well loved patterns of home.

A man could become too insular. If his writing lacked substance, that insubstantiality must stem from a lack of experience of other places, other people. How could he write convincingly about places he had never seen, people he had never met? How could his work reflect any kind of authenticity unless he moved into the mainstream of life?

He thought longingly of London, a job in a newspaper office. Fleet Street. He had saved enough money to ensure his survival for a month or two if he could find somewhere cheap to live. A rented attic room would do. He liked attics. He would exist on porridge and boiled eggs, if necessary, until he had landed himself a job. He would make a portfolio of his published work so far, to prove his writing ability.

The only snag was telling his parents that he was leaving home. He hoped his mother wouldn't cry and beg him to stay. He couldn't bear that. But he knew, deep down, that she wouldn't, that the tears she shed would be shed in the privacy of her own room. He had, after all, Grace to thank for encouraging him to write in the first place. Even so, he realized how difficult, how heart-breaking for her to contemplate the further dissolution of the once closely knit family circle. With Dulcie gone, himself and Danny, there would be only Kerry left at home, and who knew for how long if that blasted Irish tenor swept her away to the Emerald Isle?

'Oh, for heaven's sake, Danny, stop brooding! We have people coming in half an hour. Go up and get changed.'

Wilma was in what she called the lounge, arranging dishes of snacks on the coffee table, having read in one of the women's magazines she devoured assiduously from cover to cover that snacks with sherry were the hallmarks of a successful hostess. The sandwiches, pinwheel scones, and the Victoria sponge sandwich she had made earlier that day, were on the kitchen table along with the cups and saucers. These she would serve with coffee at 'half time', when the sherry supply had run out; Danny knew this, since he would be called upon to hump the trays to the sideboard.

Going upstairs to put on his best suit and a clean shirt, it struck him as ludicrous that the guests, when they arrived, would sit on unpaid-for furniture, drinking sherry and eating food which he and Wilma could not really afford to provide for them. But what use talking to her? So many rows had erupted between them over this entertaining fetish of hers that he had stopped trying.

Quietly opening the door of what Wilma referred to as the nursery, standing on the threshold, he saw that his son lay sleeping, chubby fists outflung, lost in a world of dreams peculiar to childhood. What did infants dream about? he wondered. Birds? Rabbits? Toys? Or perhaps they did not dream at all? Possibly every child's slumber was as deep and satisfying as a night without stars, an area of darkness between sleeping and waking? He hoped so. There was nothing sadder than dreaming dreams which never came true.

At least Jimmy possessed enough courage to set forth in search of his dream, but it had been a bitter pill to swallow when his brother had come round, this Sunday morning, to break the news that he was off to London next day to try his luck as a writer.

'I'll miss you,' was all he, Danny, could say, wringing Jimmy's hand at the final moment of farewell. 'Just keep in touch, that's all, and take care of yourself.'

'You too, brother.'

When Jimmy had gone, 'What was all that in aid of?' Wilma wanted to know, seating William in his high chair.

'Jimmy came to say goodbye. He's going to London the first thing tomorrow morning.'

'Oh?' Wilma shrugged uninterestedly. 'Well, I guess he'll be back before long, his tail between his legs! Huh, a bit of a laugh really, isn't it?'

'What is?' He knew, then, that she had been listening to their conversation; eavesdropping. Sick at heart, he said, 'I'm not laughing.'

'No, well, a sense of humour has never been your strong point, has it?' Then, crossly, 'Oh, for heaven's sake, child, sit still!'

William's face crumpled. He began to cry. 'Dada,' he sobbed, 'Dada!'

'That's all right, son, I'm here.'

'I suppose you know you're spoiling him to death?'

Wilma muttered savagely, slamming down a couple of rusks on the tray of the high chair. 'It's all very well for you, Danny Kingsley, you're out at work all day! You don't know what it's like for me, shut up in this house all the time, trying to cope with his tantrums. And all you can do at the weekend, is undermine my authority!'

'*Authority?* Over a *toddler?*'

At that moment, in a blinding flash of self-revelation, Danny knew that he had lied to his son, that everything was far from right between himself and the boy's mother; never had been from the beginning of their ill-fated love affair, their winter wedding and their honeymoon fiasco.

Now, Jimmy was leaving him alone in a sea of regret, of self-abnegation, and how he would miss him, that stalwart companion of his childhood days. Danny knew in his heart of hearts that, were it not for his son, Jimmy would not travel alone to London. He would have gone with him. If things were different, he would have turned his back on Wilma with a sensation of relief that he no longer had to live with a woman he not merely disliked, but thoroughly detested. But things were *not* different. They were as they were, and would remain so, because of the child his wife had borne him, because he would never willingly abandon his own flesh and blood.

'The house seems so quiet,' Grace said, as if she could hear the silence. She and Bob were in the back room. Rosa had gone to bed after supper, Kerry had not come in yet. The hands of the clock stood at half-past ten. A week had passed since Jimmy went away to London. He'd written briefly to say he'd arrived safely, had found digs near King's Cross Station and he would write more fully when he'd settled in.

'Strange, isn't it?' she sighed, 'Jimmy has always been the quietest of the four, and yet the house seems empty without him.' Glancing up at the clock, 'I wonder where Kerry has got to? She's been out since dinner-time. Did she say where she was going?'

'Not to me. Didn't she tell you?' Bob frowned.

'I'd have known, if she had.' Grace got up. 'I'll look out of the front room window, see if she's coming.'

'I wouldn't if I were you,' Bob said. 'Kerry's seventeen now. She'll be in soon, you'll see. She's probably with Betty. Perhaps they went to Peasholm Park this afternoon and Betty invited her home for tea. Afterwards, I dare say they went to the pictures.'

'This is Sunday,' Grace reminded him. 'Kerry doesn't usually go to the pictures on Sunday.'

'Oh, come on love,' Bob laughed, 'Sunday is Kerry's only free day of the week. Only natural to want to make the most of it. Besides, it's summer-time, not the middle of winter.'

'I know all that, but I can't help worrying. She's been acting very strangely; going out after supper, coming home late. Not a word about where she's been, or who with; just poking her nose round the door to say good night, then hurrying up to her room. I don't like it, Bob. I'm worried!'

Kerry had felt nervous, at first, on the switchback ride across the moors: the road before them a series of humps, curves and dizzy descents leading to the next hill, the next bend, the next downward swoop, the next seemingly insurmountable obstacle – a hill far steeper than the last.

Heading for Whitby in a car Rory had borrowed from the stage-manager, a vintage Ford A, a 'rag-top' model with wire-spoke wheels, disc clutch and a three-speed gear-box, he had laughed and told her not to worry, that he was completely in control.

Stopping the car on the outskirts of Whitby, 'What you need is a nice cup of tea,' he told her, 'and here's the very place. We'll have it in the garden, shall we? You sit down, I'll go indoors and do the ordering.'

It was a pretty stone cottage with yellow roses round the door, a crooked, hand-painted sign, 'Afternoon Tea Served Here', near the garden gate. Awaiting Rory's return to the rough wooden table on the front lawn, she noticed, with a deep inner pang of regret, that the first of the autumn flowers were in bud; the michaelmas daisies, dahlias and

335

crysanthemums, whose flowering would mark the end of summer-time, the onset of winter. Time was fast running out for herself and Rory, she realized, wishing she knew what to say or do to come closer to him, to prove how much she loved him.

After tea, Rory drove on to Whitby where they walked, hand-in-hand, about the ruins of the abbey above the sun-washed sea. There, feeling the warmth of her hand in his, he knew that he had fallen like a ton of bricks for this girl. She was so lovely to look at, so genuinely good, so physically attractive that, whenever they were close together, as they now were, he wanted her with every fibre of his being. What man in his right senses would not wish to possess that fine, slim young body of hers?

To him she epitomized 'The Kerry Dance'; that lilting melody, the ring of the piper's tune; the play of lantern light on the faces of the dancers as 'up the middle and down again' they went; those long-forgotten lads and lasses of long ago, whose laughter had once filled the air in a lamp-lit glen on a summer night. He had initially regarded 'The Kerry Dance' as a romantic pot-boiler on a par with 'Macushla' and 'I'll Take You Home Again, Kathleen'. On the other hand, the producer had insisted he should sing the kind of sentimental songs the audience expected to hear from a good-looking Irish tenor of the kind popularized by Count John McCormack, and he had gone along with that, since his livelihood depended on pleasing the public, not to mention the producer. Now, 'The Kerry Dance' had become, in a sense, his signature tune. Because of Kerry Kingsley; he put a wealth of feeling into the words when she was seated in the front row of the stalls – and even if she was not, he knew that she would be waiting for him on the starlit promenade after the final curtain.

On the road across the moors from Whitby to Scarborough, he fell silent, noticing that the great swathes of heather clothing the hills and dells as far as the eye could see, were gradually changing colour from brown to pink. And soon, he thought, that pink would turn to purple, and the moors would be covered with a great tide of deep purple blossoms heralding the final lowering of the curtain on the Bouquets' Concert Party, the end of summer-time, and his return to Ireland.

The bright summer day was fading now to the quiet of evening. Kerry, he knew, must be terribly hungry. He was too. They hadn't had a bite to eat since the scones and jam in the country cottage garden. He said casually as the lights of Scarborough came into view, 'Let's have dinner at my place, shall we?'

'*Your* place?' Kerry frowned. 'I didn't know you had a – place. I thought you lived in digs with the rest of the Company.'

'So I do,' he said blandly, 'and I'm sure the landlady will find us something to eat, however makeshift. Please say you'll come.'

'Oh, very well then, if you really want me to.' Glancing at her watch, 'But I must be home early tonight. Half-past nine at the latest. You see, well, I know my parents are worried about me, and I haven't been entirely honest with them lately.'

'Honest? In what respect?'

'Well, I haven't told them about you, for instance.'

'Oh? What about me?'

'That I'm in love with you,' she said simply.

They were on the road leading down to Peasholm Park. Fairy lights twinkled in the dusk, they could see the floodlit pagoda above the waterfall. Rory stopped the car. Facing Kerry, taking hold of her hands, 'You've never said so before.' His voice was husky.

'I thought you knew.'

'I knew you liked me, I hoped it was more than that. Oh, Kerry, darling Kerry!' Drawing her close in his arms he fastened his mouth on hers. Eyes closed, she returned his kiss in a way she had never done before, deeply, to prove how much she loved him, and trembled at the touch of his hand at her breast, the strange, hitherto unknown desire his touch evoked in her.

337

Then, 'We can't stay here,' he murmured hoarsely. 'We'll go to my room. No-one will know, if we're careful.'

She opened her eyes. Jimmy's words, 'Just you be careful, that's all,' echoed in her mind. The world, seemingly lost to her a minute ago, came back into focus. Rory's hands were now on the steering wheel, the car was moving forward. 'We'll go the Marine Drive way,' he said. 'I'll park the car on the Foreshore. We'll walk from there. My digs are in Princess Street.'

'I don't want to go to your digs.'

He laughed disbelievingly. 'But you said—'

'What did I say?'

'That you loved me.' He wasn't laughing now. But then it hadn't been a real laugh in the first place, Kerry thought, more of a chuckle with a slight edge of impatience.

'I do love you.' She was out of her depth, but she had to be honest with him and herself. This above all. 'I don't want to spoil it, that's all.'

They were on the Marine Drive now, the sea on the left as calm as a millpond beneath a starlit sky. Rory stopped the car. His arms about her, 'Hey now,' he said softly, 'what is all this? Is it afraid you are? Afraid I'll hurt you?' Cupping her face in his hands, speaking gently, 'Sure, and what's wrong with two people in love wanting to be alone together?'

'We *are* alone. We have been all afternoon,' she reminded him. 'It's just that I . . .' How to explain that she could not have borne to creep upstairs to his room like a thief in the night, afraid of being seen? Knowing she was doing wrong? 'I – I'm tired and hungry, and I want to go home.'

'What a child you are to be sure,' he said quietly, uncupping her face. She knew that he was bitterly disappointed, trying hard not to show it. 'But at least you'll not go home hungry. There's a good fish restaurant on the Foreshore – unless your scruples get in the way of my treating you to a fish-and-chip supper!'

'Please don't,' she murmured, close to tears as he restarted the engine.

'Don't what?'

'Be angry with me!' Appealingly, 'I don't want any supper. Just drive to the Spa. Please, Rory, do as I ask. I just want to talk to you, to make you understand how I feel.'

'I thought you wanted to go home?'

'I do, but I want to talk to you first.'

Driving along the Spa promenade, he stopped the car near the sea wall. 'Seems to me you want everything your own way, Kerry,' he said bitterly. Getting out of the car, he walked to the sea wall, and stood there looking down at the rocks beneath.

Laying a hand on his arm, 'I'm sorry,' Kerry said gently, 'but I meant what I said. I do love you, more than words can express.' She smiled sadly. 'I guess it happened that day of the Rose Queen ceremony, remember? When we walked along the beach together and you asked me to meet you later, after the show?'

'I remember,' he said bleakly. Then, turning to face her, the picture of misery, 'and how do you suppose I felt, singing that damned song of yours night after night? Wanting you so much it hurt! Then, when you told me you loved me too, how do you imagine I felt when you turned me down flat?'

'But, don't you see, Rory, love to me means more than a hole-in-the-corner affair? To me, love means marriage; children, an everlasting commitment between two people who really love one another.' Breathlessly, 'Don't you feel the same way too?'

'Yeah, I guess so. At least I did once, a long time ago. Of course I was very young then, living in Dublin, taking singing lessons, and earning money as best I could to pay for the lessons: washing pots, waitering, navvying. You name it, I did it! I had to. You see, I wanted to sing more than anything else in the world. I knew I had talent. I imagined . . .' He laughed bitterly, 'Oh, what's the use of talking?'

'Please, Rory, go on,' Kerry urged him gently. 'What did you imagine?'

'Why, that I'd earn fame and fortune as an operatic tenor

one of these fine days. I had my sights set on Milan, Paris, New York – and then—'

'And then?' Kerry asked. 'Then what happened?'

'Then *she* came along,' Rory said dully, 'Bridget Malone, the girl I married six years ago, the mother of my children, God help me. So now you know.' Extending his hands in a futile gesture of despair, 'But it's you I love now, mavourneen, more than I have ever loved any woman before, more than I shall ever love anyone again.' He drew in a shuddering breath of despair, 'Please don't look at me like that. What I say is true.' He held out his hands to her. 'Say something, for God's sake!'

'What do you expect me to say?' She felt cold inside. Empty, numb. 'Why did you do it? Why did you make me fall in love with you? Or is it something that happens all the time, wherever you happen to be? Whenever you meet girls willing to make fools of themselves?' She turned away abruptly, blindly, her eyes brimming with tears, seeing the spaced-out gas-lamps along the promenade through a veil of tears, unclearly, the effulgent lights blurred just, as lights, in winter, are blurred by snow.

She was walking aimlessly, like a blind woman, unaware of the curious glances of passers-by; summer visitors out for a stroll in the warm night air. In Kerry's heart the season was winter, not summer.

'Kerry! *Wait!* Please, wait!' Rory was at her side, his hand on her arm, speaking urgently.

'Leave me alone. I'm going home.'

'But I want to explain.'

Anchored by the touch of his firm warm fingers at her elbow, 'What is there to explain?' she said dully. 'You've told me all I need to know. You're married, with children.' Brushing away her tears, 'Well, so far as I'm concerned, the sooner you go back to them the better!'

'If only it were that simple, that cut and dried, but it isn't.'

'Things seldom are.' She smiled sadly, remembering Danny and Wilma; an innocent child born of a loveless marriage, 'but we can't turn our backs on the past, not when children are involved.' Facing him, 'Don't you see, Rory? You had no right to involve me in your life in the first place.'

'You think I don't know that?' He stood before her, tall and proud, so handsome that the ice about Kerry's heart melted suddenly and it was summer-time once more, 'But no matter what you think of me now, I couldn't help falling in love with you, and I shall go on loving you till the day I die!' Clasping her hands, he said, 'Every time I sing "The Kerry Dance", you'll be there. Wherever I go, whatever I do from now on, you'll be there.'

'Goodbye, Rory,' she whispered, and then she was gone. Hurrying away from him, Kerry wondered how her heart could sustain such grief and keep on beating?

Watching her retreating figure, Rory knew that their brief summer-time love affair was over and done with. Never again would he see her sitting in the front row of the stalls; never again emerge from his dressing-room to the starlit balcony to find her there, her lovely face upheld to his, awaiting his kiss. Ah well, so be it.

Turning away, returning to the car, he recalled the futility of his life so far. His own fault entirely. He had married, too soon, a girl who had never understood his ambition to become an opera singer. For her sake, and the sake of their children, he had abandoned all the years of self-discipline which might have led him to the great operatic theatres of the world. To earn money, he had embarked on a series of summer shows and winter pantomimes to feed and clothe his wife and children.

Tomorrow, he would go to early morning Mass at St Peter's Church; seek absolution for his sins from the priest in charge. 'Forgive me, Father, for I have sinned,' he would say in the confessional, remembering Kerry, deeply regretting the pain he had caused her, knowing that a thousand and one acts of atonement could never restore to him a long-lost feeling of love for his wife, the red-haired, quick-tempered girl he had married when he was far too young to know his own mind. But there would be other summer times, other girls to fall in love with.

*   *   *

Grace was in the hall, on her way to the kitchen, when Kerry came into the house. 'What is it? What's wrong?' she asked anxiously.

'Oh, Mum!' Tears streamed down the girl's cheeks unchecked.

Moving forward quickly to hold the sobbing Kerry close to her heart, 'Come on, love,' she murmured, 'bed's the best place for you, the state you're in.' Slipping a supporting arm about her waist, leading her upstairs to her room, opening the door, 'Now, get undressed and climb into bed. Meanwhile, I'll make you a hot cup of tea and a sandwich. Don't worry, just do as I say, the way you used to when you were a little girl, remember?'

Kerry remembered. Undressing, slipping into her soft warm bed, cradling her cheek against the pillows, drying her tears with a clean handkerchief, she thought how easy it was to slip back into the old familiar pattern of childhood, to seek comfort, as a child, in her mother's arms. The fact remained that she was no longer a child but a woman.

When Grace came back into the room with a tray of tea and sandwiches, 'Please, Mother, I need to talk to you,' Kerry said. Brushing aside the tray, she got out of bed, shrugging on her dressing-gown, standing tall on her own two feet. 'The fact is, I've made a fool of myself. A complete and utter fool of myself.'

Setting down the tray on the bedside table, facing her daughter, Grace said quietly, 'I'm listening.'

'I don't know where to begin.' Kerry brushed her hand through her hair, and she meant what she said. All she could remember clearly was the end of the affair. All that had happened in between seemed like shifting kaleidoscope patterns in her mind: colours, music – words that had meant everything and now meant nothing. She said, 'I didn't know he was married. He didn't tell me until tonight.'

'*He?*' Grace sat down on the bed.

'I told Jimmy about him. He told me to be careful.'

'Yes, I expect he did.'

Kerry turned to the window and looked out, a hand on the curtain, her hair cascading about her shoulders. 'I walked home. We were on the Spa. That's where we met. I was with Betty. He sang "The Kerry Dance", and I thought that's *my* song. I thought he was singing it for me. That was silly. He didn't even know me. But he did sing it for me after that night. He would leave a ticket for me at the box-office, and I would sit in the front row of the stalls. He has a lovely voice. Well, he studied in Dublin. He told me that tonight, before he told me about . . .

'We'd been to Whitby. He borrowed the stage-manager's car. It was such a lovely afternoon. We had tea at a cottage with roses round the door. I noticed that the autumn flowers were beginning to bud, and I thought – in a month from now he'll be gone and I might never see him again. I told him I loved him.

'He asked me to go to his room. He said no-one would know if we were careful. Then I thought about Jimmy, and I knew I couldn't.' She had been speaking quietly, un-emotionally. Suddenly, turning away from the window, covering her face with her hands, she sobbed harshly, 'I wish now that I had. Oh, God, I wish now that I had. Oh, Mum, help me. I don't know how to bear it.'

Then, there she was, despite her fine words, a child once more, in need of comfort, love and strength; wanting to be held close in someone's arms. And the arms that held her *were* strong. Strong yet gentle. The arms of a compassionate mother with no fault to find, no harsh, unkind words to say to a hurt child.

Kerry had not even told her the name of the man she was in love with, but this was no time for questions. Only love. Silent understanding.

Chapter Twenty-six

The heather would be in full bloom now, Kerry thought sadly. Confession was supposed to be good for the soul. Hers felt lacerated. The sparkle, the magic had gone out of her life since that night three weeks ago when she had told her mother about Rory.

Now Grace looked troubled. When Kerry asked her not to worry so much, she said, 'I can't help it, everything's in such a state.'

'Everything?'

'Dad thinks there's going to be another war with Germany. He's worried sick about it. You see, Danny and Jimmy would have to go.'

Kerry's heart gave a sudden lurch. Selfishly, she had not given a second thought to briefly glimpsed newspaper headlines concerning Adolf Hitler's increasing threat to the Peace of Europe, the terrible events that were taking place elsewhere. How could she have been so blind, so wrapped up in her own problems as not to realize the full depth of her mother's anguish?

Thank heaven Herbie would be arriving later that day. Dear Herbie, whose presence would break the tension of the past few weeks, since Jimmy's departure to London and the misery of her abortive love-affair with Rory Traherne.

Rory! Tomorrow night the final curtain would fall on the Bouquets' Concert Party. Thereafter would come the whole-sale removal of the costumes and props, the stacking of the scenery backstage. Rory had once described to her what happened after the final curtain call in theatres everywhere: the 'get out' he called it, when pandemonium broke loose in the dressing-rooms, and the wardrobe mistress held sway, demanding the swift return of every costume, every item of

344

fake jewellery, shoes, parasols and gloves to pack into the wicker hampers in the wings, and woe betide anyone who had mislaid so much as a pair of cuff-links or a cravat.

Kerry knew that she must be there, in the audience, on that final night of the Bouquets, that she must see Rory again. Then and then only would she find the peace of mind she so desperately craved, the courage to live her life without him. Above all, she desired a decent end to the affair, to wish him well for the future, to heal the wounds; tell him that she loved him and always would. How could she do otherwise? Nothing could alter the fact that he was married, but life might be easier for him too, knowing that she still loved him.

After supper, she slipped away unnoticed. Herbie was in the back room with her parents. Quickly she hurried along the Foreshore to the Spa. People were crowding round the box-office, anxious to see the last night of the show, the finale, the handing-up of bouquets. When Kerry's turn came, the girl in the ticket office told her she was lucky, all she had left were a few singles in the back row of the stalls, then the commissionaire would put up the *House Full* notice.

Edging into her seat, the old familiar thrill ran through her. This place, this theatre, was filled with remembered magic. She loved the red plush seats, the gilding, the indefinable theatre smell, an amalgam of perfume, grease-paint, packed humanity. Above all the excitement, the striking up of the orchestra, the parting of the heavy, red velvet curtains.

'Lovely to Look At'. The couples came on stage, the girls twirling their parasols. The only one Kerry saw or cared about was Rory, the way he moved, looked and smiled.

During the interval, she remembered the row when Betty found out that she was seeing Rory, the harsh words that had ended their friendship. Eyes flashing fire, bosom heaving, Betty had called her a snake-in-the-grass, a mealy-mouthed sycophant.

'I'm sorry, Betty, I never meant it to happen. You must believe me.'

'Believe *you*? Huh! I wouldn't believe you if you swore on a stack of bibles!' Scornfully, 'A fine friend you turned out to be. If I never set eyes on you again, it will be too soon!'

Rory had laughed when she told him, 'I wouldn't lose any sleep if I were you,' he advised. 'Girls like Betty are a pain in the neck.'

But Kerry had not been able to dismiss Betty so easily. It had hurt her deeply that Betty had believed her capable of subterfuge. Afterwards, she had given up her dancing lessons.

The interval over, Kerry returned to her seat. Heart pounding, she awaited the moment when Rory would appear on stage, tall, handsome, immaculate in evening dress, to begin his solo performance.

Dear God, how much she loved him. Never more than now. If only she was sitting in her old place in the front row of the stalls. If only she could turn back the clock to that day in June when they had walked together, hand-in-hand, along the sand, and she had taken off her hat the better to feel the sunshine on her face, and he had begged her to meet him, that night, after the show.

' "Macushla, Macushla, your red lips . . ." ' She was too upset to remember the rest of the words.

Kerry's eyes filled with tears. How weak she had been, how cowardly in running away from him when she should have stayed to listen. Instead, eaten up with false pride and jealousy, she had turned her back on him. Now she longed to hear once more the words of 'The Kerry Dance'. Her song! *Their* song!

'And now, ladies and gentlemen, for a very special lady in the audience tonight, a song dear to my heart . . .' Smiling down at someone in the front row, ' "The Rose of Tralee",' Rory announced tenderly.

'Excuse me, please.' Edging past a row of knees, thanking God that she was in the back row near one of the exit doors, Kerry stumbled from the theatre into the warm night air. Resting her hands on the sea wall, she stared out at the deep, dark water of the bay; saw, as one in a dream, the cold, distant light of the stars in the sky above.

It was then she realized with a cold, inner certainty, that the show was over. No need to await the finale, the handing-up of bouquets. No need to make amends, to say what she had come to say.

In a little while, she turned and walked slowly along the lamplit promenade, the way she had come. In the space of three short weeks the Kerry Dance had ceased to exist in the heart and mind of the man she loved, she thought painfully, too proud to cry. Just as well she had discovered the truth before making an even greater fool of herself, she told herself severely. And yet, in her heart of hearts, she still loved him, and it would take a very long time to forget the bittersweet memories of her first real love affair.

Herbie, Grace and Bob were in the back room, and yet the old sense of contentment was missing. The threat of war and the increasing gravity of the European crisis seemed to hover above them like a bird of prey.

If war came, Grace thought, life as they knew it would cease to exist. Memories of the first conflict were deeply rooted in her mind: the waste, the sadness of it all. And in her case, the agony of waiting for news of Bob, the terror of a sudden unexpected rat-tat on the front door of the house in Alma Square, the possible arrival of a telegram from the War Office beginning with the words, 'Regret to inform you'.

That telegram had never arrived, thank God, but if this second war happened, if her sons were taken away from her, the agony of waiting would begin all over again. Her mind felt like a mouse on a treadmill, going round and round, arriving nowhere.

Bob said in concern, 'Don't worry, love, it may never happen.'

But it *had* happened! Her peace of mind had already been shattered beyond repair. War or no war, the old sense of security she had once known was gone for ever. Danny, who had married the wrong girl, was reaping a poor harvest from his hastily sown oats in that summer-time of 1935. Jimmy had discovered, to his chagrin, that the high and mighty editors of the Fleet Street hierarchy had remained unimpressed by the portfolio of a non-member of the NUJ . . . the National Union of Journalists.

'But how the hell am I supposed to become a member of the NUJ,' he'd written in a recent letter, 'without first becoming a journalist? It doesn't make sense!'

But then, nothing made sense these days, Grace thought despondently. Why had Dulcie, for instance, given up her secure job as the Bergmann twins' nanny, to become the manageress of a café? And why, for heaven's sake *why* had her beloved little Kerry fallen head over heels in love with a married man? And what, in God's name, was going on between her mother and Aunt Fanny in that house above the fancy goods shop in South Street? Rosa seemed to know, but her lips were sealed. Indeed, it appeared to Grace that the old woman was growing dottier by the day. Kittenish, almost, smiling to herself and nodding, moving her 'sealed' lips as if holding a conversation with herself. At any rate, Grace thought, talking to oneself had certain advantages. One could not very well quarrel with one's alter-ego.

Restlessness was in the air. Grace felt unable to settle to her knitting. Herbie had made it clear that, if war came, he would enlist at once with the Green Howards. What if Bob decided to follow suit? But no, she told herself. Herbie was as free as air. Bob had a business to run, financial commitments, family responsibilities. Even so, if war came, as seemed inevitable, the choice may not be his to make. He was still a comparatively young man, lithe and healthy.

'I'm going to make some tea,' she announced, getting up, heading for the kitchen, unable to sit still a moment longer. And, 'We'll come with you,' Bob said.

When the tea was made, they sat down at the kitchen table to drink it.

'About Dulcie,' Grace said, cradling her tea-cup, deriving pleasure from its warmth, 'have you seen her lately, Herbie?'

Her question held a wistful note. 'The last we heard, she had left the Bergmann household. She didn't say why. She simply said, in her letter, that she had found herself a better job as the manageress of some café in Leeds city centre, with living accommodation above.' A slight pause, then, 'We wondered if you had heard of it?'

Herbie knew exactly what Grace was driving at, and his heart went out to her – a worried mother anxious about her daughter's welfare, as well she might be, in Dulcie's case. He said carefully, 'Oh yes, the Headrow Konditer . . . café, is quite famous, and very – er – respectable. I pop in quite often, on Saturdays, to pick up my bread and treat myself to a pot of tea and a cream cake or two.'

Feeling that he was treading on egg-shells, 'As a matter of fact, the café belongs to Klaus Bergmann's younger brother, Franz.' Dabbling a toe in deeper water, 'I dare say that Dulcie was given the job of manageress when—'

'When – *what*?' Grace persisted, puckering her forehead.

'Well, when Klaus Bergmann announced his engagement to some Swiss lass – Constanz summat or other. It was in the *Leeds Mercury*. I dare say they came up with the idea of sending the twins to boarding school; the reason why Dulcie had to find herself another job.'

'I see!' Grace emitted a sigh of relief. 'So she is still, in essence, employed by the Bergmann family?'

'Yeah, I guess so,' Herbie agreed, thinking it unnecessary to mention that Franz Bergmann's reputation was scarcely as white as driven snow so far as women were concerned: that rumour had it he had installed his latest mistress in the maisonette above the Headrow premises.

How could he possibly divulge, to the girl's mother, the woman he loved, that her elder daughter, Dulcie, was nothing more than a kept woman? To hear the truth about Dulcie would break Grace's heart, Herbie realized, in which case, far better to keep her in ignorance. The poor lass had enough problems on her mind at the moment to worry about, without adding to her burden.

He knew, for instance, that Danny's marriage had hit

rock-bottom, thanks to that greedy, insensitive wife of his, that Danny was struggling for survival beneath an overwhelming burden of debt, that Jimmy's writing talent had failed, so far, to impress the Fleet Street hierarchy, that poor, dear little Kerry had embarked on an abortive love affair with a married man. All this allied to the steadily worsening European situation, Grace's fears for the future, her deeply felt concern for Nan, Aunt Fanny, and Rosa . . .

What a bloody life, he thought feelingly, swallowing his last mouthful of tea. Then, catching Bob's eye, he smiled lopsidedly, knowing instinctively that he had not fooled, for one moment, his dear old pal of the 1914–18 war, his comrade-in-arms in the trenches of the Somme battlefields of long ago.

The door opened suddenly, and Kerry came into the kitchen, the pale oval of her face framed with golden hair. 'I'm home,' she said simply. 'Home – to stay!' And then she was gone, the sound of her footsteps dying away as she hurried upstairs to her room.

'I'd best go up to her,' Grace said, rising to her feet.

'No, love,' Bob said quietly. 'Best leave her alone. She'll come through this in her own way, in her own good time. All we can possibly do now is stand by to pick up the pieces.'

And what Bob said was true, Grace realized. All that anyone could do now was to pick up the shattered fragments of life, to try to make sense of a seemingly insoluble jigsaw puzzle of bits and pieces, to form a new pattern of life from the misshapen facets of the old.

Suddenly relief was in the air. People were smiling. The bird of prey had spread its wings and taken flight. The Prime Minister, Neville Chamberlain, had returned from a meeting with Hitler, Goering and Mussolini, in Munich, on 30 September, waving a scrap of paper – the new peace accord – telling the crowds of cameramen and reporters at Heston Aerodrome, 'I believe it is peace for our time.'

Wild applause and cheering broke out at this unexpected announcement. Then Chamberlain was swept off to London where he later appeared, with the King and Queen, on the Buckingham Palace balcony, to a tumultuous welcome from the throng surging about the palace railings.

Hearing the news on the wireless, Grace burst into tears of relief. Then, wiping away the tears, she put on her hat and coat and went out shopping. Tonight she would cook a celebration meal for the family. Something special. In the market she bought a nice, plump little chicken, potatoes, carrots and a cauliflower, a pound of cooking apples and a carton of fresh cream.

Returning home, she set to work to prepare the dinner. Her hands were in the baking bowl, covered in flour, when the phone rang. Quickly she dusted her hands on a tea-towel and rushed through to the hall to answer the call. The voice on the other end of the line sounded ghostly, disembodied almost, a long way off. Taking a chance, 'Jimmy, is that you?' she called out, her lips close to the mouthpiece.

'Yeah, Mum, it's me!' More crackling on the line. 'I just wanted you to know. I've done it. I've landed myself a job.'

'Jimmy, that's marvellous! But how?'

'I went to Heston Aerodrome early this morning. Waited about for hours. Talked to people, wrote up a quick article from the point of view of the "common" man, so to speak, and shoved it under the nose of a Fleet Street news editor. He liked it. Said it was different. Told me to wait. He had a word with the editor. Came back, said OK. Then – wait for it, Ma – he told me to report for work the first thing Monday morning, and not to worry about the union thingy, he'd make sure they'd accept me. No problem, since the paper had already accepted me as a member of staff, with a printed article to prove it!'

More crackling on the line, then Jimmy said proudly, 'I have it here in front of me now. The early edition of *The London Gazette*, my first published article under their banner – "What Peace Means to the Populace by our on-the-spot reporter"!'

'Oh, Jimmy! I'm so proud of you, my son!'

'Yes, well I just wanted you to be the first to know! Sorry,

I've got to go now. Give my love to everyone. And thanks Mum. Thanks for everything!'

The chicken, filled with home-made stuffing, was chuckling away in the oven, the bread sauce had been made, the potatoes had been parboiled, the cauliflower denuded of its outer leaves, the cinnamon-flavoured apple pie had been baked and set aside to cool when Rosa came down to the kitchen, fresh from her afternoon nap.

Sniffing the air, 'It smells like Christmas,' she said vaguely, 'the way Christmases used to smell, long ago, when dear Fanny, Nan and I were children.' Rapidly blinking her eyes, 'But it isn't Christmas, is it? Oh dear, I hope not! You see, I haven't bought any cards or presents—'

'Please don't worry, Aunt Rosa,' Grace said gently, putting the kettle on to boil, 'Christmas is a long way off. This is September.'

Sipping the tea Grace had made for her, Rosa said, with a puzzled frown, 'It's strange, isn't it, how muddled I am these days? I used not to be in the old days, when Fanny and I were together in South Street, before Nan moved in to take my place. But then, Nan was ever a trouble-maker between dear Fanny and me. She was so jealous, you see, of anyone who came between herself and Fanny.

'Of course, it was a feather in Nan's cap when your dear father asked her to marry him. Not that they were entirely suited. Far from, as I recall!' Rosa sighed deeply, lost in memories of the past. 'Oh no, they were never cut out for one another. Nan made the poor man's life a misery from start to finish. He had to toe the line, you see, to dance to her tune, otherwise his life would have been unbearable.'

'Please, Aunt Rosa, don't say any more,' Grace advised her, 'the past is over, done with and best forgotten. Remember, please, that you are speaking of my parents, that I thought the world of my father.' Rising quickly to her feet, 'And now I have work to do, if you'll excuse me. Bob and Kerry will be home soon.' She added kindly, 'You might start setting the dining-room table, if you feel up to it. That would be a great help.'

'Yes, of course I will,' the old woman replied with dignity. 'You know that I would do anything in the world for you, Grace, and that dear husband of yours, who have been so kind to a troublesome old lady such as myself.'

Alone in the kitchen, Grace opened the oven door to baste the chicken, to jettison the parboiled potatoes into the hot fat surrounding it. Putting on the panful of cauliflower to cook, she kept a wary eye on the kitchen clock; nevertheless, Grace could not help remembering Aunt Rosa's words: 'Nan made the poor man's life a misery from start to finish. He had to toe the line you see, to dance to her tune, otherwise his life would have been unbearable.'

Was that really true? she wondered. Had she and her father missed coming together because of Nan's influence? Nan's jealousy, her self-righteous attitude towards everyone standing in the way of her autocratic demand to be revered, bowed down to as the central figure in her own small universe?

And, yes, she thought, that was entirely possible.

Then the front door opened and closed, and Bob and Kerry were home to enjoy the fruits of her labour, a celebration supper of roast chicken, apple pie and fresh cream, because, miraculously, Neville Chamberlain had signed a Peace Treaty with Hitler and Mussolini; more importantly, because Jimmy had landed himself a job with a bona-fide Fleet Street newspaper.

Chapter Twenty-seven

Fanny knew that Nan had been in her room, meddling with her personal belongings, and going through her wardrobe, prying into the contents of her escritoire, reading her letters. Easy-going by nature, at times a little absent-minded, she thought at first she must be mistaken. Surely Nan would never stoop so low – a pillar of the church, the widow of a Methodist minister? But her precious letters had been re-tied carelessly, she could tell by the ribbon, and there could be only one culprit.

Never had Rosa entered her room uninvited. Theirs had been a relationship based on mutual trust and understanding. Rosa would no more have gone through Fanny's possessions than Fanny would have gone through hers. The idea would never have occurred to them. By the same token, Fanny had kept out of the kitchen when Rosa was doing the cooking. Life had been simple, uncomplicated, uneventful, when she and Rosa were together – until Nan came to live with them. Fanny could not help wondering if Nan had planned all along to oust Rosa from the South Cliff premises? If so, she had received an unpleasant surprise when Rosa had gone to live with Grace and Bob. So what had Nan in mind for Rosa? Removal to an old people's home? The Dean Road 'workhouse'?

Mulling things over in her mind, Fanny began to realize the extent of Nan's subterfuge, her power of destruction. It had all started that day way back in 1935, when Nan had announced her intention of coming to live with herself and Rosa, since when the old, well-ordered pattern of life had changed dramatically for the worse.

Fanny had not known, at the time, the extent of Nan's bitterness towards Bob Kingsley, or why she harboured so much resentment towards him. On the day of Danny's wedding, when she discovered the truth, the reason why Grace and Bob had married in haste, her sympathies had lain entirely with them. Remembering her wartime love affair with James Courtenay, how could it have been otherwise?

Then, suddenly, in high dudgeon, Nan had declared her intention of severing all family ties. In vain, she, Fanny had tried to talk her sister into a better frame of mind, had begged her to let bygones be bygones, but to no avail. In Nan's view, she had been badly mistreated by Rosa, Grace and Bob in particular; wickedly and wantonly she had shut them out of her life.

Even when Grace, Bob and dear little Kerry had come to the house one day to patch up the quarrel, Nan had been unwilling to listen. Then she, Fanny, had begun her long-time correspondence with Rosa. Just short, simple letters assuring her elder sister of her unwavering devotion towards her. They had even managed to meet, now and then, in town, for morning coffee or afternoon tea, unbeknown to Nan. At least Fanny had thought so until she realized that Nan had gained access to her private correspondence; had discovered the secrets of her past life in a way more fitting to a chambermaid than the widow of a Methodist minister. Well, something must be done about it, Fanny decided, and the sooner the better.

One evening at supper, facing Nan across the kitchen table, she delved into her handbag, withdrawing a letter, and said calmly, sweetly, 'Oh, by the way, Nan dear, this letter arrived for me this morning. It's from my friend, Mr Hodnot, inviting me to dine with him at the Pavilion Hotel next Sunday. You might as well read it now as later.'

Nan's jaw sagged. 'I don't know what you mean,' she said stiffly.

'Oh, don't you?' Fanny's eyes were bright beneath her quizzically arched eyebrows. 'I'd have thought it was as plain as the nose on your face. You have been *au fait* with the secrets of my past life for some time now, haven't you?

What did you make, I wonder, of my love-letters from James Courtenay? What did you think of the clothes in my wardrobe? The clothes I wore when I was young and slim, when our love affair was at its height?'

'I don't understand what you're driving at,' Nan countered quickly, rising swiftly to her feet. 'Have you taken leave of your senses?'

'Not at all, Nan. But please don't run away. You're rather good at that, aren't you? Sit down and listen to me. I said, *sit down*!'

Nan sat down abruptly.

At last she had everything she had ever wanted from life, Dulcie thought ecstatically, a place of her own, a well-paid job. Above all, a rich lover in whose arms she had willingly sacrificed her virginity.

The night of their first ever supper party in the flat above the Bergmann Konditorei, Franz had first told her how lovely she looked in her red velvet hostess gown. Then, following her upstairs to the dining-room, he had congratulated her warmly on her choice of food, had uncorked the bottle of champagne he had brought with him to celebrate the occasion – her house-warming tête-à-tête, he had described it laughingly as the champagne cork popped, and he poured the vintage wine into the glasses. Both had known, throughout the meal, the refilling of the glasses, that later would come a far deeper intimacy, when the wine had been drunk, the remains of the meal left on the table.

So be it, Dulcie had thought, leading her lover upstairs to her bedroom, divesting herself of the red velvet gown, praying to God that he would have no fault to find with her naked body, still plump to her way of thinking – curvaceous to say the least – with swelling breasts and thighs between a severely controlled waistline due mainly to her recent diet of lettuce leaves, grilled fish, and endless cups of black coffee.

To her everlasting gratitude and satisfaction Franz appeared to like what he saw. Lying on the bed, awaiting his coming, eyes closed, she felt, at first, his hands at her breasts, then she had heard the swift indrawing of his breath as he traced the outlines of her body with his exploratory fingertips. Finally had come the hardness of his naked body against hers, the moment of entry, the rhythm of intercourse, the initial pain of it from her point of view until, at last, she had cried out, in ecstasy, as he brought her to a thrilling climax, after which, whimpering the pleasure-pain of this, her first experience of love-making, she had fallen deeply asleep in the arms of her lover, her mouth wide open, snoring slightly. Awakened to find that he was gone . . .

Hurrying down to the kitchen, she found a scrawled note from him on the table. Reading it, she knew that she had not disappointed her lover. The note read: 'My darling, couldn't bear to disturb you. Tonight at 8.30? Franz.' All was well with her world! She knew, at last, the ecstasy of love, the value of self-denial so far as food was concerned; that all her longing, seeking, striving, had not been in vain.

Returning to the bedroom, she dressed quickly, after bathing in her own private and personal bathroom with its bewildering array of soaps, body lotions and other expensive toiletries, and went downstairs to the café to make felt her presence as the manageress of the Bergmann Konditorei.

Never in her life had she been happier than she was now, aglow with life and love; the world her oyster. No longer a virgin. No longer fat but desirable, with a rich lover in tow; a home of her own to cling to. A home of her own making, reflecting her own personality throughout.

And, one of these fine days, she thought, when she became the wife of Franz Bergmann, as she intended she would, what pleasure she would derive from cocking a snook at his mother, not to mention Klaus – who had recently become engaged to marry the plain, toothy woman she had met that day in the drawing-room of the Bergmann residence. Yes, one of these days, Dulcie thought maliciously, she would derive great pleasure from paying back Frau Bergmann and Klaus in their own coin. Not as a nursery maid, but a force to be reckoned with as the wife of the younger son of the family – as Mrs Franz Bergmann! A consummation devoutly to be wished . . .

The dire events, foreseen and dreaded by Ashley Hawthorn, came to pass in the November of 1938. Initial murmurings of dissatisfaction from the shareholders of his father's company had eventually flared into deep resentment of the Chairman and the Board of Directors' mismanagement of Company matters: the use of sub-standard bricks and mortar to increases their profit margin, the lining of their own pockets, their own standards of living.

Soon, the shareholders were up in arms against what they saw, quite rightly in Ashley's opinion, as a lack of integrity on the part of his father in particular. Inevitably, questions were being asked by solicitors involved in the intricate web of lawsuits levelled against him by a small army of householders whose homes, purchased in good faith, had developed faults inherent upon poor materials and bad workmanship. Houses whose walls and ceilings had cracked suddenly, whose chimneys had toppled, whose foundations had proved insecure, whose plumbing had failed to function.

Blood was thicker than water. Ashley loved his father. Even so, harsh words had passed between them. One day, in his father's study, facing him across the desk embellished with silver inkwell, silver-framed photographs, morocco-bound blotter, all the appurtenances of wealth in a room filled with fine antique furniture, Ashley demanded angrily 'Why the hell have you done this? Is money so important to you? If so, all I can say is, you've paid too high a price for all this! All this – sham. This house, the furniture; your bloody knighthood!'

'How dare you speak to me that way?' Rising swiftly from his chair, 'In case you've forgotten,' Sir Charles said harshly, 'you have my money to thank for giving you a damned good education, everything you wanted in life!'

'If that's what you think, you are wrong!' Ashley replied staunchly. 'The only thing I want from life is the love and respect of the girl I'm in love with.'

'*You*? In love?' Sir Charles said scornfully, 'Frankly, I'd begun to wonder if you were capable of forming a normal attachment to any woman. So why all the secrecy? Who is this girl? Why haven't we met her?'

Ashley smiled grimly. 'Mother *has* met her.'

'Then why in God's name why hasn't she mentioned it? Is there something radically wrong with her?'

'Not with the girl. Kerry Kingsley's her name, by the way. The fault is mine. I'm not good enough for her, you see.'

'Not *good* enough?' Sir Charles recoiled slightly with surprise. 'You who have everything – money, good looks, social standing, a fine education.'

Facing his father, Ashley knew that the older man had failed to grasp the seriousness of the charges of corruption levelled against him which, if proven in a court of law, might lead to a term of imprisonment. If that happened, what price then the family name, the social standing of which he was so arrogantly proud?

As ever, Sir Charles Hawthorn pinned his faith on friends in high office, his personal fortune to overcome what he obviously regarded as a matter of little or no importance. In his view, money possessed the power to settle any action brought against him. His own team of highly paid company lawyers would see to that.

Ashley said quietly, 'Kerry, the girl I'm in love with, dislikes this house, my lifestyle, as much as I do. I know because she told me so. Money means less than nothing to her. As for my education . . .' A smile touched the corners of his mouth, 'I have the feeling she knows as much and more about poetry and music, about life and love than I ever learned during my time at Oxford.' He added, 'Frankly, Father, all your money did for me was help me to waste my time when I should have kept my nose to the grindstone.'

He sighed deeply. Laying down the silver letter-opener he had been toying with, he said heavily, 'I'm leaving now, Father. My things are packed. I'll say goodbye to Mother first, of course. Afterwards, I shall find somewhere of my own to live; send you a forwarding address.'

'You mean you are quitting the Company? Leaving me in the lurch?' Sir Charles was breathing heavily now, his face jutted forward, his hands gripping the edge of the desk.

'Leaving the Company, yes,' Ashley replied levelly. 'Leaving you in the lurch – no. I thought you knew me better than that. If and when the occasion arises, I shall shoulder my share of the blame; stand up with you in Court; take whatever punishment is meted out to me. After all, Dad, blood is thicker than water.'

'*Punishment*?' Hawthorn's face sagged suddenly. 'You're surely not suggesting that I . . . ?' Words failed him.

Turning at the door, Ashley said compassionately, 'I'm sorry, Father, but it's time you faced the truth. What you have done is tantamount to theft. I knew what was happening, God help me. I tried to warn you, but you wouldn't listen.' He closed the door quietly behind him, walked upstairs to say goodbye to his mother, pausing on the landing to instruct a manservant to carry his suitcases down to the front door.

Half an hour later, in the back seat of a taxi, he glanced out of the rear window at the rapidly receding view of Glebe House.

Where he was going, he had no idea except, initially to Scarborough where, God willing, he might find himself a couple of furnished rooms with a view of the sea; a job of work to do.

In his room at Glebe House, he had left behind him on his dressing-table, his cheque book and wallet. All he had with him was four five-pound notes, some loose change. His suitcases contained one decent suit of clothes, a few clean shirts, sweaters, socks and ties, two pairs of shoes, pyjamas, a dressing-gown, shaving gear, a few books of poetry, clean handkerchiefs, shoe polish and duster, a pair of corduroy trousers, a shabby tweed jacket, and a photograph of his parents taken years ago, in their younger, happier days.

All that mattered to him, as the taxi sped towards Malton Station, was that he was free, at last, of all the sham and pretence which had coloured his life for so long. Free to carve out a new future for himself. A future which, hopefully, would include Kerry Kingsley.

Later that day, he found the rooms he sought in Marine Terrace, a backwater parade close to the amazing bulk of the Grand Hotel.

Treating him to an 'old-fashioned' look, 'I shall want a week's rent in advance,' the landlady told him, preceding him upstairs to his attic eyrie. 'It's all nice and clean, as you can see for yourself. But no female visitors, and that's flat. I have my reputation to consider.' Puckering her forehead, she knew a gentleman when she saw one. 'What's your little game, eh? Slumming, are you?'

'No, not at all, just a bit down on my luck, that's all,' he said brightly, 'hoping to find myself a job of some kind, to tide me over.'

'A job, eh?' Lena Bartliff pulled thoughtfully at her underlip, 'Well, that shouldn't prove too difficult at this time of year with the hotels wanting waiters over the Christmas period. Any good at waiting on, are yer?'

'I'm willing to give it a try,' Ashley replied, taking in the details of his accommodation; sloping ceilings, stained wallpaper; dormer window, threadbare carpet, and the narrow iron bedstead, the cracked marble wash-hand-stand, the cheap chest-of-drawers and the surprisingly lovely Victorian mahogany wardrobe facing the bed.

'Look here, young feller-me-lad,' Lena said pithily, 'no use trying to pull the wool over my eyes! I wasn't born yesterday. You'd be more at home being waited on at yon Royal Hotel than waiting on others. So what kind of a job are you really after?'

'I don't honestly know,' he confessed, chastened by his landlady's perception. 'All I care about is earning myself a decent living.'

'Hmmm,' Lena pondered. Then, 'Can you cook?' she shot forth at him. 'What I mean is, do you know the difference between fish and chips and fakey French cookery? Haddock and prawns "provincial" and the like? If so, a gentleman friend of mine might take you on as a kitchen assistant-cum-chef. It's hard, hot work, mind you, in that basement kitchen of his, and he ain't very good-tempered, but he just might take you on as a washer-up if I asked him, ever so nicely, of course. On the other hand, if you're lucky, you might end up as his "soos" chef, mixing up the "moose" and so on. Just as long as you don't cross him. Fred can't bear to be crossed when he's busy. Well, whaddayou think?'

'I think, Mrs Bartliff, that you are a gem among women,' Ashley told her sincerely, with a smile like a sunburst.

'Oh, get along with you,' she murmured modestly, fingering the five pound note he had handed her. 'I knew you was a real gent the minute I set eyes on yer. I'll bring up your change directly – and, if there's owt else I can do for you in the meanwhile, don't hesitate to arsk!'

God, but he was good-looking, she thought, on her way downstairs.

Alone, he began unpacking his belongings; remembered, without regret, the mass of expensive, faultlessly tailored suits, the drawers and cupboards filled with the kind of clothes he no longer needed or wanted; knew that he should have fought tooth and nail against entering his father's business.

Soon, he must decide what to do about his future. For the time being he was content to take whatever job he could find to feed himself and pay the rent, to keep his head above water. Darkness had fallen. When he had finished unpacking, he stood near the dormer window looking out at the pinpricks of light strung along the Spa Bridge, the pale, drowned primroses of light on wet pavements, the warm, welcoming glow of lighted windows from the massive Victorian edifice of the Grand Hotel, the twinkling red, blue and green lights of Christmas trees in the windows of the St Nicholas Square houses facing the central garden.

The small attic apartment he had chanced upon earlier that day, comprising a bed-sitting room and a tiny, boarded-off kitchen containing a sink, gas-ring, kettle, and a cupboard of mismatched cups and saucers, a cracked tea-pot, milk-jug,

362

and a slot-meter to feed the gas-supply, held a deeper meaning for him than the grandeur of Glebe House with its brightly-lit crystal chandeliers, spacious rooms, its wealth of hot-house blooms, deep carpets and polished antique furniture.

His one and only deep regret lay in his mother's distress when she knew he was leaving home, turning his back on the future she had mapped out for him. 'You must be out of your mind,' was all she could say, over and over again. 'I don't understand you, Ashley. Why are you doing this? What do you hope to gain by it?'

How could he have possibly explained that what he hoped to gain was self-respect?

Standing alone in the darkness, he thought that somewhere out there, amid the blossoming lights of Scarborough, was the girl he loved. What was she doing now? he wondered. Reading? Writing Christmas cards? Washing that long, golden hair of hers? Having supper with her family? If only he *knew*.

Suddenly there came the tap-tap of high-heeled shoes on the stairs, a knock at the door. His landlady had brought him the change from the five pound note. Entering the room, 'Why the heck haven't you lit the gas?' she demanded. 'It's fair freezing up here. Here, let me do it for you.' Kneeling, she applied a match to the ancient gas-fire, cursing under her breath at having to feel her way in the darkness. Then, 'There, that's better, ain't it? Only it won't last long unless you put a bob in the meter. An' what about the light?' Rising to her feet, she applied another match to the overhead gas-mantle within the confines of an etched-glass globe, after which, hurrying to the window, she pulled together the cretonne curtains on their sagging wires, shutting out the darkness beyond, the pale primrose-coloured reflections in the wet pavements, the shining Christmas-tree lights he loved.

Facing him, breathing heavily with exertion, 'Well,' she told him triumphantly, 'I've had a word with my friend Fred, an' he says you can have the washing-up job if you wants it, starting tomorrer night – seven o'clock till midnight – yer supper thrown in. Take it or leave it!'

'I'll take it, and thank you, Mrs Bartliff,' Ashley said gratefully.

Staring at him in amazement, 'Don't you want to know how much?'

'Yes, of course! Er – how much?' Ashley responded.

'Two and six an hour,' she told him proudly. 'Less, of course, yer stamps and yer union dues. An', of course, it's only soup and bread for supper as a rule. Moreover, it's only temper-whatsit over the Christmas season, but it's a *start*, isn't it?'

'Yes, indeed,' Ashley acknowledged thoughtfully, close to tears. He had almost forgotten that there was so much kindness in the world.

Standing at the door, fancying him like mad, Lena said breathlessly, 'If you're hungry, yer welcome to a bit of supper with me, downstairs – a bite of rabbit pie and mashed pertaters with onion gravy.' With a deeply indrawn sigh at his gentle refusal of her hospitality, 'Oh, please yerself, then. I expects yer tired an' wants ter get ter bed. Had a long day, have yer?'

'Yes, you could say that, I suppose,' he acknowledged kindly. 'Another time, perhaps?'

When she had gone, switching off the overhead lamp, and re-opening the curtains, he looked out for a while at the lights of Scarborough. Then, unbelievably tired, undressing, he visited the communal bathroom along the landing, got into bed, and lay there for a little space of time looking up at the lights on the cracked ceiling until, at last, he sank into a deep and dreamless sleep of sheer exhaustion.

Chapter Twenty-eight

Fred Jackson's premises in Westborough, rejoicing in the name of the Élysée Restaurant, catered mainly for bright young things of slender means whose fancy had been caught by the bizarrely executed wall paintings of short-skirted soubrettes and moustachioed garçons; red-and-white checked tablecloths and the smell of garlic permeating the atmosphere.

The food served up by Fred, in the basement kitchen, consisted mainly of mixed grills, steak and chips (described on the menus as *pommes frites*); thick, garlic-flavoured onion soup; pâté provençal served with hunks of hot, garlic-flavoured bread; prawns in salad cream served with lettuce, and his *spécialité de la maison*: Boeuf Bourguignonne, a kind of cottage pie to which had been added liberal quantities of herbs and rough red wine.

Fred, a short, thick-set man with a rapidly balding pate, greeted his new kitchen assistant with a marked lack of enthusiasm, showed him the sink, stacked with greasy pots and pans, and told him to get on with the washing-up 'toot sweet'. 'An' no egg smears left on the plates, mind you,' he added disagreeably. 'Washer-uppers are ten a penny, an' don't you forget it!'

Taking off his jacket, rolling back his sleeves, Ashley considered the problem confronting him. Systematically removing the clutter of pans and plates from the sink, he stacked them about him in a pyramid, filled the sink with hot water laced with Omo and soda-crystals, washed first the cutlery, then the china, and finally the pots and pans.

Smiling inwardly, what price his Oxford education now? he wondered. Curiously, he had seldom been happier in his life before than he was then – creating order from chaos for

1*s*. 6*d*. per hour. He had, after all, the independence he'd craved, a roof above his head, a bed in which to sleep, and even the formidable Fred Jackson had seemed pleasantly surprised to discover that his new employee had not merely done the washing-up in exemplary fashion but had also swabbed the still-room floor, boiled and rinsed the dishcloths and tea-towels, and hung them up to dry on the ceiling-rack in readiness for the next influx of dirty dishes.

'You're due for your supper now, I reckon,' Fred told him off-handedly. 'Onion soup suit you?'

'Yes, thank you, Mr Jackson, onion soup will suit me fine,' Ashley replied, swallowing hard, smiling at his employer. After all, why look a gift horse in the mouth? He felt he had earned his bowl of onion soup and its accompanying wedge of garlic-flavoured bread.

His dreams that night were shot through with visions of leering, moustachioed waiters pursuing simpering soubrettes down endless corridors of greasy plates.

Getting up in the early hours of the morning, he stood by the window gazing out at the pearly light of a new day staining the sky above his own private and particular wedge of sea glimpsed between the Grand Hotel and the MacBean steps leading down to the Foreshore. He saw, with a full heart, and renewal of hope and optimism, the riding lights of a small fishing-coble heading out from the harbour in the lee of the Castle Hill, and thought of Kerry, hoping perhaps that she, too, was awake and watching that brave little boat setting sail, seeing the firefly glimmer of its progress towards the distant horizon.

And yet, much as he longed to see her again, common sense warned him not to pursue her, not to pester her as he had done so often before. In any case, he had nothing now to offer her. Who knew what the future held for him? Public disgrace, possible imprisonment? He meant what he said when he told his father he would shoulder his share of the blame in the case of a public scandal, a court case in which the Hawthorn Company would be called upon to answer the charges brought against it.

In the meanwhile, he would garner and treasure all the feelings and memories inherent upon his present situation, his sharpened awareness of life, his new-found independence. He would relish the view from this window; the sloping ceilings of his attic abode, the glowing skulls of the gas-fire, the benison of a hot cup of early morning tea drunk from a chipped cup, a walk into town to purchase a loaf of bread, a slab of butter from the Meadow Dairy, a jar of honey, a bit of cheese, a newspaper, his job at the Élysée Restaurant.

Herbie had been invited to spend Christmas in Scarborough. Jimmy would be coming home. Grace had asked Danny, Wilma and William to the Castle Road house to spend Christmas Day. A specially written request to Nan and Fanny to join the family party had been posted; another to Dulcie, accompanied by a Christmas card depicting a robin redbreast against a glittering background of snow, with the simply worded message: 'Please, Dulcie, *do* come. The family circle will not be complete without you. Your ever loving Mother and Dad.'

'*I'm* not going,' Nan said disagreeably, reading Grace's letter. 'Of all the sentimental nonsense! Grace must want her brains testing if she thinks for one moment that I shall enter her house again!'

'Really?' Fanny smiled equably at her irate sister across the breakfast table. 'But, of course if you prefer to spend Christmas Day alone, that is entirely up to you.'

'Eh?' Nan's jaw sagged. 'What on earth do you mean?'

'I mean, Nan dear, exactly what my words imply. Simply, I have every intention of spending Christmas with Grace, Bob, Rosa and the rest of the family.'

'But you *can't*! What I mean to say is, you couldn't possibly leave me alone here on Christmas Day!'

Fanny sighed deeply. Some people never learned, she thought sadly. Possibly her sister Nan in particular was blind to her own shortcomings, so wrapped up in her own brand of bitterness and self-aggrandizement that nothing on earth possessed the power to shatter the self image of a woman beyond reproach: a zealot soaked in religious fervour to the exclusion of her own faults and failings as a human being.

Even the unpleasantness which had erupted when she, Fanny, had accused Nan of invading her room, of reading her private and personal correspondence, had met with little response other than Nan's shocked horror that a sister of hers had actually cheapened herself to the extent of conducting an illicit love-affair with a married man during her wartime years in London.

Even so, Fanny had never forgiven Nan's 'holier-than-thou' remark that it was just as well James Courtenay's death, in battle, had released her from an untenable situation as the man's mistress. 'Amen!'

Fanny said, across the breakfast table, 'You are wrong, Nan. I have every intention of leaving you alone here, on Christmas Day. Why worry? After all, you have the Lord on your side. Why not treat yourself to a lunch of five loaves and two fishes?'

Nan's mouth worked angrily; 'That's sacrilege!' she spat forth wrathfully. 'Utterly contemptible! To think that a sister of mine should utter such a blasphemy!'

Rising to her feet, Fanny said levelly, 'I loved you once, Nan, long ago, when we were young.' Drawing in a deep breath, 'Now that we are no longer young, God help me, I feel nothing for you but pity and dislike. I'm sorry, but that's the way it is. Now I intend living what is left of my life in my own way, with the people I love around me. Is that perfectly clear?'

Dulcie consigned her mother's Christmas card to the rubbish bin. No way would she consider spending a dreary Christmas in the bosom of her family. This was her home now, this flat which she would decorate with bauble-bedecked Christmas trees, gilded pine-cones and hot-house blooms.

Her plans were made to the last item on her shopping list; the food that she and Franz would eat, the wine they would drink, the expensive silk dressing-gown she had decided upon as his Christmas present from her. She would, moreover, treat herself to a new apricot silk nightdress and matching negligée, have her hair done in a new style.

Recently, jealously, she had read an account of the wedding of Klaus Bergmann to Constanz Olivier-Schmitt in the social column of *The Times*. The bride's father, a well known banker, had come from America to attend the ceremony. The bride had worn a gown of white *guipure* lace and carried a bouquet of crimson roses. The Bergmann twins, the bride's attendants, had worn red velvet dresses and carried ermine muffs. The honeymoon was being spent in London, Paris and Zurich.

Franz had proved unusually uncommunicative on the subject of his brother's wedding at which he, of course, had been the best man; adding to Dulcie's jealousy when she thought of him in the company of other women, being charming to them as only he knew how. Rich women, tall and slender. And yet, she consoled herself, planning their Christmas together in the flat above the Konditorei, she was the one he really wanted, really loved. Not that he had ever said so, but there were things a woman knew without being told, to do with sexual pleasure and fulfilment, the thrill and excitement engendered by their being together, his various and varied approaches to love-making. He could be tender or cruel, according to his mood of the moment, so that she never quite knew what to expect of him in bed; a lingering, almost lazy amount of foreplay leading to a tender intimacy, or a rough, dispassionate entry resulting in a quick, insensitive climax on his part, and nothing whatever to do with her own wishes and desires.

There was, nevertheless, in Franz's mastery, an element of unpredictability, a coarseness which matched her own nature, so that they seemed ideally matched – made for each other. Above all, she wanted to make this Christmas special for him, a time to remember.

It would certainly prove an occasion which Dulcie would never forget.

Grace's invitation to spend Christmas in Scarborough had come as a godsend to Herbie who, the minute the letter arrived, set about buying gifts for the family; a silk scarf for Grace, a tie for Bob, a brooch for Rosa; a toy for William; a book of poems for Kerry, a set of table-mats for Danny and Wilma, a fountain-pen for Jimmy, a box of Chanel soap for Dulcie. Not that he imagined, for one moment, the latter would be present to receive his gift. Rumour had it that Dulcie, deeply involved in a love-affair with Franz Bergmann, would certainly not be in Scarborough come Christmas.

His heart bled for Grace and Bob, in whose imagination Dulcie remained the daughter they knew and loved, certainly not the overbearing manageress of the Bergmann café, heartily disliked by all with whom she came into contact, especially the older members of staff who regarded her as nothing more than Mr Franz's 'bit on the side', a jumped-up nobody with her eye on the main chance, a woman of easy virtue who knew next to nowt about the bakery side of the business, who simply swanned about the café snapping her fingers at uncleared tables. She made the waitresses' lives a misery, 'As if she were the Queen of Sheba in her fine dresses, reeking of Chanel bloody Five perfume,' as one of the older employees put it succinctly, the day she had handed in her notice, picked up her cards, her week's wages, and quit the premises for good and all.

Just to make certain that he had gifts enough and to spare, in case of emergency, Herbie purchased from Schofield's a dozen lace-edged hankies, a box of stationery, and a box of chocolates, all of which he wrapped carefully, in red-and-gold Christmas paper. He stowed them methodically in the bottom of the suitcase containing, also, his best suit, several shirts and clean pairs of socks.

As he did so, despite Neville Chamberlain's return from Germany waving that 'Peace for our Time' agreement, Herbie's core of common sense warned him that this Christmas of 1938 might well be the end of all he had known and loved. The last Christmas he would ever spend with his friends in a world at peace, in which case, best make the most of it, no matter what the future may bring, he thought fatalistically, catching the 4.30 train to Scarborough.

Picking up a copy of the *Scarborough Evening News* from a vendor in the main street Ashley Hawthorn read, with a sick feeling in the pit of his stomach: 'Dramatic Arrest of Well Known Businessman'. The sub-titles read: 'Malton builder, Sir Charles Hawthorn, denied all charges of fraud on his arrest in the early hours of this morning at his home, Glebe House, Malton'. The item went on to sketch in Sir Charles's background and the firm of which he was the Chairman and Managing Director, and the allegations of sub-standard workmanship and materials brought against him by members of the public, leading to his present detention by Scotland Yard's Criminal Investigation Department pending further investigation of the charges. In the manner of newspaper reportage, nothing apart from the known facts was clearly stated, and yet the reporter had managed to suggest a broad path leading to destruction. Emphasis had been placed on Sir Charles' affluent lifestyle, his love of entertaining, his fondness for horse-racing.

Grimly folding the newspaper, Ashley knew that he must go to his father as quickly as possible. First thing in the morning, he would return to Glebe House to comfort and support his mother. He would then make himself available to the CID officer in charge of the case in readiness for questioning. It was the least he could do. Meanwhile, he must present himself at the Élysée Restaurant in time for the evening shift, do the job he was being paid to do to the best of his ability, then hand in his notice to Fred Jackson. Washer-uppers were, after all, ten a penny, he reminded himself. As to the flat, his little domain beneath the stars, he would decide about that later; write a note to Mrs Bartliff enclosing his remaining five pound note explaining his dilemma, asking her to accept that amount as a token of good faith, in the hope that he would, in due course, see his way clear to his return.

Glancing up at the Christ Church clock in Vernon Road, he saw that the time was five o'clock exactly. A thin rain was falling on the heads of the hurrying crowds of shoppers in the main street. The Salvation Army Band, grouped in the road near Rowntrees Department Store, were playing 'Away in a Manger'. Tears filled his eyes as he walked, unseeingly, the crowded pavements, hoping, praying for some small miracle to alleviate the bleakness of his heart, the finding of a lost penny on the pavement, perhaps, as a good luck charm, a talisman . . .

Suddenly there came the touch of a hand on his sleeve; a well-remembered voice. 'Ashley?' the voice said softly. 'Is it really you?'

Turning, knowing that miracles did happen, his heart lifting at the joy of seeing her again, 'Kerry,' he whispered. 'Oh, Kerry!'

Kindly, compassionately, she had taken charge of him. 'Let's go up to the restaurant for a cup of tea, shall we?' she suggested. 'You look half frozen.'

When they were seated at a window table, not beating about the bush, she said, 'I've seen the evening paper. How worrying for you.' Pouring the tea, 'Do you take sugar?'

He shook his head, said slowly, 'It's true, you know.'

'Is it?'

'Don't you mind?'

'Of course I mind that a friend of mine is in trouble. Here, have a slice of toast. There isn't a picking on you. What have you been doing, starving or worrying yourself to death?'

He grinned awkwardly, 'A bit of both, I reckon.'

'Then you must promise to come to Christmas dinner at our house,' she said decidedly, 'unless, of course, you have made other plans. Sorry, that was silly of me, you'll want to spend Christmas with your . . . at home.'

Looking at her radiant, flower-like face across the table,

realizing her motives, the innate sweetness of her nature, he said quietly, 'The choice might not be mine to make. I may well spend Christmas behind bars.' Scarcely able to swallow the tea, let alone the toast. 'The facts are plain and simple. I knew what was happening all along, now I must shoulder my share of the blame.' He added haltingly, 'Forgive me for saying this, Kerry, but I must. I told you once that I loved you, remember?' He paused, uncertain how to continue. 'I meant what I said, and my feelings are the same now as then. But now, my love, I have nothing in the world to offer you. In any case,' struggling to gain control of his emotions, 'you made it perfectly clear that you were far from in love with me, so there's no need for all this—'

Frowning slightly, 'All this what?'

'Kindness – sympathy. Pity.'

'*Pity?*' Her frown deepened. 'You think I feel sorry for you?'

'Don't you?'

'Well, yes, but only because you look half frozen and hungry. That's all.' Resting her elbows on the table, 'What are you doing here in Scarborough, Ashley? Why all the mystery? Please, I want to know.'

And so he told her the story from beginning to end.

Now the restaurant was beginning to empty. Taking the lift to the ground floor they walked arm-in-arm towards the main street where the rain had changed into clinging gobbets of snow as light and fluffy as mimosa.

Standing just inside the main entrance, 'You don't know what this has meant to me,' he said in a low voice. 'I had prayed for a miracle, and suddenly there you were.'

Taking hold of his hand, 'I'd like us to keep in touch,' she said simply, 'and for you to know I'm on your side whatever happens. You will let me know?' How strange, she thought, that she was no longer in awe of him. The Ashley Hawthorn she had once rejected because of his background no longer existed. She admired his courage in making a new life for himself, above all, his sense of loyalty to his father. 'I hope you'll soon come back to your flat,' she said. 'Well, I'd best be going now. Goodbye Ashley, and God be with you.'

'Before you go, Kerry, there's something I need to know,' he said urgently. 'The man you told me about – the one you're in love with.'

Looking up at him, her face caught the coloured lights of the Christmas tree above the entrance to the store. Clasping his hand more tightly, she said quietly, 'The man I *thought* I was in love with, you mean? My summer time romance? My Irish tenor?' She paused, 'I imagine he's back in Ireland now with his wife and children.'

'Oh, Kerry, I'm sorry.' He meant what he said. Sensing the pain, the bitterness of that meaningless affair of the heart, the suffering it had caused her, how could he rejoice fully that it was over and done with?

She said softly, '*I'm* not. Not now. It was just a part of growing up, I suppose. What is known as learning the hard way.' She smiled suddenly. 'What other way is there?' Impulsively, standing on tip-toe, she brushed his cold cheek with her warm young lips, and then she was gone, hurrying away from him into the snowy darkness of a winter afternoon.

When she had gone, standing alone in the shop doorway, bemusedly, Ashley touched his cheek with his fingertips, and suddenly it was spring time, not winter, in his heart.

Chapter Twenty-nine

Wilma had made plain her objections to spending Christmas Day with Danny's parents. 'It simply isn't fair on Mummy and Daddy,' she complained bitterly. 'William's *their* grandchild too, remember?'

'We can go to your parents on Boxing Day,' Danny reminded her, weary of the constant bickering.

'Oh, trust you, you selfish beast, to want everything your own way. Why can't we go to your parents on Boxing Day?'

'It's just that Jimmy will be home on Christmas Eve, and . . .' How to explain that he wanted, above all things, to experience once more the familiar table of home at this, the most important family festival of the year? How to tell his wife, without deeply offending her, that he could not bear the thought of eating his Christmas dinner in that overcrowded back room in Aberdeen Terrace, seated opposite his morose father-in-law, next to his ebullient, twittering mother-in-law when he could be at home, sharing a truly festive meal in a joyous atmosphere of love and laughter?

He could see it all clearly in his mind's eye: the crackling damask table-cloth and the best china dinner service, gleaming cutlery, the red-and-gold crackers beside each plate, the lighted Christmas tree in the front room window. There would be the happy, smiling faces of his family as they opened their presents before dinner was served, before they all trooped into the dining-room to pay their respects to the turkey, carved by his father at the head of the table, during which ceremony his mother would bustle in the tureens of vegetables and the boats of gravy and bread sauce.

Moreover, if William, seated in his high chair, splattered gravy down the front of his bib, no-one would say, 'Who's a dirty boy, then?' as Mrs Burton was wont to do when the child banged down his spoon experimentally into a dish of food.

Latching on to Danny's last remark, 'Oh, and I suppose that precious brother of yours means more to you than *I* do?' Wilma said sneeringly, clattering the breakfast pots into the washing-up water. 'Well, if that's the way of it, the choice is yours. *You* spend Christmas Day with your family if you want to. William and I are spending it with *my* parents, and there's the end of it!'

Danny had never fully comprehended before the meaning of the saying, 'the straw that broke the camel's back'. He knew it now. The last straw – that last insupportable burden of humiliation which strained a man's tolerance beyond endurance. Humiliation linked to a constant, carping criticism of his every thought and action until, curiously, with no feelings of guilt or remorse, he had reached the end of his tether.

He said slowly, calmly, 'You are right, Wilma. There's the end of it.'

Suddenly afraid, facing him, realizing that she had gone too far, still blustering, 'The end of *what*?' she demanded.

He gave her a long, pitying look. 'Our marriage, of course. That's what you want, isn't it? It's certainly what *I* want.'

Unable to think clearly, so inured to regarding herself as the injured party, to treating her husband as the dust beneath her feet, she said sharply, 'Don't be so ridiculous. All this because of a silly misunderstanding!' Even more sharply, as he turned away from her, 'Where are you going?'

His hand on the doorknob, he looked back at her. 'I'm going home,' he said simply.

In a frenzy of fear, she burst forth, 'But you can't walk out on me and William this way! Are you mad? I'm your *wife*! William is your son! Don't we mean anything at all to you?'

Looking at Wilma directly, 'My son means more than all the world to me,' Danny said quietly, 'far too much to have him used as a kind of pawn in a human game of chess. Winner take all! And we both know, don't we, who that winner will be. *You*, Wilma, because there's no end to your ambition, your greed, your meanness of spirit, your lack of humility.'

He paused momentarily, then said, 'I loved you once, long ago. I thought the sun shone out of you. Perhaps it did once, but not now. I love my son, I always shall, God help me. Now I deeply regret ever having laid eyes on you that night at the Olympia Ballroom.'

Closing the door behind him, sick at heart, he went upstairs to begin packing, pushing to the back of his mind the thought of leaving his son; clinging to the belief that the child would be better off without him. He was unable to bear any longer the stress factor of a small, innocent human being continually subjected to the state of war between his parents.

An hour or so later, Wilma came upstairs to his room. Considerably chastened, she said, 'We'll spend Christmas Day with your parents, if that's what you want, but our marriage was a mistake, I know that now. I think, in the new year, we had better start thinking in terms of a legal separation. Since you are obviously no longer in love with me, nor I with you, all that really matters is William's future – what's best for him in the long run, don't you agree?'

'Yes, of course,' Danny said calmly, remembering the night he had first held Wilma in his arms in the summer of 1935; walking her home after the last waltz from the Olympia Ballroom, the way they had kissed and clung together in that deserted shelter in the St Nicholas Gardens. But all that was over and done with now. And yet, in the heart of him, he still recalled how lovely she had looked by moon and starlight on that warm summer night long ago . . .

Thank God they would spend Christmas together as a united family, keeping up the pretence of happiness: their son in his high-chair splattering gravy to his heart's content, pulling crackers, wearing silly paper hats, eating Christmas pudding and rum sauce within the confines of the Kingsley family circle.

*　　　*　　　*

Trust Grace, Danny thought gratefully, that she, in her wisdom, had invited Wilma's parents to share the Christmas Day festivities. An invitation which they had accepted, thank God.

Calling home one day after work, he had found his mother seated at the kitchen table, working out her guest-list, and the amount of food she would need to provide for twelve hungry people: Herbie, Kerry, Rosa, Fanny, Jimmy, himself, Wilma and William, herself and Bob, plus the Burtons.

'What about Nan and Dulcie?' he'd asked in all innocence.

'One can always hope,' his mother had replied quietly.

'OK, so Dulcie is a law unto herself,' he said, 'but surely Nan is bound to come with Fanny? What I mean to say is, Nan wouldn't contemplate spending Christmas Day alone, would she?'

'I can't answer that question, son,' Grace admitted. 'Nan also is a law unto herself.' Then, biting the end of her pen, she frowned slightly. 'It has just occurred to me that I should invite Mr Hodnot. I gather that he and Fanny have become quite friendly again lately. Yes, I think that I had better invite Mr Hodnot for Fanny's sake. So that means, let me see, an eighteen-pound turkey, an extra box of crackers, two pounds of sausage-meat, a stone-and-a-half of potatoes – better make that two stone, just in case – three pounds of sprouts. The cakes and the puddings are already made, thank heaven! Oh Lord, whatever else shall I need?' She smiled up at him, 'I love you dearly, Danny, but would you mind not looking over my shoulder? Now, let me think how much bread I shall need. Oh, and I must buy a ham shank to boil for the tea-time sandwiches. And what about jellies and tinned fruit? And cream? I must order extra milk and cream from the dairyman in case I run short over the weekend. Oh please, Danny love, do go away for the time being, otherwise I shall end up in a complete mess!

'You see, son, it isn't just the food, there's beds to be seen to, a thousand and one things to do: the tree to decorate, presents to pack: silver to polish, people to feed, not just on

Christmas and Boxing Day, but now. There's mince pies to make, and Yule-bread, egg and chips to fry for tea, a trifle to prepare.' She was laughing, Danny was not. 'What is it?' she asked, 'what's wrong?'

When he told her that he and Wilma were thinking of parting, Grace sat very still for a while, her face pale and set. She was thinking of the child mainly, and the effect this would have on his young life. 'Is there no other way?' she asked. 'No other solution?'

'Apparently not. Things have been going from bad to worse lately. I'm worried about William's reaction to the atmosphere he's being subjected to, the constant rows. He doesn't understand. The poor kid looks so unhappy, and he's crying a lot these days. Wilma gets upset and slaps him, which makes things worse. William turns to me for comfort and that causes more trouble. It's like a nightmare.'

'But what will happen about the house? Surely Wilma would not want to live there without you?'

Danny said bitterly, 'Oh, I know what's in her mind. She'll go back to her parents. Frankly, I shouldn't be sorry to see the back of the place, put it up for sale. That way I'd be able to pay off the mortgage, free myself of debt. Of course I'd have to pay Wilma maintenance. I'm not trying to shirk responsibility. Oh, Mother, it's just that I can't bear the thought of William being brought up by the Burtons.'

'It hasn't come to that yet, son,' Grace said. 'There is another alternative. You come back home to live with us. We'll look after William.' Standing, she put her arms round Danny, felt the shaking of his shoulders, and knew that he was crying. 'You can have your old room.'

'It may not be as simple as that,' Danny said, brushing his hand across his eyes. 'It depends on what Wilma tells the solicitor.'

'What could she tell him?' Grace frowned. 'You've been a good husband and father.'

Danny said bitterly, 'She could say that I'd come home drunk, had had an affair with another woman, that I forced myself on her on our wedding night.' Ashamed of his tears, he turned to look out of the window.

'I don't know much about the letter of the law,' Grace said calmly, 'but show me a man who has never come home, on just one occasion, the worse for wear, and I'll show you a saint. As for that so-called affair of yours, nothing of a physical nature took place. In any case, you and Wilma made a fresh start, and so, in law, she condoned it. As for forcing yourself on her on your wedding night, I imagine any solicitor worth his salt would scarcely risk his reputation on that kind of say so. Rather, I think, he would question a woman's motives in marrying at all if . . . Well, never mind.

'Think about it, son, that's my advice, and be prepared to put forward a few questions of your own. Why, for instance, did Wilma insist on your moving in with her parents to live after the wedding? Why did she fail to provide you with decent meals at the house in Princess Street? Why, in your present home, has she squandered money on unnecessary luxuries? Above all, why vent her anger and frustration on an innocent child?'

'Thanks, Mum, I'll try.' Facing his mother, he said, 'I want you to have William. I know he'll be safe here with you, but there's one more thing I think you should know.' Drawing in a deep breath, 'I've decided to give up my job at the Town Hall, to join the Royal Air Force and train as a pilot.'

'*Danny!*' Grace's heart lurched suddenly. 'But *why*? Why?' She laid a hand on his arm as if to hold him back from some action too terrible to contemplate.

Clasping her hand, he said, 'Because there's a war in the offing. Because, when it happens, I want to be in on the action, to fight for my country.' He smiled suddenly, his eyes, his face alight with purpose, renewed hope and self-respect, a look that Grace had not seen since his cricketing days when, strong, proud and self-confident, facing the bowling, he would loft the ball to the far-off pavilion in the final over.

Grace knew, understood and accepted, at that moment,

that she had no right to stand in his way. The time had come to let go, as she had done so many times before so far as her children were concerned.

Christmas was drawing nearer. Inexorably, Grace felt, not happily.

Dulcie had sent a Christmas card with a brief message saying that she had arranged to spend Christmas with friends. By a later post, a hastily wrapped parcel had arrived containing presents for the family, which Grace placed under the Christmas tree. A card from Fanny saying that she would be coming alone on Christmas Day added to Grace's distress. The thought of Nan spending Christmas on her own was unbearable. She must do something about it.

Putting on her outdoor things, she caught a bus to the South Cliff and battled her way, in the teeth of a gale, to South Street where, ringing the bell, she waited for what seemed like an eternity until the door opened and she stood face-to-face with her mother.

'Oh, it's you! Come to gloat, have you?' Nan said coldly. 'Well, you can just go away and leave me alone, since being alone appears to be my portion in life, the cross I have to bear!'

'Nothing of the kind!' Grace felt her anger rising against her mother's self-inflicted martyrdom. 'I've come to insist that you spend Christmas with Bob and me! No way will I allow you to spend Christmas alone. Where's Aunt Fanny? I want a word with her, too.'

'She's not here,' Nan said. 'She seldom is these days, since she took up with that fancy man of hers, that Cyril Hodnot.' In a whining voice, 'Fanny doesn't care tuppence for me now. She told me so. The sooner I'm dead and gone, the better, if you ask me!'

'You may get your wish sooner than expected if you don't go indoors before we freeze to death,' Grace said crossly, sick and tired of her mother's carping, refusing to be bullied or made to feel guilty. 'I want to know what's going on here, and I won't take no for an answer.'

Grumbling, moving slowly, Nan led the way upstairs to the drawing-room where she stood, facing her daughter, planning her means of attack. 'It seems to me,' she said coldly, 'that neither you nor Fanny have the slightest respect for me. I must say that I am shocked by your attitude in particular. I am, after all, your mother. As for Fanny, the things I have discovered about her past life are shocking beyond belief.'

'Really? What kind of things?'

Nan bridled. 'Things which I should not care to divulge to a living soul.'

Refusing to be dominated, determined to discover the truth, 'More shocking, you mean, than my getting pregnant at sixteen?'

Nan quivered. 'How *dare* you bring up that disgraceful episode? Have you no shame?'

'Not a bit, since you ask. Why should I? Bob and I were in love when we married. We are still in love. Ours has been a love-affair to be proud of, not ashamed of. The guilt was yours, Mother, not mine. It was you who tried to make me feel both guilty and ashamed at the time. It was you who turned my father against me, wasn't it? Why, I wonder? Because he happened to be a Methodist minister, a man of the cloth? Because you were so bound up in religious fervour that you ignored the underlying principle of forgiveness?' Speaking quickly, she unleashed the pent-up emotion built up over the years, 'I loved my father, and I know he loved me. That time in Ireland, we were so happy together jouncing along in that donkey cart. How jealous you must have been. I can see that now. The reason why nothing was right with you, why you complained so bitterly about the food we ate, the places we stayed at. Particularly that hotel in County Kerry, remember?'

Memories flooded Grace's mind, illuminating memories, hidden away and forgotten until now. Herself clinging to her father's hand, begging him to take her to the glen to see the Kerry Dance, his whispered reply, 'I can't, my darling, your mother wouldn't like it. I must go now.'

'But, Papa! *Please*, Papa!'

'Hush, child!' A loving, backward glance over his shoulder. 'I'll see what I can do, but not a word, remember?'

Then a servant girl had come to her room, taken her hand and led her, in the wake of the glimmering lanterns, down to the glen to see the Kerry Dance, to hear the ring of the piper's tune.

Next morning, a finger was raised in warning when she had said, in all innocence, 'But Mamma, I *did* see it!' That warning finger had been her father's, a bond of secrecy between them. And to think that she had forgotten all that until now, her father's love for her undermined by her mother's far stronger, domineering personality.

Suddenly, poor Aunt Rosa's words came back to her: 'Nan made the poor man's life a misery from start to finish. He had to toe the line, you see, to dance to her tune, otherwise his life would have been unbearable.'

Nan said aggressively, 'If you have come here to rake up the past, you are wasting your time.'

Refusing to be brow-beaten, Grace retorted, 'But isn't that exactly what you are doing now? What you have done all the days of your life – raking up a past best forgiven and forgotten?' With a proud uptilt of her chin, 'If you really prefer to stay here alone on Christmas Day rather than come to me, to join in the family celebration of the Birth of Our Lord, Jesus Christ, there's nothing more I can say to make you change your mind. At least I tried.' Admitting defeat, sick at heart, 'Well, goodbye Mother,' Grace said gently, 'and – God bless you.'

Slowly she walked down the stairs to the front door to face the bitingly cold wind whistling along the Esplanade, knowing she had failed in her mission. Had she really hoped to succeed? Of course she had. She had always believed, in her heart of hearts, that where there was life there was hope.

And now it was here at last, Christmas Eve, the night sky lit with stars. All was ready. The Christmas cake had been iced and decorated, the rooms were ready for Jimmy and

Herbie, the Christmas tree lights shone from the front room window, the scent of freshly baked mince-pies permeated the house; there was a heartwarming beef stew in the oven in readiness for supper. Bob had brought home with him several bottles of medium sweet sherry and a final edition of the *Scarborough Evening News* which no-one had bothered to read.

Hard at work in the kitchen, busily engaged in making the stuffing for the turkey, and turning out batch after batch of mince-pies and Yule loaves, scarcely knowing if she was on her head or her heels, Grace awaited the ringing of the doorbell, the arrival of Herbie and Jimmy.

When the doorbell eventually rang, she ran in a fluster from the kitchen to find the pair of them standing on the doorstep, wreathed in smiles.

'Oh, my dears,' was all she could say, 'welcome home!' Then Jimmy's arms were about her, Herbie's hand clasped warmly in hers, and tears of joy were streaming down her cheeks. Then suddenly Kerry, Bob and Aunt Rosa were there beside her, a kind of welcoming committee, exchanging hugs and kisses until, sniffing the air, Grace hurried back to the kitchen to rescue a tray of maids-of-honour before they burnt black.

There was something special about Christmas Eve, Kerry thought, a kind of unfailing magic. Even the stars seemed brighter. Tonight, frost had rimed white the gravestones in St Mary's Churchyard, and the broad meadow overlooking the sea. The frost sparkled like diamonds, the scene resembled a winter wonderland of brilliant gems, with the stained glass colours of the church windows shining out to illuminate the path down which she, Jimmy and Herbie walked to the Midnight service.

Singing all the old well known carols, she thought about Ashley, and wondered if all was well with him. Scarcely likely, she supposed, wishing she'd had word of him, a note or a Christmas card from him. It was pure selfishness on her part, she realized. With so much on his mind, he would scarcely have had time to write. In any case, she hadn't thought to give him her address. Tears filled her eyes. Suddenly Jimmy's hand was on hers. 'Don't worry, kiddo,' he whispered, 'it may never happen.'

Glancing up, she caught the warmth of his smile, saw the brightness of his eyes behind his glasses. She experienced a lifting of the heart that he was there beside her, the tall, compassionate brother she loved so much, and thought of something that Ashley had said to her at their last meeting: 'I had prayed for a miracle, and suddenly you were there.'

Christmas Day dawned fair and clear. There was a sense of occasion in the air, apart from the aroma of cooking. A feeling of excitement, of expectation, a mood of gaiety.

As giddy as a girl because Fanny and her friend Mr Hodnot were coming to dinner, Aunt Rosa had dressed herself in her Sunday best blouse and skirt, and arranged her fringe in a series of kiss-curls. 'Oh dear, do I look all right?' she asked over and over again, fluttering in and out of the kitchen where Kerry was helping her mother to prepare the vegetables, at the same time keeping an eye on the Christmas pudding to make sure the water in which it was simmering didn't boil dry. And 'Yes', they reassured her, 'you look fine.'

Finally, 'I expect I'm being a silly old nuisance,' Rosa said, 'but I can't help wishing that Nan was coming, too. I really can't bear to think of her all alone at Christmas when we are having such a jolly time.'

Understanding her mother's feelings on that particular subject, and that Grace was far from looking forward to the advent of the Burtons, their presence at the festive board, Kerry said brightly, 'Don't worry, Mum, we haven't got a piano, so at least we'll be spared Mabel's rendition of "One Alone", from *The Desert Song*.'

Grace smiled at Kerry's light-hearted remark. So typical of Kerry, she thought, to show a brave face to the world despite her own misgivings. The girl knew full well that the end of Danny and Wilma's marriage was imminent, of her mother's sadness that Dulcie would not be home to share the family Christmas, her heartbreak that she had not been able to break down Nan's barrier of resistance towards her. Kerry knew all these things because Grace had confided in her, not as a mother to a child, but as one woman to another, as Kerry had once confided in her, her heartbreak over that Irish tenor. More recently, Kerry had talked of her feelings towards someone called Ashley Hawthorn, with whom she might, or might not, be in love. Only time would tell.

Thank God for the simple, certain and sure things of life, Grace thought, basting the turkey: the preparation of food, the setting of the dining-room table, the hands of the kitchen clock moving inexorably towards the midday hour. The ringing of the front door bell announced the arrival of the guests. First the Burtons, closely followed by Danny, Wilma and William, all of whom Bob – a genial host *par excellence* – shepherded into the front room. He came, minutes later, into the kitchen, his grandson in his arms, the child crowing delightedly at the sight of his grandma and his Aunt Kerry and, clamouring to be let down from Bob's embrace, he toddled forward to receive his complement of kisses.

A quarter of an hour later came another ring at the doorbell. Up to her eyebrows in steam from the various pots and pans bubbling on the stove, 'That will be Aunt Fanny and Mr Hodnot, I expect,' Grace told Kerry. 'Not to worry, your father will take care of them. I really can't be seen just now, the state I'm in, with everything just about ready: my hair's in such a mess!'

Suddenly, the kitchen door opened, and Bob stood there, smiling. Grace looked up at him askance. 'Not *now*, Bob,' she pleaded, 'can't you see I'm in no fit state to—'

He said calmly, tongue-in-cheek, 'Sorry, love, it's just that we have an extra guest for dinner, I thought I'd better tell you because of the table arrangement.'

'An *extra* guest? But *who*?'

Nan entered the kitchen, head held high, proud, undefeated. 'I decided to come after all,' she said. 'Of course, if I'm not welcome . . .'

The flat looked delightful. Dulcie had suspended gilded pine-cones from fragrant larch boughs smothered in glittering artificial snow. She had purchased glowing red lampshades to create a romantically dim atmosphere, had filled tall vases with red and white chrysanthemums the size of dinner plates, decorated the Christmas tree with red baubles and gold tinsel interspersed with white ribbon bows, and filled the larder with food enough to feed an army: a whole salmon, cold roast goose, duck and turkey, celery, tomatoes, cucumber, plus several bottles of Chablis and a variety of cheeses from Stilton to Wensleydale.

As an afterthought, she had added a loaf of bread and a slab of butter to her shopping list, in the event that Franz would require a sandwich or two in bed, between bouts of love-making. He, after all, was not on a diet. No need. His firm, leanly muscled torso carried not one ounce of surplus fat, God dammit. And so, at the last minute, she had brought upstairs, from the café, a gâteau, cream-filled, smothered with chocolate icing and flaked almonds, and a plate of profiteroles and vanilla slices.

Early on Christmas morning, she had bathed long and luxuriously in warm, scented water, after which, sitting at her dressing table, she had carefully applied her make-up and combed her latest hairstyle into place. Then, awaiting Franz's arrival, she had wandered about the flat, rearranging cushions here and there, setting the dining-room table with its centrepiece of white gardenias, and making certain that every knife, fork and spoon was in place. She was keeping an eye on the clock, hoping against hope that his Christmas present to her would be a diamond engagement ring, a solitaire diamond the size of an egg, a pullet's egg, perhaps, but an *egg* nevertheless, ensconced in a morocco box inscribed with the legend 'Tiffany' or 'Gerrard'. She didn't care which, just as long as he slipped that ring on her finger and asked her to marry him.

Eleven, twelve, one o'clock came and went, with no sign of Franz. At a quarter to two, beside herself with anxiety and frustration, she picked up the phone and rang his home number. A servant answered. 'I wish to speak to Mr Franz Bergmann,' Dulcie said icily.

'I'm sorry, madam, I'm afraid he's not here,' the servant replied.

'Then where is he?'

'In London, madam, to the best of my knowledge,' the man replied, 'at the Savoy Hotel, attending a celebration party of some kind. Would you care to leave a message?'

Not bothering to reply, Dulcie hung up the receiver. Tears flooding down her cheeks, she stood stock still for a little while, surveying the ruination of her Christmas, feeling, as a slap in the face, the loneliness of the empty flat. Then, slowly but surely, dawned on her the fact that she meant less than nothing to Franz Bergmann, that all her hard-won victories over her plumpness, all that bloody black coffee she'd drunk, all those flaming rotten salads she'd eaten to diminish her waistline, had been a waste of time and effort, just as the gilded pine-cones, the soft lights and the scented bathwater, her new hairstyle and her new apricot silk nightdress had been a waste of money.

So be it!

Entering the pantry, slicing into the loaf of bread, she first spread the slices thickly with butter. Then, with malice aforethought, she hacked off chunky slices of cold goose, duck and turkey to stuff between the bread, which she ultimately stuffed into her mouth in the manner of a starving woman dying of malnutrition. Finally, with a sigh of relief, she bit into a gigantic wedge of cream-filled gâteau, quickly followed by a couple of profiteroles and a vanilla slice.

Later, her appetite appeased, she opened a bottle of wine, which she drank to the dregs in the loneliness of her flat before going upstairs to bed to sleep off her crushing headache, the sick feeling in her stomach.

At midnight, the bedside telephone shrilled suddenly, arousing her from her drunken stupor.

Picking up the receiver, 'Who's that?' she enquired testily, feeling abominably sick and miserable.

'Dulcie, darling, is that you? It's I – Franz! I'm ringing to say how sorry I am. I meant to let you know that I couldn't spend Christmas with you, but everything happened so suddenly. Please say you forgive me. We'll spend New Year together, I promise.' A pause. 'Dulcie, are you there?'

'Of course I'm here, where else would I be? I've been here all day, on my own. Alone in this bloody flat!' With an uprush of pride, 'Well, Franz, my "darling", so far as I'm concerned, you can go to hell and pump thunder!'

So saying, she hung up on him. Seconds later she was in the bathroom spewing up the contents of her stomach, wanting her mother.

Nan's presence at the dinner table had made all the difference in the world to Grace. Leopards could not be expected to change their spots overnight, she knew that. There was now, at least, hope of a new beginning, a glimmer of hope for the future. Rosa appeared to bear no resentment towards Nan, and Fanny and Mr Hodnot were obviously happy in each other's company.

Even so, Christmas was clouded, for Grace, by the coolness between Danny and Wilma, Mr Burton's moroseness, his wife's mindless twittering, her desire to be the life and soul of the party despite the underlying tension between her daughter and son-in-law.

As for poor Kerry, Grace knew only too well the feelings and emotions of a young girl suffering the pains and pangs of the growing-up process. How bravely she had endured the ending of her summer-time love-affair with that Irish tenor. Now, despite her smiling face, her frequent dashes to the kitchen to help with the serving-up of the pudding and rum sauce, Grace knew that her daughter was far from happy, deep down, because of this Ashley Hawthorn who appeared to be in some kind of trouble.

Oh, Lord, Grace thought, carrying the pudding plates to the dining-room, if only someone would wave a magic wand and everything would come out right at last. No messing.

No more trouble. Just plain and simple happiness. Was that too much to ask?

Suddenly the doorbell rang. Kerry was in the kitchen turning out the Christmas pudding. Halfway between the kitchen and the dining-room, her hands full of plates, Grace awkwardly answered the summons, thinking it might be the Salvation Army Band wanting a donation. But the man on the doorstep, holding a sheaf of red roses, was certainly not a member of the Sally Army Band.

He said, courteously, 'I hope I've come to the right address.'

Smiling up at him, 'If your name is Ashley Hawthorn, then yes, you have,' Grace said, remembering that magic wand she had longed for. 'Kerry's in the kitchen, just along the hall, the second door on the right, coping with the Christmas pudding.'

'Then, may I?'

'Yes, of course! I'm her mother, by the way.'

'I'm delighted to meet you, Mrs Kingsley,' Ashley said gravely.

'And I you, Mr Hawthorn,' Grace replied with equal gravity. Then, 'Just don't break her heart, that's all.'

'I'll try my best not to. I love her, you see. She's the only girl in the world for me.'

'Then you'd better tell her so, hadn't you?' Grace said, liking the look of him, his charm, his manners. 'But what of the future? The court case? I'm sorry, but I really must know.'

Ashley's face fell. 'My father must stand trial, but I'm in the clear. I shall have to appear, of course, as a witness for the prosecution, God help me, but no charges have been brought against me. I should not otherwise have come here today. I intended to spend Christmas with my mother, but she has gone to Eastbourne to stay with her sister, where she intends to remain for the foreseeable future. All this has shaken her quite badly, I'm afraid.

'In fact, my home, Glebe House, is shuttered and closed now. Up for sale, as a matter of fact.' He brushed a hand

390

across his eyes. 'It all seems like a nightmare.'

'Life often does seem that way,' Grace reminded him gently, 'but if you are truly in love with Kerry, she with you, her father and I will not stand in the way of your happiness.' Grace paused, smiling. 'Go to her now, and good luck, Ashley.'

Slowly, nervously, he entered the kitchen. 'Kerry,' he said gently, 'better late than never. Are you pleased to see me?'

'*Pleased?*' Smiling, her heart in her eyes, crossing swiftly towards him, feeling the warmth, the strength of his arms about her. 'Oh, Ashley, you'll never know how much.'

'Enough to marry me one of these fine days?' he whispered, his lips against her hair, breathing in the sweet fragrance of her.

And, 'Oh yes, Ashley,' she murmured, 'if you really want me.'

'*Want* you? Oh Kerry, my darling. I wanted you from the first moment I saw you! I shall go on wanting and loving you till the day I die!'

PART FOUR

Chapter Thirty

At York Crown Court in February 1939, Sir Charles Hawthorn was found guilty of the charges brought against him, and sentenced to five years' imprisonment. Three other directors of the Hawthorn Company involved in the fraudulent conversion of Company funds had also been found guilty and given sentences of from two to four years. Five other members of the Board had been found not guilty and released from custody.

In one sense, Ashley had his father to thank that no charges whatsoever had been brought against him. Sir Charles had been adamant from the outset that his son had played no part in the collusion of senior members of the board to defraud the public and shareholders alike. Rather, during his short period of employment in the family business, he had tried repeatedly to warn himself, the Company Chairman and Director, against the use of sub-standard building materials and unskilled labourers. And yet Ashley had derived no satisfaction but a great deal of grief from his father's admission of guilt. On the other hand, he could not help but glory in what he regarded as his father's honourable desire to pay the full penalty of his folly, to face his term of imprisonment as a man, not a coward.

What he would have done without the help and support of Kerry during the past two months, Ashley dreaded to think. She had stood beside him as a rock throughout the court proceedings, had been there at his side on that terrible last day, when sentence on his father had been pronounced. It was she who had comforted him when he knew that his mother had instituted divorce proceedings against her husband, and later, when Glebe House and its contents had been put up for auction.

Meanwhile, he had returned to his attic eyrie in Marine Parade, continued his job as a washer-upper at the Élysée Restaurant, and begun writing letters of application to various schools in the vicinity, citing his teaching qualifications, his Oxford M.A. degree, with little hope of success until one day, miraculously, he received the offer of a teaching post at a small private boys' school at Scalby – a stone's throw away from Scarborough – which he gladly accepted. Not 'the sea-mark of his utmost sail', perhaps, but a beginning.

From his first month's salary he bought Kerry a small, three-stone diamond ring of Victorian vintage from a second-hand jewellers' shop in Westborough. She would accept no other. The diamonds were minuscule, the setting was old-fashioned, as it was bound to be since the ring itself was old-fashioned, but she loved it the moment she saw it, and said quietly, 'I have the feeling that this is a happy ring, worn long ago by someone who was as happy then as I am now.'

He knew she meant what she said. Kerry was incapable of lying. Then, tongue-in-cheek, and with a flirtatious upward glance at him, 'Am I to assume, then, that "one of these fine days" is really here at last? Is this an engagement ring or what?'

'You know damn fine well it is!'

'Then why don't you take it out of the box, place it on the third finger of my left hand, get down on one knee and say, "Kerry, darling, wilt thou be mine?" '

'I might just do that,' he warned her, teasingly, 'In fact—'

'Don't you *dare*, Ashley Hawthorn!'

'I will if you want me to.'

Suddenly they were clinging together, laughing despite the falling rain, the bitter wind blowing in from the sea, and the ring was on the third finger of Kerry's left hand, her eyes were as sparkling as diamonds, and Ashley was saying, 'Kerry, darling, wilt thou be mine?'

'Since thou put it that way, yes, of course I wilt – thou idiot!'

Passers-by turned to stare at them, a handsome young couple, oblivious of the rain, kissing each other in the middle of a busy thoroughfare. Just like the final fadeout of a romantic movie.

Franz had returned from London at the New Year to find Dulcie curiously lethargic, lacking the *joie de vivre* he had found amusing.

Letting himself into the flat on New Year's Eve, he found her sitting in the lounge, a box of chocolates on the table beside her. She was wearing the red housecoat, but her hair was untidy and so was the room. The vases of chrysanthemums had lost their freshness, the petals had begun to turn brown, some lay scattered on the carpet; cushions were crumpled, the Christmas tree had shed some of its needles.

He had expected fireworks, Dulcie in her Joan Crawford mood, eyes flashing, in a towering rage. He knew he had treated her badly in leaving her alone at Christmas without a word of explanation. His prerogative. Family came first. Klaus and his bride had returned from honeymoon to spend Christmas at the Savoy. Franz had taken his mother and the twins to join them there. It had been a last-minute invitation he could not ignore. Dulcie should have spent Christmas with her own family, he'd reasoned inwardly on his way to London. Surely she had not expected to monopolize him the whole of Christmas, and he had, after all, rung her up to apologize and tell her he would spend New Year with her.

Angry now, throwing down the gifts he had brought her, 'What kind of a welcome is this?' he demanded, glancing distastefully at the evidence of her neglect of both herself and the flat, her unkempt appearance, the dusty furniture, withering flowers and unswept carpet.

Glancing up at him, unsmiling, 'The kind you bloody well deserve,' she said wearily. 'What did you expect? Oh, don't bother to tell me, value for money. A grateful mistress waiting to welcome you with open arms, ready and willing to pay the price for all – this. Only I'm not willing to pay the price this time, you heartless, miserable excuse for a human being. So just pick up that load of rubbish you've brought with you and get the hell out of here!'

Franz laughed briefly, 'You seem to forget, my love, that I happen to own all this *and* you!' Arrogantly, 'Think about it, Dulcie. I've squandered a great deal of money on this little investment, this flat and your greedy little self in particular. Let's not forget that, shall we? Certainly I expect value for money. I expect more than that. Gratitude for all I've done for you these past months.' Master of the situation, he said coldly, 'You have an hour to clean up this mess, including yourself, then I'll be back.'

Dulcie had no choice other than to comply. She knew the score well enough. Never more so than now. Her job, her home, her security lay in her availability, her sexuality, her prowess between the blankets, her ability to please her lover in bed. If she failed to do so, what then? The answer came clear and simple. Mistresses were ten a penny. He would find someone else to take her place. So much for the diamond engagement ring she had hoped for, a proposal of marriage. Her apathy lay deep in the knowledge that Franz's feelings for her were less than the dust on the coffee table beside her chair.

Rising wearily to her feet, curiously tired and inert, she first consigned the fading chrysanthemums to the rubbish bin, then swept up the scattered petals and the pine needles from the Christmas tree.

There was little food left in the pantry. She had gorged most of it. The sink was full of dirty pots which she washed hastily and stacked on the draining board to dry.

Upstairs, she quickly changed and made the bed, bundling the soiled sheets and pillow-cases into the Ali-Baba basket in the bathroom. She then filled the bath with steaming hot, Chanel-scented water in which she spent less than five minutes, after which, returning to the bedroom and removing the red housecoat, she put on her new apricot silk nightdress and negligée, brushed and combed her hair, and applied her make-up. Keeping a wary eye on the clock, she realized that, in less than a quarter of an hour, Franz would be back – wanting value for money. Very well, then, she would make damn sure he had what he wanted. What, after all, had she to lose that had not already been lost beyond recall by her own greed and lack of morality?

When Franz returned to the flat, he found his mistress, as he had expected, lying in bed, beautifully groomed and scented, awaiting his embrace. And yet, undressing quickly, holding her in his arms, there was something different about her, he realized. Her waistline had thickened slightly.

He said critically, 'You've put on weight, Dulcie! Not very clever of you, my darling, under the circumstances, knowing my preference for slender women.' Impatiently, 'You've been making a pig of yourself, haven't you? Stuffing yourself with cakes and chocolates? You're a slut at heart, Dulcie.'

'At least I have a heart,' she reminded him.

The European situation was worsening day by day. On 17 March, in the House of Commons, Prime Minister Neville Chamberlain had denounced Adolf Hitler and recalled the British Ambassador to Berlin. Twelve days later, Chamberlain had announced his intention of doubling the size of the Territorial Army. His intentions were clear-cut and decisive. Great Britain was preparing to go to war with Germany. What price now his 'Peace for our Time' agreement?

The battle royal between Grace Kingsley and Mabel Burton over the custody of William, began at that time. One capricious March morning, when the house in Norwood Street had been sold and Danny had received his call-up papers for the Royal Air Force, Grace had purposefully knocked at the door of the house in Aberdeen Terrace to confront Wilma's mother.

'Let's not beat about the bush, shall we?' Grace said succinctly. 'You know as well as I do that Wilma never wanted William in the first place, and neither do you. Let's face facts, which appear to me to be clear-cut and simple.

You don't want the child. *I* do. Without him, Wilma might make a fresh start, a new beginning. In short, if you place William in my custody, you can pretend he never happened: get on with your lives as normal, as they were before that winter wedding day, remember? Well, what do you say? Are you prepared to take on the constant care and upbringing of your grandson, or not? If not, will you hand him over to me to take care of? It's your decision entirely.'

'Well, I'm not too sure,' Mabel prevaricated. 'There's a matter of maintenance, you see; Danny's responsibility towards Wilma. She's entitled to what's due to her and the child.'

'Of course,' Grace acceded, 'she'll receive every penny due to her, but you haven't answered my question.'

Mabel replied snappishly, 'Oh very well then, take the boy if you want to, the nasty-tempered little brute. Takes after his father, if you want my opinion!'

'And you'll be prepared to put that in writing?' Grace asked firmly. 'What I mean is, you know as well as I do what solicitors are like, wanting everything cut and dried.'

'Yes, of course,' Mabel declared intently, 'the sooner the better, so far as I'm concerned. Just as long as my poor little girl gets what's due to her.'

Walking down the garden path to the gate, Grace thanked God, in her heart, for the precious gift of her grandson given into her care and keeping. It was another small miracle in the sum total of small miracles which constituted the great miracle of life itself; the mere fact of breathing, of living. Of loving. Above all – loving.

When the time came, Wilma had been quite pleased with the idea of referring to Danny as 'My husband in the Air Force.' No-one need know they had parted company for reasons other than his decision to join up. Then she would tell their friends, when the new tenants moved in, that she had not wanted to live alone in the house with Danny away.

A romantic picture of herself in a nice little flat had begun to build up in her mind. The only fly in the ointment was William. Living within the cramped confines of her parents' home with an inquisitive toddler making a nuisance of himself was bound to cause problems. Nor did she like the idea of her precious furniture being stored away in the spare room. If only she could go back to her job at the Meadow Dairy, find herself an apartment in a smart area of town, and leave William with her mother to look after. Fat chance of that, Wilma thought. Knowing Mabel, she would expect her to be on hand every minute of the day to stop the kid getting into mischief.

And then, miraculously, Danny's mother had come up with the ideal solution. Of course. Why hadn't she thought of it herself? More to the point, why hadn't Danny thought of it? He had, of course, thought of it, but Grace had advised him to let her handle the situation. She had read the Burtons like a book – an Ethel M. Dell novel – and she had won! Now everyone was happy, Danny most of all, knowing his son would be properly looked after. Mabel Burton was happy, deep down, that she would not be required to accommodate a meddlesome two-year-old who might smash to smithereens her *objets-d'art*. Wilma was happy because, free of her responsibilities as a mother, she would be able to go back to work, find a place of her own to live, and begin life anew – with money to burn.

In view of his educational standards and by reason of letters of recommendation from his Town Hall employers, Danny had been accepted as officer training material by the Royal Air Force, and posted to an officers' training unit in Wiltshire to undergo preliminary tests and examination to establish his leadership qualifications. Grace had no doubt he would pass with flying colours, nor did she regret that he and Wilma had come to the parting of the ways. Their marriage had been wrong from the start. Now, hopefully, a better future lay in store for him.

She had guessed all along the name of the girl he was really in love with. There had been certain signs and signals concerning Meg Jenkins' embarrassment on fish-delivery days, a worried look on her face. Then suddenly she had stopped coming altogether. Asked why, Mr Jenkins hemmed and hawed at first, then admitted that his daughter felt guilty about coming to the house because of 'that bit of trouble in Princess Street, tha knows!'

Grace didn't know, but she didn't let on to Mr Jenkins. All she said was, 'Well, these things happen, I suppose, more's the pity.'

Sighing deeply, 'You're right there,' Jenkins said, with a shake of the head. 'Mind you, I'm attaching no blame. That son of yours is a fine lad. The pity is he married the wrong lass. Sorry, Mrs Kingsley, I shouldn't hev said that. In any case, it were nowt but a storm in a tea-cup. Meg told me so herself, an' I believed her. She's a good lass, our Meg, with a good head on her shoulders. No way would she have set out to cause trouble between husband and wife.'

Kerry and Ashley decided on an autumn wedding. She loved October more than any other month of the year because of the colour of the autumn leaves drifting down from the trees, the crystal clear, wine-sweet days bringing with them a hint of frost, so that every spider's web in the hedgerows resembled crystal-beaded Chantilly lace. Besides which, October nights scintillated with stars more clearly defined, more brilliant than at any other time, and the lights of home came on early to shine through the dusk of this town to which she had belonged all the days of her life.

This Ashley knew and understood, and so they had fixed their wedding for 10 October at St Mary's Church. Meanwhile, they had been hunting for a flat, not a house, and had found exactly what they both wanted: a top-floor apartment on the Esplanade, overlooking the sea, the main room leading to a small balcony with a view of the Spa gardens and the Holbeck Clock Tower, the whole of the South Bay.

She would wear a white satin wedding dress, Kerry decided, simply cut, with pointed sleeves, a sweetheart neckline, a shoulder-length veil, and carry a bouquet of crimson roses. She wanted no fuss, no frills, no furbelows, no bridesmaids and no honeymoon. After the wedding ceremony there would be a quiet reception in the front room at home, her immediate family around her, after which she and Ashley would drive to their own flat to begin their married life together, in the setting they had chosen with so much happiness and care.

Her father would give her away. Jimmy would be Ashley's best man. Hopefully, Danny would be given leave to attend his sister's wedding. Herbie Barrass would be there, of course. Nan, Rosa and Fanny, young William, Grandma Kingsley and Aunt Caroline, and perhaps Meg Jenkins. Mr Hodnot would come, of course, since he and Great Aunt Fanny had recently announced their own engagement, and possibly Kerry's dancing teacher, Miss Williams, whose mother had died recently. And Dulcie – pray God Dulcie – the sister Kerry still loved with all her heart despite the long years without her.

Fanny and Mr Hodnot had renewed their friendship at summer-time concerts in the Spa Grand Hall. Nan disliked music, and in any case she considered the Sunday morning pursuit of pleasure as a mark of the devil, that those Sunday morning excursions of Fanny's, wearing her best clothes, were a futile attempt to resurrect the days of her misspent youth.

As far back as she could remember, Fanny had evinced not the slightest desire to move out of the house on Sunday mornings, much less dress up to flaunt herself on the lower promenade of the Spa near the open-air bandstand. She looked for all the world like an overweight bird-of-paradise in her bizarre medley of floating dresses, colourful scarves, baubles, bangles and beads, streamers of hair dangling beneath a variety of turn-of-the-century hats trimmed with feathers or fat, pink artificial roses, carrying a *petit-point* handbag and a silver-knobbed walking stick.

There was method in Fanny's madness. Triggered by the shocking discovery of Nan's subterfuge, the reading of her private correspondence, and taking a long, hard look at her present mode of living, she had determined to make the best of her life from then on. Old and fat she may be, but she still had a brain in her head, a heart in her body. Besides which, she adored music – especially the wartime melodies she had danced to in the arms of her lover – and, despite her avoirdupois, she still possessed panache, a certain glamour.

Certainly Cyril Hodnot had appeared to think so on that Sunday morning they had met accidentally in the foyer of the Spa Grand Hall. 'Why, Fanny,' he said admiringly, 'how lovely you look. Er – may we sit together during the performance?'

'Of course, Cyril. How kind of you to ask. How are you?'

'Fine. Never better. And you?'

Smiling, 'As you see – as large as life. Perhaps larger!'

'Not at all, not at all. Certainly as lovely, even lovelier than ever!'

And that had been the beginning of their late-blossoming romance.

Later, apart from their shared love of music, they had discovered a mutual need of companionship. Hodnot's business interests were now in a minor key. Growing older, he had realized that beautiful objects – shining crystal bowls and goblets, silks and satins and gold-fringed lamp-shades – had ceased long ago to fill the empty corners of his life as successfully as they filled his flat above the shop.

Equally, Fanny began to lose interest in sewing beads onto milk-jug covers or embroidering tray-cloths that no-one wanted to buy. The South Street shop had long been a millstone round her neck financially, a fruitless venture which might have closed long ago had it not been for Nan's injection of capital. Even so, she had loved her little fancy-goods shop and the house above it when Rosa had been there to take care of her, and when Grace, Bob and their children had come on Sunday afternoons, to partake of poor Rosa's damp egg-and-cress sandwiches and her heavy-as-lead Swiss roll. Now the time had come to think in terms of selling up.

Fanny knew, in her heart, that she could no longer continue to live with Nan, whom she no longer loved or trusted. When she admitted as much to Cyril Hodnot, he had asked her to marry him.

Her immediate reaction had been, 'No! I couldn't possibly. It's kind of you, Cyril, but I confided in you as a friend. I never meant to suggest that I—'

'Fanny, my dear,' he said tenderly, 'my proposal has nothing to do with kindness. I'd have asked you to marry me a long time ago if I'd had the sense I was born with. Now, all I want is to make your life as happy as you have made mine these past months. Please don't disappoint me. You see, my dear, I am still in love with you.'

Nan would be furious, Fanny knew, the day she walked home to announce her engagement to marry Cyril Hodnot. More than furious – outraged, scornful, vituperative. Curiously, Fanny no longer cared tuppence about the stormy confrontation ahead, her sister's self-righteous anger that the shop, the house, would soon be on the market. 'But what about *me*?' would be the thought uppermost in Nan's mind. A question to which, Fanny considered coolly, there could be no immediate reply, to which she would certainly make no attempt to reply until Nan's anger had subsided somewhat. If and when it ever did subside. Fanny knew only too well her sister's predilection to harbour grudges until the bitter end, if necessary.

Fanny the kind-hearted, secure in her new-found happiness, hoped that Nan's end would not be too bitter, that she would, one day, be given the grace to confess to her own faults and failings, to seek forgiveness for all the damage she had caused to those nearest and dearest to her.

Nan arrived on the doorstep looking as if she had been blown from South Street to Castle Road by the mad March wind.

'Come in and get your breath,' Grace said, sensing trouble. 'Sit down and tell me what's wrong.' Leading the way to the kitchen, 'I'll put the kettle on.'

'Wrong? I'll tell you what's wrong. Fanny's had word this morning that the shop's been sold. The house too, and most of the furniture and fittings!' Nan's dentures seemed likely to spring from her mouth from the force of her words. 'It's nothing short of disgraceful! To think I went to live there in good faith. Now what's to become of me?'

'Please, Mother, don't distress yourself, it's bad for you at your age.'

'At *my* age! Precisely! At my age one expects a little kindness and consideration. After all I've done for Fanny. Now she doesn't care tuppence about me! All she can think of now is that fancy man of hers. A fine kettle of fish, I must say, a woman of her age behaving like a love-sick calf. Ha! It's nothing short of indecent, in my opinion, two silly old fogies wanting to get married, to share the same bed. Wanting sex – that's what it's all about!' She threw off her scarf and unbuttoned her coat, her face as red as turkey wattles. 'Huh, I wonder if Fanny has let on to her precious Cyril that she's had plenty of *that* before. Oh yes, I found out all about her carryings-on during the war, the hussy!'

'Just a minute, Mother. How do you mean, you found out?'

'That's beside the point. I came across some letters, that's all. Disgusting letters they were too. I felt ashamed reading them.'

'Perhaps you weren't meant to read them?' Grace suggested quietly.

'Oh, that's right, accuse me of spying. But I will make quite sure that Cyril Hodnot realizes the kind of woman he is thinking of marrying. I dare say he'll change his mind in a hurry when he discovers the truth about her.'

'You'll do nothing of the kind! I mean what I say, Mother! If you utter one word to spoil Aunt Fanny's happiness, I'll have nothing more to do with you, is that clear? Not ever!' Abruptly switching off the gas under the kettle, too angry to think of making tea, she faced Nan across the table, hands clenched. 'Bob and I had already decided to offer you a room here with us after Aunt Fanny's wedding. Oh, I dare say that wouldn't meet with your approval, but the offer stands as long as you leave Fanny and Mr Hodnot alone to get on with their own lives.'

'Oh, so it's come to blackmail, has it?' Rising unsteadily to her feet, Nan began rebuttoning her coat. 'Well, if you think I'd consider living under the same roof as Rosa again, you're very much mistaken.'

Swallowing her anger, 'It isn't a question of blackmail, Mother,' Grace said wearily, 'I just happen to believe that people have a right to happiness at any age. After all, you had a happy marriage. Why deny Aunt Fanny the same right?'

Primming her lips, Nan retorted, 'Oh yes, I had a happy marriage because I made it so! What your father would have done without me, I shudder to think. *I* was the power behind the throne. Your father was far too soft for his own good, especially where *you* were concerned. All you had to do was pout or cry and he would give you anything you wanted. I warned him time and time again not to give in to you, and what was the result?'

'Like the night of the Kerry Dance?' Grace said slowly.

'*Exactly!*' Nan readjusted her scarf. 'I made clear my feelings on the subject of taking you to watch that pagan ritual despite your constant begging and pleading. We had words about it. Harsh words, as I recall, but he came, at last, to my way of thinking, thank goodness. He realized, thanks to me, that a man of the cloth should think shame on himself to even consider partaking in such a ritual, much less subjecting a small child to the wickedness of such a ritual.'

'But it wasn't like that at all,' Grace said. 'The Kerry Dance was just a happy company of young people gathered together to enjoy the music, the laughter, the lantern light.'

'Oh? And how do *you* know that?'

'Because I was *there*! Because my father made it possible for me to be there!'

Nan angled her shoulders. 'It isn't true! I simply don't believe it!' She stared at Grace askance. 'How dare your father have gone against my wishes?'

'Because he knew, perhaps, more about human nature than we gave him credit for.'

'By "we" you mean *me*, I suppose?' Nan was deeply, fiercely angry, betrayed by the shaking of her voice, the trembling of her limbs.

In retrospect, Grace could see that her father had been torn between love and duty, incapable of withstanding his wife's far stronger personality. A gentle man, he had plumped for peace at any price. What other choice had there been? She said quietly, 'It all happened a long time ago. Why rake up the past?'

'As I recall, *you* have done the raking up,' Nan said bitterly.

'That isn't quite fair, Mother. You were the one who raked up Aunt Fanny's past. But she was young at the time, away from home before the war. Why not forgive and forget?'

'You are just like your father,' Nan retorted, 'every bit as soft and weak as he was! Always ready to turn the other cheek, to make allowances for the weakness in others. If it hadn't been for me and my influence, he'd have got nowhere in the ministry. What kind of a man is that?'

'A Christian?' Grace suggested quietly.

Angry beyond belief, 'How dare you say such a thing to me, your own mother?' Nan bridled with self-righteous indignation. Picking up her handbag, she walked out of the kitchen to the front door, intent on catching the next bus into town. 'Don't bother to see me out,' she flung over her shoulder, 'I am perfectly capable of taking care of myself. I shall make my own arrangements concerning my future. I shall seek the advice of the minister of the South Cliff Methodist Church.'

'Mother! Wait. Please wait.' Quickly shrugging on her coat, Grace followed Nan across the road to the bus-stop. 'I'm sorry, Mother,' was all she could say, 'I didn't mean to upset you. Bob and I really do want you, you know.'

Nan made no reply. When the bus arrived, she boarded it and sat down in a seat near the door, staring straight ahead.

In tears, Grace returned to the house. Guilt-ridden, she

knew she had failed yet again to break down the barrier of resistance between herself and her mother. But what more could she have said or done, apart from sanction Nan's determination to spoil Aunt Fanny's wedding to Mr Hodnot? And why, in heaven's name, had she brought up the subject of the Kerry Dance?

Too late now. What was done was done. One thought emerged clear and simple. Despite all her faults and failings, she still loved her mother.

Grace, Bob, Rosa, Kerry and Ashley, were having supper together when the phone rang.

'I'll answer it,' Bob said, going through to the hall.

A few minutes later, he returned. Looking at Grace, 'It's bad news, I'm afraid,' he said quietly.

'Bad news?' She rose quickly to her feet. 'Not Danny?'

'No, love, not Danny.' Crossing to her side, he placed a steadying arm about his wife's shoulders. 'It's Nan. That was Fanny on the phone from the hospital. Nan has suffered a stroke, a rather serious one, I'm afraid.' He paused a moment, then very gently he said, 'She's asking for you. I think we should hurry. I'll ring for a taxi.'

At first, Grace scarcely recognized the shrivelled figure as that of her mother, the indomitable Nan Daniel. Holding the old woman's hand, 'I'm here, Mother,' she whispered. Tears ran down her cheeks unchecked. Bob was standing near the bedside chair, his hand on his wife's shoulder, knowing the end was near.

The face on the pillow was grey, the mouth twisted with the severity of the stroke, the eye corners pulled down, and yet there was a glimmer of recognition in the old lady's eyes. The mouth worked pitiably. Bob's eyes filled with tears. He turned his head away, knowing that these last few moments belonged to Grace and her mother.

Grace bent her head closer to catch what Nan was trying to say to her.

The nurse in attendance shook her head, 'It's pretty

useless, I'm afraid,' she said quietly, 'I'm afraid that what she says won't make sense.'

Clasping his hands, Bob prayed that Nan's last words would make sense to Grace.

And then it was all over. The old woman's eyes closed. She was at peace at last, holding her daughter's hand.

Fanny, Cyril, Kerry, Ashley and Rosa were in the corridor. Clinging tightly to Bob's arm, Grace smiled at them briefly, sadly, shaking her head, and walked with him to the front steps where, head erect, drawing in gulps of fresh air, 'Take me home, Bob,' she said quietly. 'Please take me home.'

They walked silently, arm-in-arm, along Friar's Way to Castle Road, drawing strength and comfort one from the other. No need of words, until, reaching the boundary of St Mary's Church, stopping suddenly to rest her hands on the wall, she gazed out to sea, her face wet with tears, Grace said softly, 'Her last words were: "The Kerry Dance. I'm sorry."'

Chapter Thirty-one

Dulcie's world had shattered like broken glass. The new life she had created for herself was over. The New Year incident between herself and Franz had never been healed. His manner towards her had changed abruptly after his return to the flat that night, when he had referred to her as a slut.

Soon, she had realized that the thickening of her waistline had little or nothing to do with her over-indulgence at Christmas, the food she had gorged as an antidote to loneliness, her feeling of nausea, of lethargy. Other physical changes were happening also. Her breasts were fuller, her nipples swollen. She had scarcely needed a doctor to confirm the fact that she was pregnant.

Leaving the surgery, deeply shaken, she had clung to the hand-rail for support, facing the ruination of her life, the shattering of all her hopes and dreams for the future: the loss of her job, her home, her lover. She had known, even then, that the last person she could turn to for support was Franz Bergmann. Value for money, from his viewpoint, would certainly not include the care and support of an illegitimate child born of a cast-off mistress. And she was right.

Furiously, coldly angry when she told him she was pregnant, he had told her in no uncertain terms that their relationship was over and done with. Finished for good and all. His lack of concern for her welfare, and that of the child she was carrying, brought her to the full realization of his worthlessness as a human being. Pacing the drawing-room, he reached the instant decision that she must quit the flat by the end of March at the latest, leaving behind all the gifts he had given her, the jewellery, clothes and perfume.

'You needn't worry, Franz,' she said dully, 'the only gift of any worth you have given me, I shall carry with me when I go!'

'If that is a threat,' he flung at her contemptuously, 'forget it. If you imagine, for one moment, that I intend to pay through the nose for that brat of yours, you have another think coming. Blackmail, emotional or otherwise carries no weight with me. Try involving me in a scandal, and you'll wish you'd never been born!'

With a resurgence of her old spirit, she said, 'I'm beginning to wish that already. The fact remains that this child I'm carrying is yours, and you know it!' Facing him squarely, she added, 'The day may come when you'll try to lay claim to it. The boot will be on the other foot then. Furthermore, what I said to you on New Year's Eve was perfectly true – you *are* a heartless, miserable excuse for a human being!'

Trouble was in the air, and Herbie knew it. Inflamed by the latest war news, gangs of drunken youths turning out from the pubs in Leeds city centre had taken it on themselves to administer rough justice to the foreigners in their midst, particularly those with German-sounding names. The fact that the Bergmanns were Austrian, not German, mattered not at all to the gangs of stone-carrying thugs intent on shattering the shop windows of the Bergmann café on the Headrow.

On the edge of the crowd of assailants, glancing at an upstairs window, he saw a face he recognized, a frightened face gazing down at the street below – that of Dulcie Kingsley. Christ, he thought, the poor kid must be scared witless, all alone in the building.

Suddenly, dramatically, the situation worsened. The leader of the gang hurled a lighted petrol-bomb through the downstairs window. His followers cheered as the building began to burn. Soon, tongues of flame were shooting upwards to the night sky, flames fed by the café tables and chairs, the woodwork, the stairs leading to the upper premises.

Heart hammering, and with one thought in mind – to lead Dulcie to safety – Herbie raced along a narrow passageway to the rear of the building. There *must* be a back exit, a fire-escape of sorts. Thank God he was right. But the exit door was locked. Right then, he'd burst the bloody thing open! Bathed in sweat from head to foot, he relentlessly applied his full weight, like a human battering-ram to the locked door, until at last the lock splintered and he was inside the building, calling out, 'Dulcie! Dulcie, where are you? It's me, Herbie! Herbie Barrass!'

And suddenly, miraculously, she was there on the landing, a trembling, distraught figure wearing a red housecoat, tears streaming down her smoke-blackened face, reaching out her arms to him, saying over and over, 'Oh, Herbie, thank God you've come!'

Taking her hand, he led her through a maze of passages to his flat round the corner where, with trembling fingers, he opened the door with his latchkey, and drew her inside, put his arms about her and whispered soft words of comfort, like a father to a frightened child.

He knew at once that she was pregnant. A man of wide experience, he knew such things without being told. Very gently, he ran a bath for her, bundled up her smoke-blackened housecoat, gave her a clean pair of pyjamas to wear, and finally tucked her into his own bed to sleep. He would spend the night on the couch in the living-room.

But sleep would not come. His only thought was that he had somehow been instrumental in saving the life of the daughter of the woman he loved. Memory drew him back to that first morning when Grace had given him triangles of fried bread to supplement the bacon and scrambled eggs, forgiving him his trespasses of the night before, when he and Bob had landed on the doorstep the worse for wear. She had even gone to the trouble of sponging and pressing his best suit of clothes.

Dulcie slept fitfully at first, exhausted by the events of the night, the terror she had suffered when she had looked down to see that hostile gang in the street below, heard stones shattering the café windows and seen the throwing of the petrol-bomb. In the early hours, she woke suddenly, bathed in perspiration, reliving the horror of the burning building. At first she had thought the battering of the rear entrance was the gang of drunks trying to gain access, to drag her into the street to kill her. Then suddenly there was Herbie – the last person on earth she had expected to see – a man she had treated badly from the beginning, had regarded as a sponger, an interloper. How wrong she had been. But she had been wrong about so many things. Tears streamed down her face. She pressed a hand to her mouth to stifle her sobs.

She heard a voice at the door, 'I'm going to make some tea. Would you like a cup?'

In a few minutes, Herbie came in with a tray of tea and sandwiches. 'I thought you might be hungry,' he said, making room on the bedside table. 'I heard you crying. Do you take sugar?'

She nodded. No reason to diet now, she thought, drying her eyes.

Herbie perched on the end of the bed. 'Good. Sugar for shock, as the saying goes.' He grinned awkwardly. 'Did you hear the fire-engines earlier on? There'll be a right mess to clear up, I'm thinking, a few thick heads into the bargain.' He paused, 'Come on, lass, have a sandwich. They're only cheese, but they'll fill a corner.'

'Why are you being so good to me? I've always been so rotten to you.'

'Have you? I hadn't noticed.'

She said slowly, 'You must have noticed that I'm – going to have a child. The fact is, I'm not a very nice person. I didn't even go to my grandmother's funeral. All I did was send a wreath and a letter saying I couldn't get off work. That was a lie. I couldn't have gone, not in my condition. They'd all have known the kind of life I've been living. I – I couldn't bear the thought of facing my parents.'

'The father, I take it, is Franz Bergmann?' Herbie said quietly.

'Yes, but . . . how do you know?' Dulcie's hands trembled.

'Here, give me that cup before you spill it.' He paused to frame his thoughts. 'Look, love, you can trust me. I have no axe to grind. I'm neither judge nor jury. Anything you say to me will not go beyond these four walls, you have my word on that. I just think you need to talk to someone. You can't face what's happened all alone. You need help.' Handing her a clean hanky, 'Try not to cry any more, it's bad for the baby. When is it due, by the way?'

'July, I think the doctor said. I wasn't really listening at the time. All I could think of was Franz's reaction, losing my home, my job, my security.'

'Security? With a man like that?' Herbie sighed deeply. 'Let me guess. He didn't want to know. Am I right?'

Dulcie nodded, trying desperately to stem a fresh tide of rising tears. 'He told me to get out of the flat by the end of March, to take with me nothing that belonged to him – none of the presents he'd given me, the clothes, the perfume, the furniture, the jewellery.'

Herbie smiled grimly. 'Well, at least you obeyed his instructions. I'd like to be a fly on the wall when he discovers that all the fine presents he gave you are burnt to a cinder. That's what I call justice. And serve him damn well right, the bastard!'

Dulcie laughed suddenly. 'I hadn't thought of that! Oh, Herbie, to think of it. Those fur coats, the sealskin and the musquash, down to the hide. All that ruined furniture, the scorched dresses. And that perfume! Wouldn't it be heavenly if those bottles of Chanel Number Five, Je Reviens and Joie-de-Vivre exploded in the heart of the fire? Quelle pong! At least he'll have something to remember me by!'

Her laughter held a note of hysteria. Herbie said calmly, 'The thing is, what now? You can stay here for as long as you like, that goes without saying, but you must give some thought to the future, your own and the baby's.'

'I could always pray for a miscarriage,' she said with a brittle little laugh, 'or go into one of those homes for fallen women; have it adopted by a decent couple so the poor little devil need never know the kind of person his mother is – a whore! A – *slut!*' Her bravura broke suddenly. Tears poured down her cheeks. 'Oh, Herbie,' she whispered hoarsely, 'what the hell am I going to do?'

'You could always go home,' he suggested quietly, 'where you belong. Where you would find nothing but love and understanding. Your mother would welcome you with open arms, you know that as well as I do. A rare person, your mother.'

Staring at him through tear-dimmed eyes, 'You really do love her, don't you?' Dulcie asked him.

And, 'Yes,' he acknowledged softly, 'I think I loved her from the first moment I saw her, because of her beauty. But there's more to Grace than mere physical beauty. There's loyalty and truth, honesty, simplicity, sheer goodness of heart—'

'I suspected as much,' Dulcie said quietly. 'The reason why I was jealous of you, I suppose, was because I saw you as a threat to my parents' happiness. Because I knew that my mother thought the world of you, too. So did Dad, Kerry, Danny and Jimmy. It seemed to me, somehow, that you had usurped my place in her affection in particular. But then, I was never a favourite of hers. I realized that long ago. It was always Kerry she loved better than me, and Danny and Jimmy . . .' She covered her face with her hands as if to shut out memories too painful to bear.

Moving closer, Herbie prised Dulcie's hands away from her eyes. 'You're wrong if that's what you think,' he said tenderly. 'It was you who raised the barriers between yourself and your family. Think about it!'

'Why? Because I wouldn't conform? Because I was sick and tired of being the fat one of the family? The plain one? Because I wanted to prove myself a person in my own right? Because I wanted to get away from the Pavilion Hotel, to find myself a rich husband?' Angrily, she continued

'And I very nearly succeeded, didn't I? *Didn't I?*'

'Yeah.' Herbie raised a quizzical eyebrow. 'You've certainly come a short way in a long time, but the question remains – what about the future?'

Still hostile towards him because he had touched on a sore spot – the barriers she had erected between herself and her family – she said shortly, 'Since you are so clever, you tell me.'

'Very well then, I will.' Half closing his eyes, drawing in a deep breath. 'Bearing in mind, of course, that I am neither rich nor handsome; that we are far from being in love with one another, I'd make you a decent husband on the whole.'

She stared at him as if he had taken leave of his senses, her eyes wide with disbelief. 'You mean that you are asking me to *marry* you? But *why*?'

'I'd have thought that was fairly obvious,' he said calmly. 'Mainly because of the child you are carrying, because I have no wish to see it adopted by strangers; yourself in a home for "fallen women"! More to the point because, as a married woman with a wedding ring on your finger, there would be no need to explain your pregnancy to your parents, or anyone else for that matter. It would seem to me the ideal solution.' He added, 'No need to worry that I'd ever bother you physically, of course. As a matter of fact, I've joined the Territorial Army – my old unit, the Green Howards. Very soon now, I'll be on my way to a training camp in Richmond.

'When war comes, I'll be in charge of the new recruits. With luck, I'll be sent abroad sooner or later to France, Holland or Belgium, wherever I'm needed.'

He suddenly remembered the words of a clairvoyant, uttered long ago, words never forgotten, the intensity with which they had been said: 'You will travel abroad in a position of trust, even authority. There will be difficult decisions to make concerning your future at that time. I see you torn between love and duty.'

After a long pause, Dulcie said wearily, 'Very well then, Herbie, I accept your proposal. I will marry you, and the sooner the better. Then I'll go home with a wedding ring on my finger, if that's the way you want it.'

Smiling, he said, 'It's the only way, isn't it?'

The wedding was to take place in a registry office in Leeds city centre. Herbie had bought his bride a brand-new outfit to mark the occasion, from underclothing upwards, since she had been wearing nothing but that red velvet housecoat on the night of the fire. Thankfully he had his cases of samples to hand, and left her to choose what she wanted, not that Dulcie would care much for celanese, he imagined, but it seemed the obvious solution. The poor kid couldn't even go outdoors until he had bought her a dress, coat and shoes. The choice of a wedding outfit he would leave to her.

The event had begun to assume an air of unreality – a bit like one of those zany Carole Lombard movies, or *It Happened One Night*. Except that this wasn't funny. Never in his wildest dreams had Herbie imagined marrying someone he was not in love with. It must be even worse for Dulcie marrying a man old enough to be her father, ugly to boot, with no money to speak of. Far different from the future she had planned, the kind of wedding she had envisaged: in church, herself all in white, marrying a handsome, rich young man with whom she was deeply in love.

Knowing how unhappy she was, he tried his best to keep cheerful, to please her in small ways. He had even bought her a bottle of 'Soir de Paris' perfume. No way could he afford Chanel No. 5. Opening the package, she had burst into tears.

His flat had never seemed so small and cramped before, and he had a crick in his neck from sleeping on the sofa. His culinary skills ran to eggs, bacon and sausages, and mince which he cooked with vegetables and thickened with Bisto, none of which Dulcie appeared to relish. And so he had begun taking her, occasionally, to a small restaurant he knew on the Headrow, and treating her to steak and chips.

On one such occasion, a few days before the wedding, he

had tentatively suggested inviting her family to witness the ceremony. Her reaction had startled him. Eyes blazing, '*No!*' she said so vehemently that people had turned their heads to look at her. Then, less forcibly, 'That's the last thing I want. It's impossible, that's all.'

He had known, at that moment, that the whole thing was impossible. Later, at the flat, Dulcie had confirmed his suspicion. Standing before him in the little sitting-room, the picture of misery, 'I'm sorry, Herbie,' she said, 'You've been kindness itself, but I can't go through with it. I can't marry you. It wouldn't be fair on either one of us. You do see that, don't you?'

'So what are you going to do?'

Tilting up her chin, 'The decent thing for once in my life,' she said. 'I'm going home tomorrow to face the music. *Alone!* I'm going home alone to tell my parents the truth about myself!' Tears filled her eyes. 'You see, I'm sick of lying, tired of pretence. Besides, I need my mother. I've never needed anyone so desperately in my life before!'

Herbie saw her off at the station. She was wearing the dress, coat and shoes he had bought her, plus, he imagined, the celanese underwear. The rest of the garments she had chosen from his samples case he had packed into a small overnight bag along with several items of make-up and the bottle of 'Soir de Paris' perfume.

After buying her a one-way ticket to Scarborough, he slipped a five pound note into the palm of her hand. When she demurred, 'Take it,' he said with a smile, 'you might want a cup of tea, a sandwich or a bar of chocolate. I'm not having you setting off without a penny piece in your pocket.'

The train was standing at the platform. Porters were trundling hand-barrows, the engine was getting up steam, carriage doors were beginning to slam. The guard was standing by, his whistle and green flag at the ready. Herbie's heart smote him, Dulcie looked so small and defenceless, her face as pale as ivory, devoid of make-up, trying hard not to cry.

Knowing what she was going through, her dread of what lay ahead, 'It'll be all right, you'll see,' he said gently. 'You'll be welcomed with open arms. Believe me, I *know*!'

'The return of the prodigal daughter?' She attempted a smile.

'Something like that. Well, lass, best climb aboard now. Goodbye and God bless you.'

Suddenly her arms were about him, her lips on his cheek. Hugging him fiercely, she said, 'I love you, Herbie, in a special kind of way. I owe you more than I can ever hope to repay. I owe you my life, and that of my child.' Getting into the carriage, leaning out of the window, 'If it's a boy, I shall call him after you!'

As the train began to move, 'In that case,' Herbie called after her, 'let's hope he's a girl!'

Returning to his flat, the emptiness struck him like a blow in the face. Everything was too quiet, too tidy. For a little while, Dulcie had filled that emptiness with her presence. He would miss her . . . But not for long. He picked up an envelope from the doormat, a buff OHMS envelope familiar to Herbie, who had received many OHMS directives before in the course of his Army career.

The news contained in this particular envelope came as a relief. In a week from now he would be on his way to that training camp in Richmond to join his comrades of the Territorial Army as a sergeant instructor in charge of the new recruits. Refolding the missive, he looked round the flat: soon all this would be a memory, he thought.

Glad of the money Herbie had given her, tired and dispirited, too weak to walk far, Dulcie hired a taxi from the Scarborough Station forecourt to the house in Castle Road.

Mounting the steps to the front door, her heart failed her. Overcome with shame and remorse, how could she possibly face her family, the state she was in? How tell her mother the kind of life she'd been living? How confess that she had sold her body for money over and over again? That she had been living in sin? Yes, *sin*! She could see it all quite clearly now, her total disregard of decent human values as long as she got what she wanted. Above all things, money, sexual pleasure, fine clothes, jewellery and perfume.

Now, having had her fill of all those things, and pregnant with an illegitimate child, what right had she to expect forgiveness for her sins? Unable to bring herself to ring the doorbell, she turned away, clinging to the iron handrail for support, the way she had done that day outside the doctor's surgery.

Suddenly the front door opened and Grace was there on the top step, bucket and brush in hand, her hair tied back with a scarf, wearing her workaday pinafore, preparatory to swilling the steps with hot soapy water.

And then Dulcie heard the clattering down of the bucket and brush, Grace's voice calling out to her, 'Dulcie, love, is that you?'

Turning slowly, her face blotched with tears, 'Yes, Mother,' the girl said wearily, 'but I have no right to be here. I shouldn't have come.'

'Not come? Not come home where you belong?' Hurrying down the steps, gathering Dulcie into her arms, rocking her as a mother rocks a baby, 'Oh, my dear, don't you know, can't you guess how long I have waited for this moment?'

'But you don't know how wicked I've been! Mother, I'm going to have a baby!'

'Well yes, I can see that. I've had four myself, remember?'

Very gently, Grace led Dulcie up the front steps. Picking up the bucket and brush, 'The swilling can wait till tomorrow,' she said decisively, 'and so can everything else, come to that! Now, upstairs to bed with you. What you need is sleep, my girl. Your bed's all ready for you. No need to say a word right now. Not ever, if you don't want to. All I care about is that you have come back to us, my darling. Nothing else matters a damn!'

Chapter Thirty-two

Dulcie had slept until four o'clock in the afternoon, when Grace came in with tea and hot buttered toast. Vaguely, in her sleep, the girl had been aware of the familiar sounds of home, the ringing of the doorbell, quiet footsteps on the stairs, like a soothing lullaby, a kind of background music to slumber.

The sheets and pillow-cases smelt of lavender, not Chanel No. 5, and the bed was well aired, as though her mother had anticipated her arrival at any time during her long absence. Nothing could have touched Dulcie more deeply than this evidence of Grace's love for her. Sitting up to drink the tea, 'Has Dad come in yet?' she asked anxiously.

'No, he and Kerry won't be in until supper-time, but you mustn't worry, love, I'll tell them you're here.'

'Oh, God,' Dulcie whispered fearfully, 'what will they say when they know about the baby? Will Dad be very angry? And what about Kerry?'

Grace smiled, 'Your father will be too relieved you're home to be angry. As for Kerry, she's a woman now, not a child. In any case, what has Kerry to be angry about? She's missed you so much – more than you realize. She'll be so happy to see you again, to know you'll be here for her wedding.'

'Kerry's getting married?' Dulcie frowned perplexedly, 'I didn't know.'

'Oh, didn't you receive her letter?'

Dulcie admitted, shame-faced, 'I may have done. I – you see – I didn't always bother to read letters from home.' She paused, close to tears. 'My guilty conscience, I suppose. You don't seem to realize how truly wicked I've been, how selfish.'

Grace said quietly, 'I was "wicked" myself once, a long time ago.' The time had come to confess that she had been pregnant at the time of her marriage. 'I was just sixteen at the time. Your father was about to go overseas, to France. I leave you to imagine my parents' reaction when I told them I was pregnant. Nan's in particular. So you see, Dulcie, I do understand a little of what you are going through right now.' She smiled, picking up the tea things. 'All I'm saying, this isn't the end of the world. Babies bring with them a special kind of love, their own brand of innocence which has nothing whatever to do with the circumstances in which they were conceived. Just keep on believing, my love, that your child, when it is born, will bring you untold joy and happiness. Then the rest will be all forgotten, over and done with for ever.'

Her hand on the doorknob, 'Go back to sleep now, Dulcie,' Grace said softly. 'All will be well, you'll see.'

Dulcie had no idea of the time when, opening her eyes, she heard the creaking of her sister's bed-springs. 'Kerry, is that you?' she murmured drowsily.

'Oh, Dulcie, I'm sorry, I didn't mean to disturb you.'

There came a faint rustling sound, then Kerry, in dressing-gown and slippers, was on the bed beside her, holding her close, smothering her face with kisses, saying breathlessly, 'It's just like old times, isn't it? Remember the night we went to see *The Merry Widow* at the Futurist cinema? How cross you were when you saw me standing at the window with the curtains drawn back? That was the night we heard footsteps on the landing and thought it was a burglar. Remember when you had your hair permed and you treated me to a fish-and-chip supper on the Foreshore afterwards? How long ago that seems now.'

Suddenly, tears flooded down Dulcie's face, triggered by memories of those far-off days that would never come again, which she had thrown away as carelessly, as wantonly as a spoilt child throws aside an unwanted toy.

'Oh please, Dulcie, don't cry! I didn't mean to upset you. I was just trying to be funny, that's all.'

Dulcie said bitterly, 'I suppose you know that I'm going to have a baby?'

'Yes, of course I do. Mum told me. I'm hoping to have one of my own soon after Ashley and I are married.' Kerry switched on the bedside light, revealing Dulcie's tear-stained face. 'Oh God,' she said, startled by her sister's appearance, 'What have you been doing? Starving yourself to death?'

'Something like that,' Dulcie admitted. 'So what's wrong with losing weight? Has it ever occurred to you how sick and tired I was of being the fat, ugly misfit of the family?'

Wrinkling her forehead, 'No, never,' Kerry said truthfully. 'To me you were just Dulcie. A bit awkward and snappish at times, but what difference did that make? You were still my sister.'

'I was jealous of you. As far back as I can remember, I was jealous because you had a kind of – oh, I don't know. You seemed to dance everywhere. All I could do was plod after you like a horse and cart.'

'Don't talk so daft. In any case, you look like a racehorse now.'

'Not for very long,' Dulcie reminded her. Then, 'Oh God, what will people think when they see me?'

'What people are we talking about?' Kerry asked, tucking up her legs.

'The great aunts, the neighbours, the girls I went to school with. Everyone who knew me before I went away. The Burtons, Wilma. Danny, Jimmy—'

'You're worrying yourself unnecessarily,' Kerry said decisively. 'Great Aunt Rosa already knows. She's looking forward to knitting baby clothes. Great Aunt Fanny is too busy planning her wedding to care much about other people at the moment. In any case, she's broad-minded enough to understand. The same applies to Jimmy. As for Danny, he's up to his eyebrows in his own troubles at present since he and Wilma came to the parting of the ways. A good thing, too, if you ask me – Danny and Wilma calling it a day, I mean. Besides, we've already got one baby in the house. Not that William's a baby exactly, not now he's toddling and into everything.'

'You mean William's living here, not with the Burtons?'

'Yes. I thought you knew. Mum saw to *that*. So you see, the Burtons have nothing to crow about, and neither has Wilma. In fact they're keeping the whole affair hushed up. As far as I can make out, Mabel is spreading it around that Danny and Wilma are still happily married. I imagine she's told everyone that William is living here because "Daddy", being a "Transport Official", needs peace and quiet.' Kerry laughed. 'Trust Mrs Burton to think up a good scenario. She should try writing a romantic novel herself one of these days!

'As for the neighbours, they're not a bad lot on the whole, just curious. Mum will deal with them in her own inimitable way. Knowing her, she'll probably invite them in for afternoon tea and say "By the way, our daughter Dulcie is expecting a baby, isn't that splendid? You're all invited to the christening." It's what's called "taking the bull by the horns".'

Bob entered the room at that moment, after a discreet knock at the door. Dulcie glanced at him fearfully. Above all, she had dreaded her father's reaction to her pregnancy, knowing how deeply he had objected to her leaving home in the first place. She had to face the realization that his misgivings had been well founded now that she had brought disgrace to the family name.

She need not have worried. Quickly crossing the room, gathering Dulcie into his arms, 'I'm so pleased to see you, my lass,' he murmured.

Quietly, Kerry went back to her own bed, knowing this moment belonged to Dulcie and their father alone. No-one else in the world. Snuggling down in bed, turning her face away from the light, dreamily content, she heard the murmur of voices as the sound of waves washing in on the seashore. Half asleep, she gave thanks in her heart that her sister was safely home at last.

*   *   *

425

'I'm sorry, my darling. I never meant it to happen. It just happened, that's all,' Ashley murmured contritely. 'You see, the school has a long-standing naval tradition: sea-scouts and all that. Only natural, I suppose, since the headmaster is a retired sea captain. So when this jolly old bosun came to give us a pep talk about joining the Naval Reserve, I simply added my name to the list along with the rest of the staff. There was really no alternative, with the headmaster breathing down our necks.'

'So what you're really saying is, if war comes, you'll be among the first to go?' Kerry asked him faintly.

'Well, yes,' Ashley admitted. 'But the fact must be faced, in the event of war, God forbid, at my age I'd be among the first to be called up anyway and, frankly, darling, I'd rather go into the Navy than the Army or the Air Force.'

'A fine comfort that is,' she said bitterly, hiding her face against his shoulder.

'Oh come on, love,' he said gently, smoothing her hair, 'this isn't like you. I hoped you'd feel proud of me.'

'Of course I feel proud of you. I just can't bear the thought of losing you, that's all!'

Holding her close, 'You couldn't lose me now if you tried for a million years,' he said tenderly, 'I thought you knew that. This love-affair of ours will last for ever.'

They were in the living-room of their flat, making a start on the decorating. Daylight was fading, lights springing up along the Esplanade. They could see the necklace of coloured lights outlining the bay.

'It's coming, isn't it?' she said helplessly. 'The war, I mean.'

'Perhaps not. Mr Chamberlain might pull another rabbit out of the hat.' Ashley smiled, 'He did last year, remember?'

'It just seems so much closer now, with Danny and Herbie in uniform. Now this. I suppose they'll be sending you on manoeuvres.'

'Well, not manoeuvres exactly, just to a training camp of sorts I expect, the odd weekend now and then to learn how to tie short sheepshanks and reef knots. It's hardly likely the

headmaster would want his staff slogging it out at Scapa
Flow. We'll probably end up in a rowing boat in the
harbour.' He was making light of things for Kerry's sake.

They came to the flat whenever possible, mainly after
work, to start cleaning the rooms in readiness for furnishing
when the time came. They had started saving for the
essentials. Unlike Wilma, Kerry had no desire for brand-new
furniture bought on tick, rather good quality second-hand
stuff from the local salerooms. She wanted a home, not a
show-place, and Ashley felt the same way. She would
make the curtains and loose-covers herself now that she
knew all about taking measurements and the cutting and
matching of the material. Mr Hodnot had some lovely
patterns in stock, and she would receive discount as a
member of staff. She had also decided to make her own
wedding dress.

Kneeling down, she dipped her paintbrush into a tin of
cream paint and started work on the skirting board. Ashley
was doing the fiddly bits round the french windows leading
to the balcony. His optimism had rubbed off on her. 'Hey,'
she called out to him, 'know what?'

'Hmmm?' He turned to look at her. 'What?'

'I love you.'

Love was in the air. Fanny and Mr Hodnot were married in
St Martin's Church the following Saturday. This was,
perhaps, the loveliest church in Scarborough, with its Burne-
Jones stained-glass windows and richly gilded altar screens.
It was the perfect setting for a larger-than-life bride. Fanny
wore a many-layered pink chiffon dress surmounted with a
wide-brimmed, matching straw and chiffon hat encircled
with fat, pink chiffon roses, and carried her *petit-point*
handbag containing a lace-trimmed hanky and a bottle of
smelling-salts.

She entered the church on Bob's arm, smiling to left and
right, like royalty, gold chains and lorgnette dangling,
pushing back, with her free hand, the mink stole about her
shoulders – a wedding gift from the bridegroom, who was

standing near the altar steps as though awaiting the arrival of the Queen of Sheba.

As a spinster of the parish, Fanny had felt it her right to be married in a Church of England setting. Methodism held no charm for the rebellious Fanny Mallory and never had done, despite her upbringing. She much preferred stained glass and gilding, the romantic rather than the mundane, far better suited to her own romantic, flamboyant personality.

On her way down the aisle, she thought affectionately of poor Nancy. How shocked she would be if she could see her now, a-flutter with pink chiffon, aglow with happiness, about to marry the man she loved, with a honeymoon in Paris to look forward to; a reception at the Royal Hotel.

Cyril had been so good to her, so considerate, even to the extent of suggesting a postponement of the wedding, following the death of her sister, if she so wished. But to what purpose? Time was growing shorter by the minute, and Fanny loved life, which she intended to live to the full from now on. She'd had her fill of heartbreak along the way. Now was the time for a new beginning.

Following the cutting of the cake, the champagne toasts to the long life and happiness of the bride and groom, Fanny could not help noticing the deep unhappiness of one member of her family – her great niece Dulcie – obviously pregnant, who had slipped away to the powder room at the height of the celebration.

Laying a hand on her bridegroom's arm, 'Forgive me, my dear,' she said quietly, 'I'll be back in a little while.'

Entering the powder room, Fanny discovered Dulcie all alone, sobbing her heart out. Conscience-stricken, knowing that she had never cared very deeply for Dulcie, and wanting to make amends, she sat down beside her and placed her arm about the girl's shoulders. 'Forgive me, my dear, I couldn't help noticing—'

'I'm not surprised! It is pretty obvious, isn't it?' Dabbing her eyes with a handkerchief. 'I've made a damned fool of myself, haven't I? My own fault entirely.' Dulcie laughed bitterly. 'I wanted nice clothes, money, a position in society, a rich husband. This is how it all ended, so you needn't waste your sympathy on me.'

'I imagine most girls want the same things,' Fanny said slowly. 'I know I did at your age.' Looking into the past, she continued, 'London was the place I wanted to be. I was ambitious, quite attractive in those days before the war. It was even harder then for young women wanting to break away from their home environment, but I never was a conventional type of person. I knew what I wanted and nothing on earth would stop me.

'I moved in with a friend of mine who had a tiny flat in Bloomsbury. Very soon, I found myself a job at a fashion house in Bond Street. It was such fun. We went to parties, picnics, the theatre. Escorts were thick on the ground.' She smiled reflectively. 'I had several quite innocent romances with nice, ordinary young men, until . . .' her smile faded, tears filled her eyes, 'I met someone who was not in the least ordinary. Oh, I knew he was married, but that didn't stop me falling in love with him. It was love at first sight for both of us. Right and wrong didn't enter into it at first. We were so joyously in love, and yet . . .' She blinked back her tears. 'There was a price to be paid. James had responsibilities: two sons whom he adored. I knew that there could be no question of marriage between us, that he would never forsake his family. And so I became his mistress. Does that shock you, Dulcie? It would have shocked my family, had they known.'

Dulcie shook her head. Fanny continued, 'I'm telling you all this because I wanted you to know that you are not alone. I, too, became pregnant. Oh yes. And I have never told this to a living soul before – not even James. He was abroad at the time of my miscarriage, in the early stages of my pregnancy. He was a diplomat, you see, attached to the Foreign Office, often away from home. I thought it best not to tell him. I was so afraid that it might make a difference to our relationship. I didn't want to lose him, but ah, how

429

much I regretted losing our baby. This was the cross I had to bear, the cross I've borne ever since.'

'Oh, Great Aunt Fanny, I'm so sorry. And then what happened?'

'The war happened,' Fanny said softly. 'Don't ask me what it was like. I could never describe, in a thousand years, the agony the women endured watching their menfolk marching off to fight, most of them never to return. The last thing on earth I imagined, was that James, at his age, would join the Army. We had been together for such a long, long time, spending our snatched time together at my flat in Bruton Street, still as deeply in love as we were the moment we first set eyes on each other.'

She recalled, mistily, the last night they had spent together at the Savoy Hotel; how handsome James had appeared in his Army officer's uniform, the way they had danced together until dawn, she in a gown of midnight-blue chiffon encrusted with sparkling paillettes which had shimmered beneath the lights of the crystal chandeliers. Tired of dancing, they had finally gone up to their room to cling together, in the little time left to them, until it was time to say goodbye.

'I knew in my heart that I would never see him again in this life,' Fanny said quietly, 'and I was right. He was killed in the first Battle of the Somme.' Holding Dulcie's hand, she said, 'What happened to me is not important now. What *is* important is that you should cherish the child you are carrying. Never let go of it, I beg of you! Oh, I know what some people will say. Life has never been easy for the rebels of this world, but you are home now, among your own people, your family who love you, and you have been given the greatest gift that life has to offer – a child to love and to cherish all the days of your life.'

Fanny rose to her feet. 'Well, Dulcie, it's time I went back to the reception. Will you come with me?'

Clasping her hand, 'Yes, I'll come with you,' Dulcie said quietly. 'And, thank you, Great Aunt Fanny.'

They walked down the long curving staircase together, hand-in-hand.

Entering the reception room, glancing at the people gathered there, Fanny thought tenderly how tall and lovely Kerry had grown, and how happy and confident she looked standing beside that handsome fiancé of hers. Pray God nothing would happen to spoil their happiness. And how smart Danny looked in his Air Force officer's uniform. A pity his marriage had not worked out well.

Jimmy was doing well now apparently, and he had lost that youthful gaucheness of his of the old Sunday afternoon tea-party days when she had wondered if he was getting enough to eat.

And there was Rosa in the new lilac costume Fanny had helped her choose for the wedding, the amethyst brooch pinned to the lapel, looking positively radiant, cheeks flushed pink with excitement, talking animatedly to Grace and Bob, who had been so good to her.

Dear Grace and Bob, whose relationship stood as a shining example of what marriage was all about: undying love and faith between two people, the facing together of life's problems, taking the rough with the smooth – and there had been plenty of rough patches, Fanny knew. There may be many more to come. But that was life. Never easy, smooth or straightforward. Possibly even she and Cyril would hit the occasional whirlpool. At their age, she scarcely thought so, but how could one be sure?

Of one thing she was entirely sure. Crossing towards her bridegroom, seeing his face light up as she came towards him, Fanny knew that this was the happiest day of her life.

Much later, after the happy couple had set forth on their honeymoon, when Kerry and Ashley had gone to the flat to decorate, Aunt Rosa had gone to bed tired out, and Danny and Jimmy had gone out together for a couple of pints of beer at the Albion, Dulcie was alone with her parents in the back room. 'I want you to know what happened,' she said. 'The whole story from beginning to end.'

'There's really no need, love,' Bob demurred. 'No use upsetting yourself. What's done is done.'

'But you have a right to know, and I'll feel easier in my mind. You see, Dad, I know you thought it was Klaus Bergmann I was after – and so I was. I thought he wanted me, too, but I was wrong. What I mean is, he didn't want *me*, he wanted a nursemaid for his children.

'His mother saw through me from the start. She knew what I was after right enough – a rich husband – and she made my life a misery. Well, I started dieting to make myself more attractive to Klaus. I used his children to make him more aware of me. Then, one day, I went down to the drawing-room and there he was with this other woman, the one he eventually married.

'Meanwhile, his brother Franz came home from a trip to America.' Dulcie's voice faltered. 'Franz, not Klaus, is the father of my baby. It was Franz who offered me the job as manageress of the Headrow café, who set me up there as his mistress, who gave me everything I'd ever wanted.'

'No need to go on,' Grace said compassionately.

'But there *is*,' Dulcie said in a low voice hoarse with emotion. 'When I told Franz about the baby, he didn't want to know. He told me to get out of the flat over the café, to get out of his life. Then, one night a gang of drunken youths set fire to the house, and there I was, alone in the place, thinking my end had come.'

'Christ Almighty!' Bob muttered savagely. 'The swine! The absolute swine!' He rose to his feet unsteadily, hands clenched. 'I've a damned good mind to knock his teeth down his throat!' Pacing the room, he threatened, 'And I'll do just that if ever he dares show up on my doorstep! I'll make him wish he'd never been born!'

'Please, Bob, sit down and listen.' Grace had never known her husband so angry before, and yet she knew that his anger was justified. 'Go on, Dulcie. What happened next?'

'Herbie happened next,' Dulcie said simply. 'It was Herbie who battered down the fire-escape door and led me to safety. It was Herbie, realizing the mess I was in, who offered to

432

marry me, to make an honest woman of me because of the baby, because I lacked the guts to come home alone to tell you the truth about myself.'

'But you *did* come home alone,' Grace reminded her gently.

'Yes,' Dulcie sighed wearily, 'because I didn't want to mess up Herbie's life as well as my own. So now you know, and I'm glad! Glad you know the truth about me at last, the kind of woman I really am. A whore at heart. A *slut*. That's what Franz Bergmann called me, and he was right.' Tears filled her eyes. 'That's why I don't really belong here any more, why I don't deserve your kindness, your love.'

Grace said quietly, getting up from her chair, 'God help us all if we received our just desserts from life. Isn't that so, Bob? Now I'm going to make some tea and sandwiches. Remember you are eating for two now, Dulcie love.'

Staring at her mother with anguished eyes, 'Is that really all you have to say to me after all the pain and misery I've caused you?'

Grace smiled, 'Well yes, I suppose so, except, would you prefer ham or cheese?'

Getting ready for bed, Grace said, 'I bless the day you brought Herbie home with you that night four years ago. If it weren't for him, Dulcie might have died in that fire.' Her hands were trembling at the thought of what might have happened. 'And to think he was prepared to marry her, to help her make a fresh start, to give her child a name.'

'I always knew he had a heart of gold,' Bob said gruffly. 'I only hope he's done the right thing, joining up again at his age. Thank God he's near enough to come home occasionally.'

Home, Grace thought. Here to this house where he belonged as part of their lives, their family.

433

Chapter Thirty-three

The Spa was crowded for the Crowning of the Rose Queen ceremony. Home on leave, Herbie walked with Kerry to watch the proceedings. Memory drew him back to the first time they had come this way on that Sunday afternoon, four years ago, after the South Cliff tea-party.

Kerry was 14 at the time, a dancing, bright-eyed little lass skipping along beside him, her heart set on one day becoming the Rose Queen of Scarborough, and he had told her that in another four years she would be the loveliest Rose Queen of them all. And he had been right. At eighteen, Kerry was the prettiest girl he had ever seen. A pity she had never entered the competition. He could see her, in his mind's eye, walking down that long flight of stone steps to the promenade, tall and slender, in a flowing dress, carrying a bouquet of roses.

When he reminded her, she laughed and said that wanting to be the Rose Queen was just a childhood dream of hers, like wanting to dance 'The Merry Widow Waltz' in the arms of a handsome hussar, and yet Herbie discerned a certain wistfulness about her, a faraway look in her eyes.

'You're worried about Ashley, aren't you?' he asked her as they mingled with the crowd of onlookers awaiting the arrival of the decorated floats, the Battle of Flowers.

'Yes,' she said simply, 'you see he's joined the Naval Reserve, and things look pretty grim right now. The war news, I mean. It *is* grim, isn't it Herbie?'

'Well, put it this way, it isn't good,' he said truthfully, 'now the Conscription Bill has been introduced in Parliament, and with Hitler and Mussolini on the rampage, I'd be daft to tell you otherwise.'

Holding on to his hand, 'Thanks, Herbie,' she said

gratefully, 'I knew I could depend on you.' She smiled. 'I always have. Remember Sid Hannay? That Sunday evening crossing the Spa Bridge?'

Herbie grinned, 'How could I ever forget? What became of him, by the way?'

'Sid? Oh, he married the girl from Boots the Chemist.'

'The one with the loud-hailer voice?'

'That's the one!'

'Hmmm,' Herbie murmured reflectively, 'the poor sod, that's all I can say.'

Kerry said carefully, 'I happen to know that you asked Dulcie to marry you.'

'Yeah,' Herbie gave a lop-sided grin, 'and she turned me down flat. Can't say I blame her. No oil-painting, am I?'

'From where I'm standing, you're a masterpiece by Michelangelo,' Kerry said quietly. Then, quickly changing the subject, 'Have you heard about my love-affair of last summer? My Irish tenor?'

'Not in any great depth,' Herbie replied cautiously, as the first of the floats appeared on the peninsula. 'Why? Do you want to tell me about it?'

'There's nothing much to tell, in any great depth. It was shallow, meaningless, I know that now. I made a complete fool of myself, that's all. I fell for the obvious, the voice, the charisma, the charm of the man, the theatre setting; the secret meetings by moonlight.' She sighed deeply. 'I didn't know he was married. I really thought he was in love with me.'

'I'm sure he was,' Herbie responded quietly. 'I mean, how could any man not fall in love with a girl like you?'

'The thing is, I might have landed myself in the same kind of fix as Dulcie if it hadn't been for something Jimmy said to me, which brought me to my senses just in time.'

'Good for Jimmy,' Herbie said. 'I'm glad he's doing so well. He has a good head on his shoulders, that lad. It must have taken a great deal of courage to leave home, to take on those London newspaper editors the way he did. More power to his elbow!'

The air about them was now filled with whirling rose petals thrown by the girls on the floats in their colourful dresses, a laughing bevy of beauties with not a care in the world, who rode into battle on a tide of carelessly flung rose petals, streamers and pink and white confetti, not knowing, not realizing that this Battle of Flowers might be the last for a very long time, when the tanks and guns of a very different kind of battle flared into action.

Dulcie's baby was born, on 15 July, in the hospital where Nan had died. Last-minute complications had arisen, and Dulcie was taken to hospital on 13 July. After hours of anxious waiting for those nearest and dearest to her, the child, a boy, was born by Caesarean section.

A month later, on the day that Adolf Hitler closed the border with Poland in Upper Silesia, Dulcie had had her son christened Herbert Robert Daniel James Kingsley at a simple ceremony in St Mary's Church, as if she could scarcely wait, Grace thought, to lay claim to the child without a shadow of doubt that this was *her* child. Hers and hers alone. As if Franz Bergmann had never existed.

And this, Grace realized, was a new Dulcie, a devoted woman whose suffering had borne good fruit, a bright-eyed young mother whose eyes misted over with tears of happiness whenever she held young Herbie close in her arms to feed him with the milk of human kindness.

Even so, the bird of prey of last September had returned to hover above the house-top, to cast its remorseless shadow over the comings and goings of ordinary, decent human beings whose thoughts were centred on peace, not war.

The decorating finished, Kerry and Ashley had begun to furnish their flat with items bid for at the salerooms: solid tables and chairs, a Georgian sideboard bought for a song because it was scratched in places: faults easily rectified by the application of beeswax polish and elbow grease. Kerry had covered a second-hand settee and matching armchairs with deep rose-pink velvet to match the living-room curtains, and to complement the cream paintwork and the plain, cream-tinted walls on which were hung two seascapes by an up-and-coming artist, Laura Knight.

The carpets were all second-hand, threadbare in places, but glowing with colour. There were small antique tables beside the settee and armchairs, bedecked with the rose-shaded lamps which Cyril Hodnot had bestowed upon Kerry as a pre-wedding gift. His main gift, he had assured her – a canteen of silver cutlery – would come later, each item bearing the intertwined initials of the happy couple. Kerry and Ashley.

Deep down, Kerry knew that Ashley was far from happy. Apart from the steadily worsening war news, he had taken badly his mother's decision to begin divorce proceedings immediately following his father's prison sentence.

'How could she have done such a thing?' he'd repeated over and over again, half wild with despair. 'I thought my parents' marriage was rock-solid. I never dreamt for one moment that Mother would desert Father in his hour of need!'

'Try not to judge her too harshly, darling. She had grown used to a certain lifestyle, a position in society. I think she wanted to dissociate herself from the scandal, and divorce seemed the only way to do that. Think about it Ashley, how impossible it would have been for her to stay on at Glebe House.'

'You are right, of course. She said much the same when I went to see her.'

'I'm sorry she felt unable to accept our wedding invitation,' Kerry said. 'I know how much it would have meant to you to have her there on the day.'

'Perhaps,' Ashley admitted, 'but the way I've been accepted into your family has meant a great deal to me.' He smiled. 'Not long to wait now. October the tenth isn't far off. Oh, darling, I can hardly wait to see you in your wedding dress.'

* * *

But there would be no 10 October wedding for Kerry and Ashley.

On 31 August, Neville Chamberlain announced the call-up of the Army, Air Force and Royal Naval reserves in view of the grave international situation. Three days later, on Sunday 3 September, the British nation, gathered close to their wireless sets, heard the weary voice of the Prime Minister declare that a state of war now existed between Great Britain and Germany.

Following the announcement, Kerry hurried up to the flat on the Esplanade to find Ashley, who had been living there recently, packing his belongings into a small suitcase.

'I'm so sorry, my darling,' he said, the picture of misery, and holding her close in his arms, 'I have to report to the naval barracks at Rosyth by 0800 hours tomorrow morning.'

'But what about us, Ashley? What about *us*? Our wedding?'

'I'm afraid I can't answer that right now,' he said wearily.

'But it isn't fair! It just isn't fair!'

'You think I don't feel that too? Oh, Kerry, I can't bear leaving you like this. I love you so much, so very much.'

'How long have you got?'

'There's a train at four o'clock. It's bound to be packed. I'm not sure about trains from York to Rosyth, I'll just have to trust to luck I'll get there on time.'

'That means you'll be travelling all night. You'll need sandwiches. I'll make you some; go to the station with you.'

'No, Kerry, I'd rather you didn't! I want to remember you here, at home, as you look now, not as a face in the crowd. You understand?'

'Oh yes, of course I do.'

Time was running out for them. In two hours from now he would be gone. She wanted to fill those hours with memories to last a lifetime; the feel of his arms about her, his lips on hers. Who knew when they would meet again? Perhaps never.

They made love passionately, tenderly, without inhibition – as two other people had made love once a long time ago, as a prelude to parting, in a shelter in the Italian Gardens.

When the loving was over, 'Walk with me a little way,' Ashley said gently. 'I'll go to the station across the Spa Bridge. It's such a lovely day.'

And so it was, that warm September Sunday with the autumn flowers in full bloom in the Spa gardens, the sky a brilliant blue above, the deep blue sea as calm as a millpond. Hand-in-hand they walked slowly down the winding paths leading to the long stone staircase down which so many lovely young girls had descended to receive their glittering paste-diamond crown as the Rose Queen of Scarborough.

Glancing up at an iron wrought balcony overlooking the promenade, Ashley recalled that summer afternoon, four years ago, when he had thrown a red rose at the feet of a nervous ballerina. 'Do you remember?' he asked.

'Of course I remember. I still have that rose. Somehow, I could never bear to part with it. I wonder why?' Kerry said, knowing the time had come to part with the love of her life, not knowing what to say or do at this moment of leave-taking. She simply buried her head against his shoulder and whispered, 'Take care of yourself, my love.'

'You too, my darling. Now, please go. Don't look back. Promise me you won't look back.'

'I promise.'

Turning away, she hurried back up the long flight of stone steps, sobbing as if her heart would break.

'Please, Mum, don't be upset,' Kerry told Grace, 'but I've decided to move into the flat for the time being. It's just that I—'

'No need to explain, love. I think I understand why.'

Tomorrow would have been her wedding day.

'Mr Hodnot said I could have the day off if I wanted to,' Kerry attempted a smile, 'but I'd sooner go to work as usual, then go to the flat afterwards. I think I'd feel closer to Ashley there. I – I'll take my wedding things with me.'

'I'll give you a hand to pack the dress,' Grace said. 'I've got a long cardboard box and plenty of tissue paper. And you'll need some milk, bread and butter, tea and so on. I'll make up a little hamper.'

'Oh, Mum!' Trust Grace to think of the practicalities, to smooth her path.

'You'd better take a taxi. Dad will go with you to lend a hand at the other end.'

'My word,' Bob said, when the various boxes and bags had been safely delivered, 'you've made a grand job of this place. It feels like home.'

'Ashley did most of the decorating,' Kerry said proudly. 'All the fiddly bits anyway. I just stuck to the skirting boards – quite literally, at times!'

'And what a view!' Standing on the balcony, looking down, 'The Spa looks like a miniature from this height. It reminds me of a painting, the colours of the trees and all, the bandstand and that stone staircase.' He laughed. 'Must be getting poetical in my old age.' Stepping inside, he said, 'Well, I'd best be getting back now. Sure you'll be all right? Don't forget about the blackout, will you?'

'No, Dad, I won't forget, and I'll be fine, just fine.'

'You won't starve, that's for sure,' he chuckled, 'with all the tinned stuff Mum packed into that hamper. She even thought to put in a tin-opener.'

'Thanks, Dad. Thanks for everything.'

Cupping her face in his hands, 'Good night, love, and don't worry. Ashley will be home soon, then we'll have a wedding day to remember.'

When her father had gone, Kerry unpacked her wedding dress and hung it on the wardrobe door. That way, it would be the first thing she saw in the morning.

All day long she went about the business of serving customers, producing pattern books for their consideration, longing for the solitude that night would bring.

It was such a glorious day, warm and sunny, as clear as crystal, the kind of day she had envisaged for her wedding to Ashley. Memories arose of the cool interior of St Mary's

Church patterned with the intricate colours of the stained-glass windows, burnished with the glowing wings of the lectern-eagle; filled with the scent of autumn flowers.

All day long she had been hoping for a message from Ashley, but none had arrived. Slowly, she walked home to the flat. Darkness had not yet fallen, nor would the sky be entirely dark tonight, with a full moon in ascendence, a panoply of stars overhead. Stars as clear cut as diamonds in a heaven as soft as blue velvet.

Loneliness overwhelmed her. Oh Ashley, she thought, where are you? It seemed to her that the world had suddenly gone dark. The necklace of coloured lights no longer beaded the bay, the firefly gas-lamps no longer outlined the bridge into town.

Suddenly, the doorbell rang . . . She hurried downstairs.

'Hello, Kerry love,' Herbie said. 'These are for you.' He handed her a bouquet of red roses. 'They're from Ashley. He sent them to the wrong address.'

With tear-filled eyes, Kerry read the attached message: 'On this, our Wedding Day, all the love in the world, my darling. The best is yet to come.'

Upstairs in the living-room, 'I'm what you might call on embarkation leave,' Herbie told her. 'Not that I mind, it's what I've wanted all along, to feel useful again. Better than selling celanese underwear any day of the week, wouldn't you say?'

'Oh, Herbie, I don't know. I don't honestly know. You've been the best, the kindest friend I've ever had. I can't bear to think of you far away from home.'

He said quietly, 'Know what would please me most, right now? Remember the last time we met? We were on the Spa at the time, watching the Crowning of the Rose Queen?'

'Yes, of course I remember, but—'

'Call me daft, if you like, but I'd like to remember you walking down that stone staircase in your wedding dress, holding your bouquet, a memory to treasure all the days of my life.'

A small frisson of fear touched Kerry's heart, 'You're not thinking of doing anything daft, are you?'

'Like getting myself killed, you mean? Naw,' he laughed, 'I'm too old to be a hero, except—'

'Except what?'

'You know that book of Jimmy's? Well, I'm not supposed to let on, but he's rewritten it and there's a good chance of it being accepted.'

'Oh Herbie, that's wonderful!'

'He'll be telling you himself when he's certain. A great lad, your brother. We've always kept in touch, you know.' Herbie paused. 'I don't suppose he's let on about the other thing either.'

'What other thing?'

'He's joining some kind of special Army unit as a reporter, what they call a correspondent.'

'But he'll be in the thick of the fighting!'

'We'll all be in that sooner or later,' Herbie said. 'Even civilians. This war won't be anything like the last. That's why I'd like to see you in your wedding dress, walking down that flight of steps – to remind me of the happy times.' He grinned awkwardly, 'A kind of dream come true. For yourself as well, maybe? Am I right?'

'Perhaps. All right, Herbie. You win.'

'You look a picture,' Herbie said.

'I feel a bit of a fool,' Kerry told him. 'Suppose someone sees me?'

'I wish they could. I wish it was summer-time and all the paths were crowded with visitors. I wish there was music!'

The staircase seemed as clear as day by the light of the moon and stars. And suddenly the air seemed filled with the sunshine and laughter of long-gone summers, and there were rose petals, not autumn leaves drifting on the warm October breeze; the far-off sound of phantom music played by the Scots' Greys Band marching along the promenade. The silver threads of the heralds' trumpets blowing a fanfare.

There was other music, too. Beyond the wash of the sea on the rocks below, came the words of 'The Kerry Dance' sung by an Irish tenor: 'Oh the days of the Kerry dancing, oh the ring of the piper's tune. Oh for one of those hours of gladness, gone, alas, like our youth, too soon'.

Head held high, she slowly walked down the staircase, her wedding dress whispering about her ankles, her arms filled with crimson roses, remembering all the stepping stones of life leading to this moment: happy times, and sad – the richness of the interwoven tapestry of her days on earth, the kaleidoscope of swiftly changing colours, patterns and impressions which had marked her progress from childhood to maturity. Life itself, she thought, was a bit like the Kerry Dance, a cotillion danced to the music of time, up the middle and down again. No telling how the dance had begun or how it would end.

It was simply a matter of faith that love would triumph in the end. Smiling, she remembered those words from James Elroy Flecker's *The Golden Journey to Samarkand*: 'We are the pilgrims, master; we shall go Always a little further: it may be Beyond that last blue mountain barred with snow'. She had once imagined setting off alone on that journey to Samarkand, not understanding, not realizing that there was no need to cross blue mountains barred with snow to achieve her heart's desire. That it was here she belonged and always would.

She stood near the sea wall with Herbie, gazing at the path of moonlight on the water, inhaling the fragrance of her bouquet, and plucked from it a single, perfect rose. Close to tears, she threw the rest of the flowers, one by one, into the shimmering sea below, and stood there watching as they floated away on the receding tide. No need of explanation. Herbie, the compassionate, knew that each flower represented the people Kerry loved best: Grace and Bob, Danny, Jimmy, Dulcie, Rosa, Fanny, Nan Daniel, young William and little Herbie. Himself. The single rose she had kept aside for Ashley.

He said hoarsely, 'I'll see you home now, Kerry love.'

'No, Herbie, if you don't mind, I'd rather be on my own for a little while. You understand?'

'Yes,' gruffly, 'of course I do.' On impulse, drawing her close to his heart, kissing her cheek, he said, 'You are your mother's daughter. I can pay you no greater compliment than that.'

'Take good care of yourself,' she whispered. And then she was gone, a ghost-like figure in white hurrying up the moonlit paths towards home.

Undressing, Kerry hung her wedding gown on the wardrobe door. Then, getting into bed, she placed the single, perfect rose she had kept for Ashley on the empty pillow beside her, knowing its fragrance would invade her dreams just as surely as his physical presence had, so blessedly, invaded her life, and remembered, on the brink of sleep, the flowers she had cast into the sea, as an act of faith, a tribute to her loved ones.

'Cast thy bread upon the water . . .' She had cast, not bread but roses.

Ashley would understand.

THE END

THE JERICHO YEARS
by Aileen Armitage

Jericho Farm, high in the Pennines, had been in the Hemingway family for generations. Life on the farm was hard, yet the place had a rugged compulsion for those who lived and worked there. But now James Hemingway was thinking of breaking with tradition and selling up. With his wife tragically dead, David, his son, making a separate career as an artist, and his daughter, Ellen, a strange, withdrawn and troubled girl, there seemed little point in staying on at Jericho.

The David, the beloved and only son, was struck by a fatal illness and with Lisa, the girl he wanted to marry, came back to Jericho, to the house and land that he loved. As the new family coped with fresh tragedy and began to try and weld together once more, so an entirely unexpected and unconventional relationship exploded into their lives, one that offered hope to James, to Lisa, and to Jericho Farm.

0 552 14049 X

PROUD HARVEST
by Janet Haslam

Hannah Critchlow, orphaned after a storm which carried away her beloved father and destroyed her home, was given refuge by the notorious Bunting family at their remote hilltop farm, Bunting's Tor. The three men of the family were feared and hated in the area: George, the autocratic and brutal patriarch; Jed, his profligate and much-favoured elder son; and Sam, the best and most steadfast of the three, who had to grow up believing that he was tainted because of his deformed hand – a deformity which had cruelly led the locals to rename the farm Bunting's Claw.

Sam had come to believe that no woman would ever want his love, and that no children would ever be born to inherit the great farmhouse and rolling acres. Only Hannah, proud and self-willed, could see the real Sam beneath his imperfect body, and only she could bring new love and hope to the doomed family.

0 552 14138 0

THE LONDONERS
by Margaret Pemberton

Magnolia Square in South London was a friendly and vibrant place to live, not least for Kate Voigt and her father. Carl Voigt had been a prisoner of war during the First World War, had married a cockney girl and never gone back. Now widowed, he and Kate were part of the London life of the square with all its rumbustious and colourful characters. Then came the war.

Suddenly it seemed the Voigts were outcasts because of their German blood. When Carl was interned, Kate's only support was her best friend Carrie, and Toby, the RAF pilot whom she loved. Finally, when Toby was killed, and even Carrie turned against her, she found herself pregnant and totally alone.

Late one Christmas Eve, during the Blitz, she was approached by a wounded sailor asking for lodgings. Leon Emmerson, like Kate, was also a lonely misfit because of his parentage. It was to be the beginning of a new friendship, of startling and dramatic events in Kate's life. And as the war progressed, as the Londoners fought to help each other while their city was bombed and burned, so the rifts in the community were healed, and Kate and those she loved became, once more, part of Magnolia Square.

0 552 14123 2

A SELECTED LIST OF FINE NOVELS
AVAILABLE FROM CORGI BOOKS

14058 9	MIST OVER THE MERSEY	Lyn Andrews	£4.99
14049 X	THE JERICHO YEARS	Aileen Armitage	£4.99
13992 0	LIGHT ME THE MOON	Angela Arney	£4.99
12850 3	TOO MUCH TOO SOON	Jacqueline Briskin	£5.99
14261 1	INTIMATE	Elizabeth Gage	£4.99
14231 X	ADDICTED	Jill Gascoine	£4.99
14382 0	THE TREACHERY OF TIME	Anna Gilbert	£4.99
13255 1	GARDEN OF LIES	Eileen Goudge	£5.99
14095 3	ARIAN	Iris Gower	£4.99
13897 5	BILLY LONDON'S GIRLS	Ruth Hamilton	£4.99
13872 X	LEGACY OF LOVE	Caroline Harvey	£4.99
14138 0	PROUD HARVEST	Janet Haslam	£4.99
14284 0	DROWNING IN HONEY	Kate Hatfield	£4.99
14220 4	CAPEL BELLS	Joan Hessayon	£4.99
14207 7	DADDY'S GIRL	Janet Inglis	£5.99
14262 X	MARIANA	Susanna Kearsley	£4.99
14045 7	THE SUGAR PAVILION	Rosalind Laker	£5.99
14331 6	THE SECRET YEARS	Judith Lennox	£4.99
14002 3	FOOL'S CURTAIN	Claire Lorrimer	£4.99
13737 5	EMERALD	Elisabeth Luard	£5.99
13910 6	BLUEBIRDS	Margaret Mayhew	£5.99
13972 6	LARA'S CHILD	Alexander Mollin	£5.99
10249 0	BRIDE OF TANCRED	Diane Pearson	£2.99
14123 2	THE LONDONERS	Margaret Pemberton	£4.99
14057 0	THE BRIGHT ONE	Elvi Rhodes	£4.99
14298 0	THE LADY OF KYNACHAN	James Irvine Robertson	£5.99
14318 9	WATER UNDER THE BRIDGE	Susan Sallis	£4.99
14375 8	ECHOES OF YESTERDAY	Mary Jane Staples	£4.99
14296 4	THE LAND OF NIGHTINGALES	Sally Stewart	£4.99
14263 8	ANNIE	Valerie Wood	£4.99